I0771270

RECKONING

Other Books by Vincent M. Wales

Wish You Were Here

One Nation Under God

RECKONING

THE MANY DEATHS OF DYNAMISTRESS

BOOK ONE

Dinah Geof-Craigs
with
Vincent M. Wales

DGC PRESS • SACRAMENTO

Acknowledgments

I'm indebted to the people (too many to list) who read sample chapters early on, before I even knew what I was doing. A few, however, went the extra mile: Blair, Debbie, Mike, and Sabrina, I thank you.

I'd also like to thank the members of my writing group in Sacramento – the H Street Irregulars – who provided much needed advice at early stages of the book's development: Bill, Eve, Janna, Jason, Paul, and William.

Special thanks to my sister, Sue Wales, and also to Gabe Howard, Jacquie Jean, and Sheree Lowe for helping make this happen.

Appreciation to my long-time friend, Jon, for the quote that opens Chapter Twenty-Three.

The characters of Devilgirl and Hellion were co-created by Erica Stratten.
The character of Sinta was co-created by M. Young.
The character of Zero-Point was co-created by Miguel Tarrats.
My deepest gratitude to you all for allowing them to live in my world.

DEDICATION

This book is dedicated with great fondness to a particular group of online gamers, without whom this book would not exist. It was great while it lasted, and I miss you all very much.

"Show me a hero and I will write you a tragedy."
~F. Scott Fitzgerald

FOREWORD

As most readers know, *Supers* magazine spotlights a "Super of the Month" in every issue, featuring an exclusive interview and photos. A handful of years ago, on our weekly teleconference, one of our stringers suggested a particular individual for this honor. Everyone was probably thinking the same thing, though I was the only one to give voice to it. *"Who the hell is Dynamistress?"* I said.

I looked at the promo photo she'd sent, which she told me had been an unsolicited submission from our slush pile. It's common for the new metas to contact us, in hopes of finding fame. It seems to never occur to them that we're a magazine that reports on those who are already famous.

She took a good photo, though, I had to admit. It was a typical cheesecake pose, leaning against a wall, one leg bent, a stiletto-heeled boot resting against the bricks. But her costume was much more modest than her name would imply.

I read the attached brief as my reporter told me what she'd dug up on her. Evidently, she'd been part of the Nevada Incident. That was newsworthy enough, but the other information she'd found was... intriguing.

I clicked back to the photo, staring at the piercing blue eyes that seemed to carry both pain and humor. *"Do the interview,"* I said. *"Then I'll decide."*

Well. You know how I decided.

The January 2008 issue was our best selling ever, aside from "memorial" issues honoring the fallen. And it's the one most often requested as a back issue in our circulations department. (We're sold out, by the way. Try eBay.)

I've read hundreds of books about metas, from boastful recitations of exploits to poorly ghostwritten "autobiographies" to scandalous, unauthorized exposés. But this book – Dyna's book – is one of the very few that I'll actually recommend to friends.

And strangers, too. Buy this book. Read this book. It's not what you'd expect.

And stay safe out there.

Malcolm Goodman
Publisher / Editor-in-Chief
Supers

ONE

"We do not remember days, we remember moments. The richness of life lies in memories we have forgotten."
~Cesare Pavese

Every moment of our lives is an iceberg. The moment we call "now" is just the tip of things, the short sliver visible of all those other moments that have led to it. The rest lay drowned in the past, out of sight, out of mind. Only upon close inspection does the magnitude of "now" really slam into us.

My "Titanic moment" was my sixteenth birthday, February 12, 1987. It had been a good day, I suppose. It was a weekday, so I spent it in school. Afterward, it was dinner at my favorite restaurant with my family: Mom, Dad, and my brother, Dana.

Dana was in grad school on the other side of the state, in Philadelphia. I practically idolized him. He was smart, funny, and always treated me like his equal, despite me being seven years younger. And he'd do anything for me, including ditching two important days of classes.

After dinner, it was cake and ice cream back at home. And presents. Mom, as usual, had gotten me a new dress and shoes. Dad bought me a new stereo, complete with one of them newfangled compact disc players. And, of course, Dana got me some CDs.

Dana helped me set up the stereo in my room, and we sat there on my bed, listening to Duran Duran. And even though it was more than two decades ago, I remember our conversation like it happened yesterday.

"Sweet Sixteen," he said in that teasing, older brother kind of way. I rolled my eyes and told him to shut up. "And no girlfriend to share it with?"

That's how close we were. He knew of my attraction to girls. He'd never judged me, and was totally accepting of it. Of *me*.

I just shook my head and said, "I wish."

Our hometown was small. The population was of European descent and not much else. Two thousand people, the vast majority of which were conservative. Not the freaky, wingnut, gun-fetish variety, but the old-fashioned, family-centric, God-fearing variety. Still, despite the outward friendliness, it was clear that certain people weren't treated with the same amount of Christian love. Anyone of non-hetero inclination was deep in the closet. No one I knew of was "out." AIDS was still "the homosexual disease," and "gay" and "lesbian" were insults, not attributes. Non-heterosexuality was regarded as just as much of a mutation as those other, more flamboyant, examples on the nightly news.

Dana gave me a reassuring hug. "Someday," he said. He was always telling me how much more open-minded the college environment was, and I was so looking forward to actual communities made up of those who wouldn't condemn me.

Then Dana stopped smiling and said, "Dinah... there's something I need to tell you. But you have to promise not to let Mom and Dad find out I told you."

"Okay," I said, frowning. I was used to this weird family trait. Any non-vital news that might upset someone was glossed over or kept quiet altogether. Our last surviving grandparent died when I was in third grade. But I didn't find out his death was a suicide until I was thirteen, and that was by overhearing a conversation not meant for my ears. I found it insulting that our parents often thought I shouldn't know something or other, but history had taught me to be more concerned than angry.

Dana got all serious and stood up from my bed and paced. I didn't think people actually did that, except in movies. But there he was. Pacing. I would have laughed, had it not been for the look on his face.

Finally, he stopped and leaned against my dresser, not looking at me. His voice was barely audible. "You're not the only one in the family who has a secret."

I was stunned. What secret could he have that Mom and Dad wouldn't want me to know about? My mind raced, trying to figure it out before he told me. I knew he wasn't gay. He'd had a girlfriend up until about six months before, when she tore his heart out. And I knew of one other girl he'd "gone all the way" with. Bisexual, maybe? I offered this as my guess.

"Bigger," he said softly.

"Bigger" meant "worse." And there were only two things worse than being gay, as far as our folks were concerned. One of these things, Dana had already owned up to, years before.

I'm eight years old. I'm supposed to be playing in my room before going to bed, but I'm crouching at the top of the stairs, eavesdropping on the conversation below. It goes more or less like this:

Our father says, "Seems pretty odd that you only get sick on Sunday mornings, but feel better once the rest of us return from church."

There's only silence in response. I can picture Dana shrugging his shoulders.

Our mother says, "Don't you like going to church anymore?"

"I've never liked going to church," my brother says in the semi-whine that all teenagers seem to share.

"Son," Dad says, "you'll find there are lots of things in life that we need to do, even though we don't like to."

"I know... but going to church isn't one of them."

"Bite your tongue!" our mother hisses.

"But I don't believe that stuff!"

There's another silence, during which I imagine my parents are staring at Dana in shock. I know I'm stunned by his words.

Mother breaks the silence. "What do you mean?"

"I mean I don't believe in God. God's every bit as imaginary as Santa Claus!"

Now I'm aghast. I wait for Mom or Dad to refute him, to confirm that God and Santa are just as real as anyone.

"Richard, our son's going to hell."

"Now, Margaret..."

"Like you didn't already think I was going there, anyway," Dana sneers. I have no idea what he means, but don't have time to think about it before Dad speaks again.

"Son, I know you think you know better than everyone else. But that sort of arrogance will cause you nothing but trouble. Now, we'll hear no more of this talk."

"Especially around your sister!" Mom says. "She believes every word you say, so don't you let her hear that you've forsaken the Lord! And she still believes in Santa Claus, so keep your nasty mouth shut about that, too."

And there it is, from my mother's own lips: confirmation that Santa is just a figment of someone's imagination. The rest of the conversation is lost to me, as I shuffle back to my room. But resuming my pretend life with Barbie and the Rockers has no appeal for me. I look down at my dolls, in the little wooden house Santa had...

No.

Santa hadn't brought me this dollhouse. Santa wasn't real. My dad, though, was quite real. And I'd seen him make things with his tools in the garage. He'd made Mom those pretty planter boxes for outside her windows. He'd made the bookshelves in Dana's room. I look at the wooden house again with fresh eyes.

So if Santa wasn't real... then neither was the Easter Bunny. Or the Tooth Fairy. So what about God? Was Dana right about that? I shake my head. I'd pretty much always equated Santa Claus and God. If Santa wasn't all-knowing, I couldn't figure out how else he could have the naughty or nice list. But only God knew everything, I was told in Sunday School.

By the time Mom comes to tuck me into bed, I, too, am an atheist.

Eight years later, on that very same bed, I stared at my brother, finally seeing the rest of the iceberg. I know now what Dana had meant, all those years ago, by the going to hell comment. It's the other thing "bigger" than being gay.

My heart almost burst as I blurted it out. "You're a *mutant?*"

He winced at the word. "Meta. I'm a meta."

I was glad I was sitting down, or I might have fallen to the floor. I couldn't believe it. I *didn't* believe it. "Show me!" I pleaded.

"Not so loud!" he said, and then I remembered the promise he'd asked of me. Our parents never had anything nice to say about metahumans. Not even the ones who clearly deserved to have nice things said about them.

Dana glanced at my dresser. Then, right before my eyes, my lip balm tube floated up into the air and over to me. When it dropped into my hand, I about peed myself. It was the most amazing thing I'd ever seen. There was, despite Dana's concerns, a hint of pride on his face. *Pretty cool, huh?*

Without thinking, I said, "Yeah!"

It was only after I'd replied that I realized his lips hadn't moved. I'd heard his voice inside my head. And I boggled again. Telekinesis *and* telepathy! Dana had struck the mutant gene jackpot, as far as I was concerned.

Lucky bastard.

There is much disagreement about when super-powered metahumans began to appear. Most scientists believe the first births were in the '40s, perhaps the '30s, although there is a small (but vocal) minority claiming they have always been among us. Certainly, by the time I entered the world in 1971, metahumans were firmly in the public eye.

And they weren't just in the press, but in popular culture. Comic books had long detailed the exploits of super-powered, costumed folk doing heroic or nefarious deeds, dressed in bright costumes and sporting outlandish names. They were entertaining, I suppose, despite the silly and unrealistic dialogue. But when you could see the real thing on television, why would you buy hand-drawn fiction? Regardless, in a case of life imitating art, the media began attaching colorful names to different metahumans. And eventually, the government got involved, as it always does.

Whatever the timeline, the conservative estimate is that one out of every hundred thousand births will be a metahuman.

Now, mutations happen all the time, the vast majority of which are utterly benign. In many cases, without examining one's DNA, it would be impossible to tell there was even a mutation there. Other mutations are simply what we call "birth defects" or "congenital abnormalities." And many of these are innocuous. A common one is crooked pinky fingers, where the tips angle toward the ring fingers, after the outermost knuckle. Clinodactyly, it's called. About ten percent of the population has this, to one degree or another.

Other mutations are far more severe. Muscular dystrophy, for example, is the result of a mutation. And of course, some mutations are fatal, either before birth or at an early age.

But a small percentage of mutations are helpful. That's what drives evolution: mutations that allow us to adapt to our environment, giving us a better chance at survival. One example is a community of people in Italy who are seemingly immune to atherosclerosis, amazingly enough. This has been traced to a genetic mutation of a particular ancestor, who was even identified. Another example is that some people have a genetic mutation that makes them highly resistant to contracting HIV.

As beneficial as both of these mutations are, they're subtle and passive. But there are other mutations whose benefits are more blatant. There are instances of individuals who are unable to feel pain or are seemingly immune to extremes of hot or cold or even electric shock. Conversely, there are some who can generate heat, or manipulate magnetic fields. There are some blind persons who can use echolocation to "see." There are some whose "super" brains are capable of accessing much more information than the average person's, including some with "perfect" visual memory. There are those whose reflexes are abnormally fast and accurate and others whose muscles seem to remain undamaged from normal usage, enabling them to continue working or running essentially until they pass out from lack of sleep. Then again, there are those who don't seem to need sleep.

The average human would regard these as superhuman abilities, but the mutations themselves are still what we consider normal. Rare, of course, and undeniably interesting. But still "normal."

However, "meta mutations," as they've come to be called, make these remarkable abilities look positively mundane, and have thrown long-held scientific beliefs into chaos.

And as happens whenever such disruption to what is "known" occurs, research exploded in many scientific fields. When a human being can do things that should be utterly impossible, we have no choice but to either prove it's done with smoke and mirrors, or consider that maybe the laws of physics have more loopholes than we thought.

Oddly enough, despite all we've learned, all we can actually demonstrate, there are plenty of people in the world who still insist that it's all fake. I assume these are the same people who deny that we've set foot on the moon or claim the Holocaust never happened. To these people, the scientists who've made the breakthroughs in the past decade or so in discovering how metahuman abilities work are all conspirators, fleecing the public for reasons I can't even begin to imagine. I'm just not that paranoid.

But then, I suppose it's fair to say I'm biased.

Most kids develop a fixation with something by the age of ten. For my brother, it had been dinosaurs. I'm told that, at ten, he could recite a ridiculous number of facts about countless Cretaceous creatures, in much the same way that our father could rattle off endless sports statistics or our mother could quote lengthy passages of scripture, verbatim.

And me? By the time I was eleven, I could name probably a hundred of the known metas in America and list their metahuman abilities. I could tell you which metas composed any given team. Metas ranked right up there with movie stars and musicians, in the eyes of the public.

Well, most of the public, anyway. There were always people who didn't think too highly of musicians or movie stars and for those folks, metas were maybe the lowest of the low. Among those with this attitude was our mother.

Father's attitude was that they were all attention-seeking grandstanders, not deserving of respect, let alone adulation. Mother, on the other hand, regarded them as abominations. She ignored the idea that this was the next stage in human evolution because, religious fundamentalist that she is, she didn't accept the truth of evolution.

But at least they were realistic about our exposure to them. They recognized the fact that, if we weren't watching the metas on TV, we'd find out about them in other ways. Schools talked about them, after all. The whole field of biology was under the microscope, so to speak, and teachers lectured excitedly on the ideas behind human-to-metahuman evolution. By the last quarter of the twentieth century, it was flat-out impossible to ignore the metahuman contingent and its effect on society, though many wished otherwise.

The metas' effect on me was profound. I wanted more than anything to be one of them, much as kids a decade before might have dreamed of becoming astronauts. I dreamed about it while sleeping and fantasized about it during school. I tore off Barbie's clothes and painted a costume on her, hiding it again under her outfit. And of course, I put on a domino mask, tied a towel around my neck as a cape, and pinned a big letter "D" to my chest. I tried to put a matching cape on our dog, so he could be my sidekick, but he would have none of it. And always, I was imagining what abilities I might have, once puberty had its way with me. I guess you could say I was single-minded about the future. Or at least, *my* future.

The day I began my first period was a day of high excitement for me. After the initial panic, of course. No matter how much you prepare for it, you're never quite ready to see blood on your underpants for the first time.

For a month, I woke up eagerly, expecting to feel different, with whatever changes were happening inside me. I'd read the interviews with other metas. I knew that the changes took different forms and felt differently from one meta to another. I didn't know what to expect... just that *something* would be different.

Even though I didn't feel at all out of the norm, I tried to do things. I would concentrate until I gave myself a headache, trying to make my hands burst into flame, or to levitate off the ground. At least I had sense enough not to jump out of my second-story bedroom window, trying to fly.

But I finally had to admit, with the heaviest of hearts, that puberty had come and gone, and I was still just plain old Dinah Geof-Craigs, girl geek. More specifically, I was an *aimless* girl geek. So certain had I been that I'd develop superhuman abilities that I never gave a moment's thought to anything else I might want to do with my life. I was not only single-minded, but short-sighted.

As one might expect, my education wasn't of high importance to me. Oh, I got decent grades. But I wasn't the whiz kid Dana had been when he'd graced those halls of middle education, seven years earlier, and my teachers never failed to remind me of this little bit of trivia whenever I'd barely get a "B" on a quiz.

Despite this, I loved school. It was my social outlet. I relished the life of a teenage girl, even though I wasn't a member of the popular crowd. It didn't matter. Even unpopular girls could engage in the same mindless idiocy as the cool kids. We gossiped, shared makeup, traded clothing, and generally behaved like the superficial, material girls we were.

And that's how it was for me, up until Dana's confession. It seemed so wonderful at the time, that my awesome brother was even more awesome. But slowly, the wound his admission inflicted became more evident.

The iceberg tore a gaping hole in me. Only it wasn't cold seawater that came rushing in. It was something much more vile.

I wonder, sometimes, about the perceptiveness of parents. Teenagers, I think, typically assume their parents are clueless to the point of being socially embarrassing. I know I certainly held that opinion of mine, and they did little to prove me wrong. Mother's attitude toward anything outside the status quo bothered me immensely, as did my father's passivity. Even when he disagreed with her, he rarely spoke up.

I've never been able to understand how anyone could have a real understanding of the world, of people, and still hold closed-minded opinions toward those who, for example, didn't believe in God, who were attracted to the same gender, or had a genetic mutation that they certainly couldn't do anything about.

Yet, in retrospect, I wonder if my parents didn't know me better than I'd thought they did. Maybe their reasons for demanding that Dana not tell me about his mutation weren't just the same old reasons. Maybe it was because they knew how I'd really react.

Yes, at first, I was thrilled. I wanted to brag to all my friends about Dana's abilities. I didn't, of course. I knew what repercussions a public "outing" could have for him. But after a time, this filial pride was replaced by something I'd never felt before: sibling envy.

As much as I'd always loved and admired him, I'd never felt envy, because he always made me feel so good about myself. But our closeness was disrupted by the physical distance of him being away at college, which inevitably led to a growing emotional distance. As the years progressed, he came home on weekends less frequently, and even took summer classes some years.

I missed him. He'd always been my best friend, and now that I knew of his abilities, I wanted him around even more. I wanted to watch him float things around. Hell, I wanted him to float *me* around. I wanted him to read other peoples' minds and use his telepathic "inside voice" to tell me what they were thinking. Every time he "spoke" in my mind, I got a thrill. I figured if I couldn't be a meta, myself, I at least wanted to be one vicariously through him.

But he was two hundred miles away.

I'm sure this distance contributed to my feelings, but I'm not sure things would have been much different if he'd still lived at home. The truth is, I'd been so obsessed with metahumans, so convinced that I was going to be one, that it probably bordered on psychosis. When puberty came and went and I wasn't gifted with superhuman abilities, I was devastated. But I accepted it. What other choice did I have?

But there he was, with his abilities. Him. Not me.

But the worst part was that he didn't even seem happy to have his abilities. He just kept going to school, working toward his Ph.D. It was the height of insult, really. Given how rare meta-mutations are, we certainly had no reason to expect that our little town would produce one. And how ironic was it that the one who'd gained abilities was someone who didn't particularly care to have them?

And my envy grew to resentment.

I didn't understand. Didn't he want to be famous? Didn't he want to be on the cover of *Supers* magazine? Featured on *Biography*? Didn't he want to be a member of The Liberty League, or any of the other teams of metahumans? Didn't he want to be loved by the masses?

I couldn't imagine anyone would *not* want these things. Being famous was what I craved more than anything. And I began to view it as a cosmic injustice that he'd been graced with abilities that he didn't want and wouldn't use, while I was denied exactly the same thing, when it's what I most wanted in life.

Did I ever confront him about this? Sort of. Once. On one of his visits home, I casually mentioned my envy. His reaction? "It's not worth feeling envious, Dinah. Believe me... It's not all you think it is."

When I asked why he felt that way, he waved it off and wouldn't discuss it any further. I was hurt that he treated it – treated *me* – so dismissively. It was adding insult to injury, as the saying goes.

If I'd been a believer, I would have been supremely pissed at God. But I wasn't. So instead, I turned my resentment and anger to Dana. I was no longer bothered by the distance separating us. Not seeing him made it easier to maintain the negative feelings.

I suppose one good thing did come of this. I stopped being aimless. I knew what I was going to do with my life. I knew enough about biology to know that we had the ability to induce mutations. So it seemed only reasonable to believe that we could induce meta-mutations.

My goal in life now was to become a brilliant geneticist, to study human to metahuman evolution, and to find a way to induce meta-mutation. In myself.

My brother might not want the fame, the glory, the adoration... but *I* did.

And I was damn well going to have it.

Two

"When one creates phantoms for oneself, one puts vampires into the world, and one must nourish these children of a voluntary nightmare with one's blood, one's life, one's intelligence, and one's reason, without ever satisfying them."

~*Eliphas Lévi*

I have a lot of nightmares. I don't remember dreams every night, but for each nice dream I can recall, there are probably two or three bad ones. When I was little, most of my bad dreams were those that most kids seem to have. Being chased, for example, usually by a monster of some sort. I can probably thank my brother's boy-child fascination with monster movies for that one. Other nightmares involved falling or being physically hurt in some way. For that, I suppose I can just blame my own clumsiness, combined with being a hyperactive tomboy. I was always skinning my knees or elbows, bumping my head on anything in its way, or tripping over my two left feet.

I don't have monster chase dreams, anymore, even though I routinely encounter creatures today that most would call monsters. Nor do I have dreams of falling or being hurt, although I actually do both a lot more often, and a lot more severely, than I did as a girl. But then, we fear the unfamiliar, and these things are commonplace for me, now.

But the nightmare that was worst in my childhood, and that still sometimes wakes me in a panic, was of being lost. My shrink isn't at all surprised that I have these dreams, but I think she's frustrated that they haven't gone away, yet. It's not a reflection on her skills as a therapist. I'm just not very good at working through my own crap.

I try, though. I do a lot of journaling. I'd kept a diary in my early teens, but it was the typical superficial stuff you'd expect of a girl that age. My therapist urged me long ago to get back into the journaling process, and to really go deep... to not simply write accounts of what's going on in my life, but to mine my emotions, to dig out what I'm feeling and see what might be lying underneath. I guess that's part of why I agreed to write this book. It's all part of my ongoing effort to find myself.

Okay, there is one other nightmare I have a lot. Can you call it a nightmare if it's a memory of an actual event?

By the beginning of my senior year in high school, I've developed "that attitude" that so many teens seem to have. I think I know better than anyone else. I wield sarcasm like a bludgeon instead of a rapier. I consider the eye roll sublimely eloquent. In other words, I'm a brat.

On this particular day, I'm in a snit over something or other and Mom has done or said something to exacerbate it. We get into a fight.

"I've had about enough of your attitude, young lady. The Bible says to honor your parents, and you're doing anything but!"

"Whatever." Eye roll.

"No, not 'whatever'! Do not disrespect the word of God!"

"I haven't believed in God since I was eight years old!" My voice quavers only a little as I say this. I'd imagined having "the religion talk" with her for years, so in some sense, I'm ready for it. But like the blood in the underpants, it still comes as a shock when it finally happens.

I know the proclamation will hurt her, and it does. So I land the first blow. Despite the butterflies in my stomach, I'm inwardly thrilled to see how appalled she is. Her mouth hangs open in comic shock, and I nearly laugh.

She stares at me, then deflects. "Your brother did this to you!"

"I have a mind of my own, thank you!" Dana always gets the credit for things. Of course, in a way, she's right. But I'm not about to admit that.

"The devil's in him, Dinah! Don't you listen to him!"

"There's no such thing as the devil, mother! And Dana has a great gift!"

And there's my second shot, straight to the gut. I knock the wind out of her. Now she knows that I know, and I'm glad of it. This woman needs to have her insulated little world knocked off-kilter, and I'm elated to do it.

She's near apoplectic, by this point, face red, words jamming up in her throat. Finally, she spits out, "It's a curse!"

I roll my eyes again at her primitive beliefs. "You're hopeless. He has fantastic abilities, and I hate the fact that I don't have powers, too."

Now she stares at me, clearly appalled. "It's bad enough you're questioning your faith. I don't need you wishing to be corrupt."

Still high with the power I seem to have over her, I decide it's time to put her down for the count. "Corrupt? You want corrupt? Guess what, Mom... I'm a lesbian! How's that for corrupt?"

There it is. The haymaker. It comes out easily enough, but my heart is pounding like mad. I'd never planned to tell her about my sexuality, but I can't resist the thrill of being able to render her speechless. If anything, it freaks her out even more than the admission of atheism. I continue my roll. "Didn't you ever wonder why I only have posters of girls on my walls?" I say. "Why I prefer to hang Brooke Shields there instead of Tom Selleck? I swear, you're so obtuse sometimes."

She's reeling, and I wait smugly for her to crumple to the mat. Instead, she surprises me, as parents often do, by being the one to deliver the knockout. Her face screws up in an expression I'd never seen on her before.... a combination of pain, revulsion, and anger. Her eyes flare as she hauls off with a vicious slap across my face.

Time stands still for me... the sound of the slap echoing off the walls, or perhaps just in my mind. I feel the bright, stinging flush fill my cheek, and we stand there staring at each other... she radiating righteous indignation, and I... hurt. Devastated. Knowing that nothing will ever be the same.

When I wake from that dream, I can still feel the imprint of her hand on my cheek. So, yeah. I think I can call that a nightmare.

I went to Penn State for my undergraduate degree. I wanted to go directly to the main campus right away, but that wasn't an option for my major. So I spent my first two years at the DuBois campus, about a twenty-minute drive from home. But even that was an improvement, especially since I now had my own car.

When I'd graduated high school, my father told me he'd match whatever money I was able to save toward the purchase. So I'd gotten a job working as a cashier at the Rexall. By September, I'd managed to save enough, with my father's matching input, to buy a 1983 Renault Alliance. It was gold. And not a cheery, yellow gold, but an ostentatious metallic gold. Even had it not been dulled from years in the sun, it would still have been a ridiculous color for a car. Especially one as boxy and unglamorous as the Alliance. Its horn sounded like the Roadrunner, but I was certain Wile E. Coyote could outrun this little thing.

I named it "Baby." Not because it was an adorable little thing, but because that's what I had to do to it to keep it running. It was ugly and abused, with over 70,000 miles on it, but it was mine. And with a car, of course, comes freedom. In my case, it wasn't freedom to hit the open road, but freedom to avoid going home.

After classes, I'd head to the local Perkins restaurant and study while eating fries with gravy and sipping bad coffee. I'd go home at ten or eleven o'clock, and if my parents were still awake, I'd simply say goodnight and head to bed.

It was just easier that way. Mother and I were going weeks at a stretch without saying ten words to each other. And Dad... well... I don't think he knew what to do. When a man has to choose sides between his wife and his daughter, there's just no correct side to take. So he kept out of it, for the most part.

As for my dear brother, he was working on his doctorate, so money was tight for him, living on student loans. He rarely drove the four and a half hours home to visit. I used this as more reason to be upset with him.

What really bothered me, though, was that although our mother clearly viewed Dana as being "corrupt," to use her own term, he was still the darling of the family. I didn't know how to explain that. Was it that whole mother/daughter competition thing? Was it because Dana was the firstborn? Whatever the reason, it just seemed wrong that he was still the golden child and I was the black sheep. I resented both of them for that.

But Dana had been right about college. It really was far more of an accepting environment for those of us who lived and loved outside the box. For the first time, I saw in public those who were clearly "out" about their sexuality. True, there weren't many. But it was still encouraging.

As for my dating life there... I wanted a girlfriend, but dating intimidated me. I didn't find myself attractive, so I didn't want to set myself up for rejections. Not one girl asked me out, either, in two years there.

A few boys, on the other hand, did. Usually, I just said no, and that was that. There was one, however, who was persistent to the point of irritation. I'd told him no, twice. This third time, I just rolled my eyes. At which point, he called me a dyke. I laughed and in my most snarky fashion, informed him that yes, I was, but that even if straight, I'd still say no to him.

Some guys... I don't know. It's as though they're threatened by girls who like girls. Or insulted, maybe. Men are prone to arrogance, I've found, and I think some are just appalled that not all women think the penis is deserving of adulation. So they get a little pissy. They say it's because we're afraid of men, or that we've never had a good fuck, or whatever.

Not that I owed them, or anyone, any clarification, but let me set the record straight. I was not a virgin. I took care of that little detail at the age of fifteen. I decided I needed to be sure that boys weren't my thing, so I seduced a guy I knew. It helped that he was really drunk at the time. No, I'm not going to reveal his name. We're still friends, and the last thing I want is for his buddies to say, "Way to go, dude... you turned her gay!" He doesn't need that sort of attention, nor would he want any other sort, either.

And yes, I actually enjoyed sex with him. Despite being drunk, he knew what he was doing and made me feel really good, including my first orgasm that wasn't self-induced. So it's not that I had a bad experience. It's not that guys gross me out. I can admire a handsome man easily enough, but no man has ever taken my breath away, mesmerized me to the point of distraction, or made me ache with desire just to be close to him.

Plenty of girls in high school made me feel that way. But by the time I got to college, my mind was on other things. I had a goal, now, and the details of it were beginning to gel in my head. I focused on studying everything I could that would help me achieve it. Dating was a very low priority, by comparison.

I had no social life during these two years. I didn't really have any close friends. I'd grown apart from my junior high friends and of course, many of my acquaintances went off to schools out of town or out of state. I saw no real benefit in trying to make friends at the branch campus, as I was only going to be there for two years. So it was no great intrusion on my social life to continue working weekends at the drug store.

The store was rarely busy. But even when slow, there were too many distractions to actually study. However, I could leaf through magazines to my heart's content. My daydreams, fueled by the magazines, were pretty much my social outlet.

Supers magazine was always my favorite. Sure, there were other magazines devoted to the metas. *SuperPeople. Teen Hero. Them.* But *Supers* was the best, with actual interviews of substance, rather than just gossip and paparazzi pics. I'd fantasize about being one of those interviewees, of having my picture on the cover.

They weren't just fantasies, though. They were, and always had been, plans. Back in grade school, my girlfriends would talk about which movie star or pop singer they were going to marry. I'd talk about which superteam I'd be joining.

In retrospect, maybe it's not surprising that I had few friends.

Truthfully, though, I've never liked the way the vast majority of superteams were created, here in the States. Once the government puts its greasy finger into something, logic and common sense seem to slide away like beads of water. So the superteams best known to the public are those that have been deliberately put together in an inorganic fashion, saddled with "themes" that are often corny, or at least unimaginative.

I mentioned The Liberty League, already. Everyone knows that one, the premiere patriotic-themed group from Philadelphia. Slightly less well known is the all-female group, The Liberty Belles. Like I said, corny.

I hate nationalism. I find it disgusting and feel it does far more harm than good in the world. It reinforces separatism and xenophobia. But then, I often feel our government wants this. Our leaders may be idiots, but they're not stupid.

Outside of Philadelphia, the best-known Pennsylvania team is The Keystones. Today's generation doesn't really remember it, but I remember seeing old black and white comic films from the early 20th Century featuring The Keystone Cops. This group of inept officers – sometimes in feature films, sometimes supporting Charlie Chaplin or others – was known for long, bumbling chase scenes. I used to think The Keystones, for this reason, chose an unfortunate name, notwithstanding the fact that Pennsylvania is "the keystone state." But after watching them for years, perhaps the name is fitting. Their track record isn't very impressive.

But there are a lot of teams. There's even a "team" for retired metas: The Goldens. They often appear on TV – usually local channels, not cable – for supermarket openings and such.

I'd estimate that most metas... or at least, most of the ones not actively criminal... work for the government in some capacity, a fact that never thrilled me. The government formed most groups, be it federal, state, or local. The Secret Service is comprised almost entirely of metas. And it's pretty much taken for granted that governments around the world utilize metas as assassins. It's fortunate, I guess, that very few metas have ever allied themselves with terrorist organizations. Yet.

There were, of course, a few teams of metas put together of their own free will, rather than some governmental decree, bound together by a common ideology, rather than by an imposed "theme" or their location. But they were few and far between.

I had never been very studious in high school. My grades had always been decent, and I'd always enjoyed learning, but even in the late '80s, I knew the schools weren't concentrating on things that really mattered. Seriously, why does anyone need to know what our Gross National Product is, or the major imports and exports of Brazil?

I will, however, defend one practice that a lot of people don't seem to understand. Why, they lament, when kids today all have computers, are we still filling their heads with advanced mathematics? It's simply not necessary, they claim, to teach them how to do calculus. But they're wrong. If we stopped teaching it, we'd never advance. No one would be able to take math in new directions.

Memorizing the terms of office of all the U.S. presidents, however, will always be pointless.

At any rate, I think my professors were a bit astounded. After all, for these first two years, I was taking just the basics in biology. But after class, I'd pick their brains about the latest things. The automated gene sequencer had been invented recently, and I had all sorts of questions about that. There was talk about a Human Genome Project soon to be beginning, and I asked almost daily if they'd heard anything new about it. I badgered them about the finer points of the regulation of gene expression. And I think they got tired of my incessant questioning about point mutations.

But I didn't much care if others thought I was odd. It was the life I wanted, at that point... working on weekends, spending weekdays in classes taking as many credits as allowed, and passing my nights by avoiding home as much as possible. I was in my own little world, avoiding my family, and becoming estranged from those I used to call friends.

Talk about establishing a bad precedent.

THREE

"Ever has it been that love knows not its own depth until the hour of separation."

~Kahlil Gibran

Pennsylvanians often joke about the colorful names that grace many of our towns. One long-standing quip is that to get to Paradise, you have to go through Blue Ball, Bird-in-Hand, and Intercourse. It's not actually geographically accurate, but it's amusing. Funnier still is that Climax is on the other side of the state, nearly four hours from Intercourse. Talk about stamina. And no, there's no town called Stamina. Surprisingly.

In contrast to these interesting names, other location names are mundanely unimaginative. For example, the county smack-dab in the middle of the state is called Centre County. Found here is the main campus of Penn State, which has its own ZIP code and is known as University Park. The town surrounding the school is named – I kid you not – State College.

The name may have been boring, but State College itself had a population nearly twenty times the size of my hometown. And that wasn't counting a student population that was probably even larger. A virtual metropolis, by comparison. I was thrilled when I could finally make the transfer from the DuBois campus.

State College was only about a ninety-minute drive from home, but it may as well have been halfway around the world. I was out from under my parents' roof, and thrilled to be so. I think they were glad to be rid of me, too, for that matter.

The idea of living in the dorms, surrounded by drunken football freaks, bordered on being one of my previously mentioned nightmares. I snagged a studio apartment a five-minute walk from the edge of campus and, for the sake of my own sanity, decided to live by myself, despite the financial burden.

To reduce that burden, I took a job at a specialty foods market about five blocks from my apartment. It carried bulk items like sugar, flour, dried legumes, and rice, the requisite organic foods that were just becoming in vogue, as well as a wide assortment of vitamins and other supplements. I was responsible for the bulk products, the beverage cooler, and the produce.

It was a dull job, honestly, but I learned a lot about fruits and veggies. It paid terribly, but then, most students were happy to work for nothing more than beer money. I considered "barely above minimum wage" to be better than average.

Besides, in addition to getting a great employee discount, it's also where I met Sharon.

It's always bothered me when clichés are borne out. Like the old "if you quit looking for love, it'll find you" cliché. And I honestly wasn't looking for love or a relationship. Unlike many, I really was in school to learn. Relationships, I told myself, would do nothing but detract from that.

But the moment I laid eyes on Sharon, I was captivated. It was her eyes. There was something exotic about them. Something feral. This was oddly contradicted by her perfectly coiffed hair.

I thought she looked like she should be modeling Jordache jeans in a magazine ad, so yeah, she might have had that sort of "too perfect" appearance. But those eyes... They're the windows to the soul, to go all cliché again. But that one, too, is more often true than not. Sharon's eyes reminded me of a cat's, playful but wild. Or maybe I just think that because, the first time I met her, she was wearing a leopard print blouse under her leather blazer.

She looked nothing like the typical customer in the store, which was nice. Most of the "health food" set back then were gaunt and looked as though they were made of tofu.

Sharon shopped there mainly for the coffee, which was one of my bulk food items. And, obsessive freak that I am, I'd been learning as much as I could about coffee since working there, which included sampling all the varieties we carried.

This was, after all, before there was a Starbucks on every other corner, and most grocery stores then carried nothing but cans of ground B-grade coffee. My father drank two pots of Maxwell House a day, black. I grew up hating even the smell of coffee. In fact, it wasn't until I'd started working at this store that I began to do more than just tolerate the beverage. Our beans moved quickly, because they really were the freshest and best in town.

That first day, Sharon ordered a pound of Guatemala Hermosa. "Excellent choice," I said as I began measuring out her order. She smiled, her eyes glinting, and the next thing I knew, I could barely breathe. "How would you like it ground?" I managed to say.

She shook her head. "I grind my own."

"Me, too," I said, and actually blushed, as though this were in some way intensely personal and too private to share with a stranger. I felt the flush in my cheeks and then became embarrassed that I was blushing, which only made my pale complexion redden further. Sharon noticed, of course. How could she not?

But instead of laughing at me, she extended her hand. "Sharon," she said.

After a moment of shocked hesitation, I took her hand... that smooth, warm, soft hand... and tried not to blush even more. "Dinah," I said, then winced. "Just... like it says on my badge."

Now she laughed, but it was at the humor of the situation, not at me. Her laugh made me smile, and I knew I'd do almost anything to hear it again.

"Here you go," I said, placing the bag on the counter in front of her. "Anything else?"

"Do you like Turkish?" she said simply.

"Oh, sure," I said. "Especially the banana flavor."

She laughed again. (Success!) "Not Turkish *Taffy*! Turkish *coffee*, silly."

I smiled faintly, glad she got the joke. "Never had it. What's it like?"

Her eyes, I swear, glowed when she said, "Black as hell, strong as death, and sweet as love." As I absorbed that, she pulled a small notepad and pen from her purse and jotted something down. She tore it off and handed it to me. "You free around eight?" I nodded dumbly as I took the paper. "Great," she said, picking up her coffee. "See you then."

I watched as she glided up to the cashier and, eventually, I remembered to breathe again. I glanced at the slip of paper and my heart stuttered. It was an address. But not of a restaurant or café, I knew. For one thing, there weren't any on Waupelani Drive. For another, the address included her apartment number.

What the paper *didn't* include was her phone number. So when I had my anxious freak-out at around six-thirty, I didn't even have an out. I couldn't call her to cancel, but I wasn't going to stand her up.

I stood in front of the bathroom mirror, not knowing what to do with the mess that was me. Just out of the shower, my dirty blonde hair draped like soggy seaweed over my shoulders, not quite reaching my decidedly unimpressive B-cup breasts, which sat above my paunchy tummy.

I'd experienced the "Freshman Ten." And the "Sophomore Twenty," for that matter. Chalk that up to all those nights avoiding the home front by staying out eating fries and gravy at Perkins. I really didn't want the "Junior Thirty," but the newfound joy of pizza delivery definitely had me headed in that direction.

What a lump I was.

I tore my gaze from my midsection and focused on my hair as I blew it dry. Should I wear it up or down? Down, I decided. Mainly because the only way "up" that I ever really did my hair was in a high ponytail. And I looked about fourteen when I did that. Definitely not the impression I wanted to give, tonight.

Then came the wardrobe, such as it was. I stood there in front of my tiny closet and suddenly realized what was happening. I finally understood all those movies and TV shows where the girl was nervous about going out with a guy. I'd always found it totally weird, before. But here I was, butterflies breeding exponentially in my stomach, a sense of dread washing over me in the form of a cold sweat.

I couldn't do this. I had to cancel. How dare she not give me her number? I didn't even know her last name! What the hell was I doing?

Freaking out. Yeah.

After equivocating for twenty minutes, I settled on my one pair of designer jeans and a light blue sweater. A quick return to the mirror for judicious application of makeup (an art I rarely dabbled in, and it showed), and out the door I went.

I barely made the bus.

Sharon lived on the fifth floor of a complex called Imperial Towers. It was a plain brick structure, and the name didn't fit at all. Then again, we've already determined that naming conventions in this area left much to be desired.

On the inside, however, the apartment was quite nice. It certainly made mine look like a hovel. As I walked down the hall toward her unit, I noted that each floor apparently had its own laundry room. My own building had one laundry room for the entirety of the occupants. Granted, it was a much smaller building, but I still found myself doing laundry at odd hours in order to increase the chance of finding open machines.

Finally, I stood in front of her door. The butterflies were out on maneuvers and I seriously thought about turning and walking away. Instead, I knocked. A moment later, Sharon opened the door, and the butterflies broke formation and went in all sorts of directions. She smiled, eyes shining. "Hey," she said.

I tried to smile, but am not sure I succeeded. "Hi," I croaked.

She invited me inside and I stepped through, into the kitchen. "I'm glad you came," she said. "I was afraid you might stand me up."

"No," I said. "I..."

"You would have, if I'd given you my number." She said this casually, as she led me through and into the living and dining area. My stomach knotted as she said it. How could she read me so easily? "Which is why I didn't give it to you," she said.

"Nice place," I said, not wanting to talk about it.

"Thanks," she said, and gave me a quick tour of the rest of the unit.

I saw the door to a second bedroom. I wanted her to say she lived alone, that the other room was an art studio or some other impractical thing that almost no student could afford.

"And that's Jackie's room. She's on a date, tonight."

Okay, a roommate. And she was on a date. At first, I automatically assumed it was a date with a boy. But then I questioned myself. What if she had a date with a girl? What if she had a thing for Sharon? What if Sharon had a thing for her? Did I have competition with a home court advantage?

Worse, what if Sharon was actually straight? What if she was merely being friendly, not flirty? Was I on the verge of making a total fool out of myself? My gaydar had never steered me wrong, before, but...

"So," I said, hoping Sharon wouldn't sense how nervous I was, "what about Jackie's roommate?"

Sharon looked at me suspiciously, but with a smirk. "What about Jackie's roommate?"

I cleared my throat and asked, "Is she on a date, too?"

She laughed again, and I felt giddy hearing it. "Sure looks that way," she said. And I breathed a silent sigh of relief. I'd been afraid she'd be offended at the suggestion that she might (a) be into girls and (b) be attracted to me. She was just too... too perfect. But the gaydar was still working. I was just insecure.

Yes, that little voice was still there... the one saying I didn't need this, didn't want this, that it would take my attention away from my studies, and so on. I mentally told that voice to piss off. Because I *did* want this. The rest might be true, but oh, how I wanted it.

"So where do we go to get Turkish coffee?" I asked, as we returned to the kitchen.

"I make it myself," she said as she pulled a strange little pot from her cupboard. It was made of copper, she told me, lined with tin. The outside was enameled, decorated with beautiful designs in bright colors. It had a long, wooden handle and was oddly shaped... fat on the bottom, tapering quickly at the neck. It looked like it would hold no more than a cup of liquid.

Next, she got out what looked like a big, brass peppermill. She opened it up and filled it with coffee beans, then added a couple cloves and a cardamom pod. She ground it all into a small bowl.

"Geez," I said. "That's a fine grind!" It was even finer than an espresso grind. It was more like coffee powder.

"It has to be," she said. She scooped two ridiculously heaping teaspoons of the ground, spiced coffee into the pot, followed by two of sugar. From the fridge, she pulled a pitcher of chilled water and filled the pot carefully to about an inch below the lip. She stirred the contents with a fork, making sure there were no clumps of coffee, then put the pot on a stove burner on low.

And then we waited. And talked.

Before I knew it was even coming out of my mouth, I heard myself say, "Why me?" Sharon gave me an odd look, obviously not sure what I was asking. "I mean... you said... or implied... that we were on a date. And... I'm really... I don't understand why me."

She just smiled. "Why *not* you?"

"Because!" I blurted. "I'm so... so plain! And you're so... so *wow*."

I didn't think I was being funny, but she laughed... that incredible, tinkling bell laugh, and it put me a bit more at ease. "You assume a lot, y'know."

"I do?"

"Mm hm," she nodded. "First, you assume that everyone finds you to be as plain as you think you are. Second, you assume that someone who is 'wow' won't find someone 'not wow' to be attractive. And third, you assume that my attraction to you has anything at all to do with your wow factor."

I blinked, a bit taken aback. "So... you're a psych major."

Again, the laugh, and this time, I smiled, too. "Education." She continued watching the pot. "You have a problem with psych majors?"

"Just one. My brother."

"Oh? Does he go here?"

"No," I said. "He practices in Philadelphia."

I glanced at the pot – she called it an *ibrik* – and saw the coffee had formed a thick mass atop the water. "Jackie's a psych major," she said.

I nodded, having nothing to say about that. We watched the motionless liquid in the pot for a bit. Then I said, "So... what is the attraction?"

Another quick glance, this one not mirthful, but serious. "Wow, you've got it bad, don't you?"

"Got what?"

"Low self-esteem."

It's true that I didn't think I was anything spectacular, but I'd never felt I had poor self-esteem. But I held back my automatic denial and replayed in my head what I'd been saying so far this evening and had to admit, it sure sounded as though I did. And then I began second-guessing myself.

"Ooh, here we go!" she said, and I looked to see the liquid in the pot begin to foam. It wasn't boiling, exactly, but tiny bubbles of dark froth were growing up the neck of the pot, surfacing around the edges of the island of coffee. Then the island sank, the foam taking over. Sharon removed it from the burner just before it overflowed. "That's it, baby," she cooed to the coffee, then waited for about thirty seconds while the foam receded before returning it to the heat under her watchful eye. Without looking at me, she said, "You're awfully quiet."

"Just... watching what you're doing."

"And berating yourself."

"No, I..." But I stopped. She was right, after all. "Yeah."

"Don't. Now come over here."

I stepped to her side, prepared to assist with whatever arcane step was next in the coffee-making process. Standing next to her, I looked down into the pot. It was decidedly unappealing. The foamy substance was a reddish brown and looked like nothing so much as mud. It did, however, smell amazing. The cloves and cardamom mixed with the coffee aroma and I found my mouth watering at the thought of drinking this stuff, no matter what it looked like.

Just then, it began to rise a second time and Sharon again removed it from the heat, let it cool again, and returned it to the burner. She inhaled, a look of ecstasy on her face.

"How many times does it have to do that?"

"Depends who you ask," she said. "The longer you can keep it at the foaming point, the more foam you have, and I love the foam, especially when it's nice and thick."

"Tricky process," I said.

"Oh, sweetie, it's so worth it. This is the foreplay leading up to the main event. You can't rush it."

Call me sheltered, but never in a million years would I have compared coffee to sex. But as I looked at her face, I could see she was quite serious about the analogy. I cleared my throat, trying also to clear my head of certain other images. "So, what did you need me to do?"

She grinned. "Nothing. I just wanted you closer to me." And then she kissed me on the cheek.

I'd never blushed so much in one day in my entire life.

The coffee began foaming up a third time and now Sharon removed it from the heat and turned off the burner. "The grounds will settle out a little, now," she said as she reached past me to retrieve two demitasse cups and saucers from the cupboard, decorated identically to the *ibrik*. "Take these to the table?"

I did so and she followed behind me, carrying the coffee and a trivet. She placed them on the table and we sat. She inserted a spoon into the pot, lifting out about half the foam. "This is the stuff," she said, and deposited the aromatic mass into one of the cups. She placed the rest into the other, then began pouring the coffee itself.

It looked like hot tar. She must have seen the slight revulsion on my face. "Yeah, that's how I reacted, the first time I saw it." She finished pouring and put the pot back on the trivet. "Don't drink the sludge on the bottom."

"You're not making this more appealing," I said.

"Trust me," she said.

I looked at the layer of foam atop my cup, so different looking from the *crema* of an espresso. Thicker, darker... and as Sharon said... sludgier. I lifted it to my lips.

What did it taste like?

Like you'd imagine sex should taste.

Sharon and I didn't have a great deal in common, honestly. Nevertheless, we really enjoyed each other's company, and did a lot of things together. We'd go out to movies. We'd stay in, watch TV, and eat popcorn. We'd go out to dinner. The normal stuff. And yes, we became lovers. The sex was... well, it was like you'd expect Turkish coffee to feel.

Quite often, Jackie was included in our non-sexual activities. Especially on TV nights, since I didn't own one, myself.

Jackie and I got along great. We had a tremendous amount in common. We liked the same music, the same books. Jackie was a stark contrast to Sharon's Cosmo cover girl glamour. She was somewhat plain looking, wore virtually no makeup, and had light brown hair that hung mostly straight. Not quite "mousy." Sharon said Jackie was beautiful. I found her oddly pretty, and her face totally lit up when she smiled, but most people wouldn't look twice at her when passing by on the street. Their loss.

The girls delighted in showing me around town and the campus. And there were certainly treasures to be found, such as The Creamery. If you love ice cream, this was the place to go. In fact, it was the place to go if you wanted to learn how to make ice cream, too. Penn State is renowned for its dairy program. Just ask Ben & Jerry. They learned their trade through PSU. Needless to say, we went there often.

Life was good, I have to say. Classes were going well. Things with Sharon were wonderful. And Jackie had become one of my best friends. Not bad for only being halfway through the first semester of the year.

Of course, just when you think all is running smoothly, life has a way of complicating things. In this case, it occurred during one of the TV and popcorn nights. Jackie was taking a potty break during a commercial, and Sharon and I had gone into the kitchen to refill the popcorn and drinks.

"Jackie really likes you," Sharon said.

"She's awesome," I said as I refilled our bowl of popcorn. "I like her, too."

Sharon pulled a pitcher of iced tea from the refrigerator and refilled our glasses. "She's shy, though."

I looked at Sharon, wondering what relevance this had to the conversation. "Um... okay?"

She put the tea away and smiled enigmatically. Then she put her hands on my shoulders and kissed me on the nose. "You're so naïve, it's cute. She *likes* you."

You could have knocked me over with a piece of popcorn at that point. I stood there, totally speechless. It's not that I had nothing to say; I just couldn't decide which of the many reactions needed to come out, first.

"Hey, the show's back on," Jackie said from behind me. Sharon let go of me and picked up our drinks, handing one to each of us. "Coming, Dinah?" Jackie said, and I slowly turned around, picked up the popcorn, and headed back to the couch.

I took my now uncomfortable spot between the two, sitting there with the bowl in my lap as the two of them leaned against me and ate from it, laughing at the episode of *Cheers*. Sharon, to my consternation, seemed amused by my discomfort. Jackie didn't notice... or at least, not right away. But when the next commercial break came, and I just sat there like a statue, she spoke up. "You okay, Dinah?"

The only thing I'd been able to think of had been Sharon's nonchalance in the kitchen. She seemed to be perfectly okay with the idea that Jackie "liked" me. That could only mean one thing. I turned to face Sharon, my eyes stinging. "Are you breaking up with me?" I blurted.

Sharon blinked, obviously shocked. Then her face softened and she sighed. "Oh... sweetie, no..." She picked up the remote and turned off the TV, turning to face me, cross-legged on the couch. Jackie did the same on the other side, both staring at me. I felt like a specimen on a slide. "I'm so sorry," Sharon said. "I thought you knew."

Flustered, I shook my head. "Knew what?" The girls exchanged slightly nervous glances, then started talking.

I sat, mouth zipped, and listened. I already knew some of it. I knew they were from the same town. I knew they'd gone to high school together. But the fact that they were also lovers was news to me.

"Semi-open," they called their relationship. To me, this sounded like "a little bit pregnant," but they gently explained to me that they were, in fact, in a very committed relationship. It just wasn't exclusive. They didn't believe that love was something that could or should be limited.

"We don't own each other," Sharon said.

"Right," Jackie agreed. "And there's nothing keeping us together, aside from desire. Either of us could say tomorrow that we're done, and that's that." She smiled softly. "So every day we're together is a day we're grateful for."

"On the other hand," Sharon said, "we understand being attracted to others. So if I want to go out on a date, I do."

"And then she tells me all about it," Jackie said with a suggestive smile, "which is usually entertaining."

They weren't promiscuous, they explained. They weren't swingers. One always got the other's okay before becoming physical with a new interest, on those rare occasions when the outside relationships got serious.

They explained all this to me in a careful and caring fashion, and then Jackie openly admitted her feelings for me. And she and Sharon proposed that we form a triad. Assuming, that is, that Jackie and I hit it off romantically. They both wanted me to be their girlfriend, while they continued their own relationship.

I sat there, stunned, for a moment. Then I reacted exactly as most people would have. I got up and went home.

I didn't wait for the bus. It was only about a mile and a half to my place and I needed to do some serious thinking. So I walked.

What bothered me most was that much of what they said made sense to me. "Why end a good relationship just because you want to start another one?" That was Sharon's rhetorical question, and I certainly didn't have any kind of answer that was more reasonable than, "Because that's how it's done!"

And let's face it... I'm not exactly Little Miss Traditional.

Sharon was still as captivating to me as ever. But I had to be honest. If I'd met Jackie without having known Sharon, I'd have gone out with her, had she asked. Well, she was asking now.

I trudged up the stairs to my apartment and went inside, standing with my back against the door for a minute. Then I called Jackie and asked her out for pizza the next night.

The following months were the most emotionally fulfilling months of my life, up to that point. I'll spare you the juicy details, but suffice to say that yes, we became a triad. None of us had any outside relationships. A few casual dates here and there for Sharon, but nothing serious. And to my surprise, I wasn't more than just a smidgeon jealous. Because neither of them for a moment allowed me to feel like they weren't as crazy about me as I was about them.

I practically lived with them, staying at their place several nights per week, sometimes sleeping with Sharon, sometimes with Jackie. Sometimes with both of them. We got along fantastically well, and I wondered how I'd gotten so lucky.

Further, my worries about having a relationship proved unfounded. Despite my deep involvement with the girls, school was productive. My grades were good. Rather than distracting me from my studies, my relationship actually made things better.

I'd been unhappy for so long that it had become my *status quo*. I'd pretty much forgotten what it was even like to be happy, until Sharon entered my life, bringing Jackie with her. So yeah, I was happy. And a happy Dinah is a productive Dinah.

Not only was I learning everything I could about biology and chemistry, but I was also discovering the scientific path I knew I was going to follow. I'd given up on the idea of replicating my brother's abilities. There just wasn't enough known to determine which genes might control mental abilities such as telekinesis and telepathy. I was going to have to work with what was known, and it was around this time that I became obsessed with the subject of metabolism, the process of converting matter to energy inside our bodies.

So many things about the human animal are fascinating. The idea that we can eat, say, a slice of pizza, and have this culinary masterpiece stripped down to its essential components and transformed into fuel that our cells need... well... we might understand how it happens, but that doesn't take away one bit from how amazing it is.

Naturally, I kept quiet about my ideas. When pressed about my interests in the field, I'd say I was studying metabolism with the hopes of using genetic manipulation to control human obesity. This was true, but not the whole truth. To state that I wanted to create metahuman abilities would've gotten me strange looks, to say the least. I didn't even tell Sharon or Jackie. The last thing I wanted was for either of them to think I had a screw loose.

The point, though, is that I was deliriously happy. I spoke to my family more often and didn't allow my mother's evangelical ramblings to get under my skin. I even decided to do something I swore I'd never do again. I went home for Christmas.

My little town is, truth be told, a lovely little place. It sits in a small valley, and has many parts of it that are picture postcard perfect. Winter can be brutal, with high humidity and heavy snows due to the lake effect from Lake Erie. But there are times when it's quite beautiful. Christmas Eve, this year, was one of those times.

Our parents had gone to a midnight church service. Dana and Elizabeth, his girlfriend, had gone with them, which rather shocked me. Dana was very much a non-believer and hated church, but Elizabeth was evidently okay with going to services, enjoying the music and feeling of amity that came from such gatherings. I declined, of course. Instead, I decided to go for a walk.

It was cold, well below freezing, so I'd bundled up. It was a clear night, with some snow on the ground from earlier in the day. At midnight, most homes had turned their colorful lights off, but there were still some lit. I remember standing in the middle of a deserted Main Street, just listening to... nothing. It was dead quiet, but not in that creepy way. It was just silent, still, and peaceful. I'd forgotten how quiet our town could be, after living in a noisy college town.

I breathed in the air, which was well past "crisp" and practically crystallized my sinuses, but I didn't care. It was pure and invigorating. In that moment, I had no cares in the world. I berated myself for thinking I wasn't able to enjoy life, and swore then and there that I was going to stop being such a bitter person. A whole week before New Year's, I had my resolution.

Before going back into the house, I stood there on the sidewalk, filled with what can only be described as joy. I felt new. I felt centered. I felt like a little girl, again.

The day after Christmas, I decided to tell my family about Sharon and Jackie. I did so in a halting, almost nervous way. I wanted them to understand and, yes, to approve. This was, in retrospect, undeniably foolish of me.

I don't think my father fully understood what our relationship was. He just looked at me strangely as I described it, shrugged his shoulders, and returned to his newspaper.

Dana and Elizabeth exchanged inscrutable looks before he said he was happy for me.

Mother, of course, blew a gasket. "Sinful," she called it. I didn't believe in the concept of sin, of course, so this didn't mean anything to me. "Selfish and disgraceful" were her next adjectives. "Abomination" was her final say on the subject.

At that point, I nearly broke my resolution. I felt the sneer forming on my face and barely caught the insulting words before they flew from my mouth. I looked at her, then the rest of my family. Dad was still behind the sports section. Dana wore a frown aimed at Mother, but said nothing. Elizabeth gave me a sorrowful look. But I didn't know whether she was expressing sympathy for my plight or pity for me and my lifestyle choices.

I was proud of myself for not ripping into Mother. And I didn't want this to destroy the good feelings I'd so recently found. So, to preserve those, I packed up and drove back to State College.

Not that the good feelings were going to last for long, anyway.

By the time the new year was barely a month old, my mood had begun to sour. By March, I was miserable. Why? Because Jackie and Sharon were seniors, and they weren't staying local after graduation.

They were headed to Pittsburgh. And naturally, our first thought was for me to go to grad school there, too. Jackie showed me her catalog from Carnegie Mellon and I ordered catalogs from the other major schools in the area and scoured them for information. But none of the programs offered at that time were really in line with what I wanted to pursue.

But that didn't matter. I'd find something close enough to what I wanted, just so I could be with them. I told myself this for a month. But in the end, the obsession I'd had since my teens outweighed my obsession with Sharon and Jackie.

In May, they graduated. I helped them pack their apartment into little boxes spotted with teardrops. And then, they were gone, leaving me to face my own senior year... alone.

Over the summer, I continued to work at the store. Sharon and Jackie spent the months with their respective families. We'd talk on weekends and sometimes write letters.

I tried to remain positive, to tell myself that we could make the long-distance thing work. Pittsburgh was only about two and a half hours from State College. Not a big deal.

Had it been a handful of years later, when Internet access was readily available to most and computers were semi-affordable, we might have done it.

Sure, once the fall semester started, there were letters and calls aplenty, and the occasional weekend visit. But by Thanksgiving, all this had lessened. Jackie's grad studies took up most of her free time and Sharon was teaching elementary school in the area. Their lives became much busier, understandably. And we drifted apart. I don't know how the two of them took that. Better than I did, I'm sure. They still had each other. And I was alone again.

I plunged into a deep depression, unable to deal with the loss of these two amazing women from my daily life, unable to accept that they simply didn't need me, as I needed them.

I knew I needed help, so I turned to find solace in another group of friends.

Spiritual friends.

Mainly rum.

FOUR

"The truth that many people never understand, until it is too late, is that the more you try to avoid suffering the more you suffer because smaller and more insignificant things begin to torture you in proportion to your fear of being hurt."

~Thomas Merton

Many things people eat and drink are evidently beyond my ability to appreciate. My father, for example, is one of those who will immediately reach for the salt and pepper before even tasting anything on his plate. And he'll cover everything to the same degree.

In grade school, I'd watch other kids hoard packets of ketchup, taking extras from the cafeteria and begging other students for theirs. They'd consume it in equal ratio to the fries, it seemed. Today, I watch people do the same thing with ranch dressing, which more or less makes me gag.

I already mentioned being unable to appreciate coffee in my pre-college years. The same can be said for alcohol. My father kept a case of Old Milwaukee in the house during the summer, and would sometimes enjoy a cold one after mowing our lawn. I had a taste, once, and just couldn't understand the appeal. It was exactly as I'd imagine carbonated urine to taste.

But alcohol consumption is a major pastime of college students, who consider beer a major food group, along with instant ramen, frozen pizza, and anything cheap and deep fried.

And age doesn't matter. If there's an underage college student alive who doesn't know how to obtain liquor with a minimum of effort, I haven't met her. In my case, it was through an arrangement with a graduate student named Liam who lived across the hall from me. I'd give him twenty bucks and he'd buy me a fifth of something, keeping the change as his "delivery charge." I fully expected him to maximize his profit by purchasing bargain-basement brands. The first time I took him up on the offer, I asked him to buy me some vodka, the flavor of which I could mask with whatever I poured it into. But instead of the vodka-esque equivalent of paint thinner, Liam returned with Smirnoff. Not a premium brand, by any stretch, but certainly better than the mystery spirits of the bottom shelf. Another time, though, he brought me a bottle of Finlandia. "It was on sale," he said. Even so, I knew it was pricier than Smirnoff, but he didn't care.

At any rate, it was because of his relative generosity that I was able to appreciate the differences between brands and styles. His own selection of liquor was impressive. Even more impressive was the fact that I don't remember ever seeing him drunk. Every once in a while, he'd invite me over for a tasting session. He'd have four or more examples of, say, Scotch. And he'd explain to me, as I tasted them, just what was responsible for the differences in flavor, texture, and so on.

For my twenty-first birthday, he presented me with a ridiculously extravagant gift: a bottle of Appleton Estate 21-year aged rum. I would have assumed he was trying to get into my pants, if I hadn't known he was gay.

I may have been drowning my sorrows, but at least I was doing it in style.

But I suffered, on several levels. I suffered from the loss of an incredible relationship, and from frequent hangovers. My grades suffered, as did my relationship with my family. Again.

When the triad ended, I didn't share the news. Even if I'd just told Dana, he would've told our mother, and I wasn't willing to endure that scene. She would have happily hopped on her high horse, hit me with a round of guilt, saying those evil women had just used me for my body and discarded me when they grew bored, and that I should have expected such things from *lesbians...* a word she always said in a voice dripping with disgust.

Nope. Not something I needed. So I suffered alone.

Eventually, though, my life of muddling through classes, being a zombie at work, and moping at home came to an abrupt end when I realized in a panic that I hadn't yet applied to graduate school. I'd equivocated while trying to decide whether to apply to a school in Pittsburgh, and then after the girls moved, I'd been too depressed to even think about it.

Because I'd waited so long, I chose to play things safely and apply for a master's program rather than go directly into the doctorate. And I did one of those things you're not "supposed" to do. I applied at the same school where I was getting my undergraduate degree. Honestly, given the deterioration of my performance during my senior year, I was just hoping they'd even want to keep me around. But then, even though my grades were fading, my student loans weren't. So I got in.

I wasn't stupid, of course. I was quite aware that I was screwing up, allowing depression to get the better of me. And I knew I wasn't doing myself any favors by praying at the porcelain altar on a regular basis. One night, after a particularly enthusiastic session of worship, there was a knock on my door. I staggered to the living room. It was Liam.

"Hey," I said quietly, my head pounding. "I'm really not up for anything, tonight."

"Listen," he said. "It's none of my business, but..." And he handed me a business card.

It was for CAPS. Penn State's Counseling and Psychological Services.

Despite the fact that my brother was a psychologist – or perhaps in part because of this – I wasn't exactly enamored of the idea of therapy. At first, I dismissed the whole idea, and even got angry with Liam for suggesting it. How dare he? But the look of concern on his face kept coming back to me. So I made an appointment.

In the assessment interview, I begrudgingly explained what had been going on in my life, focusing mainly on the ending of the relationship. At first, I was hesitant to explain the fact that it was a triad, rather than a "normal" two-person thing. But I did.

When we were through, the intake counselor recommended individual counseling for me, explaining that I would qualify for ten sessions at no charge. Beyond that, I could continue for a fee.

My first appointment was a week later. And I was a bit annoyed, because my therapist wasn't the counselor I'd seen in the intake assessment. That shouldn't have surprised me, but it did. I wasn't very good at opening up to strangers, and I hated that I'd now have to go through it all a second time. And I wasn't a good patient. It would take me half the session to open up. And by the time I really felt at ease, the session would be over.

My counselor soon diagnosed me with chronic depression. And since he couldn't prescribe medication, he suggested I break out of some ruts, shake up my world a little bit.

I thought that was ironic. It was having my world shaken up that put me in the depression in the first place, I told him. He disagreed. He said I'd probably had depression since I was young, but was only now having a really bad streak.

And as soon as he said it, I knew he was right. I hadn't been truly happy, more than briefly, as long as I could remember. I was always, at best, just okay. But even then, there was a constant hum of unhappiness underneath.

Dysthymia, it's called. A perpetual, low-level depression punctuated by occasional major depressive episodes. My counselor suggested seeing a psychiatrist to pursue a medication-based treatment. I declined. Drugs and alcohol don't mix, and I wasn't ready to give up the liquid crutch.

But I decided to follow his advice. Another shake up, but this time on my terms.

My first step was to quit my job at the market. I didn't need the constant reminder of where I'd met Sharon. I didn't need to be working around coffee, either. Every time someone ordered Hermosa, I'd be in a funk the rest of the day.

To replace this income, and now being twenty-one, I took a job at Zeno's. Zeno's was, and probably still is, a dark little basement pub just off campus on the corner of College Avenue and Allen Street. Though there were more attractive bars in town, and probably ones that would net me bigger tips, Zeno's was the only one that played music I could tolerate for hours at a time. Lots of classic rock, not the Top 40 dance crap that was ubiquitous in the early '90s.

Zeno's was only a few blocks from the market job I'd just left, but it was such a different world, in both good and bad ways. The music, obviously, was good. The smoke, however, was bad. No establishments were smoke-free, back then. Then there was the clientele. Both better and worse. No more snooty dorks asking, "Do you have rennet-less cheese?" But plenty of inebriated college students.

I was able to indulge my compulsive learning personality by diving into mixology. Gone were the days of making nothing more complicated than a gin and tonic or a (bad) martini in my apartment.

The popular drink the girls were ordering at the time was the Cosmopolitan, so I quickly mastered it. The Cosmo was invented to showcase the then-new Absolut Citron vodka. The original recipe also used Rose's sweetened lime juice instead of fresh squeezed. And, contrary to how you often see the drink served these days, it should be pink, not red.

The thing many people don't realize is that making a drink isn't an art. Or rather, it's an art in the same way cooking is an art. There's a science to it, too. You can't just throw flour, eggs, sugar, and some other stuff in a bowl at random, mix it up, and expect to bake yummy cookies. There are proportions, proper choices of ingredients, methods of mixing, and so on. It's no different with alcohol.

James Bond's preferences notwithstanding, a proper martini should be stirred, not shaken. And no, it has nothing to do with "bruising" the gin, but with how much water the drink will contain. And yes, water is an important ingredient in cocktails. Shaking a drink puts more water in it from the agitation of the ice. A brief stir and strain imparts less.

Balance is important.

During the last semester of my senior year, I worked almost every day at the bar, socking away as much money as possible. And I started cracking the books again, determined to pull out of the scholastic nosedive I'd begun when the girls left. As for my emotional trauma... I just stopped thinking about it.

Avoidance, however, isn't a method of recovery. Instead, it wraps the agony in a shell, where it hides until some event cracks it open. And then the perfectly preserved pain is born anew.

I also berated myself for having gone against my previous inclinations to avoid relationships while in school. And frequently in my alcohol-induced misery, I'd do the unthinkable: admit that maybe my mother was right. Maybe they really *had* used me.

Sober, though, this didn't stand up to the evidence. And in some ways, that was worse. If I'd really believed myself a victim, it would have been easier to take. I could have channeled the sorrow into anger, at least. But no. I wasn't a victim of anything more than Cupid's sneak attack.

The truth I had to accept was quite simple, really. The girls had treated our relationship pragmatically. They knew going in that it was likely to be temporary. Foolishly, I wasn't thinking that way.

At the end of the year, I took stock of my life.

Grades – Not bad. Not great, or even what I'd call "good," but certainly improved. I felt sure that I could pull my GPA up in my final semester as an undergrad.

Work – I had a nice little nest egg growing. I was enjoying my job and getting my feet wet as a bartender during slow times.

Meta-Research – Between studying like crazy and working my tail off, I didn't have much time to put into it. And I was often discouraged, feeling like I was trying to do the impossible.

Emotional recovery – Though I wasn't devastated, anymore, I'd withdrawn from any social life at all, outside of work. I convinced myself that the bar was enough, even though becoming familiar with the regulars was limited to joking around with them for a minute here and there while I did my job.

Pity I couldn't get a degree in self-deception. I'd have aced that with ease.

In April of 1992, a month before I graduated with my B.S. in biology, one of my professors announced the sad news that Peter D. Mitchell had just passed away. Mitchell had been a British biochemist, winner of the Nobel Prize in Chemistry in '78 for his Chemiosmotic Theory, and I'd always fantasized about interviewing him, to discuss the finer points of his work. Clearly, that dream wasn't going to come true.

Mitchell's theory dealt with the production of adenosine triphosphate, or "ATP," through cellular respiration. ATP is, among several other things, a source of chemical energy in the body. In short, he'd discovered a basic process governing the generation and transfer of energy within cells. Naturally, this was one of the big pieces of the puzzle I'd been putting together in my quest to turn myself into a meta.

Another piece was fat.

The human body has two types of fat: white fat and brown fat. Brown fat is loaded with mitochondria, little cellular power plants, which generate a large amount of ATP. The main purpose of brown fat in infants is to produce heat, since hypothermia is a risk for little ones. But babies are also growing at a rapid rate. Growth requires constant energy. Why do you think babies just seem to eat and sleep? They're burning lots of energy, constantly active, even though they're "just lying there."

Very efficient stuff, brown fat. I found it fascinating, and wished that brown fat didn't virtually disappear in adults. But white fat is a much better insulator and cushion than brown fat, and evolution compensated, since that's what adults needed in the rough, lean millennia before our modern lives became so easy.

Today, of course, we'd be much better off if we could retain the brown fat and dispense with most of the white fat. If nothing else, it would pretty much eliminate the obesity epidemic. For that matter, I often wondered whether there might be, somewhere in nature, another kind of energy producing tissue even more efficient than brown fat.

The Chemiosmotic Theory and brown fat were interesting enough for the production and storage of energy, but when it came to actually doing something with that power, I looked at nature's oldest known battery: the electric eel.

This amazing creature, which isn't an eel at all, not only manufactures energy, but can store it and discharge it without self-damage. And it can zap in sufficient power to kill other creatures, including some much larger than itself, with repeated shocks. It can zap and zap for an hour or more without seeming to tire.

I still had no idea if I could ever figure out how to mimic that ability, but then, I had a lot to learn. There were so many things on the horizon that I knew would be instrumental in my research. In 1992, we were still half a dozen years away from isolating human embryonic stem cells. The government had banned experimentation using fetal tissue. Progress would be made, with or without federal consent. It didn't have to be in our country, after all. One thing was certain: the advent of metas in the world really kicked scientific research into high gear.

Despite metas being everywhere in the public eye, it was difficult to know what was going on with them. I couldn't seem to find any hard data on research or the official activities of the government groups.

So I filled out a request under the Freedom of Information Act to learn a few things. But the government's response was, "We are unable to fulfill your information request due to the interests of national security."

I had former President Reagan to thank for that one. In 1982, he signed an executive order severely limiting the Freedom of Information Act, allowing federal agencies to withhold ridiculous amounts of information under this pretense.

"National Security" my butt.

In May, I graduated. I didn't attend the ceremony, choosing instead to have my diploma mailed to me. Dana sent me a "Congraduations" card with a nice note. My parents sent me a more formal card, but it was devoid of any personal touches, unless you count the religious tracts my mother insisted on sending me at least once a month. My card was stuffed with them.

Time seemed to accelerate after graduation. Summer zipped past and then I was in my first year of grad school. It was hard, but I really got into it. I was determined to excel, now, and studied like crazy. Work was hectic, and that was fine. Lots of thirsty students meant lots of tips. And for some reason, I got really good tips.

I spent much of my free time at Pattee Library, especially at the circulation desk, eagerly reading every issue of the *Journal of Cellular Biochemistry*, *Cell*, *Science*, *Nature*, and any other magazine that might hold relevant information or inspiration.

Thanksgiving soon arrived. I didn't go home. Same for Christmas and New Year's. Mother sent me a nastygram condemning me for not spending the holidays with them, while simultaneously admitting that the house was much less stressful in my absence.

Before I knew it, I'd finished my first year of graduate school. The last semester of my program would involve an internship. Mine would be at GACTech, a biotechnology firm in nearby Bellefonte. I'd get to know some scientists who had far more than theoretical knowledge, but hands-on experience with the sort of things I was planning to do.

Well, not *exactly* what I was planning to do. No one had that experience, to my awareness.

GACTech was not the only biotech firm in the area, but most of the others dealt with agriculture or dairy cattle and/or milk products. Not surprising, since central Pennsylvania has lots of farms. Go five miles outside of State College in any direction, and you're pretty much in farmland. Penn State, in fact, began as an agricultural school.

Had I wanted to play around with cows and crops, I'm sure I could have gotten an internship at one of those other firms. But GACTech was where I wanted to work. It was the only local firm exploring medical biotech.

The other half of my final semester would be a research paper. The nice thing about metabolism research is that it can apply to so many different things. I knew I'd be able to write my paper on obesity and mitochondria practically off the top of my head.

Mother continued to send her religious tracts, sometimes accompanied by letters. But most of the letters really were only more of the same, with quote after quote from her televangelist *du jour*. I skimmed them, at best. Sometimes, I just threw them away, unread.

Maybe that's why I was blindsided, at summer's end, by the arrival of Dana and Elizabeth's wedding invitation, with a date set in October.

It was a strange feeling, I have to admit. I never really pictured Dana as the "get married and settle down" type of guy. I think what bothered me the most, though, was that I hadn't known it was coming. And I don't mean by virtue of Mother telling me, but because he and I didn't talk. I knew this was my doing, but it still upset me that he hadn't told me.

The wedding took place in a suburb of Philadelphia, the bride's hometown, on an unseasonably warm Saturday. It was a nice wedding, I suppose. The short, secular ceremony was outdoors, officiated by a judge, with a harpist and flautist as the musical accompaniment. The seats were arranged in a semi-circle, and from mine at the far end of the first row, I could observe most of the other guests. I noted especially the reactions of Elizabeth's family.

They didn't seem very happy. Even from across the lawn, I could tell her mother's smile was fake. Every so often, it would disappear completely and she would clench her fist in her lap, holding a handkerchief that never came near her eyes.

At the reception, I exchanged pleasantries with the few guests I knew, but couldn't stop glancing at the table where my brother's new in-laws sat. After my second trip to the buffet, I made my way to stand within earshot of them. It didn't take much eavesdropping to conclude that Elizabeth's mother was a bit tipsy... a heck of an accomplishment at a dry party.

More interesting than a drunk mother-in-law, though, were the snippets I overheard, which confirmed the earlier visual cues. They weren't happy about the marriage, because they didn't approve of Dana. He was an admitted atheist, after all, and they couldn't stand the idea of their daughter marrying someone who was so misguided and damned. Elizabeth's mother and mine would probably have gotten along well. Dana was sure in for an interesting marriage.

I soon extricated myself from the festivities and "Baby" and I made the three hour drive back to State College. During the trip, all I could do was think of how happy Dana and Elizabeth looked, despite the negativity from her family. I wondered if I'd looked that happy when I was with Sharon and Jackie. I wondered if I ever would look that happy again. And I wondered when I'd stop thinking such thoughts.

The term "abandonment issues" typically brings to mind a tragically orphaned child or an infant left in a basket on someone's doorstep, never knowing the comforts of a biological family while growing up. Truth is, though, you can live with your birth parents your whole life and still have these issues.

According to my therapist, abandonment issues become attachment issues in most people, leading us to take rejection very badly, and even perceive things as rejection that truly aren't. They often lead a person to feel unworthy of love and even to push away those who offer it. The idea there is that it's easier to dump someone than to be the one dumped, which we believe to be inevitable. And even aside from the romantic arena, attachment issues may even lead us to take the blame for things that aren't our fault, or at least to take on the bulk of the blame for no good reason.

All this, I found interesting and enlightening, to a degree. But understanding why I was this way didn't really help me *stop* being this way.

These issues were the focal point of my therapy sessions. "Tell me," my counselor said one day, "about when you had a good relationship with your mother. Give me a nice story from that time."

"I can't," I said. And he gave me that look that meant he knew I was just being lazy. So I thought about it. I have some scattered memories of my early childhood where it seems as though things with us were as a healthy mother/daughter relationship should be. I remember sitting in her lap, watching TV. I remember helping her stir cake batter in the big steel bowl and her letting me lick the spoon. Things like that. But they're rare.

More often, I remember coming home from school, eager to tell her about my day, and her reacting with, at best, feigned interest. I remember fidgeting in the pew next to her at church and her pinching my leg to get me to settle down. And of course, I remember all the nastiness of later years, after I threw my sexuality in her face. Thereafter, we lived in the same house, but she was a stranger to me.

"Okay," I finally said. "When I was six, I got the chicken pox really bad. Even had them in my mouth. And my mother treated me like a princess the whole time, putting lotion on me, making my favorite meals and dessert every day. And when they finally cleared up, and I wasn't in constant misery, we spent an entire weekend doing things together. We went shopping, had ice cream cones, went to the movies... It was a lot of fun."

"And how long after this did you begin to feel the distancing?"

"Um... less than a year. My sixth birthday was the last where I had a birthday party at my house. For my seventh, she said I couldn't have one."

"So, during that year, what happened?"

"Well, it was around that time that she started to get really religious, going to church a lot, watching the televangelists and so on."

"And what do you think was behind that?"

"I have no idea."

"Any issues in her life, or your father's life? Marital problems, for example?"

"Not that I ever knew of," I said.

"Any problems with your father's job?" No. "Death in the extended family?" No. "Problem with your brother?"

I started to deny that one, too, but paused. Quick addition... I was six, so Dana would've been... "Maybe," I mumbled.

Dana once told me that he was thirteen when Mother learned of his telekinetic abilities. It was still some time before our parents learned of his telepathy. And even though our parents aren't exactly Mensa candidates, they're not ignorant of what it meant to have a child develop meta-abilities at puberty. They knew it meant the other child was at higher risk for it.

So, when she learned of Dana's mutation, they started to worry about me being similarly "afflicted." And even though I didn't develop abilities the way Dana had, by the time that was obvious, she had already put up a wall between us. Once a wall is up, it takes quite a lot to tear it down. And as we've already determined, I didn't exactly give her much cause to do anything other than reinforce it.

This is just a working hypothesis, of course. The reality could be that my mother's just a bitch.

FIVE

"If we want to be loved, we must disclose ourselves. If we want to love someone, he must permit us to know him. This would seem to be obvious. Yet most of us spend a great part of our lives thinking up ways to avoid becoming known."

~Sidney Jourard

When I was growing up, back in the days before virtual online communities, kids generally had two sets of friends: the ones at school and the ones at home. Some were lucky enough to have the two groups overlap, but I had geography against me.

Our house sat on a dead-end street, flanked on one side by a large creek with flood control dikes and on the other by railroad tracks with a patch of woods in between. So my "neighborhood" consisted only of the dozen or so homes along that short stretch of macadam.

My brother, at least, had the good fortune of growing up with three or four other families on the street with children his age. But by the time I was ten, the other kids were either almost driving or barely walking.

The one school friend I sometimes saw outside the classroom was Rhonda. Our mothers were friends, and would sometimes visit the other across town, with daughter in tow. And often, Rhonda would come over to my house after school and we'd play for a couple hours until her dad picked her up after work. We were close up until about twelve or thirteen.

Maybe because of this insulated childhood, I was never good at forming friendships in college. Or maybe it's because I was too busy for them. But by my mid-twenties, I was desperate for friends. I wanted someone to watch movies with, share pizza with, get drunk with, cry with. A girlfriend in the platonic sense. As children, it doesn't take much to form a bond. *"You like Rainbow Brite? Me too! Let's be friends!"* Easy peasy.

But as we grow up, we seem to develop a detailed list of qualifications that must be met before we let someone inside our circle. We expect more than just instant gratification; we want a long-term payoff for our investment of time and effort. We want friends who are clearly going to benefit us in a noticeable and substantial way.

Or maybe that was just me.

Either way, my ability to meet potential friends in college wasn't great. If I wasn't in class, I was studying, working on my theories, or tending bar at Zeno's. But I had to go with what I had.

I put myself in the kid frame of mind. At the bar, I noted what songs on the jukebox people played or sang to, what they ordered to drink (and what they didn't), and what they would chat about.

And it's funny how things work out, sometimes. One of my fellow bartenders, Brent, liked Alice Cooper. So one day, I played "Caught in a Dream" on the jukebox and even sang along with it. Not one of his better-known songs, but always one of my favorites.

Brent was impressed. "I think you're the first girl I've ever met who was into Alice Cooper," he said.

"My brother is about your age. I grew up listening to whatever he had in his collection."

"Well, you tell your brother he has good taste in music," he said, and moved off to serve a new customer.

That was when the brunette at the bar said, "I saw Alice Cooper on *The Muppet Show*."

I laughed. "Yeah! Me, too!"

She smiled. "You're a really good singer."

"Thanks." I noticed her glass was empty and poured her another Captain and Coke.

And that's how Lee and I became friends. Easy peasy.

Lee never did become much of a fan of Alice Cooper, but we had plenty of mutual interests outside of music. We had complementary outlooks on society. We liked a lot of the same books and movies. We both enjoyed playing board games and cards. And we both loved to shoot pool. We spent hours playing at The Corner Pocket, which was the pool room downstairs at the Hetzel Union Building on campus. There were other pool halls downtown, but I liked this smaller, quieter location.

Lee was exactly the kind of friend I needed. We shopped, had drinks over lunch, saw movies, and so on. We talked about relationships. She was seeing a guy, but he didn't seem to want it to become as serious as she wanted. I wasn't seeing anyone, and that's how I wanted it. Sure, I sometimes got lonely, and self-gratification didn't always satisfy. I told her, as I'd told myself before, that a romance would interfere too much, even though it hadn't with Sharon and Jackie. But really, I was just trying to prevent the heartache of separation, again.

This didn't stop Lee from frequently trying to fix me up with someone. She had a few lesbian friends, and I showed my gratitude by going out on the occasional date. But nothing came of any of them.

Though Lee was completely okay with my sexual preferences, the one topic she had a hard time talking about was my relationship with Sharon and Jackie. She dismissed such a polyamorous lifestyle as naïve and idealistic, and said I was just fooling myself about my relationship with the girls, even if a hundred and fifty miles hadn't separated us. "We're not cut out for that sort of thing," she said. "Humans are possessive and territorial."

I didn't argue the point. Maybe she was right. That relationship was more than two years past. I sometimes doubted, myself, that it had been as amazing as I'd built it up to be.

In December, I received my master's degree in genetics. It was a proud moment for me, and one that I'd rather hoped my family would share. Dana and Elizabeth sent a card, but my parents didn't even acknowledge the accomplishment.

Lee threw me a surprise party at Zeno's. It celebrated not just my degree, but also my new job: lab assistant at GACTech.

In January of '94, the Northridge Earthquake rocked L.A. Though it's doubtful the metas prevented many deaths, it's certain they rescued hundreds more quickly than emergency responders could have. And several assisted with the cleanup afterward.

Metas often help out in natural disasters. In March, four southeastern states were hit with what has been called the Palm Sunday tornado outbreak. Twenty-seven tornadoes in the space of nine hours.

Unfortunately, there are always the paranoid folks in the population. Following the tornados, one prominent anti-meta group suggested that such a disaster must have been caused by metahumans. It was common knowledge that some metas could control weather to a limited degree. Though not a view embraced by many, the minority was quite loud. And now there was a brand new shouting forum for them: the World Wide Web. Sites popped up spouting all sorts of wild ideas about how metas were behind everything from the Rwandan genocide to your kid's case of colic.

And even more unfortunately, sometimes metas did deserve the lambasting.

That summer, the media pummeled the nation with diatribes about the "problem" of teen metas, set off by a rash of high-profile incidents involving a group in Los Angeles. Ironically self-named The Defenders, this adolescent team tended toward grandstanding, brutality, and excessive property damage in their alleged pursuit of justice.

Naturally, reporters were quick to focus on the fact that they were adolescents, and it gave the term "hormonal teens" an all-new meaning. And it added to the growing public opinion that all too many metas were interested primarily in personal gain and/or inflating their egos. Some said it wasn't so much a matter of their youth, but the fact that they weren't a government-run group. They lacked the accountability that other groups had, and were therefore prone to do whatever they liked, no matter the consequences.

The Defenders' actions were enough to cause a previously split Congress to pass a bill requiring all metahumans to register with the government, to be entered into a national database and issued a federal metahuman I.D. card. These cards were equipped with RFID tags that could be scanned by any government agent from a distance of up to one hundred feet, allegedly, and would contain all sorts of personal data, including known meta abilities and weaknesses.

To my dismay, President Clinton actually signed it, and it was scheduled to go into effect the following year.

All in all, a heinous result, but one good thing did come of The Defenders debacle. It reminded me to add another element to my own research.

The vast majority of metahuman abilities manifested at puberty. Sure, there were exceptions. Some mutations were triggered by trauma, including some that preceded puberty. (Thankfully, super-powered toddlers are virtually unheard of.)

Until this point, I'd been focusing purely on genetic manipulation to trigger my own mutation. I hadn't particularly thought much about hormones. But now it was squarely in my mind.

The stage of life we call puberty is actually a sequence of hormonal actions. First, the hypothalamus secretes one hormone, prodding the pituitary into releasing two other hormones, which in turn occasion the ovaries and tickle the testes to release gender-specific hormones that lead to all those traits and side effects we know and love... cracking voices, zits, and having to shave hair from locations we might have preferred to remain bald. I knew now that I couldn't afford to dismiss the idea of additional hormone treatments.

And as with most research, I was continually discovering some unexpected things that could potentially result from the final experiment.

Sirtuins, for example, are a class of protein that plays a part in metabolism. But they affect much more than metabolism. It was conceivable,

I reasoned, that in addition to boosting my production of energy, sirtuins could also aid in DNA repair. Talk about handy. When you're looking to muck about with your genetic code, it helps to have something there to maybe fix your less egregious mistakes.

Most of my focus was on mitochondria, of course. I aimed to increase the performance of the little organelles, and increase the number of them in my cells. Turns out, there are several ways to do both, one of which doesn't require a degree in genetics.

It's called exercise.

Joining a gym was Lee's idea. I just wanted to take up jogging or something. But she hated jogging and wanted us to work out together.

It's not that I was opposed to gyms. I was just opposed to paying money for something that I could get free, essentially.

And maybe that's because I grew up in a one-income family. Our dad didn't make a lot of money and mother didn't work any sort of steady job. Her limited income, from accepting a few bucks for doing her friends' hair or for selling Avon, mostly went to the collection plate at church. Sure, the monthly mortgage on our house was less than I currently pay for my cell phone bill, but one income was still just one income. Dad was frugal because a family of four wasn't easy to support. So I grew up having a great respect for money. Or perhaps it was more a fear of not having it.

I worried like mad about finances. I was dreading having to begin repaying the massive student loan debt I was accumulating. But I would put that off for as long as possible. If I could've become a professional student, I'd have done it.

Also that summer, Lee and I became roommates. It was her idea, but I agreed to it happily. I wasn't saving anywhere near as much money as I'd hoped, so reducing my rent would have been enticing enough. But Lee and I got along so well, I couldn't really see any huge negatives to the proposition.

It meant moving to a two-bedroom apartment, of course. That was fine, though. Even with the higher rent, we both saved money over our previous living arrangements.

Lee and I hit the gym every day, first thing in the morning. But despite her desire to have a workout partner, our routines differed quite a bit. She did almost exclusively cardio, whereas I did mostly strength training. For cardio, I still preferred running outdoors.

At some point, I learned that the gym offered yoga classes. I persuaded Lee to sign up with me. True to form, though, I only took yoga for a few months. Like running, I could do this on my own without paying someone, once I learned the *asanas* I wanted to practice.

In the fall of '94, I began working on my doctorate, my third degree at Penn State. I was beginning to feel like I lived in Mueller Lab.

I took to the program well, soaking up the classes and texts, which allowed me to make tremendous inroads on my own research. The professors were great, and I liked that they regarded the doctoral students with respect.

Meanwhile, out in the "real" world, relations between metas and the rest of society weren't going so well.

The Meta Registration Act went into effect in January of '95. As expected, many metahumans refused to register. Some left the U.S. for Canada or other friendly nations. Some went into hiding.

Not that hiding did much good. Some metas had the ability to detect others. And the government put them to good use, tracking down known metas who had not registered by the January 31 deadline.

On the other hand, the U.S. at that time had about 2500 metas. That figure, by the way, isn't from any sort of census, but based purely on the average estimated rate of metahuman births. And although quite a lot of metas were publicly known in one way or another, quite a few were unknowns. Those whose mutations didn't result in some sort of obvious deformity could hide in plain sight and no one would know the difference, Meta Registration Act or no Meta Registration Act.

The anti-meta segment of the population was becoming more vocal and demanding that the government do something about them. The registration business wasn't the only result of this. During this same period, the use of metas in police departments and other agencies began to fall apart. The non-meta agents began to resent the metas, and as a result, the metas were given their own departments within the agencies.

Segregation had begun. Even among those on the same "team."

I'm in second grade, standing backstage in my school's auditorium, peeking through the side curtain at the crowd, all full of people – grownups! – waiting to watch me when it's my turn to go out.

My teacher puts her hand on my shoulder, urging me to step back from the curtain. I bounce on my toes and gesture toward the crowd. "Mrs. Martin! My mama and dad and Dana are here!"

She smiles kindly down at me. "Yes, I saw them come in. Ready to impress them, you little diva?"

I frown. "What's a diva?"

"Never mind, honey. Just get ready."

Turning back, I see my classmates, most of them nervous about performing a skit or routine in our end-of-year talent show. But not me. I'm excited, eager to perform. I'm a good singer and I know it. I'm going to impress the heck out of everyone. They'll love me.

The act before mine ends and the curtain closes. Someone – our principal, I think – introduces my act. The music begins as the curtain parts.

I strut out to the front of the stage, the spotlight hitting me full in the face, my golden locks glowing. It's hot, but I pay no attention as I bop up to the microphone, the music cueing me to sing.

With gusto, I break into the Rose Royce disco tune, "Car Wash." I think I get the lyrics right, but there's no denying my enthusiasm. And I can see the audience is enjoying it. They could see that I was talented and pretty.

I bob my head, making my pigtails bounce as I prance around the stage. But in no time, the song is over. I bask in the applause, warm from the adulation. I find my family's faces in the crowd. Mother claps politely, Dad with more enthusiasm... and Dana laughs and cheers.

I bow and turn around, paying no attention to the six other children who'd danced with me, rags and water buckets flailing, as they sang backup to my lead. I skip offstage, feeling like I'm flying.

My last year in school was for my dissertation. I supposed I had an advantage over most of the other students, as I'd essentially been working on it for quite a long time. *Induced Mutation to Effect Meta-Biogenesis* was the title. Defending this largely speculative work felt more like a hazing than an academic process. But the review board was impressed, especially Professor Gray. He said it was the most fascinating thing he'd read in years.

So now I was "Doctor Dinah," as Lee insisted on calling me.

And speaking of calling, Dana did so, to offer his sincere congratulations on my degree. We had an awkward but not unpleasant conversation. My resentment toward him, I realized, had lessened, largely because of my work, whether or not it was viable. I was proud of the work I was doing.

Most of the time, anyway.

Abandonment issues often translate into self-doubt or low self-esteem, as Sharon had so accurately noted. The underlying, usually unconscious, idea behind these feelings is that *we* were somehow to blame for being abandoned, because we were bad, or unlovable, or something. And we go through life looking for that missing love from childhood, all the while still thinking we're losers.

There were plenty of times I was sure I was wasting my time and money. Hell, wasting my life, really. There was no way I'd ever be successful. And I'd not even considered any sort of contingency plan, should my meta-research be a wash. Usually, I didn't think about such scenarios, but whenever something would throw me into a state of doubt, this lack of backup would add a nice little layer of panic to my emotions.

I wish I could say that I handled these slips with some sort of dignity, but I didn't. Before meeting Lee, I would just become despondent and drink heavily. But since I'd shared my plans with Lee, I could whine to her. And I did.

She was a good friend, always able to coax me into a better frame of mind. She was also a practical friend. She'd lock the liquor cabinet and hide the key.

There were two major episodes where her influence was particularly pivotal. The first was about a year after I received my Ph.D. I was now a full research scientist at GACTech. I had my own office and unrestricted access to pretty much everything in the facility. After everyone else had gone home, I'd stay late into the night, using the technology at my disposal to work on my project.

I'd been refining my theory for close to a decade and had a few of what I believed to be brilliant ideas. But, as with many great theories, there were a couple large gaps. After one particularly frustrating afternoon in the lab, when one of my ideas failed spectacularly (it had looked so good on paper, too), I angrily stormed out and headed to the nearest bar.

There's not a lot I remember about that night. I remember bumping into Dr. Gray there, and probably embarrassing him by talking his ear off between shots. I think his date wanted to kill me. Or him. Or both of us.

The wise bartender had taken my keys at some point. He offered to get me a cab, but instead, I called Lee to come pick me up. She poured me into the car and drove me home in silence.

We were barely inside when she lit into me. "You've got to stop doing this, Dinah! Can't you see what you're doing to yourself? Or to me?"

I blinked. "To you?" I practically fell into an armchair in the living room and sat there, gripping the cushioned arms even though I knew the room wasn't *really* spinning. "What am I...?" I let the sentence fade as I choked back a bit of nausea.

Lee stood in front of me, arms crossed, with a look of pain on her face. "Don't you think it *hurts* me to see you abusing yourself like this? You're so *angry* all the time! And I'm tired of having you take it out on me."

I shook my head, which was a mistake. Wincing, I said, "How?"

She turned her head away and her expression softened. "Dinah... I care for you."

I nodded. Another mistake. "Look," I drawled, "unless you're speaking on behalf of my liver, you don't need to feel hurt."

She looked at me, then at the floor. She muttered to herself, but I heard her. "Wrong organ," she said, and walked off toward her room.

I sat there for a few minutes and let my brain chew on it all. I was hurting her... somehow. A joke about budding alcoholism elicited a comment about another organ. Which organ? Brain? Lungs? Pancreas?

I care for you. Not *I care* about *you.*

She'd broken up with her boyfriend. She hadn't tried for months to set me up with girls she knew...

Suddenly, I felt all kinds of weird.

I got up and went to her room. I entered without knocking, to find her sitting on the edge of her bed, looking rather despondent. I sat beside her.

After a minute of silence, I said, "So..."

Lee shrugged. "Yeah."

"Really?"

She gave me a sidelong glance that was hurt and scared and a hundred other things. At least, that's what my rum-soaked eyes saw.

That, and her delicious lips.

SIX

"There is no such thing as a 'failed experiment,' only experiments with unexpected outcomes."
~R. Buckminster Fuller

I'm in first grade. Our teacher is writing on the blackboard when the classroom door opens. Twenty-five pairs of eyes turn to see the school nurse standing there, the faint smile on her stern face seeming to mock the terror gripping the room full of children. The arrival of the school nurse only ever meant one thing: a visit from the town doctor. And a visit from the town doctor only meant one thing: we were about to get a shot.

Knots forming in our stomachs, we trudge single-file down the hallway to the cafeteria, where a score of other students stand in line, arms bared for whatever inoculation is on the menu. I look at the girl next to me in line, wondering if my eyes hold the same fear as hers, knowing quite well they must.

An eternity later, I stand in front of the doctor, panic mounting as he swabs my arm with alcohol. "This won't hurt a bit," he says. I want to call him a liar. But before I can open my mouth, the needle pierces my flesh. A moment later, a grinding pain makes me gasp.

"Ow! You hit the bone!"

"Oh, I did not, young lady. You're all done. You can go, now."

Fighting back tears, I make my way back to my room and take my seat. My arm is throbbing, and I sit there, waiting for the rest of my classmates to return so that class can resume.

Minutes pass. I feel woozy. My arm still hurts and I absently reach out to rub it. My hand touches something slick. I look to see my upper arm soaked with blood.

The boy next to me sees it, too. He screams for me, since I'm too weak to do so, about to pass out. The teacher rushes to my side, then fetches paper towels to sop up my blood. I'm ushered to the nurse's office, where I'm bandaged up and given an ice pack to hold on my arm.

No one can ever tell me again that shots aren't so bad.

Lee was a good sounding board for my ideas, mainly because she knew almost nothing about my field of science. Her questions, being basic, often required lengthy explanations, and these would sometimes cause me to think of some new part of the process I'd need to address.

But sometimes, her impact was more direct. One day, she asked me straight out, "So, how long will it all take?"

I shrugged and said, "The rest of my life. As science advances, there will always be new things for me to try."

"Right, but how do you do... you know... the part not on paper."

"Well," I said, then hesitated, realizing this would be the first time I'd ever spoken the process aloud. "In a very small nutshell, I'll extract stem cells from my blood and... manipulate them." It sounded so different when I vocalized it, so much more far-fetched than the ideas in my head and on paper. "And then re-inject them. Then I sit back and wait."

"Wait?"

"The altered cells need to make their way into the bone marrow, which will take a while, even with a vector host or lipid solution to aid them. Then even longer for them to replicate and – assuming I'm right – cause my body to produce only the mutated form from here on out." I shrugged again. "I expect it to be years before I see any real results."

Lee sat there in silence for a minute, staring at me. I don't think she really understood the scope of what I was doing until that moment. Finally, she said, "So... when will you do it?"

"I'm not sure," I said. "I want to make sure the time is right."

"When will that be?" Lee asked. "I mean, technology and science advance so quickly... If you wait for the perfect time, you'll never do anything."

I hate it when others say things I should be thinking. Lee was right. I was procrastinating. Why? Was it fear? Yes, I admit there was some of that. Just don't ask me what I was afraid of, failure or success. I don't think I can tell you.

"I just want to be sure," I said.

"Dinah... You've been sure of this since you were a teenager."

And that's the second way she critically influenced my life. I *was* ready. There was never the "perfect" time to do many things in life, whether it was something as dangerous as my Dr. Jekyll experiment, or something as innocuous as starting a new relationship.

I'd like to be able to say that becoming romantically involved with Lee was the best thing I ever did, that it felt perfectly "right" from the start, and that my life improved in short order. But who would believe that, even if it were true?

As I've said, Lee was a great friend. But our relationship was never without – at least on my part – a good deal of trepidation. I kept thinking about her condemnation of my relationship with Sharon and Jackie. "Naïve and idealistic" were her labels of choice.

I think she believed that I'd put that whole silly thing behind me and was ready to settle down with just one person. But I didn't ask, because... well, because in truth, I honestly believed – and still do – that open and honest non-monogamy is a viable relationship paradigm, one that made sense, and one with which I identified. That being said, I still regarded that triad as a fluke, something highly unlikely ever to happen to me again. And since that was the case, why put doubts in her head unnecessarily by mentioning how I felt?

Yes, this was rationalization. But it wasn't so much lying to Lee as it was not being honest with myself.

Besides, I further rationalized, it's not as though she'd asked me, either way, whether I could be monogamous. So for her to assume I was prepared to be monogamous and hop into a relationship with me was foolish on her part.

Clearly, I was looking for any way to avoid responsibility for this thing not working out. And I suppose that also means that I was, on some level, convinced that it wouldn't. Probably not the best mindset to be in when beginning a relationship.

Just after Thanksgiving, I received a call from my brother. When I recognized his number on the Caller I.D., I thought about just letting the machine pick up. But then I remembered the halfway decent conversation we'd had after I received my doctorate. So I answered.

"Hey," he said quietly, in a tone I knew well.

"Hey. What's going on?"

In a voice that hid little of his pain, he said, "Lizzie and I split up."

I don't know why, but I was shocked. Not that I really had any idea of how their relationship was, but I never expected Dana, of all people, to have a marriage disintegrate.

"Oh," I said. "I'm sorry." There was an uncomfortable silence for a few long seconds. "So... what now?"

"I'm moving," he said. "To California."

"Seriously?" Dana was so *not* the beach bum type.

"I just need to get far away for a while," he said. "Everything here reminds me of her."

I nodded to myself, fully understanding. "When?" I said.

"January, probably. After the holidays. Are you coming home for Christmas?"

Not a chance, I thought. "I haven't decided," I said, hoping his telepathy didn't work over telephone lines.

"I'd really like to see you," he said. "If you can't make it home, maybe I could swing by there before I go?"

"Maybe," I said, and even without telepathy, I knew he could tell it wasn't going to happen.

"Yeah," he said, the disappointment clear in his voice. "Okay."

The body produces stem cells naturally in certain quantities, but I was going to need a bumper crop of them for my work. The good news is there's filgrastim, a drug that increases production. The bad news is it's not a pill.

I'd been denying the fact that there would be a few occasions where I'd have to be stuck with needles. This would be the first of them.

Obtaining the drug was tricky enough and, of course, not entirely legal. My source for it was not a physician. Had it been, I would have asked them to give me the injections. But my source was the kind of guy you'd never trust with a sharp object, so I resigned to doing it myself.

I'm sure Lee would've done it, had I asked her. But I didn't. Instead, I turned to my spiritual friends again to assist me. Poking a needle into my body promised to go a lot smoother with that particular lubricant.

On Christmas Day, I called home. I wished the men in my family a happy holiday. My timing was perfect. Mother was busy preparing the meal and didn't come to the phone.

After the call, I went into the lab at GACTech for the next step involving needles. If you've ever donated plasma, you know how an aphaeresis machine works. You sit for a good while with needles in each arm. Blood flows from one arm into the machine, which separates the plasma – or in this case, white blood cells, some of which would be stem cells – from the rest, which is then returned to the body via the other arm.

Two needles. Large ones. Stuck in my arms for an hour and a half. That's how I spent Christmas.

The following morning, my phone rang. Normally, I'd have at least screened the call to see who it was, but I just wanted the ringing to stop. So I answered it with a hoarse voice and a slurred hello.

"You're drunk!" my mother said.

"Hung over," I said, though her assessment was closer to the truth.

"*Dinah!*"

"Hey, I hadda toast Jesus, didn't I?"

She was quiet a moment, probably asking the birthday boy for the strength to deal with me. "You know your brother is moving. You couldn't at least come home to see him?"

"Why? I know what he looks like."

The exasperation was as clear in her voice as the alcohol in mine. "I just don't understand you, Dinah."

"Really. I didn't know that."

"Do *not* be sarcastic with me! It's disrespectful!"

When I'm drunk, I snort, rather than laugh. So I snorted. "Well, I don't have any respect for you, so..."

"Or for anyone," she shot back. "Including yourself."

"Whatever," I drawled, knowing she hated that expression.

"I pray that God..."

"Just *stop*, Mother! No praying! No proselytizing! No fake feelings for me!"

Her silence seemed to last a full minute. Then she said, "Goodbye, Dinah."

The line went dead and, despite myself, I was surprised. I expected the praying and the proselytizing. But I wasn't one to take small favors for granted. I hung up and returned to my drunkover.

That evening, against my better judgment, I called Dana and told him to come to State College.

He arrived in the afternoon the following day, looking as bad as he'd sounded on the phone. He was gaunt, and his eyes were bloodshot with dark circles beneath.

He greeted me with a desperate hug that made me uncomfortable. He didn't seem to notice that my return embrace was purely for posterity's sake.

But we talked. Mainly, we talked about his marriage and the deterioration thereof. The specifics were probably not much different from other dysfunctional relationships, but one thought nagged at me the entire time he spoke. Finally, I couldn't hold it back.

"I'm sorry," I said, putting down my coffee cup, "but how the hell could communication be a problem in your relationship? You're a telepath!"

He looked at me sadly. "That doesn't matter."

"How can it not matter? You can read minds. You can share—"

"It's not like that!" The outburst surprised both of us. Then he sighed and said, "I never use my abilities on someone without their permission."

"Your own wife wouldn't give you permission?"

"She did," he said, "early on. But as time went by, she appreciated it less and less, and I found it more and more... unsettling." I must have looked confused, so he summed it up for me. "There's something that can happen with telepaths," he said. "A sort of telepathic bond that can happen in certain circumstances." He took a deep breath, then spoke hurriedly, avoiding my gaze. "It can happen when, while telepathically linked, something traumatic happens. Well, not necessarily traumatic. Just... something that causes intense emotional reactions in both parties."

I put two and two together. "Like having sex," I said.

He glanced up at me and nodded. "Yeah." He ventured a small grin. "Sex while linked is amazing, actually." Then the grin faded. "But that link was never supposed to remain permanent. It formed on our honeymoon," he said.

"So... what was the problem?"

His forehead knotted and he looked at me with pained eyes. "Dinah... that sort of thing is beyond intimate. I mean, really, it's... intrusive... voyeuristic..." He stopped, then stared at the floor again. "Let's just say that no one wants someone to know their every thought."

I just nodded. It might sound appealing on the surface, but I wouldn't want anyone knowing my innermost thoughts anytime they wanted.

"Before too long," he continued, "she became so disturbed by the bond that she insisted I break it."

"How do you do that?"

Dana hesitated and lowered his eyes. "Let's just say it involves an even more intrusive bit of mental manipulation. Psychic surgery, in a sense."

"But you did it?" He nodded, shifting uncomfortably on the couch. "And things got better?"

"For a while," he said. "But we never got back to how we once were. I don't think she ever believed the link was completely gone. She became suspicious that I was reading her thoughts, almost to the point of paranoia." He sighed and shook his head.

"Well," I said, "couldn't you have used your abilities to... I dunno... help fix things somehow?"

"By that point, she'd become irate if I even did a mental one-way communication with her. Broadcasting, not receiving."

And with that, I was out of things to say, other than the obvious. "I'm so sorry." And I really was. I might not have felt much love for Dana, but I had no desire to see him in such pain.

We talked about the future. His future, anyway. He admitted he was moving not only to get away from the memories associated with his years with Elizabeth, but also to put physical distance between them for a more practical reason. Telepathy is limited by distance. The truth is, she wanted him as far from her as possible. California would suffice, it seemed. So Dana was going to start in Sacramento, as he had a buddy from college who lived there, then see where things took him.

Late that night, after a dinner of delivery pizza, he finally brought up the subject I'd hoped he wouldn't. "I think I know the answer to this, but I'm going to ask, anyway." He looked me in the eye. "What happened with us? Why did we drift apart?"

I averted my gaze. "I don't think 'drift' is the right word."

"All right," he said. "Why did you push me away?"

I just frowned. "I'm sure you do know the answer. No sense belaboring it."

He let out a deep sigh. "Dinah... I'm so sorry. I knew at the time it was a terrible idea, but..."

"It wasn't," I said. "I don't care if I wasn't supposed to know. I'm glad you told me."

Dana gave me a confused look. "Told you what?"

"About your abilities," I said, stating what I thought was obvious.

"Wait," he said, shifting to sit more erect on the couch. "Are you telling me that, all these years, you've been cold toward me because of *envy?*"

He said this with such incredulity that it stunned me. I hesitated a moment, then nodded. "Well... basically. It was more than that, but... What did you *think* was the reason?"

He just stared at me, then shook his head. "I can't believe this."

"Why not? You know that being a meta was what I've wanted more than anything since I was little."

He gave a short, ironic chuckle. "And when I was eight, I wanted to be a magician. But it wasn't a serious thing... just a normal childhood fantasy."

I glared at him. "Well, mine wasn't."

"Whatever! The fact is that you're not. And that's not my fault. Why take it out on me?"

"Because!" I fought back the welling tears. "I admired the hell out of you. You know I did!" He nodded. "But after you told me about your abilities... and it became clear that you didn't seem to want to use them..." I shook my head and threw my hands up in exasperation. "I couldn't figure out why. Was it fear? Of public ridicule, maybe? Of government control? Of our parents' condemnations?"

"Well..." he began.

"And speaking of them," I interrupted, worked up and on a roll, "why is it that they always treated you so nicely – even though you were an 'abomination' – and I was treated like shit? That always pissed me off!"

"Mainly because..."

"You know what? It doesn't matter. I'm fine with being treated like crap by Mother, because, frankly, I don't like her. But you... You shouldn't have been afraid to use your abilities! You should've been proud! Defiant! You should have accepted that you're better than those without abilities and never be afraid to use them! But you chose to hide your gifts, to deny them." I let out a breath, tired from my own ranting. "Because of that, I couldn't respect you, anymore. Yes, I envied you. But I resented you, too."

Dana just sat there, staring at me. I tried to read the expression on his face. Was it disgust or disbelief? Sadness or pity? All of the above, probably. Finally, he stood. "Well." He looked at me for another long moment. "Sorry I haven't lived up to your expectations." He put on his coat, grabbed his overnight bag, and headed for the door. Before walking out, he turned and said, "For someone who claims to know so much about the meta population, you're pretty ignorant of the fact that not all metas are treated equally." He opened the door. "Maybe when you get that, you'll understand why I was treated differently at home." Then he stepped out of my life again.

Keeping cells alive outside the body is a delicate matter. There are all sorts of things to address: temperature, pH level, oxygenation, humidity, and feeding the cells the right mix of nutrients and growth factors. Basically, you've got to create body conditions in a Petri dish.

Furthermore, I wasn't just keeping them alive. I was mucking about with the DNA, then cloning the mutated cells, in order to further muck about with them. I made only one point mutation at a time, before cloning the cells. Each generation carried the chance of spontaneous cell death. And there are a *lot* of generations.

Just a few of the things I was trying to accomplish: improving the efficiency of the mitochondria (by increasing their size and quantity), increasing the production of ATP by ADP, increasing sensitivity to adrenaline, maximizing the expression of SIRT3 to increase cellular respiration. And quite a bit more.

And I wasn't just playing with DNA. I was also experimenting with brown fat, in an attempt to produce more of it. I was playing with proteins that can act like batteries. I was researching every possible thing to strengthen my mitochondria, including astaxanthin, acetyl-L-carnitine, and more. I was even looking at tweaking my Mitochondrial Aldehyde Dehydrogenase, in order to better metabolize my fuel of choice: alcohol.

None of this happened overnight, of course. Sure, I'd been working for years on some of this, but now I was looking to take it from the theoretical to the practical.

By late summer of '98, I was ready. On paper, anyway. In my head... that was completely different. Because, now that the reality was staring me in the face, I was paying more attention than ever to the inherent dangers in what I was doing.

Yes, they were my own cells, so the chance of my body rejecting them was slim, even altered as they were. Short of chemotherapy, there wasn't a lot I could do to prevent it. If it was going to happen, it was going to happen.

But having all this work destroyed by my own body was the least of my concerns. A bigger worry was that I'd succeed, but more than I wanted to.

In chemical reactions, there is an event called "runaway," where the reaction essentially goes into an uncontrolled acceleration, usually ending badly. If you're old enough to remember the Union Carbide pesticide plant disaster in Bhopal, India, back in '84... that was the result of a runaway effect. Thousands of people died within a couple days, due to the release of toxic substances.

I could comfort myself with the fact that, should I go into a runaway, the only one to die would be me.

Probably.

Finally, the day arrived. The point of no return. Once the new and improved cells were back in my body, nothing could stop whatever was going to happen. I could be committing suicide, for all I knew. I didn't think it was likely, but I couldn't dismiss the idea, either.

The I.V. bag hung above me, ready to disgorge its mutant payload into my ghost white arm. The pointed delivery nozzle glinted at me as I held it shakily in my right hand.

I glanced at the bottle of nerve tonic on the counter and quickly refilled my glass, then just as quickly emptied it, relishing its warm, spicy-sweet burn.

Deep breath.

I positioned the needle above the vein and, in a now-familiar action, plunged it home.

But the alcohol hadn't calmed me enough. My hand twitched and I missed the vein completely. I yanked the needle from my inner elbow, jaw clenched at the pain, and prepared to do it again.

Another drink. Another deep breath. Another botched effort.

I got up and paced the lab, rubbing at the errant punctures and, I'm sure, cursing up a storm.

I had to pee, and headed down the hall to the rest room. I sat in the stall, berating myself. This was what I wanted, wasn't it? Years of research had gone into this. I wasn't going to chicken out, now, was I?

I washed my hands and stared at myself in the mirror. I looked like shit. Damn nerves. Third time's the charm, I told myself, returning to the lab and the needle. Drink, breathe, stab. And this one, mercifully, went directly into the vein. I slapped on a piece of tape to secure it, then slumped against the counter, a cold sweat breaking out.

I remember staring at the needle in my arm, feeling slightly sick, expecting it to erupt in a blood fountain. I looked at the bag, at the fluid waiting to course through the tubing. It hung there, daring me to finish the job.

I reached up and opened the nozzle, watching as the tube carried my cells to the short stainless steel tunnel on their way home to my bloodstream. My heart raced. I stared at the holes left by the two failed attempts, blood caked around them.

And I thought again about that grinding pain more than two decades ago as the needle hit the bone. I could almost feel the wooziness from when I bled all down my arm. My stomach did a flop and I regretted not having anything to eat all day before deciding to drink.

When the bag was finally empty, I closed the nozzle and slid the needle from my arm. Definitely no turning back, now. I needed to get out of the lab, get some food in my stomach, or maybe just go home and sleep. I stood to reach for the empty bag, but evidently did so too quickly. Everything went black as I fell to the floor.

When I woke, I was outside.

And the lab was in flames.

SEVEN

"Compromise is but the sacrifice of one right or good in the hope of retaining another – too often ending in the loss of both."
~Tryon Edwards

One of the elective courses I took in college was a film appreciation class. We watched, discussed, and analyzed classic films in almost every genre, from comedy to horror. Great class, really. But one of the things that struck me most about older movies is just how many of them featured reporters as the protagonists.

News, way back when – whether in the daily papers or on television – was not like news today. Once upon a time, being a reporter was a noble profession. Investigative journalism brought down heads of state. Men like Edward R. Murrow and Walter Cronkite were the truth-seekers and the trustworthy.

I don't see many of those people in today's world. Instead, we have the ubiquity of the paparazzi, the embarrassment of tabloid TV, and the empty beauty of talking heads reading from teleprompters.

Real news, real reporting, is still out there, of course. But it's so overshadowed by the trash that almost no one knows about it. We're more aware of why movie stars are divorcing than we are of the schisms between nations. We consider newsworthy the TV shows about the lifestyles of the rich and shameless, while regarding as inconsequential the plight of the poor and homeless on our local streets.

Of course, one thing that has always been and always will be newsworthy and capturing of our attention is a disaster. It could be tidal waves and terrorism... it could be plane crashes and school shootings...

Or it could be a small laboratory catching fire under mysterious circumstances.

News cameras caught the leaping flames for the viewers at home. Reporters eagerly waited for the EMT to leave me, so they could aim those accusing eyes at mine.

They asked me the same questions that were bouncing around inside my woozy head. How did the fire start? Was there an explosion? Was there anyone else in the building?

I gave them the same answers I'd later repeat for the police.

I don't know.

I don't know.

I don't know.

At some point, those three little words would make it sound as though I had something to hide. But for that night, at least, "I don't know" sufficed. They grilled me, but allowed me to leave before I was completely cooked. Even so, I knew it was just a matter of time.

What surprised me was the one question no one asked. What was I doing there? Perhaps the press and police assumed that we scientists all burn the midnight oil. I knew the truth would come out at some point, but for the moment, I was grateful for not having to answer that one.

There was one question no one needed to ask, though. The friendly, caring EMT reported to the police that he'd smelled alcohol on my breath. A Breathalyzer supported his accusation.

Naturally, I was fired. Not because of the blaze, which was still considered accidental at that point, but because of violating the company policy of using company equipment for unapproved projects. Dr. Gray seemed genuinely sorry to let me go. Small consolation. Other biotech firms in the area knew about the fire, and the firing. None of them would hire me. So I went full-time at Zeno's.

In the months that followed, I mentally replayed the events of that night so often that I regularly dreamt about it. But I still couldn't remember how the fire had started or how I'd gotten out of the building.

In desperation, I even tried hypnotic regression, despite my skepticism of it. But I still recalled nothing more. It appeared I truly had been unconscious when the fire began.

But why? I'd been drinking, yes, but I was nowhere near that drunk. A natural gas leak that rendered me unconscious before catching fire? That would be handy, but it wouldn't explain how I got outside.

When the fire investigation team released their preliminary report, I knew the loss of my job was just the beginning of my problems. Though they had not yet identified a specific cause of the blaze, it was obvious that the point of origin was in the lab in which I'd been working, as it was the most heavily damaged.

I found a lawyer with experience defending clients against employers. She told me up front that my biggest concern was whether the fire inspectors found evidence of arson. If that happened, I'd be arrested and tried in criminal court. Even without that, it was still pretty much guaranteed that GACTech's insurer would sue me for damages due to negligence. Either way, I still needed legal representation, so I hired her.

It took a while for the fire inspectors to release their final report. To my great relief, I wasn't arrested. But shortly thereafter, I did receive notification of the civil suit we'd expected. Though it was not being considered arson, my bottle of alcohol acted as an accelerant, once it was ignited. There was no consensus on how that happened.

My attorney assured me that we could settle out of court. She said there was no way they'd take it to trial; I simply didn't have the money to make such a thing worthwhile.

But she was wrong. They wanted to make an example out of me, possibly out of fear that others might wish to follow in my footsteps and do some after-hours experimentation and cost insurers tons of money. There would be no settlement. They were going for the throat. They were accusing me of arson.

So my astounded lawyer and I started working on my defense. It meant lots of late nights discussing details. It also meant actually having to pay her. My savings were dwindling fast. In addition to the attorney's fees and rent, I had other living expenses, not to mention three degrees worth of student loans to pay off. So I hired myself out as a bartender for office parties and other events, which brought in a good bit of extra cash during the holidays. I even took short-term clerical jobs.

My sleep was terrible. I was losing weight. Yes, I needed to slim down, but stress wasn't the way I wanted to do it. I put in probably fifty hours a week at the bar, as many hours as I could doing temp work, and then on Sundays, I worked at a shoe store at the Nittany Mall.

This left little time for my relationship with Lee. She'd be asleep by the time I got home from the bar. And our mornings were so rushed that we often didn't even have time to share a pot of coffee before one or both of us had to go to work. But I reasoned we'd been together long enough to coast for a while, until I was through the whole mess. I might have been right, too, except that I naïvely thought it would be over quickly. Lawsuits, I learned, have a way of dragging.

I've never understood people who say they have no regrets in life. "Regrets are a waste of energy," they say. Or, "No regrets, only lessons." I think this is nothing but a form of denial, a way to avoid admitting that you've done something you wish you hadn't. Yes, you should learn from your mistakes. No, you shouldn't spend your life dwelling on them. But you shouldn't brush them off, either.

I could give all sorts of reasons for what happened that year. I could blame it on all the stress. I could blame it on not seeing much of Lee. I could blame it on my low self-image resulting from the lawsuit. And as always, I could blame it on the booze. And while all of these played a part, they're still just excuses. The real blame lay solely on me and me alone.

In retrospect, I guess I should have hired a different attorney.

I was just finishing up a day shift at Zeno's when she called on my cell with some good news, for a change. There would be no criminal trial, as the prosecution decided they just didn't have enough evidence. So it would be a civil trial only.

I suggested we celebrate the small victory. As luck would have it, she was calling from her car and wasn't far from Zeno's, so she said she'd stop by for a quick drink.

One drink became several, and my emotions got all wonky. Not for the first time, I noticed that my attorney was a very attractive woman. But this time, I told her so. She looked me in the eye, a strange expression on her face, then said she had to pee.

A minute later, I finished my drink and followed her to the restroom.

It was just that once. Neither of us ever mentioned it, afterward. Even so, I knew immediately that I couldn't keep it from Lee. I'd do the right thing, I decided. I'd own up to it, confess. Better that she hear it from me than find out some other way.

She sat there in our living room, staring at me. Her jaw was clenched in justifiable anger. I waited for the inevitable explosion. When she finally spoke, her voice was quiet and measured. "When we first got together, I told you that if you ever cheated on me, the one thing you had to do was make sure I never found out about it."

I blinked, having forgotten all about that conversation. I'd thought nothing of it at the time. "You were serious about that?"

"Yes, goddammit!" Finally, the explosion. "Why would I ever want to know it? If it's over, why did I need to know?" And now, the tears. "Jesus, Dinah. You never take me seriously."

"What? Of course I do!"

"No. You don't. You've always got to have things your way! Even this. You get to fuck someone else, and then purge your guilt by confessing, like that's going to make it all better." I shook my head and tried to correct her, but she wouldn't let me. "So now you feel better and I get to feel like shit. Nice job." Lee got up and stormed out of the apartment.

My hope was that she'd blow off some steam for an hour or three, then come back home, and we'd make up. I'd apologize again, feel like an asshole for a month or two, she'd forgive me, and we'd work past it.

Instead, she came back in half an hour and said, "I think you should move out."

Even if I could have afforded to live on my own, I didn't want to move out. I wanted to be with her. This was the crux of the argument that ensued, lasting until we were both stupid with exhaustion. Maybe sleep deprivation was why she gave in. She didn't forgive me. She was still angry. I'd have to move back into my old bedroom-*cum*-junk room. But she let me stay.

The civil trial was long. It was draining. It was ugly. I'd pretty much given up on remembering any more details about the fire. I probably looked like an idiot under questioning. Thankfully, the whole thing is just a distant haze in my memory, now.

Sometime during the trial, Lee allowed me to move back into "our" bedroom. She still hadn't forgiven me, nor did I really expect her to. But she saw what the trial was doing to me and, I think, felt sorry for me.

Still, it didn't mean our relationship was healthy. When I could spare a few minutes to actually look at it, I didn't like what I saw. Lee and I hadn't made love in months. And to be honest, we hadn't truly been friends in even longer. Not the kind of friends we once were, anyway. That fact saddened me the most. I'd never been one to believe that a romantic relationship that blossomed from a friendship could ruin the friendship when it ended. If the friendship was solid, I reasoned, it could withstand such an event. But how solid was our friendship?

The trial ended in April. Lee came to court on the last day. She sat in the back row, wanting to be as far away from my attorney as possible. Guess I couldn't blame her. She'd hoped I'd fire the woman and get a different one to represent me, but I didn't. I had too much time invested.

In the end, I was found culpable and ordered to pay restitution to GACTech and its insurer for damages. I expected to be paying the installments until my hair went white.

When that last gavel banged, my attorney put a consoling hand on my shoulder. I hugged her. When I looked to the back of the room to where Lee had been sitting, all I saw was her back as she headed out the door.

With the stress of the trial behind me, I could devote more time to our relationship. I was still working all the time, but we made efforts to improve things. She'd join me for my lunch breaks when she could, especially on weekends. She'd come to Zeno's when I was working, too.

But I soon deduced that she wasn't there because she wanted to spend more time with me. She was afraid I was still seeing my former attorney. She was at Zeno's to make sure I really was working, not sleeping around.

At the bar, every time I was friendly with a female customer, she thought I was flirting. Every time a woman greeted me by name, she assumed something was going on between us.

This went on all summer and into the fall. By the time the holidays rolled around, I was convinced that living together was a bad idea. I just couldn't handle the jealousy. When she returned from visiting her family after New Year's, we had "the talk."

I'm not sure which is uglier: dealing with your girlfriend's jealousy issues or confronting her about them. "The talk" was hideous. Suffice to say that I accepted the blame for our relationship falling apart. I moved out a week later into a one-bedroom apartment I couldn't really afford. I considered that part of my penance.

What an awful start to the year, I remember thinking. But this was 2001. The year was only going to get worse.

About a month and a half after I moved out, Lee began calling me. She was sorry, she said. She knew her jealousy had been out of control. She wanted to give us another try. I apologized, but told her I felt separating was the best for both of us.

She called often. I rarely heard her except on voice mail. Clearly, she was just going through a bad time, having difficulty adjusting to the single life again. But the more time went on, the more desperate she sounded. She was often crying when she called.

And eventually, she started calling in the middle of the night, no longer having enough consideration to allow me to sleep. So I changed my phone number.

Then she started showing up at Zeno's, wanting to talk. I politely explained that I didn't want to talk about our relationship in front of customers. When that didn't work, I told her the same thing, but less politely, threatening to have the bouncers prevent her from entering. This seemed to work. For a couple months, there was no contact, to my great relief.

Then, on September 11, terrorists attacked the World Trade Center and the Pentagon. And America went nuts. Yes, there was the standard "patriotic" posturing that always happens. Flags everywhere. Talk of "revenge" instead of justice. But there was more. There was anti-Islam violence. And, sadly, an anti-meta backlash.

A very small, but vocal, faction insisted that 9/11 was an inside job, the work of metas. Don't ask me how they justify this; I'm not willing to wade through their lengthy, paranoid rants. I guess it was just easier to swallow than the idea that terrorists could take over jumbo jets with nothing but box cutters.

And there was an even larger faction blaming metas for not stopping the attacks. The same folks who screamed the loudest for meta registration were now screaming that metas didn't do enough. I stopped watching the news.

Lee's father worked in the World Trade Center. Thankfully, he was one of those who got out in time, I learned when I called her. But the conversation bothered me. She seemed quiet. Distant. I took this to mean that she was no longer convinced that we could work out, and now she was in the acceptance phase of grieving the loss of the relationship.

If only.

On October 11, Lee stood on the balcony of our former apartment and jumped off.

EIGHT

"We all lose friends... we lose them in death, to distance and over time. But even though they may be lost, hope is not. The key is to keep them in your heart, and when the time is right, you can pick up the friendship right where you left off. Even the lost find their way home when you leave the light on."
~Amy Marie Walz

"No one wants someone to know their every thought," Dana had said. And I had to admit, it took me a long time to extrapolate that concept outside of our conversation about the deterioration and ending of his marriage.

It embarrassed me that my brother, who didn't exactly embrace his metahuman abilities nor show much interest in metas in general, knew more about metas than I did, in some respects. Sure, I knew the stats. I could blow your mind with trivia about metas and their teams. But it was all superficial knowledge. I didn't grasp the full scope of their interaction with society. I was only interested in the fame and the famous. But Dana understood.

As I've mentioned, there was a sizeable and noisy segment of the general populace that held a distrust of all metas. But when the meta in question was one of a telepathic bent, the distrust became screaming paranoia. When I was a kid, I remember there being a common, joking, expression: "The devil made me do it." These days, one can hear similar statements. "The telepath made me do it." Sometimes it was a joke. Sometimes not. Claiming to be under the influence of a telepath became a popular defense among criminals. Hearing voices was no longer automatically an indicator of possible schizophrenia. How can you prove a telepath *wasn't* influencing a person?

I learned that there were a number of bills often put forth in congress to enact strict observation of telepathic metas, in effect elevating them to the level of suspected terrorist in the government's eyes. And the public's.

And I finally got it. I finally understood Dana's words to me as he left that day, and the pained look in his eyes. Mother treated Dana like a prince to his face not because she thought he was. She did it because she was afraid of what he might do to her if she didn't treat him that way. She and Dad were terrified that Dana would... I don't know... perform psychic lobotomies on them or something. Bend them to his will. They thought this of their own son. In some ways, I suppose that was worse than how they treated me. Being regarded as a huge disappointment, or an embarrassment, was one thing. Being feared as dangerous is quite another.

Still, it's always been my opinion that a little telepathy might be a good thing. So many people struggle to be understood. Why not make it easier? Even a little?

I suppose it's a slippery slope sort of argument. All I know is that I'd have given anything to have known Lee's intentions before she carried them out.

The weather, the day of the funeral, was obnoxiously pleasant, almost insulting so. Fallen leaves tumbled with the breeze. There was the smell of burning wood in the air from someone's fireplace nearby.

I stood apart from the others, back from the graveside. I could hear only the minister's mumble as I stood there, staring at the casket, suspended above that gaping hole in the ground.

Every so often, I'd glance at Lee's family. Her parents were often staring back at me, their glares telling me that they thought I was somehow responsible. Who knows what Lee had told them out of her pain, her anger at me? For that matter, who knows whether it wasn't true?

I stood apart not only to avoid those direct stares, but also so as to not make them uncomfortable. And so they wouldn't notice I wasn't entirely sober.

The truth is, I blamed myself, too, at least to a degree. It's a common feeling for those who lose loved ones to suicide. There are always the "what if" scenarios... What if I'd been there? What if I'd known? And then the blame... Why didn't I see this might happen? If I hadn't done this, they wouldn't have done that.

Why didn't I see Lee's erratic behavior as being a danger to her? And if I hadn't cheated on her, and then told her about it, she might still be alive.

Finally, the minister shut up and the casket began its descent. I waited, anxiety mounting, as the others filed by, one by one, dropping dirt and flowers into the hole before shuffling back to their vehicles. Only when they were gone did I have the nerve to step forward.

But as I stood there, I wasn't looking down into Lee's grave. I was staring into my own personal abyss. And if I fell, it wouldn't be like the casket's gentle, supported descent, down a few feet to rest in the earth. It would be a plummet, like the one Lee took from her balcony, but endless.

Is that how Lee had felt? Out of control, with nothing to support her?

I edged closer, teetering on the edge of the void. I waited for someone to reach out and pull me back. To save me.

But no one did. No one could. No one had for Lee; why would anyone for me?

My vision clouded and all I could see was her face, as I'd stared at it in the drawer at the morgue. That beautiful, broken face. What had gone through her mind as she'd stood on that balcony? What had she felt as she'd surrendered to gravity?

My knees buckled and I crumpled, pitching forward on the lawn. My face landed so close the edge of the grave... so close to the edge of... whatever it was, helpless against its pull.

Helplessness is a horrid feeling... a combination of weakness, shame, panic, desperation, and more. No one should have to feel that way, I told myself. Ever. People needed to reach out for help when they needed it. And others needed to be there to help them. Without that support, what was the point of friendship? Of love? Of family?

But there, lying in the grass, looking down into the depths... I was alone.

I looked down at the casket, comfortable in its new, shallow home, sprinkled with soil and roses.

And I looked inside myself, at my life, lying there in its own shallowness, drowning in grief and regret.

From somewhere, I found the strength to stand. I chose a lily from the vase and dropped it into the hole, saying farewell to my lover... my friend.

And as I shuffled through the leaves back to my car, I thought about friendship... and love... and family.

After Lee's suicide, I'd called home. No matter the separation, spatial or emotional, family is family, and I needed someone. Dad was sympathetic, but didn't know what to say. Mother started in on our conversation by mentioning some distant cousin who'd died, one of the victims of letters containing anthrax spores that had been mailed about a week after 9/11. I'd never even heard of this person before, and told her so. I had another loss that was a bit more traumatic for me, I told her. A which point, she just quoted scripture and told me that Lee's suicide was God's message to me.

I hung up on her.

Later, I received a sympathy card from them. But it was in my father's handwriting, and I know that my mother had no part of it. She'd never acknowledged Lee when alive; she certainly wouldn't start after she died.

Dana, though... Dana was genuinely sorry, even though he'd never met Lee. For weeks after her death, he called me daily. We had good talks.

He referred me to a colleague of his in my area for grief counseling. He was really there for me, even after my childish resentment of him for most of our adult lives.

Naturally, this made me feel like a complete shit.

On one of our calls, I tried to assuage that feeling. I apologized, tripping over my tongue even more than usual for me. I can't remember the apology itself, but I do remember the rest of the conversation.

"I never realized," he said, "how much of an obsession the whole meta thing was for you."

I found this hard to believe. "You don't remember how much I talked about it as a kid?"

"Dinah, I went off to college when you were ten. Your interest in metas, from my perspective, wasn't any more obsessive than your interest in other things."

"Like what?" I asked, truly not thinking any of my childhood interests could come close.

"When you were seven, you told me, quite emphatically, that you were going to be the next Donna Summer. You played her 'Bad Girls' record to death."

"Eight-track," I corrected, chuckling at the memory.

He laughed. "I wanted to throw your stereo out the window."

"That explains the headphones you gave me for my birthday when I was eight."

We laughed together, and then he said, "I always thought you should have pursued that. You loved to sing. And you were really good."

"Thanks," I said, remembering my second grade talent show and Dana's enthusiastic applause. And he was right. I *had* wanted to be a singer. But once I discovered the world of metahumans, being a singer just didn't hold the same appeal. "I think I'm a really good scientist, too," I said.

"I'm sure you are," he said. "But... Has it been worth it? The obsession?"

I thought about that for a while, but I couldn't answer the question. Not yet. So I changed the subject again. "How difficult was it for you to move across the country?"

Dana sighed. "Very. But it was necessary. Everything in Philly was reminding me of Lizzie, so I had to get out of there. You considering that sort of change?"

"Just as you said... Everything in State College reminds me of either Lee or the fire. I need a fresh start, I think. I just don't know where to go."

I did see the counselor Dana suggested. It was difficult, talking about Lee. I was blaming myself for her death and nothing the counselor said seemed to make a difference. He tried to convince me to go home for Thanksgiving, but there was no way I could have handled another of my mother's self-righteous, told-you-so sermons. But spending it alone with my guilt turned out to be horrible.

Christmas was worse. I spent it mostly drunk.

In January, I called Dana on his birthday. "Honestly," I said with a bit of shame, "it's been so long since I've even sent you a card for your birthday, I wouldn't have a clue what gift to buy you."

"Want a suggestion?" he said.

I blinked in surprise. I'd expected him to say I didn't need to get him anything. "Uh... sure?"

"I'm going on a trip, and I'd rather not go alone. Come with me?"

"A trip."

"Yeah," he said. "To Europe."

I snorted. "Dana, I can't afford a trip to Europe."

"Your gift is keeping me company. The trip is on me."

I hesitated. Was he serious? "When?"

"Leave February 8, return March 12."

"A *month*? Are you crazy?"

"That's never been formally diagnosed," he said. "Come on. It'll be a blast." Dana described a tour beginning and ending in London, but covering a dozen other European cities.

My protests were only half-hearted. It did, in fact, sound like a blast. And the protests that were most valid (all involving money) were overridden.

Dana sent me a check big enough to cover my rent and all my bills for about three months. So in one of the more impetuous decisions of my life, I quit my jobs. I dug out my still unused passport, took care of necessary details, and before I knew it, we were headed to Heathrow.

About three hours into the flight, I glanced around at my nearby passengers, then said quietly, "So... you were thirteen when Mom and Dad discovered...?"

Dana tore his gaze from the window and nodded. "Yeah."

"Mom walked in on you... and a model airplane?"

His cheeks reddened slightly. "Um... I may have told you that, but no." He cleared his throat and spoke quietly. "It wasn't an airplane. It was Scooter."

I burst out laughing, picturing our beloved terrier-poodle mix sailing around Dana's room, ears flopping and tongue hanging out. In my mind, he was wearing a cape made from a hand towel. "I bet Mom about shit."

"Oh, yeah," Dana chuckled. "I thought she was gonna call Father Louis for an exorcism right there on the spot."

I laughed harder. "What!" Our family wasn't Catholic.

"I know! That's how horrified she was."

I was now close to peeing myself. Other passengers were staring, so I did my best to stifle my laughter. Once I was in no danger of an embarrassment of a bladderly nature, I said, "So how did they find out about... the other bit?"

Dana's smile faded and he looked down at his hands. "You sure you want to know?"

I frowned. "Why wouldn't I?"

When he looked up at me again, it was with sadness in his eyes. "It was a couple years later," he said. "At the time, I could only pick up something from someone in a highly emotional state." Dana paused, clearly uncomfortable with the story. "We were at dinner. And Mom casually asked Dad why he'd been working so late at the office recently." My heart skipped a beat. I knew what he was going to say, but surely it couldn't be. "Dad talked about this complex project under a deadline, but as he said it, I picked up on something else. And I just sat there, not eating, staring at Dad. I was confused, knowing he'd just lied, and finally Dad said, 'What are you looking at me like that for?' And I just said, 'Who's Charlotte?' And he just stared at me. Mom stared at me. They stared at each other. Then Mom told you and me to go to our rooms."

"I don't remember that at all."

"Well, it wasn't a significant moment for you."

"Charlotte was his secretary, right?"

Dana nodded. "Yeah. They'd been having an affair for months."

I tried to wrap my head around this, tried to give my mother some slack. Was this part of why she was a total bitch toward most people? Maybe, I conceded. But it's still not a valid excuse. Plenty of women – and men – are cheated on and don't take it out on the rest of the world.

Of course, I felt sorry for her. No one deserves that, not even her. It didn't make me feel closer to her, though. It simply added a wedge between me and my father.

We flew on in silence for a while, then I said, "I was hoping you could help me with something." I took a deep breath. "I've never been able to figure out what started the fire in the lab. Do you think, maybe, you could... you know... explore that?"

Dana nodded slowly. "If you really want me to, I can try." I nodded. "I can't promise anything," he warned.

"Of course. Can you... do it now? Or do you have to prepare or something?"

"No, I can do it now," he said, and then I heard his voice inside my head, as I had so long ago in my bedroom. *Just relax*, he urged, and so I did.

I don't know how much time passed. I think I fell asleep. Or perhaps he put me to sleep. But when I came back to awareness, Dana was frowning. "What?" I asked.

He replied using his "inside voice," so as to prevent our fellow passengers from hearing. *I'm sorry. I got nothing more than you've told me. So I don't think it's something you've repressed. Your consciousness just faded, then nothing until you came around outside.*

I didn't think I'd had that much to drink, I thought back at him.

I don't think you did, actually. I counted how many drinks you had, and it was a lot, but not enough to put you out.

I chewed on that for a while. "Thanks," I said.

Dana squeezed my hand. I smiled, looking down at our entwined fingers and realizing again just how much I'd missed our closeness. Then I settled back into my seat for the remainder of the flight.

Over the following week, our sightseeing was enhanced by getting to know each other again, as we ate and drank our way through northern Europe. But it wasn't all bonding and *bière*, photos and *fromage*. Somewhere between Brussels and Amsterdam, I began feeling jumpy and weird. I started drinking more to take the edge off (Dana had gotten me hooked on Belgian ales, so I was drinking more, anyway), but if anything, it seemed alcohol only made it worse. It wasn't until we were back in London that my blonde moment finally passed.

"It's happening," I told Dana as we sat in the Abbey Road Café. Yes, *that* Abbey Road. Dana's a huge Beatles fan.

"What is?" he said, wiping scone crumbs from his beard.

I sat there, bouncing my foot as though I had Restless Leg Syndrome, and drumming my fingers on the tabletop as we spoke. "My... experiment," I said. "It's working."

Dana looked at me for a moment, clearly not sure what I was talking about. Then his eyes narrowed. "You're kidding," he said flatly.

I shook my head. "One of the fundamental parts of the process is that my body will begin producing greater and greater amounts of energy. That's why I'm feeling like this."

Dana was quiet for what seemed a long time, just staring at me with a surprised look on his face. Then I looked deeper and felt my stomach drop.

He didn't believe me.

My life's work, everything I'd spent my entire education to accomplish... he'd never taken any of it seriously. Whether he viewed it as something impossible to attain or something I was foolish for wanting, I didn't know. Even if his interest was now piqued, so was my resentment.

He must have seen this on my face, though, because the next thing I knew, his "inside voice" was ringing in my brain. *Please*, he said. *I'm sorry. I really want to know.*

Dana's inside voice – at least with me – is very calm and soothing. It's a sure way for him to calm me down if I'm upset. But at that point, I wanted to be upset. And when a telepath – so Dana told me – was broadcasting to a person, he was typically also in "receiving" mode, "listening" for a reply. And I wanted to give him a headache. So I mentally shouted, *Why should I believe you?*

He winced, then took a deep breath and spoke aloud. "Because I'm your brother," he said gently. "And I love you."

I stared at him, hurt and angry. But his contrition was real. I could feel it. So I nodded, reminding myself that I didn't have any room to talk when it came to bad behavior toward a sibling. Then I slowly told him about my research, carefully explaining in layman's terms what I did, why I did it, and what I expected to come of it. He interrupted often with questions and I answered them gladly. He really was interested.

"Wait a minute," he said at one point. "I'm following you on the whole generation of energy thing. But how do you plan to discharge it? You mentioned electric eels, but don't they have special organs for that?"

It was just like Dana to pinpoint the one area of my planning that was the weakest. I sighed and gave a slight nod. "Yeah, well... I'm sort of going on faith that my body will just figure that out on its own."

Dana stared at me with the most incredulous look on his face. "But, if it doesn't... instead of being... I dunno... DynaGirl or whatever, you might just be... Hyperactive Woman?" I gave a bemused smile at "DynaGirl," causing Dana to chuckle. "Sorry," he said. "Couldn't resist. And hey, you'll need a name, right?"

"Yeah. But not that one."

Given the public fascination with metahumans, the TV networks have always tried to cash in on them. However, licensing of actual metas' names and likenesses are almost impossible to appropriate, so writers would invent their own. This is how, when I was five years old, the talents of Sid and Marty Krofft graced Saturday mornings with *ElectraWoman and DynaGirl*. It was campy and corny, but it's my earliest clear memory of regular exposure to metas (even if only fake ones) in my household. I guess our parents missed that one in the *TV Guide*. I got hooked on the show and watched it every week. Well, for sixteen weeks, anyway, until it was cancelled. But then I moved on to the real metas.

No, the name "DynaGirl" was off-limits, out of respect for a silly, fictitious character that, oddly enough, meant a lot to me as a child. Besides...

"I'm a little old to be called a 'girl,' don't you think?"

"Well... I wouldn't say that," Dana drawled. "But you might consider your first superteam application to be to The Goldens."

I bounced a chunk of my biscotti off his forehead. He was laughing too hard to stop it telekinetically.

On our final night in London, we went out for drinks at The Savoy. It was my idea. Dana's mostly a beer drinker, but even he couldn't pass up having some historic cocktails in the bar where they were created. We noshed appetizers and worked our way through many, many drinks... the Hanky Panky, the White Lady, the Wolfram, the Moonwalk, the Speedbird, and more.

When Dana gets sozzled, it exaggerates whatever sort of mood he's already in. If he's in a good mood, being tipsy brings him out of his shell and he's delightfully entertaining. If he's in a downer of a mood, though, being drunk makes him withdraw and grow morose. This night, he was in a reflective mood. We'd been talking about the past quite a bit. Specifically, we'd been discussing our long estrangement.

"Pretty much why I ended up with Lizzie," he said as we made our way back to the hotel.

"Wait. What?"

Dana shrugged and stumbled a bit. I caught his arm and supported him as we walked. And he haltingly explained that when I pushed him away, it devastated him. And even though he knew deep down that he and Elizabeth weren't suited for each other in the long run, he clung to her so as not to drown in his own desolation.

"Never could handle rejection well," he said as we rode the elevator up to our floor in the hotel. "Like with Jennifer." This was the college girlfriend who ripped his heart out when she broke up with him. I remembered it well.

He'd come home that weekend. It was the only other time I'd seen him drunk. And it was of the morose variety. He'd poured his heart out to me and cried on my shoulder, making references to our mother that I didn't understand at the time. He'd told me how much he loved me and how important I was to him. But I hadn't been mature enough... No. I *was* mature enough to understand. But I was too selfish to make the effort.

Now he looked at me with eyes filled with remorse and tears waiting to fall. But before he could speak, I held a finger to his lips. "Enough," I said as we entered his room. "We're on vacation. We're going to Liverpool tomorrow!" He smiled faintly. "No regrets. Okay?" He nodded boozily as I sat him down on his bed. I kissed him on the forehead. At which point, he passed out.

I lifted his feet up onto the bed, pulled off his shoes, and laid a blanket over him. Then I went next door to my room, taking with me enough regret for the both of us.

In Liverpool, we had a Magical Mystery Tour of the Beatles' birthplace. Dana was in high spirits all day, and I wondered if he even remembered our conversation from the night before. I sort of hoped he didn't.

Then we went over to Wales, from where we started working our way south. In the town of Aberteifi, we rented a small cottage, rather than staying in a bed and breakfast, as had been our plan, in order to have more privacy. Much of our conversation regarded the onset of my abilities, and we didn't want much of that to be overheard.

We'd been in town for two days, and I was expecting Dana to tell me at any time where our next stop on the trail was to be. But it turned out he really liked the place. And I couldn't blame him. We spent our time out for walks along the river out to Cardigan Bay. We bought folding camp chairs and would sit for hours looking out over the water, just talking. It was nice that it was so easy to get away from people altogether to talk freely and test my abilities.

The tests mainly involved me concentrating on the energies I could now feel accumulating within me, trying (unsuccessfully) to release them. For the sake of safety, we did this on the beach, away from any structures or people, should I somehow manage to succeed.

I knew it was unlikely, honestly. To say the odds were against me was a hell of an understatement. I'd already used up far more than my share of luck in getting as far as I had in this experiment. The one area I couldn't force to happen – manipulating a mechanism for the discharge of all the energy I was generating – should be my downfall. And quite possibly my death.

But I didn't believe that. I *couldn't* believe that.

All those "real" metas... how did *they* do it? There was no obvious mechanism for so many of the metas to fly. Or transform their bodies from flesh to flame. Or turn freaking *invisible*. And yet, they did, somehow. Obviously, there was more going on within us than we could discern. When the meta-mutations began, all bets, it seemed, were off.

So I *had* to believe, irrational though it was.

I wish I could say the vacation was entirely relaxing for me, but it wasn't. My nightmares were with me on the trip. Mainly, they focused on Lee's death.

"Why do people kill themselves?" I asked Dana one morning over breakfast.

He looked at me with a sympathetic expression, then shifted into counselor mode. "Well, there are a lot of reasons. They might be terminally ill, for example, and choose to die on their own terms rather than suffer."

I nodded. "Yeah, I get that. And I don't mean the ones that are the result of something going wrong... unintentional overdoses or autoerotic asphyxiation gone awry."

"Don't forget cries for help that go wrong, too."

"What do you mean?"

"Sometimes someone will do something they don't even realize will kill them in order to make others notice that they need help or attention. I had a client once, a fifteen year-old girl, who swallowed half a bottle of Tylenol." He frowned in disgust. "It bothers me to no end that the public isn't more aware of what acetaminophen can do. I imagine this girl figured she'd be rushed to the hospital and be fine." He shook his head and sighed. "From what her mother told me, she got scared a few hours after taking the pills and told her dad what she'd done. But by the time they got her to the hospital, it was too late. Her liver was permanently damaged and began to fail. It took her three days to die a very painful death."

"I'm sorry," I said, seeing how this still affected him.

"Anyway," he continued, "I assume you also don't mean suicide by stupidity."

"Meaning?"

He shrugged and sipped his tea. "Like the guy who gets drunk and morose because he's been dumped and does something impulsive due to his compromised mental state."

I considered this. Had this been what Lee had done? There hadn't been any mention of alcohol or drugs in her system. At least, not that I heard. But no, I decided. Her behavior leading up to that didn't indicate such an impulsive act.

"What else, then? Depression, obviously."

"Absolutely. Severe depression is the leading cause of suicide. It completely messes with how your thinking works. Everything is warped, seen through the filter of believing the world would be better without you or whatever. I tell you, Dinah, I long for the day when the public stops equating depression with sadness. Until that time, it'll never be regarded as the killer disease it really is."

I nodded. "Anything else?"

"Well… yeah. Being psychotic." I raised an eyebrow and he elaborated. "Schizophrenia, for example, can cause people to hear voices telling them they're worthless, urging them to kill themselves, and so on." He paused for a moment. "Like our grandfather."

"Really?"

He nodded. "From what I've heard, yes." He thought for a minute. "Anyway, those would be pretty much all the reasons, I think." He looked at me with concern. "And you're wondering which of those categories applied to Lee."

"Yeah," I said, pushing food around my plate.

"I'm afraid you'll never know for certain. But from what you described to me, it sounds like she did have a psychotic break of some sort." I lowered my head. "But you couldn't have known that, Dinah."

"Why not? We'd been together for years. I *knew* her!"

Dana reached over and squeezed my hand as tears ran down my face. It wouldn't be for the last time.

We often spent our evenings in one of the pubs in town. Dana loved the place because they not only had some excellent local beer on tap but because they also held trivia contests two or three nights per week. Dana's calm demeanor, and head full of useless information, went far to endear him to the locals.

So did his off-the-cuff counseling skills. If I weren't with him at the pub, he'd sit at the bar. And, as people are prone to do, they pour out their woes to the bartender. Dana would overhear and toss in some advice.

One evening, he and I went in together. A few drinks into our evening (and trivia), one of the locals came over to our table with a beery smile, put a hand on Dana's shoulder and thanked him.

"Glad it helped, Alun," Dana said.

Confused, I looked between the two men.

Alun laughed and nodded to me. "He's a right sage, he is." The man smiled and left.

I looked at my brother. "Aw, isn't that sweet? You're a sage! Can I sprinkle you on my eggs in the morning?"

"Oh, shut up," he said with a chuckle, sipping his beer.

"No, no… I think we have a name for *you*, now! You're the Sage of Cardigan!"

Dana rolled his eyes, but I called him "Sage" for the rest of the night. Yeah, I'm that kind of little sister. Even as kids, we'd lovingly pick on each other, tossing around insults and embarrassments that we found funny only because we knew neither of us meant it at all.

Maybe because I teased him so much that night, he drank more than usual. And by that, I mean that he had maybe five beers instead of his usual three (downed, inexplicably, with a steak and kidney pie). And as we were walking back to our cottage, he insisted on coming up with a name for me, since I'd now labeled him with one.

I'd had more than my usual, too, and was feeling particularly energetic and not the least bit drunk. My body was converting alcohol to energy before it had a chance to intoxicate. One thing I wasn't in the mood for, though, was picking out a "dynamic" name for Dinah.

But I figured I could indulge him a little, after the ribbing I'd given him. So I listened as he rattled off one "Dyna" name after another. I'd respond with "already in use" or "no way" or whatever. It's not like he was coming up with any I'd not thought of before.

Except one.

"Um... Dyna...mistress?"

I stopped in my tracks and turned to look at him, mouth agape. "Excuse me?"

He looked at me with a sheepish smile and repeated himself. "Dynamistress?"

"Am I gonna be running around in stilettos and a corset? Am I gonna be *spanking* bad guys? Will I use nipple clips instead of handcuffs?"

Dana opened his mouth, then paused, possibly picturing such a scenario. "Hmm..."

"No!" I said, and backhanded his shoulder.

"*Ow!*" Dana cried, rubbing his arm where I'd slapped him.

I scoffed at his exaggeration. "Seriously, does that even remotely fit me?"

"Well," he said, still rubbing at his feigned injury, "isn't that kind of the point? Make your public persona and private identity as different as possible?"

I stood there, utterly torn. On the one hand, he made a very valid point. On the other, did I really want to be saddled with that name?

Dynamistress.

"Can we get back, now? I gotta pee," he said, and hurried along.

Back at the cottage, as Dana attended to business, I stood outside, thinking more about this. It was cold out, I knew, but only because I could see my breath easily. I didn't feel cold.

Dynamistress.

I could feel the energy flowing inside me, as though looking for somewhere to go. I stretched, holding my hands up to frame where the moon hid behind the clouds. I laced my fingers together and cracked my knuckles.

As they popped, I thought I saw a faint flash of bluish-white light around my hands. It startled me and I jumped. Then, from inside the cottage, "*Jesus, Dinah!*"

I dashed inside to find Dana standing in front of the bathroom mirror, his shirt off. His shoulder, where I'd casually struck him, was a mottled purple and red bruise. I put a hand to my mouth, feeling absolutely horrible as he turned to face me.

He smirked. "Remind me not to get you really pissed at me... Dynamistress."

My hand fell from my mouth as a tear rolled down my cheek. I wrapped my arms around him and buried my head in his chest.

I laughed... I wept...

I was sorry... I was relieved...

I was excited... I was scared...

I was Dynamistress.

NINE

"I have often found in travelling in a stagecoach, that it is often a comfort to shift one's position, and be bruised in a new place."
~Washington Irving

Human beings are social creatures, and you don't need an anthropologist to tell you this. Sure, these days it seems we're more social online than in person. And I'm as guilty of that as anyone, having a firmly established online presence. But physical presence is very important. This is why certain cities have a much higher queer population than others. A questioning kid in a small community without a support network isn't likely to stick around. She's probably going to move to where she can be with others like her. It's the same for metas, which is why Atlanta has nearly a hundred identified metas when it should "naturally" have fewer than fifty. Yes, part of it is that metas want to be where the action is, but never underestimate the appeal of being able to sit and talk with someone else who just "gets" what it is to be like you.

This was one of the factors I considered when deciding where to move after returning from Europe. The others were general population (the bigger, the better), proximity to State College (the farther away, the better) and general attitude toward the LGBT and meta communities. There's a lot of overlap in these attitudes, but they're not identical. Houston, for example, is gay-friendly, but meta-nasty.

Many cities have big meta and gay populations and are friendly to both. Several of these cities are far away from all the painful memories associated with State College and Pennsylvania in general. I won't go into all the details of my pro/con list, but in the end, my decision came down to my tiebreaker factor: weather. I really hate hot and humid weather, and similarly dislike bitterly cold weather, having grown up in an area that has both. And that's why I didn't move to New York, Los Angeles, Chicago, or Atlanta, and instead came to live in San Francisco.

I sold as many of my unnecessary belongings as I could and packed up the rest. Dana insisted on helping me move, flying out from California. We rented a U-Haul and began our trek across the country, making sure to do some sightseeing along the way. We visited the Rock and Roll Museum in Cleveland and spent a day kicking around Chicago. In the middle of the trip, we veered north off Interstate 80 to see Mt. Rushmore and the perpetually in-progress Crazy Horse Monument, which, to my curiosity, Dana disliked immensely.

"Crazy Horse would have hated this," he said. "This mountain would have been sacred to him. To carve it into an homage that he wouldn't even have wanted..." He shook his head. "Kinda sad, really."

I just nodded. I knew nothing about Crazy Horse, other than the band that played with Neil Young. And then I wondered what the Lakota Chief would have thought of *that*.

From there, it was over to Yellowstone for a day, then a return south to the interstate. We visited the Great Salt Lake, drove across the salt flats, did a little gambling in Reno, and finally arrived in Sacramento, ten days after leaving State College.

Sacramento is about ninety miles from San Francisco. We made the trip several times, looking for an apartment and job for me. On June 1, I moved into what passed for a cheap apartment on Turk Street in the Tenderloin area of the city. Dana insisted on covering my deposit and first month's rent, and to help out whenever I needed it. I grudgingly accepted his offer, though I really wanted to be able to stand on my own two feet.

San Francisco was a different universe from State College. Aside from my trip to Europe with Dana and our recent cross-country jaunt, I hadn't traveled much, nor had much exposure to large cities. Lee and I had once taken a weekend trip to New York to see *Les Misérables* on Broadway, but we didn't do much else there. She didn't care for large cities in any regard, really.

So I was utterly fascinated with San Francisco. Exploring the neighborhoods was my mission for the first few months. I was astounded by the disparity between them, and how abruptly one neighborhood changed into another, without so much as a transitional zone. Naturally, I had to explore Chinatown. To this day, I don't understand how so many stores can sell the same Asian-themed kitsch and remain in business. I will say, though, that the first time I encountered a Chinatown tea shop, I thought it was the coolest thing in the world. An entire wall of shelves filled with jars of loose tea, and a bar at which to sample them. I must have tried fifty different teas my first month in the city.

My neighborhood, the Tenderloin, is a bit on the seedy side. The saving grace, for me, is the great Indian and Pakistani food. The neighborhood also has its own resident meta, The Maltese Falcon. Serious fans of Dashiell Hammett will know that his book was set in the Tenderloin. Hammett lived over on Post Street, and that's where he had his detective live, too. Or so Falcon once informed me. He's a nice guy, if a bit obsessive about his literary homage.

It's fitting that such a hardboiled detective as Sam Spade should work out of the Tenderloin. It's possibly the highest crime district in the city. After sundown, on any given street corner, you'll find drug dealers, prostitutes, or homeless people talking to people only they can see. Maybe all three.

Despite this, I quickly fell in love with the city, and even with my neighborhood. When I had money to spare, or when my mood was particularly low, I'd head over to Original Joe's on Taylor Street. I've always loved diner food, and if you were looking for comfort food, there was no place better. I can't tell you how many times I'd sit at the counter with my meat loaf and mashed potatoes, drowning my sorrows in gravy and melted butter. If I wanted to drown them in something else, I'd generally head to the Edinburgh Castle Pub for a fine selection of Scotch. Last time I counted, they had forty different bottles. My spirit of choice is actually rum, but it's not easy to find a bar stocked with a selection of high quality rums.

I'm often asked about my very first experience on the streets as Dynamistress. I wish I could give an entertaining, action-packed account of the event, but I can't. At least, not without ridiculous amounts of exaggeration.

But one thing I can write about without stretching the truth is the fear. Those early days were scary. My abilities were still limited to energy-enhanced punches. I had no defensive abilities. A gunshot would, I suspected, kill me just as quickly then as it would have ten years earlier. The Maltese Falcon could get away with dressing like a big, black bird, complete with billowing cape and beaked hood. He had ceramic and Kevlar body armor practically head-to-talon. I would have felt a lot safer decked out that way, but since I couldn't yet afford to stand out in a crowd, I had to be a bit more casual. I found a black leather vest and faux leather leggings at a thrift store. For some anonymity, I wore sleek sunglasses and a black leather head wrap. I rounded it all out with accessories like a leather choker and wristbands. And impractical shoes. Ankle boots, in fact... the kind with sharp heels and pointy toes. The outfit was just edgy enough to hint at the "mistress" part of my name.

Dana just stared, speechless, when he saw the full ensemble. "You said I should go for something *not* me," I reminded him.

"Mission accomplished," he said. "You look like a cross between a biker and a hooker."

"So... I'm a booker?"

"Or a hiker," he said.

I shook my head. "Not in these shoes."

I did most of my "patrols" in the afternoon. These were limited to "accidentally" stumbling upon the occasional alleyway mugging or, more often, a drug deal. The way it typically worked went like this: I would spy the crime in progress and walk seemingly obliviously into the nook or alleyway in which it was taking place. Usually, I'd be pretending to be talking on my cell phone. I used a broken one I'd found at a flea market, since I couldn't afford a real one at the time. Sometimes they'd ignore me, sometimes they'd yell at me to beat it. But most of the time, I'd be able to get within arm's reach. And that's all I needed.

Nine times out of ten, I was able to end the encounter with one energy-laced punch. If to the gut, it would knock the wind right out of him. If to the head, he'd be unconscious before he hit the ground. I will say, though, that the first time I broke a guy's jaw, the sound nearly made me vomit. By the third or fourth time, I got used to it.

I didn't patrol at night. It seemed that the bluish-white flash I thought I'd seen back in the U.K. had been no hallucination. The effect was definitely there. I didn't quite know what to make of it, but I knew that a light show in the dark of night would draw the sort of attention I didn't want, yet. Daylight hid it, mostly.

But those nights weren't wasted. For one thing, I joined a gym and took boxing lessons. That was fine for teaching me how to punch and so on, but I also needed somewhere big and empty, away from the public, for the sort of workout I couldn't do at a gym. The abandoned Public Health Service Hospital over in the Presidio suited nicely. Today, it's the Presidio Landmark Apartments, but back then, it was still vacant and condemned.

I chose one of the more modern wings of the old hospital, not the original '30s era building. I planned to do a little architectural remodeling of my own, and didn't want to touch such an interesting work. The wings, by comparison, were ugly as hell. Evidently, the architects who did the renovation agreed, as they tore them down. I've often wondered what they made of the many fist-sized and foot-shaped holes in many of the concrete walls on the lowest floors.

I worked as a fill-in bartender at several establishments in the city. I was like a substitute teacher, stepping in when the regular bartender was sick or on vacation, or when the bar was having a big event in need of more hands. Most of these jobs weren't within walking distance, so I relied on public transportation. I'd sold Baby to help cover the costs of moving. Of course, even if I hadn't, parking rates in the city are exorbitant. As is the rent, but I wasn't prepared to live in the streets.

Dana visited me often when I first moved there. I think it was mainly to make sure the small town girl wasn't being overwhelmed by the big city. One weekend while he was visiting, I was asked to finish a shift at a local gay bar for another bartender who'd gone home sick. Dana decided to tag along and keep me company.

He sat at the bar and watched me mix drinks and surprised me by asking for a cocktail instead of his usual beer. In fact, he asked me to create a cocktail on the spot, just for him.

It was an afternoon shift, and not busy at all. Only one other patron was at the bar. He looked vaguely familiar to me, but I couldn't place why. He was big, well over six feet tall. He was burly, blond, and a bodybuilder type, complete with what appeared to be a Lycra tank top. He soon began checking out Dana. I wanted some amusement, so I waited for him to make a pass.

For Dana's drink, I thought about another bar we'd been in together, back in Aberteifi. So I decided to do something in honor of his "Sage of Cardigan" days. I made him a drink with gin, pomegranate juice, a dash of orange bitters, a touch of grenadine, and a squeeze of fresh lime. I called it the Welsh Dragon. He loved it. The blond guy evidently thought it sounded good, too, so he asked for one. He smiled at Dana as he lifted his drink in a silent toast.

"I'm Marcus," he said to us both, though mainly to Dana. We introduced ourselves, and Marcus smiled. He nodded at me. "Nice to meet you," he said. "And very nice to meet you," he said to Dana.

It occurs to me that I've not described my brother's appearance. He's just shy of six feet tall. Like me, he struggled with his weight when he was younger. He was still husky, you could say. He shaved his head, had a Van Dyck beard, and was, to be blunt, extremely hairy. In other words, he could easily be taken for one of the "bears" in the gay community, if he were sitting in a gay bar.

Which he was.

I busied myself with wiping down my station, already smirking at what I expected to be the most humorously awkward situation in which I'd ever seen my brother. And I'd do what I could to make it more awkward. Again, that's the kind of sister I am. Dana noticed my amusement and glared at me.

"I haven't seen you here before," Marcus said.

"Never been here before," Dana replied. "Which might explain that."

Marcus chuckled and sipped his drink. "Then I won't ask if you come here often."

Dana smiled slightly. "Just here visiting Dinah." He said it in a way that implied we were "together," to avoid having to fend off any of Marcus's advances. But I wasn't going to let him sidestep it so easily.

"Oh, now, I've been telling you to get out of your shell, sweetie," I said. I turned to Marcus. "You know how hard it is, at first," I said.

What are you up to? Dana's inside voice said. I just smirked at him.

"Yes, I do," Marcus said. He smiled at Dana again. "How long ago did you come out?"

Dana narrowed his eyes at me. "Marcus, I'm flattered by the attention, but I really am straight. Dinah is messing with you, trying to embarrass me. She's my sister, and, well... it's what she does."

Marcus looked between us. "You... look nothing alike."

I snorted at Dana. "You expected him to believe that?" Now Dana's inside voice was demanding I knock it off. "It's a gay bar," I said. "You can let your hair down. So to speak."

"Cute," he said, lifting his drink.

Poor Marcus kept looking back and forth between us. "Okay, I'm confused. Are you or aren't you?"

Dana swallowed his drink and started to reply. But before he could, I decided to play my last card. I leaned over the bar and kissed him full on the mouth. He about fell off his stool as he recoiled, staring at me with eyes wide. "Dinah! What the hell?"

I turned to Marcus. "Now does that look like a straight guy to you?"

He shook his head. "No straight man I know would react that way to a kiss from you."

Dana regained some composure, though his entire head was flushed. "Just... surprised," he said. "Dinah's the gay one."

"So she's *not* your sister."

"Oh, she's my sister, all right," Dana said. And his inside voice said something I won't put in print.

Both men were staring at me, now. I thought about another ruse, but figured I couldn't top that one. So I let it go and finished cleaning up my station.

Marcus blinked. To Dana, he said, "I was going to apologize for making you uncomfortable, but I think she outdid me on that one."

"No worries," Dana said. "It's not the first time."

"Didn't you even have a client hit on you, once?" I said.

Dana nodded. "Yeah. I never realized I put out such a gay vibe."

"Client?" Marcus asked.

"I'm a psychologist."

"I see." The big man nodded. "I think your sister should be your next one. 'Cuz she's messed up."

"You're telling me," Dana said.

I just laughed.

We spent the rest of my shift talking. Marcus was a really nice guy. He and Dana got along great, engaging in a discussion about California things unfamiliar to me. And drinking. Marcus got pretty tipsy and giggly and began telling one awful joke after another. We politely laughed at each one.

"Hey," he said. "Whaddaya call a group of large, hairy, gay men with no teeth?"

Dana and I exchanged glances. "What?" we both said.

Marcus could hardly contain his laughter as he blurted, "Gummy bears!"

As Dana groaned, I shook my head. "That's it. No more for booze for you."

Finally, my replacement arrived and I prepared to leave.

"I want tacos," Dana said.

"Of course you do," I said. He always craves tacos after a few drinks.

"Mmm, tacos," Marcus said.

So we walked to a taqueria between the bar and my apartment. We sat inside the hole-in-the-wall and ate our fill, Marcus expressing some surprise at how much food I could put away. Then we stepped outside into the darkening streets and prepared to say our farewells to him, since he had parked back in the other direction.

"You sure you should be driving?" I asked.

Marcus opened his mouth to speak, but the voice I heard came from behind me.

"You ain't drivin' nowhere, man."

Someone wrenched my arms behind me and yanked me away from the others. I could see two thugs doing the same to Dana. A quick count revealed eight males: one holding me, two holding Dana, and five in a semi-circle around Marcus, two with guns drawn, two with knives, and one holding a length of steel pipe. I didn't realize steel pipes were still in fashion.

Marcus was looking directly at me, clearly afraid for my safety.

Sweet of him. But I wear heels for a reason.

A crushing, energy-enhanced stomp on my captor's foot set me free, and a power punch to his face stopped his yowling. I only had to hear the crunch to know that he'd be no more threat. A glance at Dana shocked me, as I saw both of his attackers sailing telekinetically through the air to slam into the brick wall of the market next to the taqueria.

The others turned at the commotion, and then everything seemed to slow down. I looked up, and all I could see was the gun aimed at my face. My heart hammered and fear paralyzed me, so certain was I that my brains were about to decorate the street behind me.

Two gunshots, almost simultaneous. They weren't as loud as in the movies, but the blast of air in my ear as the bullet ripped past was loud enough to scare me out of my deer-in-the-headlights freeze.

Time returned to normal just as I heard the growl.

The gunmen and I looked to Marcus, the source of the growl, who was now suffused in a golden glow, his body transformed to a massive creature. I nearly felt sorry for the remaining thugs.

Now I knew why he'd looked familiar to me. And why he was wearing stretchy clothes. Marcus Aurelius Jones, a.k.a. The Golden Bear. Sacramento's resident meta, and one of the only ones I knew of in California who had a public identity. I could barely contain my excitement!

I won't describe what happened next, other than to say it was over very, very quickly. And then, the big bear began to laugh. As Marcus morphed back to human form, he looked at the two of us with a huge smile.

"Now, what are the odds that they'd decide to attack me while I was with two other heroes?"

I grinned and turned to Dana, who was holding his head. My excitement vanished. "You okay?"

Dana nodded painfully and held out his hand, displaying a bullet. "Stopping these *really* gives me a headache," he whispered. I boggled at him, not only because he could do it, but because his words sort of implied he'd done it before.

Marcus explained to us that the attackers were members of the *Norteños*, a Latin American gang. Steel pipe dude was the brother of a guy Marcus had put in the hospital, and then jail, the previous month.

While our new friend called the authorities to come pick up the gang, Dana said seriously to me, "Dinah... you need to be careful. You pack quite a punch." He indicated the unconscious guy I'd hit. "You could kill someone."

I shrugged. "Better them than me, right?"

Marcus had ended his call and was securing the payload for the police with some zip ties he carried with him. To my surprise, the police arrived very quickly. But then, a hero named after the animal on the state's flag probably carried some serious clout, I figured.

Dana and I kept to the shadows as Marcus dealt with the officer in charge. When they were through and the *Norteños* carted off, the three of us headed to my apartment.

"I'm sorry about all that," Marcus said. "Still, it's always nice to see such teamwork. Who are you guys with?"

"Um... nobody," I said. "I'm just starting out. Not registered, even. And Dana's a psychologist, not a hero."

Marcus frowned and looked at both of us. "Not registered? Why not?"

"Because I'm not ready."

To Dana, he said, "I have to assume you're not in the business by choice... even though what I just saw tells me you'd be one hell of a force to reckon with."

"Thanks," Dana said, still rubbing his temples. "We help others in our own ways."

Back at my place, Marcus wasted no time in voicing his opinions on our situation. He picked on Dana, first. "Maybe I'm old fashioned," he said, "but I do believe that if you have a gift, you should use it for the greater good. Now, being a counselor is fine, but you could do so much more."

"So much more in the way of overtly visible good, you mean," Dana replied. "Marcus, I applaud your work. You prevent people from suffering more than they otherwise would at the hands of people like those punks who attacked us. But half my clients are their victims. I help them heal from the psychological trauma they've already endured. And I think that's pretty important."

"Certainly," Marcus agreed. "But there are plenty of non-metas who are doing that."

"And there are plenty of non-metas who do what you do, too. Do you tell them they should stop fighting crime and go be a doctor or teacher?"

"That's different."

"Is it? They might find a cure for cancer, or inspire a student to become the doctor who does. But fighting crime is their passion. Counseling is mine." As Marcus chewed on that, Dana handed him his business card. "I also counsel metas."

Marcus accepted the card with a little smile that conceded the argument. Then he turned to me. "So. Not registered why?"

I spoke with no little amount of embarrassment. "You saw me out there. I froze. I'm just lucky he missed." I shook my head. "I'm not good enough."

"Dinah," Marcus chided. "Registration has nothing to do with your ability as a hero. It has to do with the ability God gave you."

I wanted to – but didn't – refute the "God-given" aspect of his argument, but had to admit that he was basically correct. The definition of "metahuman" in the Meta Registration Act didn't limit it only to those who, like Dana or Marcus, had been born with abilities that manifested at some point in their lives. It also included those who gained abilities through accidental or deliberate means, organic, chemical, or even mechanical in nature. Thus, the ones zipping around in armored super-suits were required to register, too, even if they had no physical or mental meta-abilities of their own. Of course, some argued that the ability to design and build such a suit was, in itself, a superhuman ability. And it didn't matter how tremendous or insignificant your abilities were. It didn't matter whether you used them to fight crime or didn't use them at all. You still had to register.

"I know," I said. "I just feel the mandatory registration thing is so… Big Brother-ish."

Marcus sighed. "Well… it is," he acknowledged. "But I don't think it's going away. And the repercussions for not registering can be severe."

He was right, again. Unregistered metas were poked and prodded until the full nature of their abilities was known. A corrupt system usually "connected" the meta with some crime or other, and the unsuspecting meta was sentenced to prison. And not just any prison. A prison for metas, complete with the latest gizmos and gadgets designed to nullify or compensate for meta-abilities. Cell walls made of foot-thick steel. Dampening fields to prevent energy powers of all sorts. The worst subjugations, though, were reserved for those like Dana. Those with mental powers were kept in a state of semi-sedation, to the point where they could manage basic bodily functions, but couldn't put any strength into their abilities. It was inhumane, but so far, the public outcry about it was pretty quiet.

"Look, Dinah… I don't like it any more than you do, but until we can get the law changed, it's wiser for us to play along. Some of the true loners can get away with it. But for those of us with families and loved ones…" He shook his head. "It's just not worth it."

I'd wanted to be famous, ever since I was a kid. I still did. And I couldn't do that by hiding. I thanked Marcus for prodding me. Whether I was ready or not, it was time to register.

TEN

"If history repeats itself, and the unexpected always happens, how incapable must Man be of learning from experience."
~George Bernard Shaw

June 30, 1908. An extremely powerful explosion rocks the area now known as Krasnoyarsk Krai, Russia, estimated at about one thousand times more powerful than the bomb dropped on Hiroshima. The "Tunguska event," as it is known, has many hypotheses put forward to explain its cause. A meteoroid. A comet. A black hole. Natural gas. Deuterium from space. Some blame it on Tesla. Some blame it on aliens. But no bits of downed UFO, or anything else, are ever found.

January 18, 1994. Witnesses to an explosion in Cando, Spain, report a fireball in the sky. Hypotheses differ on the cause of the explosion, with one being a meteor strike. No fragments are ever recovered.

June 6, 2002. A mid-air explosion splits the sky over the Mediterranean Sea with a force equivalent to a small atomic bomb. The official report of the "Eastern Mediterranean event" attributes it to an asteroid disintegrating in our atmosphere. Once again, no pieces are ever found to support the report.

September 25, 2002. An explosion occurs near the town of Bodaybo, Russia, with a force estimated very broadly to be between one-fifth to one-half kiloton by the Americans and four to five kilotons by the Russians. The "Vitim event," as it is called, is suggested to have been caused by a comet. No remnants are ever found, though water and snow in the vicinity contain unusually high amounts of radioactive cobalt, hydrogen, and cesium isotopes.

The year 2003 was an interesting year for metas in the news. And by "interesting," I mean "horrid." Though metas still had a loyal fan base, negative sentiment against us was becoming more prominent and we were blamed for all sorts of things.

In February, the space shuttle Columbia burned up on reentry from orbit. Though it is virtually certain the accident was the result of damage suffered to the heat shield on takeoff, many believed it to be a deliberate act of a meta – probably from China – working on behalf of a government that wanted the U.S. space program to grind to a halt.

In April, the Human Genome Project reached completion. The announcement thrilled me, but I wasn't in the majority on that feeling. There was now a good bit known about the genes involved in the "meta mutation," but the public resented the very idea that this could be a "natural" thing. Scientists were ridiculed and "out" metas were reviled.

The month of May saw more tornadoes than any month in U.S. history (five hundred forty-two, nearly four hundred of which happened within the first twelve days of the month). Climate change? Of course not. This was "obviously" the work of those awful weather-manipulating metas!

But it wasn't all bad… at least, not for me. In June, I received an email from my old colleague, Dr. Gray. He and I had kept in touch for a while after the lab fire, but I hadn't heard from him in years. To my amazement, he asked me to co-author a paper on a genetic approach to dealing with the obesity epidemic. He said he'd always been impressed with my ideas on the topic, especially my concept of "black fat," a genetically manufactured type of fat that would theoretically store even more energy than "brown fat" does. He very much wanted to incorporate this and other ideas of mine into his paper.

To say I was surprised is an understatement. I reminded him that I was no longer actively working in the field. He realized that, he said, but surely I was keeping abreast of the latest research and watching the trends.

And, of course, I was. I visited the library weekly to read all the scientific journals I could. I scoured science news online for anything I thought would help me in the years to come. I knew there was bound to be some additional tweaking needed to refine whatever abilities I'd gain, after all. It was just a happy coincidence that much of my research dealing with metabolism could also be used to attack obesity.

He offered to fly me back to Pennsylvania for some face-time, but it didn't take much to convince him to come to San Francisco, instead.

He came for a long weekend and when he and I weren't talking about the scope of the paper and what parts he wanted me to cover, we were sightseeing and spending nights on the town. On his nickel, obviously, as I was barely scraping by.

"Dinah, I feel awful about what happened back at GACTech," he said one night over dinner and sake at Sanraku. Then, seeing me stiffen, he said, "I'm sorry... I guess that's still a sore subject."

"Not at all," I drawled. "I look forward to having twenty-five percent of my wages garnisheed until the day I die."

Dr. Gray sighed. "I tried to talk the Board out of the lawsuit, but their concern was the increased premiums to our insurer, evidently."

"And being blacklisted helped that how, exactly?"

"Blacklisted? Why do you say that?"

"What would you call it when not a single biotech firm from Pittsburgh to Philadelphia would even give me an interview?"

He frowned quizzically and said, "Well, immediately following the fire, your name was all over the news and probably known to other companies. But I assure you, GACTech never did anything to influence anyone about hiring you. Surely, now that so much time has passed..."

"Even so," I said, not really believing him, "firms here are handing out pink slips like crazy."

"Back home, too, but not for clinical researchers. They're still needed."

I conceded that, but pointed out that *"GACTech, 1994 to 1998, when I burned it to the ground"* doesn't look so good in the employment history section of a resume.

"Still," he said, "I think you should look into it."

I smiled. "Yeah. Probably so."

I wake up on the hard floor of a laboratory. I'm stiff and my stomach feels on the verge of upchucking. Flames rise around me. Acrid fumes threaten to suffocate me. But I can't move, can't scream for help. Panic flares with each surge of flame. Then I feel myself rising, lifted, and everything goes dark again.

I hadn't had a nightmare about the fire in years, but given Dr. Gray's presence, and especially our discussion of it the previous day, I wasn't surprised to have one. I woke in a panic, sweating, heart pounding. Just like every other time.

The lifting bit was new, though.

Despite the nightmares, my talks with Dr. Gray only served to get me excited about the possibility of working in a lab again. "The black fat idea hasn't quite panned out, yet," I told him over coffee the morning before he flew back east. "Though I think it would be possible to increase the amount of brown fat in our bodies."

"By what method?"

"Well, it's all about the hypothalamus, right? It regulates everything from thirst to body temperature. And what's the purpose of brown fat? To keep infants from freezing to death."

"Energy balance," he said.

"Right. And adipose tissue is adipose tissue. What makes it brown or white – or my hypothetical black – is just a matter of whatever the hypothalamus tells it to be."

Dr. Gray nodded, hanging on every word. "So you think we can program the hypothalamus to create brown fat instead of white."

"Or even convert existing white to brown," I said. "Neuropeptide Y seems the obvious way to go for that. But really," I said, "for treating weight issues, a better first step is probably to address the genetic factors we know are linked to obesity."

"I've been looking into a glyoxylate shunt in the liver..."

"...to increase fatty acid oxidation," I finished for him. "Yes. Lots of potential for that, I think. But I was thinking more about directly editing the genes themselves."

Dr. Gray stared at me. "Genome editing? Dinah, that's still a long way off." I nodded, keeping my mouth shut. He didn't need to know that living proof of successful human genome editing was sipping a cappuccino across the table from him. "Unless," he continued, "your experiment succeeded."

I stiffened, mid-sip. "What?"

He smiled casually. "Dinah, I read your dissertation, remember? After months of trying to figure what you might have been doing in the lab after hours, it just made sense. Am I wrong?"

I frowned. Dr. Gray had always been interested in my work. Excited, even. But I was still surprised. "No," I admitted. "You're not."

He leaned forward, nearly spilling his coffee. "And? Was it a success?"

I hesitated, then put on a dejected look. "I'm a bartender."

He looked at me for a long moment before nodding and easing back into his seat.

It was less than a week after Dr. Gray left that I discovered another layer of success to my experiment. The same night I met the Maltese Falcon.

Naturally, I'd heard of him. I'd even spied his rooftop silhouette a couple times. The circumstance of our meeting was a simple convenience store holdup on Hyde Street.

As luck would have it, we both happened upon the scene of the crime-in-progress at the same time. The clerk on duty had been able to trip the silent alarm and I overheard the police call through the earphone of the tiny scanner I carried. The Falcon, of course, has his scanner handily built into the electronics of his helmet.

He swooped down, landing directly in front of me as I casually strolled toward the door. "Bad time for shopping," he said, waving me off. I was perfectly okay with sitting this one out, since it gave me the opportunity to see a seasoned pro in action. I was as excited as I was as a teen when a new issue of *Supers* magazine came out.

Despite his warning, I followed him to the door. As soon as he opened it, a piercing screech erupted from him. I still don't know whether it's mechanically produced or a sound he can make on his own. Either way, the effect it has is to hammer on eardrums. I was glad to be behind him, since those in the path of the sound – in this case, the robber and the cashier – were temporarily deafened. Each immediately covered his ears in pain, which was all the opening the Falcon needed to take out the gunman with a swooping punch. He can't fly, but he's very fast. He cleared the distance from the door to the bad guy's jaw before I could even move.

As the Falcon scanned the store for accomplices, I strode in, intent on introducing myself to him in the hopes of having my first ally in the city. That was when the second kid with a gun leaped out from the candy aisle. The next thing I knew, he was behind me, his pistol to my head and my neck in a chokehold.

As he screamed at Falcon to get out, I made one of my less intelligent decisions. I swung my fist up, pivoting at the elbow. In the movies, the fist always connects with the bad guy's face and knocks him out. In my case, it did succeed in knocking the gun away from my head, but my assailant only jerked back a bit. I spun, intending to follow up with the knockout, but he saw my intentions and, to my horror, shot me in the chest.

I fell backward to the floor in more pain than I thought was possible to feel. I heard the Falcon shriek again to take out the second guy. I felt it pummel my eardrums, but that pain was nothing compared to being shot. I could hear only my own ragged gasps as I stared up at the fluorescent lights on the ceiling, a dead panic gripping me. Then the lights were blocked out by the hood and masked face of the Maltese Falcon. He scooped his arms under me, but as he started to lift, he stopped, staring at my chest.

He spoke to me, then, but I couldn't hear more than a faint mumbling. As my hearing slowly returned, I felt the Falcon tugging at my vest. Surely he wasn't going to try to stop the bleeding right here on the floor, I thought. Then I figured that was probably better than dying en route to the emergency room. But he just knelt there, looking at me. "You okay?" I heard him say.

My brain immediately offered up its standard sarcastic response, urging me to point out that I had a bullet lodged inside my chest and was bleeding to death. But all I managed to do was look at him like he was speaking in tongues. He glanced at the floor, then reached down and seemed to pick something up. Then he coaxed me into a sitting position, which only made the pain worse. Then he held out his hand. "Your souvenir," he said. In his palm was a flattened bullet. I reached toward my wound, only to find my skin intact. I looked down, seeing no blood. I touched my chest, then flinched from the pain. "Probably bruised your sternum," he said casually as he helped me to my feet.

I'd taken a handgun round from a distance of maybe three feet and now stood there with only a growing bruise to show for it. A damn painful bruise, to be sure, but I was alive.

Falcon told the clerk to call the cops as he bound the would-be robbers. Then he looked at me. "I imagine I'll see you again," he said. And then he was out the door.

It appeared that I owed my life to something I once feared might kill me. The "runaway" effect. I'd previously concluded that what was really going on inside me was a sort of constant, semi-controlled state of runaway, as my body was producing more energy than a normal human would ever expend except in the most ridiculous of circumstances... an amount that would destroy every cell in my body unless it was expended. And I did expend a good bit, but sometimes I still felt jumpy, which proceeded to discomfort and even pain. I had to expend energy regularly. Sometimes, I'd wake in the middle of the night, not having to pee, but to work out.

In recent weeks, I'd learned how to vent energy in a passive fashion, which was essentially to let it "leak" out around me. Apparently, this full-body leak had the potential to act as a sort of energy shield, so to speak.

At home, I put an ice pack on my chest and lay in bed thinking of ways to control this newfound ability, rather than hope my subconscious adrenaline rush would continue to save me, as it had that night.

Once I'd healed, I enlisted Dana to help me test my newfound protection. I couldn't convince him to obtain a gun. "Are you fucking kidding?" were his exact words when I suggested he shoot me. But I was able to get him to telekinetically batter me with less lethal objects. With concentration, I was able to make the passive protection even stronger. So much so that, eventually, I could have speeding bricks bounce off me with only the mildest discomfort.

My life in the streets changed considerably at this point. I no longer had to be as careful. Now I could actively dive into danger, like the Falcon and the other "real" metas out there.

My newfound bravado in the streets worried Dana. A lot. And I guess that was his duty as my big brother. I didn't want him stressing over it, but I didn't know how to stop it. Especially since he had every right to be worried.

Caution? Thrown to the wind. Hey, I was bullet-proof! What did I have to worry about? So I pushed myself like an Olympic hopeful. My goal, of course, was to catch the attention of the media, to start climbing the ladder of fame. The fact that public sentiment about metas was in the crapper seemed to escape me. I was going to be famous, now. I just knew it.

One of the drawbacks of my particular abilities is that energy doesn't just come from nowhere. Humans get energy from food. My altered cells were more efficient at converting food to energy, but I still needed to eat a lot. In fact, if I were to recount my average daily food intake, it would astound you. Suffice to say that hobbits have nothing on me.

I don't adhere to the standard three meals a day regimen. In fact, I eat fewer full meals than most people do. Instead, I eat several calorie-dense mini-meals throughout the course of the day. I supplement with high doses of vitamins because sometimes I go a week without eating vegetables. Not out of any dislike for them, but because they fill me up without giving me the calories I need. On days when I'm "off duty," I'll often eat nothing but veggies, in fact.

I won't lie. I do love the fact that I'm able to eat whatever I like without gaining weight. A couple pints of Ben & Jerry's every day? Don't mind if I do. For a previously overweight girl, it was a dream come true.

Except when it was a nightmare. Like the time I ran out of energy while fighting the meta known as Blacknight. For those of you who don't remember him (he died of cancer in 2006), he focused mainly on jewelry store jobs. He wore sleek black armor, including a medieval-style helmet. Probably not the best get-up for a thief who needs to get away and stay out of sight, but no one ever accused those on the other side of the law of being intelligentsia.

In my battle with him, I'd expended a lot of energy. His armor was darned effective. Eventually, I landed a blow that cracked the fitting of his helmet, causing the faceplate to come loose. But it was the last I had in me. I literally felt my energy level plummet and knew I was spent.

So I bluffed. When the visor fell away from his face, I looked him in the eye, fist poised for another crushing blow, and growled something at him. He knew one of my punches to his naked face would result in a huge dental bill, so he surrendered. Luckily for me.

After that, I swore I'd find a way to prevent such power outages without having to eat an elephant for breakfast every day. I have a firm rule never to eat anything larger than my head. Besides, stores near me don't carry elephant.

Dr. Gray and I corresponded a lot after his visit, and our discussions continually gave me new ideas for improvements in the long term. But in the short term, I needed something more. My work had previously focused on converting calories to energy, but I realized I needed to learn all I could about calories themselves.

Without going into the tedious details, I spent months coming up with a formula for a super-high calorie supplement. There are many out on the market, including over-the-counter powders for bodybuilders and products manufactured for hospital use. I used these last as starting points since, unsurprisingly, there are too many of the OTC products that are scams.

After playing around with glucose polymer chains and whatnot, I eventually came up with a super-dense, high-calorie substance with the consistency – and flavor – of library paste. I added flavoring, of course, in the form of honey or chocolate or peanut butter. Nothing lacking calories. I packaged the stuff in snack-size zipper bags and carried half a dozen or so with me on patrol, which wasn't easy with my outfit. I find it funny that the snack bags are advertised as being perfect for holding the trendy 100-calorie portions of snacks. Filled with Dynapaste, each bag holds about 3,000 calories. And no, I don't really call it that.

Okay, yes, I do.

As revolting as the stuff was, even with flavor added, it really did work. Over the next several months, I deliberately pushed myself to the brink of energy failure. And sucking down a baggie of the paste never failed to restore me quickly. I was pretty proud of myself for coming up with it. Naturally, I filed the paperwork to patent the formula. That sort of thing is drilled into us scientists.

On October 7, 2003, the people of California voted to toss out their current governor and put bodybuilder/movie star Arnold Schwarzenegger in the office. And that wasn't even the weirdest thing that happened that month.

Two days later, there was an explosion over Groom Lake in Nevada. The dry lake is part of what is known as "Area 51." Like other mysterious explosions around the world, it was presumed to be caused by a piece of comet or meteor, but no remnants of either were found. The explosion did leave evidence, though, in the form of a hole. But not a hole in the ground.

It left a hole in the sky.

ELEVEN

"Everybody has a world, and that world is completely hidden until we begin to inquire. As soon as we do, that entire world opens to us and yields itself. And you see how full and complex it is."
~David Guterson

Three noteworthy events took place on my thirty-third birthday, February 12, 2004. One was that the first same-sex marriage took place in San Francisco, after the mayor, in an act of civil disobedience, proclaimed that denying such marriages actually violated the Constitution. The courts didn't agree with him and it all stopped a month later, but by that time, almost four thousand same-sex couples had married.

Politics has never been something that could hold my interest, but certain causes do stir up passion in me. In all honesty, I don't see any appeal in the institution of marriage, but I definitely understand the desire for equal treatment under the law.

As I watched the news coverage of same-sex marriage during this month, I couldn't help but think about Sharon and Jackie. Were they still together? Did they still live in Pennsylvania? Or had they moved to Canada to legally marry? I had no idea, but I knew that if they wanted to do such a thing, they should have the right.

Seeing the outrage by the conservative factions around the nation made me think, too, about how metas were treated, how we were subjected to indignities that non-metas were not. Dana's words of years ago kept coming back to me. I understood that all these reactions were based on fear. We fear what we don't understand.

This lack of understanding fuels most of the hatred on this planet, whether it's of GLBT people, people of other nationalities, atheists (still the most hated minority), or those who subscribe to other religions. Lack of understanding is behind the belief in supernatural things and the distrust of science.

Being a scientist, I'm particularly frustrated by Americans' profound lack of comprehension of even basic scientific principles. If they were more educated, they wouldn't believe nonsensical things, such as the idea that a nuclear meltdown can reach the center of the earth and destroy the planet, or that an experiment in particle physics could create a black hole that would eat the earth, and so on. But they embrace these apocalyptic beliefs, implying that, when it comes right down to it, science is nothing but trouble. We should stop mucking about with such things.

Not counting those who choose to remain ignorant out of laziness, humans are a naturally curious bunch of folks. We want to understand things. The stranger it is, the more we want to figure it out. And an apparent rip in the very fabric of space is about as strange as they come.

The existence of Area 51 had been denied by the government up until July of the previous year. So when something mighty odd occurred there only seven months later, the conspiracy theorists went even loopier. The government finally 'fessed up, these people said, because they knew something was going to happen to reveal its existence to the world in a big way.

The explosion took place on the northern end of the dry lake, raising a small mushroom cloud of dust and dirt. Explosions in that area weren't exactly uncommon, since Area 51's western border is shared with the Nevada Test Site, where several hundred nuclear tests have been conducted over the years. But this wasn't one of those tests.

Given all the resources available between the military and NTS, there were plenty of energy experts and other scientists on hand to examine the phenomenon, and physicists from several universities were flown in. The initial "hole" was described as being perfectly circular, about twenty feet in diameter, with an edge that glowed and crackled with energy. The bottom was about ten feet off the ground when they found it. However, the rift was shrinking. Within weeks, it was gone.

What had those soldiers and scientists seen as they looked into this gaping circle in the sky? Whatever it was, it was enough for the military to immediately give it the highest level of confidentiality, the somewhat comical "Top Secret" designation. But someone at Groom Lake was scared enough to contact the media. He or she wasn't one of those privy to a first-hand look at it, but gave enough information for the media to run with. It was all over the news. And predictably, those who didn't believe it was the product of secret government work, or of aliens, blamed it on the metas. I suppose it's hard to blame them. After all, such things aren't known to be "natural." Metas are a convenient and often plausible explanation. This was the slant most of the media gave the story.

Mainstream media let go of the story after a few weeks. The oddity had disappeared and public worry over impending doom had abated. There was no story to the story, anymore, so they moved on to the next hot topic. But of course, there was always the online world, where news never truly gets old or disappears, especially when there's a conspiracy theory involved.

Some of these sources claimed that the anomaly had not completely disappeared. They said there was still something left behind, something similar to the "hole" in the ozone. It was a thinning, rather than an outright rip in the sky. Some sources claimed the experts – the soldiers and scientists – had performed any number of examinations, captured untold numbers of readings, which led to them being able to stabilize the "thin spot" of the sky by erecting a sort of mechanical "frame" around it. Physics isn't usually the forte of conspiracy theorists, so I have no idea how they believe it worked, but the framework somehow kept that thin area from disappearing altogether. And naturally, we were doing whatever we could to open it again, for some reason.

All in all, it did sound like something we would do, if we could. But that's what makes for a good conspiracy theory. It sounds just plausible enough for people to think there might be something to it.

The second noteworthy birthday event – noteworthy to me, anyway – was the discovery of an unexpected side effect of my new abilities. My hair was rapidly losing color. I wasn't clear on why, but I chalk it up to my hair follicles being affected by the massive amounts of energy constantly suffusing my body. Whatever the reason, by the summer of 2004, any trace of blonde was gone. My hair became a shockingly pure white, from split ends to roots. Yes, all of my hair. Even my eyelashes.

It wasn't that the follicles were being destroyed by the energy. If anything, they were being prodded to new levels of productivity. My hair and nails were growing much faster than before. To test just how fast, on the first of May, I cropped my hair very short, into a sort of retro shag look. By the 4th of July, it was down to my shoulders. The platinum look worked for me and I rather liked it. But it did make keeping my identity secret a little more difficult. There simply weren't all that many women under the age of seventy walking around with pure white hair.

At first, I'd tried dying it, but that only worked for about a day or two. I'd have to do my roots every single day, and that was just too much of a pain. Mascara, however, was fine for my lashes, since I was used to daily applications of that, and it didn't take much more effort to color my eyebrows. But I was glad to stop that process.

I began a routine of visiting half a dozen different hair salons, mainly because I didn't want the attention and questions that would come of weekly visits to the same one, displaying on each visit the equivalent of six weeks of growth. I had to increase my bartending hours just to pay for all the haircuts. Yes, I did try to learn how to cut my own. The results were awful, and I was glad it grew out quickly.

The third event? The Senate introduced a bill requiring all hospitals to perform genetic tests on newborns to determine if their DNA held the "meta gene" mutation. It was introduced with little fanfare. Civil rights groups didn't learn of it far enough in advance to raise public awareness, but once it passed, they pitched a royal fit. For all the good it did.

A major turning point for me was a blatant daytime mugging in the Tenderloin. Two guys grabbed a man who'd just stepped out of his Porsche, hustling him into an alley. Before they could rough him up too badly, I sprinted in and snarled something threatening. Like most other things, my running speed was boosted by my energy levels, so my approach was usually startling. They got off a couple shots before I could reach them, but both missed.

I took them down quickly, with one punch each. From behind me, I heard an expletive or two just before more gunshots. Two more men had entered the mouth of the alley and were unloading on me.

By this time, I could put enough power into my shields so that bullets from handguns were painful, but not to the point of incapacitation. Still, since I'm not exactly a masochist, I intended to quickly take out the gunmen. Then I heard a familiar screech. I looked up to see the Maltese Falcon descending on the two, who'd stopped firing and were holding their heads in pain. He subdued the pair and quickly bound their hands and feet. I did the same with my pair, using the zip ties I now carried with me, while the Porsche driver rushed back to his vehicle and drove off.

"You okay?" Falcon asked as he approached, though he was looking in the opposite direction, at the vanishing sports car.

"Yeah, sure," I said. "Nice to see you again." I extended a hand, which he shook out of courtesy. "The name's Dynamistress."

Falcon looked at the fallen thugs and sighed. "Right. Listen," he said, "you've got guts. But I don't know that this is for you."

I stared at him, jaw hanging open. "You've got to be kidding," I said.

He shook his head. "Look what happened tonight. These four could easily have been twice that many."

"For a *mugging*?"

Falcon frowned. "The guy with the Porsche was 'Mutt' McArdle." I stared at him, the name meaning nothing. "Of the Lanza gang?" he prodded. I said nothing. "See? You need to know these things. McArdle had a contract out on him."

"Okay, but I stopped it! Why don't you think I'm cut out for this?"

He shook his beaked head. "I meant that the solo act may not be for you. But you might do okay on a team."

A team! My heart leapt inside me. "I like the sound of that! Are the Gatekeepers recruiting?" I could easily see myself in the ranks of the city's premiere meta group.

"The Gate–" Falcon shook his head and might have even chuckled. "I was thinking more along the lines of the Bay Scouts. I can introduce you to Scoutmaster, if you like."

My heart stopped leaping, tripped, and fell. The Bay Scouts. There was nothing wrong with them, of course. But they were a far cry from the Gatekeepers. Definitely second string. Or third. "Thanks," I said with forced enthusiasm. "That would be great."

Around this time, I got an email from Dr. Gray, with a copy of "our" paper attached. He wanted me to read it, fill in a couple blanks, and give him any final feedback before he submitted it. I'd been co-author on a couple papers during my years in graduate school, but this was different. The others were mostly analyses of existing procedures and one or two reviews of analytical tools. But Dr. Gray's paper – *our* paper – proposed new things, things no one else seemed to be addressing.

But one section of the paper made me stop. Dr. Gray had mentioned targeted genome editing as a treatment for obesity. But he provided nothing to support the concept. I frowned. This was one hell of a blank he wanted me to fill in.

This put me in an uncomfortable spot. No journal would publish the paper without studies to support the claim that genome editing could be safely used to treat obesity. We had no animal studies to reference, let alone human. We had nothing but our assertion.

I couldn't very well use myself as a case study, either, as I worked alone on that "project," had no control subject, and therefore my data would be laughed at, even if I were inclined to share it.

I said all this in my reply to Dr. Gray. "Sadly," I wrote, "I think we need to omit the reference to genome editing for now. Maybe in our next paper?"

I sent the email off to him, knowing it was the only thing to do. Despite this, I still felt bad for letting him down.

Falcon made good on his promise. He arranged a meeting for me with Scoutmaster, leader of the Bay Scouts. We met in the headquarters of the group, an underground bunker left over from the Cold War era.

How can I describe Scoutmaster without using stereotypes? I'm not sure I can. He was a step or two down from a drill sergeant, a by-the-book, no nonsense, always prepared leader. He didn't demand respect, but even in my short meeting with him, he inspired it. Pretty impressive for someone who was only in his late twenties.

The same cannot be said of the reverse. His entire demeanor told me he was only conducting the interview as a favor to Falcon, and he felt I was a complete pretender, unworthy of his team and unlikely to ever deserve his respect.

"How old are you?" he asked, looking closely at the visible part of my face.

"Thirty-three," I said.

He frowned. "Bit old to be just beginning."

The doubt on his face caused me to squirm a little. "My abilities... um... didn't manifest until recently."

I tried not to seem nervous as he sized me up. "How do you expect to catch someone on foot when you're wearing those things?" he said, indicating my stiletto-heeled boots. "No one's gonna come help you when you break a heel or get stuck in a sidewalk crack."

It was a valid observation. I knew he was wrong, though. I'd never so much as turned my ankle in the boots. I began to explain, but he continued.

"And what's with the leathers? You a hero or a gang banger?" He shook his head. "We're the good guys and we need to look like good guys, not like... whatever it is you're trying to look like." He frowned, then said, "Still... Falcon wouldn't send me someone who wasn't worth a full interview. So let's see what you can do." He toggled a police-style radio on his shoulder and spoke into it. "We've got a Code Green, kids. Meet me in the Break Room."

Code Green. It meant a rookie recruit was seeking membership. And the Break Room wasn't where you went for coffee. It was where they took the rookies to break them.

The room itself was enormous... nearly the size of a football field. Appropriately, the first thing Scoutmaster did was pull out a football. "Go long," he said, and hurled the ball with his impressive strength.

I sprinted over the uneven ground. And ground it was... not concrete or wood, just raw earth, grassless and rocky. I put every ounce of energy I could into the dash, just to catch up to the ball. And I did... but failed to catch it.

Scoutmaster had begun walking across the field to meet me, but stopped after only a few yards. He knelt to the ground and stared at the dirt. I jogged back to see what he found so fascinating.

"Interesting," he said, indicating my footprints. To my surprise, the expected imprints of the shoes, including the heels, were flanked by other marks, arcs of compressed earth a couple inches across, from heel to toe. I could only assume the arcs were made by my energy field. Somehow, the field was stabilizing my gait, without my awareness. I certainly couldn't feel any sign of it.

"Okay... let's have you meet some folks," Scoutmaster continued. I stood and looked toward the entrance, where two other Bay Scouts stood. We walked over to them and I was introduced.

The first was Sinta, a petite, timid girl of about thirteen with what appeared to be a layer of fine, black fur. Her face was mostly human, save for the feline ears and the eyes with irises that dilated like a cat's. The other was a tall, handsome guy a few years younger than I. He had movie star looks and was introduced to me by the unusual name of Zero-Point.

"We'll see how you fare against these two," Scoutmaster said. "Sinta first."

As the men backed away, Sinta smiled and bowed politely to me. But when she raised her head, her face was stern and her pupils wide. A moment later, she pounced.

She hit me like a linebacker, knocking the wind out of me. She was slight, but it was all muscle. We slammed to the ground, Sinta on top of me, hands drawing back to strike. That's when I noticed the claws where fingernails should have been. They flashed downward and I could feel them "catch" in my shield. The next blow did the same, and I wondered what would happen with repeated blows to the same spot. Would my protection falter? I wasn't eager to find out.

I shoved and Sinta sailed backward, executing a perfect flip to land gracefully and immediately shot into another charge. I readied a power punch to deliver before she struck. But this was a child, I told myself. I didn't want to hurt her. I let the energy drain from my fist.

Not that it mattered. Sinta landed in front of me and bounced into a judo kick to my stomach. As I doubled over, she pummeled on the back of my head. Disoriented, I jumped backward. My vision cleared as I hit the ground, stumbling slightly. I was shocked to see I'd somehow jumped about fifteen feet. I didn't have long to absorb that, since Sinta was halfway across that distance to me. This time, I didn't hold back. As she neared, I rushed forward and landed a solid blow that slammed her into the ground.

As she rose, Scoutmaster yelled, "Stop!"

Sinta immediately relaxed and smiled up at me. "Good hit!" she said, rubbing her head.

I didn't know whether to thank her or apologize.

As she jogged back to the corner with Scoutmaster, Zero-Point carefully walked out. We stared at each other. He'd had the benefit of seeing how I handled myself against Sinta, but I knew nothing about him or his abilities. He nodded respectfully, which only made me more apprehensive. I waited for him to make the first move. But he didn't.

"Ladies first," he said, without a hint of condescension.

Polite and respectful though he was, he was still going to put the hurt on me. He wasn't the most powerfully built guy by any means. But that meant little with metas. And what did "zero-point" mean, anyway?

Since he wasn't seeming about to do anything, I had to. I was the one being tested, after all. I closed in on him and took a standard boxing stance.

"What the heck is that?" Scoutmaster shouted. "You're not fighting Mike Tyson!"

Great impression I was making. Hammered by a little girl and mocked by Scoutmaster. I clenched my jaw and dove in on Zero-Point, swinging a roundhouse to his jaw. He jerked his head back and my punch didn't even graze him. Before I could recover to send a second shot his way, he reached out and grabbed me by the shoulder.

His touch was cold, in a deep, bone-chilling way. A wave of weakness hit me and instead of a follow-up swing, I staggered, tripped over my feet, and landed in the dirt.

From the ground, I glared at him, wondering just what the heck had happened. I wanted to look to Scoutmaster, but knew he was probably frowning at me. No way was I going to make the team. I was defeated, if not completely physically, certainly psychologically. My energy had returned, but if this guy could just suck it out of me with a touch... well... let's say I saw "zero point" in continuing. I sighed, feeling sorry for myself.

"You okay?" Zero-Point said.

I nodded, looking up at the man I couldn't touch. "Yeah," I said, and slowly rose to my feet. I glanced at Scoutmaster and saw the unimpressed expression I expected. I looked back at the man I couldn't...

Wait a moment, I thought. This was a man I didn't *need* to touch!

A shield can also be a weapon, I remembered. I stood slowly, concentrated, and put as much energy as I could into the shield. Since the shield was, essentially, merely a constant venting of energy all around my body, I might be able to "extend" it like a bubble if I just increased the output. I did so, and moved toward Zero-Point. As I reached him, I "shoved" with the shield and, as I'd hoped, he staggered backward.

I strode toward him, continually pushing him with the shield until he was up against a wall. But then he extended his hands, braced against the wall, and pushed back. During a moment of equilibrium, Scoutmaster again yelled, "Stop!"

We both relaxed. "Interesting," Zero-Point said as we walked over to his boss.

"Thank you both," Scoutmaster said to his teammates, dismissing them. Zero-Point nodded politely, while Sinta bounced out with a wave and a cheery farewell.

Scoutmaster faced me, inscrutable. Before he could dismiss me, I asked, "Why did you stop us so quickly?"

"I saw enough."

"I could have beaten Sinta," I said.

"Not likely," he replied. "But this wasn't about your ability to beat either of them. It was about your ability to adapt. And you did okay, especially with Jack." Before pride could fill me, he said, "But you took far too long. He could have killed you ten times over while you were on the ground figuring out what to do next."

I nodded, knowing he was right. "Yeah," I said.

"Your mind is your greatest weapon out there, not your fists or whatever other abilities you might have. It's your ability to think quickly, and of course, react quickly. Teams take on more dangerous threats than the street thugs you've been fighting. If you don't think fast, you die."

I nodded again. "Yes, sir." Bad enough that I'd botched the trial. Now I was getting a lecture.

"Speed, accuracy, stamina... all of these are important, and you'll be working on all of them. But none of them will do you any good if you're hesitant. You understand?"

I began to nod again, until I realized what he'd said. "Wait... working on them? You mean I passed? I'm in?"

He raised an eyebrow at me. "It's not a country club. But yes, you did. Welcome to the Bay Scouts."

TWELVE

"The image is one thing and the human being is another. It's very hard to live up to an image, put it that way."
~Elvis Presley

Images are hard to shake, and the most difficult to shed are the ones we have of ourselves. Yes, sometimes we hold onto a self-conception because it's a good one, even if no longer applicable. The balding fellow with the middle-aged spread who maintains an air of confidence in his looks may still see himself in the mirror as the high school jock. The cougar prowling for college boys might be clinging to her days as the hottie all the boys drooled over. As illusory as these images are, and as much denial as these people swim in, the fact is they feel better about themselves than they otherwise might.

On the other hand, negative self-images linger, even when they also no longer apply, and the effects are often devastating. The unattractive, socially awkward youth becomes the man convinced he's undesirable to women because of his inability to get a girlfriend in high school. Or the fat girl who, twenty years later, still has a negative body image even though she's manipulated her genes and has less than twenty percent body fat, but is embarrassed every time she goes out on patrol in a skin-tight outfit.

I admit I was put off by Scoutmaster's insistence that, should I become a full-fledged Bay Scout, I'd need to adopt a different look. Not that I was in love with the leather look, but his "suggestion" was for me to look into the form-fitting costume. Turns out there was a reason, and it had nothing to do with looking sexy.

The "Spandex Set," as metas are often called, are not a bunch of fetishists and exhibitionists. (Only a small minority, really.) The truth of the matter is that these costumes are part of the goodies available to those who are official members of one of the government teams. The Bay Scouts were attached to the Coast Guard, as it happens.

The tight uniforms are fitted with a number of electrodes that record body functions, up to and including brain activity. The data is constantly transmitted back to the computers at the team's base of operations so the team monitor (sometimes human, usually some sort of computer artificial intelligence) will know when a member is panicking, injured, unconscious, or worse. The tight costumes hold the electrodes to the skin, and removes the tedious process of applying them before getting dressed.

This body process monitoring is directly tied into one of the most critical benefits. Those freaky geniuses at DARPA came up with the Trauma Pod, an unmanned, mobile life support unit. The Pods reside at select trauma centers in major cities and can be dispatched by a team's monitor. The Pods are electrically powered, remotely piloted vehicles with a fairly short flight range. When the Pod reaches an injured meta, he or she gets inside (or more likely is placed inside by teammates), where computer and video assessment is done and treatment performed by robotic surgical tools. Many actions are performed automatically, but some are controlled by surgeons on staff at the Pod's home trauma center, whose sole job is to be a Pod Doc. These units are strictly for quick patch jobs while the unit is en route to the home trauma center.

The costumes also store such things as communication devices, cameras, LED torches, and so on. Some goodies are even incorporated into eyewear. This can be anything from simple treated lenses that enhance vision (often simply by reducing glare from fire or energy flashes in battle) to contact lenses that display a virtual reality overlay, which can be immensely helpful in maintaining a sense of direction in less than ideal circumstances.

Then there are the capes. Stylish? Obviously. Practical? More than you might think. For one thing, most capes have pockets on the inside, for carrying vital emergency supplies and other items. Many are lined with MPET – that shiny material used in emergency blankets – as an additional survival tool. Others, such as the one worn by the Maltese Falcon, are made of Kevlar, giving an additional level of protection.

None of this was news to me. I'd read about all this and more. Even so, it was hard to get past how the costumes were perceived by the general public: as flamboyant, "look at me" outfits.

At any rate, my probationary period in the Scouts was the meta equivalent of boot camp. It was tough. Really tough. And I learned a lot. At the end of that month-long torture, I was accepted as a full member of the team.

To this day, I'm not sure whether that was a good thing.

The Bay Scouts wasn't a large group. It was small – at the time I joined, there were eight others – and close, like a family, with Scoutmaster, obviously, the father figure and Zero-Point the number one son. Sinta was the spunky youngest child.

Two others, in fact, *were* family: the twins, Pyro and Hydro, originally from Texas. As their names heavily imply, they had fire and water abilities. Nice guys, both of them, but not the sharpest knives in the block.

Then there was El Martillo. For those who don't know Spanish, that means "the hammer." And it's an apt name for him, as anyone who's been hit by one of his fists will attest. The twins had adopted the slightly younger Mexican as a sort of kid brother. They referred to their little trio as "Tex-Mex."

The only native San Franciscan in the group was Ping Song, a reserved Chinese-American girl of about twenty-five. Though skilled in any number of martial arts, Song's most impressive ability had to do with machines. Not only was she a mechanical and computer wizard, she could, to a certain degree, control machinery. She did so by, believe it or not, singing to them. Well, she called it singing, but to me it was more of a sing-song of clicks and buzzing noises than music. Naturally, she was our team's base monitor. In the family structure, Song was a little detached... more like the favorite cousin, rather than a sibling.

The eighth member was Valora. An Amazonian blonde, Val was one of those heroes who seemed to have it all: beauty, brains, and brawn. Her position in the "family" wasn't as the mother figure, as there was little motherly about her, save for being a protector figure. Valora's flesh behaved like a non-Newtonian fluid, similar to a mixture of corn starch and water that turns momentarily solid if you smack it with your first, but remains a soft goo if you push your finger in slowly. This made her incredibly resistant to any strong impact, including bullets. Val appeared to be second-in-command, though that was just my perception, not an official standing.

And me? I had no idea where I'd fit in, yet. After all, I didn't have any personal exposure to what a healthy family dynamic looked like. Dana and I were close again after all those years of estrangement, but I was still alienated from our parents. I looked at Scoutmaster and saw no qualities in him that my father shared, other than being male. I didn't have a lot of respect for my father, since he had no spine when it came to dealing with my mother. I could see in his eyes when he felt she was in the wrong, but such sentiments never passed his lips.

Not that the Bay Scouts were without dysfunction. It was pretty much inevitable when you mixed people from such disparate backgrounds. Billy and Bobby had a decided "good ol' boy" aspect to them, which often grated on everyone, it seemed, except Sinta. (Nothing seemed to bother her.) Even Esteban occasionally seemed put off by the behavior of his "brothers." Especially when they thought it was funny to call him "Armadillo."

The twins didn't pay any real attention to Song, which appeared to be fine with her. And I would occasionally hear them make statements about Zero-Point behind his back. They seemed to have an issue with intellectual types. Jack's intellect was obvious, and everyone knew about his science background. Only Daniel knew about mine, which is probably why the twins didn't take issue with me. On the other hand, their ill-concealed lewd looks told me where I stood in their eyes.

But the real dysfunction, it seemed to me, was in the friction between Scoutmaster and Valora. It was subtle, and took me some time to see, but Valora didn't hold Scoutmaster in high esteem, as the others did. I got the distinct impression that she felt she should be the team's leader, and that she resented that a younger and weaker person was her "boss." The fact that her "superior" was also male was the proverbial insult to her perceived injury.

One notable drawback of being with a government team is that most of the activity is assignment-based. So my days of looking for random trouble were effectively over. Things now were organized, regimented, and under orders. And as police officers around the world know, many of the assignments aren't as intriguing as what we see on TV shows.

The first assignment given us after I joined the Bay Scouts, for example, made me wonder whether the government actually appreciated metas and their abilities. We were tasked with investigating an unusual smell coming from a recently discovered cave near Tennessee Cove. That's not a typo. A *smell*.

Our investigative team consisted of Scoutmaster, Sinta, and me. We flew out to the site in our own Coast Guard-supplied helicopter, with Scoutmaster as the pilot. Once we arrived, it was easy to understand why this cave was "recently discovered." A section of earth had collapsed, revealing the hidden cave through an opening barely large enough for an adult human to pass. But plenty big enough for someone of Sinta's stature.

And yes, it smelled. It was a musty, organic odor, like rotting leaves. But mixed in was something else, something acrid and piercing. Once we got a whiff of that, we all fit ourselves with nose filters.

Scoutmaster nodded to me and I followed Sinta inside, barely squeezing my leather-clad self through the rock. "There's a drop," Sinta said from in front of me. We both wore LED lamps strapped to our foreheads and I soon saw what she meant. The drop was probably fifteen feet to the cave floor. Sinta hopped down with ease, landing lightly. "I'm in," she said. "Be careful, Dyna," she finished, as I followed.

The cave was a mycologist's paradise. Mushrooms and other fungi grew everywhere, some big, some small. A virtual carpet of them stretched in all directions. The walls and ceiling, too, seemed to be coated with tiny mushrooms and dark slime. I pulled out one nose filter and quickly determined the stench was mainly produced by the layer of slime, which I reported over my comm unit to Scoutmaster, who asked me to get a sample. "Ooh, lucky you," Sinta said as she pulled out a small specimen kit and tossed it to me before moving deeper into the cave.

As I scraped a bunch of the gunk into a tiny dish, I couldn't help but wonder what the hell I was doing. Sure, a cave full of odd fungi appealed to my curiosity as a scientist, but from the vantage point of a would-be hero, this wasn't a good use of my time. I snapped the dish closed and stashed it in the specimen kit, then went off after Sinta.

A short way further on, I noticed a patch of what appeared to be puff ball fungi along one wall. This piqued my curiosity, since this sort of environment wasn't hospitable to the puff balls I knew. But I'd never seen any like these, with mottled red and yellow coloration. I stopped to examine them, intrigued by the dry, paper-like bodies.

As I gently squeezed one of the globes to test its consistency, it burst open in a spray of spores. Startled, I jumped back, coughing from the cloud of spores. And in case you're curious, the spores didn't taste like mushrooms at all.

I hurried to catch up to Sinta, rounding a corner to find her standing still, staring further down the passage. "What's up?" I asked, and hacked again.

Sinta nodded down the way and I looked more closely. The light from our lamps, normally only visible when striking something, appeared as two fuzzy lines about twenty feet away.

"Well, that's weird," I said between coughs.

Sinta looked at me. "Are you okay?"

I nodded, still coughing. She glanced down the hall again, then back at me, before taking my arm and leading me out.

I gave Scoutmaster his vial of goop and we both reported on what we'd seen. I suggested that scientists should be called in, not super teams. Scoutmaster just shrugged. "Get used to this sort of assignment," he said.

I frowned, doubting that the Gatekeepers ever had to investigate random stench.

Scoutmaster was so serious about requiring me to change my look, despite my hesitation, that he made an appointment for me with a costume consultant. I'd had no idea such a profession even existed. Upon reflection, though, it was obvious that there was a need for it. One only had to see the outfits worn by those who seemed to be color blind. I know it was popular in the '90s, but please... orange and pink do not play well together. But color wasn't the only area where some metas needed help. Basic design was a problem for some, from those who insisted on wearing barely more than a bikini to those who incorporated such clashing elements as hi-tech robotics and medieval-style armor in the same costume.

Jasen was a retired meta, having once gone by the name of Sea Lion. No, he wasn't black and blubbery. He'd taken his name from the fact that he had a huge mane of golden hair and a beard to match. And gills. He'd been one of the founding members of the Gatekeepers, retiring in the early 80s after taking a blow to the neck that left half his gills a mass of scar tissue. But he had one heck of a lucrative post-retirement profession. He charged steeply for his services, but guaranteed satisfaction.

"Oh, honey," he said to me. "With eyes like yours, you simply must get rid of the shades. And leather is so yesterday. Yes, we're going to remake you, from your snow-capped top to your very shapely bottom."

When I protested mildly, asserting that I didn't want to look slutty, he became quite defensive – and rightly so – of his work. He frowned when I told him I didn't like the idea of much exposed flesh, but promised I'd look "classic," yet still sexy.

And he kept his word. When the costume was complete, I stood in his private store, looking at myself in a floor-length mirror. The costume left no skin at all exposed, other than parts of my head. The blue mask left my hair flowing free, but covered most of my forehead and cheeks. My eyes were uncovered, allowing their bright blue to "pop," as Jasen put it.

The rest of the outfit was, as expected, skin tight, with all the sensors fixed in place. The boots were stiletto heels. The color scheme was blue and white. (Over the years, we went through a few different patterns before settling on one with a nifty DNA double-helix design.)

And I got my cape. I hid my excitement pretty well, but couldn't help examining it closely. Near the throat of the chest section of the outfit, there was a silver ornament with a large, light blue gemstone inset. This unsnapped and lifted forward on a hinge, revealing a hook underneath. Aluminum rings sewn into the ends of the cape hooked over the ring and the gem setting snapped back in place, securing them.

I liked nearly everything about it, with a couple exceptions.

"Why the cuffed gloves and boots?"

"Scoutmaster told me about how you seem to have energy coming out your feet or calves or whatever to stabilize you when you run in heels." I nodded, beginning to understand. "The uppers and the turned-down cuffs are reinforced, which Scoutmaster suggested might help to focus the energy. I made the gloves match because, well, they should match. And because he said you expel energy from your hands, too."

Expel wasn't quite the right word, I thought, but nodded. Then I frowned. With no gaps between boot and pants, as I'd had up until this point, would I be ripping up my costume every time I used my abilities? I examined the glove material more closely and realized it wasn't leather. "Energy-transparent fabric," I said, impressed. "I've heard about it."

Jasen nodded. "In fact, the entire outfit is made of it, except for those reinforcements, obviously. What do you think?"

I smiled. "It's great," I said. "Except for this." The fabric of the mask fit well, for the most part, but I indicated the loose flaps at the forehead.

"Right." He reached into his satchel and pulled out the solution.

Appalled, I pointed at the object in his hand: a silver band with a gem set into the front, the same color as the one on the chest. "Oh, come on... that's a *tiara!*"

"Well, more of a circlet, really," he said.

"Whatever!" My stomach dropped. I could only imagine the teasing I was going to get. "Princess Dinah" would probably be the least of it. I stood, dumbstruck, as Jasen slid the silver band into my forehead. It was snug, but not uncomfortably so. And it did the trick, holding the mask neatly to my head. "And of course, it multi-tasks." Jasen reached up and pressed the gemstone. Immediately, a bright beam of bluish white light shot forth. The "gem" was actually just colored glass over a high-intensity LED matrix. "Takes flat cell batteries, which load in the back of the setting," Jasen said.

"Great. I'm a princess... and I'm a miner."

He reached into his satchel again and pulled out a metal belt, complete with yet another, even larger gem in the clasp.

"And what's this do?" I asked.

"Makes you look stylish."

I chuckled. "And?"

"The clasp holds a comm unit that will connect with your base computer. Built in USB port. The 'gem' holds the battery. It's removable and plugs in for charging. And the belt as a whole acts as an antenna booster for your sensors."

I had to admit, he'd done a great job.

I was going to look awesome on magazine covers.

THIRTEEN

"Illness has always brought me nearer to a state of grace."
~Abbé Pierre

One of Dana's areas of interest is the human inclination to collect things. Our dad collected baseball cards as a kid and still had many of them. Our mother hoards a variety of knick-knacks, especially anything having to do with bluebirds. Dana himself has about a hundred beer glasses from breweries all over the world, mostly Belgian.

Metas tend to collect souvenirs from their escapades. For example, I still have the bullet that Falcon picked up off the floor of the convenience store all those years ago. I occasionally wear it on a chain around my neck. Another item hangs in a frame on a wall in my apartment: a shooting range target with a huge hole in the center of its chest.

I put the hole there. From a distance of about fifty feet.

It took me a couple months of deliberate trying, but I was finally able to project a blast of energy from my hands, rather than just collect it around my fist like a boxing glove. I've often been asked what it feels like when I do it, but I've never found any words to adequately describe it. There's a certain amount of tension to the process during the build-up and a sense of release when it goes off. But those are overall body sensations. In my hand itself, it's different. There's a tingling, almost like when your hand falls asleep. There is also a throbbing, though not painful. I believe it's a sort of energy oscillation under the skin. And when the shot goes off, there is a brief feeling of cold. But of course, all of these sensations happen in the course of about a second or two. So try to imagine that and maybe you'll have an idea.

The reinforced gloves really did help to focus the blasts and control the aim, as the center mass hole attests. And the fabric of the gloves didn't impede the flow (or get shredded) at all. Over time, and with the friendly (sometimes overly so) help of the twins, I learned to control the blasts in different ways. For example, with concentration and time to aim, I can fire off a small but powerful burst with solid accuracy up to half a football field away. I can also produce an intense, prolonged burst for up close and personal shots. My standard, though, is a moderate strength blast in the twenty- to thirty-yard range. I can keep that sort of thing up for quite a while.

Just as physical activities can be built up by pushing oneself to greater achievement, metas can often build up stamina for their meta-abilities. So I spent a lot of my free time expending as much of my energy as I could, pushing myself to do it longer and with more intensity with each session.

And also as any athlete can tell you, a lot of training is psychological. It's a matter of mind over body to get past "the wall." So I worked out a lot, focusing on body and mind. And on my footwork.

Not boxing, but blasting. With practice, the "stabilizing field" that Scoutmaster had deduced became an energy springboard. Before long, by essentially blasting from my feet, I could propel myself in a big leap, easily able to land on the roof of a short building.

Of course, it's not a good idea to vault into a place where you can't see your landing site, such as the day I came down in a tangle of rooftop laundry lines. Caught off-guard and panicking slightly, my force field faltered and I knocked myself out when I hit the roof itself. After regaining consciousness, head pounding, all I could do was make my way home and be thankful no one had witnessed my klutziness.

The headache lessened but was still there the next day. And it was joined by some vomiting.

"Concussions are nothing to take lightly," Scoutmaster told me as I sat in the Bay Scouts' infirmary. The emergency department doctor had said the same thing and told me to stay hydrated and get plenty of rest. Scoutmaster went a step further. He grounded me. No assignments until the doc gave me a clean bill of health.

Dana insisted on coming to visit, once I confessed to him about the concussion. I regretted telling him almost immediately, but wasn't going to complain about him visiting. Not just because he's my brother, but because I knew he'd treat me to dinner every night. And he did. But he also expressed – repeatedly – his concern for my safety. Sometimes he took his role of big brother too seriously.

Things had begun to change for metas in the country, and I don't mean just the growing distrust of them and the stupid laws requiring registration and all that. I mean that the number of metas on the "bad guy" side seemed to be increasing at a substantial rate. It used to be that only the "good guys" were famous, but now there were more and more self-proclaimed meta-villains who'd become household names. And sometimes their infamy came from killing a hero. Dana was justifiably worried that I might become such a statistic, given how inexperienced I was in this line of work.

"I'm sure that's one of the reasons Scoutmaster sidelined me," I told him over pasta at Venticello. "Have you bumped into Marcus, lately?" I asked.

"About a week ago, yeah. At a burger joint a couple blocks from my place. He asked about you."

"I like Marcus," I said. "Almost as much as I like these meatballs."

No sooner were the words out of my mouth than another bout of nausea hit. I dashed to the rest room. The vomiting, aside from putting me off dessert, exacerbated the headache that had insisted on lingering.

Dana was frowning when I returned. He paid for the meal and escorted me out to his car. "You need to rest," he said, and I couldn't disagree. "When's your next doctor's appointment?"

"The doc said I'd only need a follow-up if the symptoms got worse. And they haven't. They just haven't gotten much better."

"You have insurance, right?"

"Yeah... TRICARE Meta."

"Okay. Just wanted to make sure you weren't ignoring your health because of money."

Money. I hated thinking about money. When I first moved to San Francisco, I lived off Dana's donations. Mostly, anyway. The truth is, his money only went so far and part-time bartending didn't pay very well. I'd had to pay for a lot of necessities on my credit cards. I was drowning in debt, made worse by my repayment of the GACTech settlement, but was too proud to mention this to him.

Being a member of a government-sponsored team did put some cash in my hand. At this point in time, I was making the utterly unimpressive base salary of about $35,000 per year. In San Francisco, that was about thirty percent below the individual median income. Active duty pay kicked up that rate, but while on my medical suspension, it was still just the base salary.

Other symptoms had manifested, too. After lunch at my apartment, one day, I passed out while carrying dishes to the kitchen. Dana caught me telekinetically (and yes, the dishes, too), so I didn't smack my head again. He told me I was unconscious for about two minutes before I came around. Then he insisted I see a doctor.

"Have the headaches gotten worse?" was the doc's first question.

"No, not really," I said as he looked at my pupils with his little flashlight.

"Any seizures? Convulsions?"

"Just the passing out, that one time."

"Speech problems? Confusion? Agitation? Loss of coordination?"

"Well... No." The doctor noted my hesitation. "The initial injury was due to a bit of clumsiness on my part, but..."

He nodded. "Any general weakness? Anything numb on your body?"

"No."

"You said you've been vomiting. How often?"

"Daily," I said. "Once or twice."

The doctor sighed. "The vomiting concerns me. But the truth is, in some cases, it can take weeks or even months to recover from a concussion."

"Great," I frowned.

"I want you to continue resting. Stay hydrated. No alcohol. Acetaminophen for the headaches. And if they get worse, contact me."

I promised I would.

After this, I began to spend more time at the Bay Scouts base, rather than my apartment. Dana had gone back to Sacramento, and I didn't want to be alone. I spent a lot of time with Zero-Point, who was our team medic. Initially, I'd assumed that this just meant that Jack had taken more first aid, CPR, and other such classes than anyone else. But it turns out Scoutmaster had the most merit badges on that front. Jack, I soon learned, was a healer. And when it comes to metas, the word "healer" takes on its own freaky meaning.

Like anything else, healing abilities come in a range of effectiveness, from the ability to impart a sense of general wellbeing to bringing someone back from the brink of death. There have always been rumors of those who could even reverse death itself, though I still regard them as apocryphal.

Jack's abilities were toward the middle. He couldn't knit bones back together, but he could heal most soft tissue damage: lacerations, punctures, and so on, and limited organ damage. Nerve damage was typically beyond his abilities. One of his more useful tricks, though, was that he could trigger adrenaline surges in others, allowing them to continue the fight even when they'd felt spent only moments earlier.

We spent a lot of my downtime together, mainly sitting in the base lounge, drinking tea and talking about science. "Zero-point energy," he replied to my eventual inquiry, "is the energy remaining after you've removed all the other energy from a system."

"But... if you remove all the energy, there's no energy left," I said, stating the obvious.

"Except that zero-point energy can't be removed."

"Why not?"

"It's a quantum mechanics/Heisenberg uncertainty sort of thing," he said with a smile.

"Which means you don't understand it, either."

"Basically." He chuckled, then said, "Okay. What happens when you take, say, helium and lower its temperature to absolute zero?"

I frowned. Helium. "It... stays liquid. It doesn't freeze. At normal pressure, anyway."

"Right," Jack nodded. "And it stays liquid because of the zero-point energy that remains in it."

"You're talking about the weak forces between the atoms."

"Exactly."

I sipped my tea. "And you've found a way to harness that energy?"

Jack stirred his cup absently. "Not exactly. Not yet, anyway, though obviously that's my ultimate goal. But as well as I can determine, I'm able to reduce things to their ground state."

"Sorry?"

"The lowest energy state that something has. Like something at absolute zero will have less energy than something in an excited state."

"So... you freeze things?"

"Well... no. As you experienced, it's quite cold, but not absolute zero cold." He shrugged. "Anyway, I can't harness it, exactly, but I seem to have the ability to tap into it, transfer it, extract it, and so on. That sounds a lot cooler than it actually is, though."

"Oh, come on. It's plenty cool!"

"Thanks." He smiled at me, almost shyly, to my surprise. Then I saw a hint of a blush in his cheek and my stomach dropped.

Jack had a crush on me.

When I was eleven years old, I got sick. Lots of body aches, sometimes shooting pains. Mother said it was "growing pains." When it didn't pass after a few days, she said I was just trying to get attention.

Eventually, Dad told her to take me to the doctor, who poked and prodded me, took my temperature, looked down my throat, and ultimately urged her to take me to the hospital for tests. She complained about it the whole way there and left shortly after I was admitted, leaving me in my bed for the doctors to poke and prod me some more. As she left, she gave me a look of disapproval, still thinking I was faking it.

Back then, outpatient treatment wasn't as common as it is today. Hospitals kept you longer, and I was bed-bound for five days while they ran test after test. I spent those days scared and alone, in pain and fear, punctuated by nurse visits, hospital food, and the occasional television show on a tiny screen near the ceiling. Mother dutifully visited daily, for about fifteen minutes. Dad was busy working and Dana was off at college.

Sometimes I thought I was dying. I was convinced I had some horrible condition that the doctors didn't want to tell me about because I couldn't be saved. Oddly enough, the dying part didn't freak me out. I just didn't want to die alone in a hospital bed.

Ultimately, though, I was discharged, with no diagnosis at all, only because the pain had suddenly vanished. I woke up that last morning and had no pain at all. Which only cemented in Mother's mind that it had been a ruse the whole time.

Shortly thereafter, I had my first period. This brought out the only sign that mother might accept that I hadn't been faking it. But it caused her to think I had no pain tolerance whatsoever, if I couldn't handle PMS.

My second hospital experience began when I became sicker. Though I wasn't vomiting as frequently, my cognition was declining. I was often confused and would black out occasionally. My doctor feared – as did I – that there was more going on than a concussion. In the hospital, they stuck my head in the MRI machines, drew my blood, had me pee in a cup, performed a full allergy panel, and served me awful food.

I required copious quantities of calories, even when not "active." Up to this point, my doctor didn't know I was a meta. It took showing him my registration card to convince him that my requests for ludicrous amounts of food weren't a symptom of my condition. "Believe me," I said, "I have no love for hospital food. I just need the calories."

He left for a few minutes and returned with a chocolate shake. "It's a calorie-dense drink," he explained. "We use them for eating disorder cases, mostly."

Not as many calories as Dynapaste, but it definitely tasted better.

Dana returned to the city and stayed in my apartment, visiting me daily. Jack visited, too, but only for a few days, before he had to leave town on business. To my surprise, Song visited me a few times, too. She was a calming presence, and not without a certain warmth. Her concern for my health was obvious, but she didn't dwell on it, as Dana tended to.

Song kept me apprised of what was going on in the meta world. Unsurprisingly, metas knew far more of such things than the media reported. "I'm afraid another hero has flipped," she said on one visit, referring to a recent trend of good guys turning bad, who chose, for example, robbing banks instead of stopping others from doing so. Song and I agreed that the increasingly restrictive legislation toward metas was responsible. The government was practically hanging the criminal carrot in front of our noses. We couldn't understand why the legislators didn't see the irony of the situation. Their laws resulted from public fear, causing some frustrated metas to operate on the other side of the law, thereby increasing crime and, therefore, raising public fear, which then resulted in more laws... It was a nightmare.

"Who was it this time?" I asked.

"Kimera."

"No way!" Kimera was a long-standing member of the Gatekeepers, well-respected and popular. I'd never met her, but Scoutmaster spoke highly of her. "Daniel must be devastated," I said.

Song nodded. "But he's more worried about you," she said. "He won't say so, of course. He's got to be the stolid leader. But he asks me about you every day."

I smiled faintly, but didn't admit to her that I was worried about me, too. None of the test results showed anything, so they were performing more and more unusual tests. Eventually, they started testing for things that they had no real reason to test for. More blood draws, urine samples, and this time, a spinal tap.

That's when they found it.

"Dinah, it's very rare to find this in anyone who doesn't have a severely compromised immune system," my doctor told me, "such as an AIDS patient. It simply wasn't something we'd normally test for. The good news is that, although yours is an advanced case, you're otherwise healthy and should respond well to an aggressive treatment."

Cryptococcal meningitis is what he was talking about.

"So... how'd I get it and how do we get rid of it?"

"Well, a common way to contract it is through the inhalation of dried bird droppings."

Try as I might, I couldn't think of any situation where I'd have breathed in powdered pigeon poop.

"As for getting rid of it, we'll get you started on a regimen of antifungal drugs. Because your immune system isn't compromised, we should be able to eradicate it completely and you'll be good as new."

"Antifungals," I said, then sighed. The cave, of course. The burst puff ball. I'd inhaled the spores. Sidelined for three months because of an assignment to investigate a bad smell. It was almost funny.

But not quite.

My treatment consisted of two weeks of daily doses of intravenous amphotericin B and oral flucytosine. This was accompanied by lots of puking and repeated spinal taps (I prefer that term to "lumbar puncture," which is far too vivid for my liking). I was discharged in mid-November. Dana picked me up and drove me home, continuing to stay with me through Thanksgiving. I had twelve weeks of oral fluconazole to go after that, but by this point, I was feeling fine.

But I figured it would be years before I'd eat mushrooms again.

FOURTEEN

"Whenever technical progress opened a new window into the surrounding world, I felt the urge to look through this window, hoping to see something unexpected."

~Bruno Rossi

When you least expect it, expect it.
Expect the unexpected.
The only constant is change.
The more things change, the more they stay the same.

Clichés, all of them. And all of them true, especially in my line of work. And I don't mean just the obvious things, such as how you can go from living to dead rather unexpectedly. Some of the changes are desired and some of the unexpected things are for the better. A few such things were in store for me in 2005.

The first was a natural progression of my abilities. Or as natural as could be, all things considered. Despite that, it was still unexpected, because I honestly didn't think it would be possible. I'm referring to the one ability I wanted probably more than anything, the one ability that made wearing a cape truly cool.

Flight.

The only reason I even suspected it could be attained – no matter how long of a shot it might be – was my powered leaping ability. I reasoned that if I could jump up to a rooftop (preferably one without laundry lines), I could eventually achieve a rocket-type flight.

The development of this ability took much concerted effort and many failed attempts before I discovered the trick to it. For the longest time, I'd assumed that I had to approach it like a rocket, with the most intense, prolonged bursts from my feet for propulsion and my hands for lift. And while that worked, I couldn't maintain such a thing for long enough to make flight practical. I'd be exhausted after one short flight with no energy left for anything else.

Nevertheless, I practiced my takeoffs and landings, sometimes with vertical "launches" and other times with the time-honored "running jump" technique. In either case, I'd blast until I felt slightly weak, then do a braking thrust before touchdown. With a somewhat horizontal flight, this required a bit of aerobatics in order to position my feet correctly. And believe me when I say I had plenty of less-than-graceful landings.

As with most discoveries, my success came unexpectedly. A few seconds into one flight, I inhaled some soot or something, causing me to sneeze. And I sneezed twice because, well, mine always seem to come in pairs.

I'd had sense enough not to put a hand to my mouth. They were, after all, helping to keep me aloft. But when you sneeze, your body tenses up. And when I tense up, it changes the entire flow of energy. The only analogy I can think of is the nozzle of a garden hose. When you squeeze it completely, which opens the nozzle the whole way, you get an intense, focused stream. Ease up on it, restricting the flow, and you get a broader dispersal, allowing coverage of a wider area, though with less intensity. It was sort of like that. The tensing during the sneeze restricted the flow, making for a "spray nozzle" effect, which turned out to be the key to controlled, sustained flight. As with an airplane, the heaviest thrust is always needed to get the vehicle aloft, not to keep it there. For me, broad dispersal, using less energy but covering more area, did the trick.

Of course, the human body isn't particularly aerodynamic, so quite a lot of in-flight adjustments always need to be made, in the positions of my hands, the angle of my feet, and so on. Early on, I'm sure I looked like an ungainly clown in the sky, arms twitching this way and that. Over time, though, I learned the subtleties of such things, using simple movements of my wrists and ankles. I also discovered that my energy shield served quite well as goggles over my eyes.

Flying is... well, it's absolutely as breathtaking as I expected it to be. And that's all I have to say about that.

✧   ✧   ✧

My development of this ability led to an unexpected conversation with Valora, who had not shown any inclination before this to get to know me at all. Admittedly, I hadn't exactly reached out to her, either, which made her approach all the more surprising.

"Your abilities are progressing at an impressive rate, Dyna," she said. "And flight!" She shook her head. "You have no idea how I envy you."

"Thanks," I said. She was complimenting me, but making me feel guilty at the same time. After an awkward silence, I said, "Your abilities are pretty impressive, though."

Valora nodded. "Yes."

"And you're so modest!" I said before I could stop myself.

After a flash of defensiveness, she snorted and gave a small smile. "My apologies. I admit to being a bit egocentric. I don't mean to offend."

"You know," I offered, "I often have the sense that you don't think Daniel's a good leader."

Val bristled slightly, then relaxed. "Daniel is a good man, and I strongly respect his sense of justice and morality. And the others do, too, which makes him the right person to lead this group." She hesitated, then said, "On the other hand, the Bay Scouts is not much of a team."

"Why is that, do you think?"

"Two reasons," she said. "First, the government doesn't need it to be. They have groups like the Gatekeepers to be the high profile teams. We're the grunts. Second, Daniel is content to keep it that way."

I frowned. "Does he have a choice?"

Valora looked into my eyes. "There is *always* choice." She frowned. "Daniel is just unwilling to deal with the consequences of making the Bay Scouts into an aggressive team. He and I exemplify two sides of the same coin. He is a soldier. He does as he's told. I am a warrior. I do what needs to be done."

"Which am I?" I asked, though I really didn't know why.

"You?" She smiled slightly. "You're a good ally," she said, putting her hand on my shoulder. "But I think you're more of a mercenary."

With that, she walked off, leaving me to figure out how she meant that.

Sometime in late November, Song went missing. We didn't realize it immediately, of course. When she didn't show up for a team meeting, we found it odd. It wasn't like her not to let us know she couldn't make it. But when several days went by with no word, Daniel went to her apartment to check on her. The only disturbing thing he found there, though, was a very hungry cat.

We put out the APB, alerting Bay Area teams and police departments of her missing status. Though there was always a bit of competition between groups, they were united when it came to protecting one of their own. Or finding them, as the case may be.

Sinta took in the cat. Daniel and the others contacted all of Song's known friends. I felt a bit useless, since I didn't know enough about Song to know who her friends or family were. So I did the only thing I could do. I buried myself in work.

Ever since joining the Bay Scouts, I hadn't done much in the way of patrolling my neighborhood, assuming the Maltese Falcon could handle the Tenderloin by himself. And he could, really. But it had been a while since I'd seen him, so I thought I'd impress him with a visit.

I found him, as expected, on a rooftop. He spun around as I landed behind him. I grinned. "So what do you think?"

"About what?"

"Well, that I can fly, now, for one thing."

I could imagine the frown under his mask. "Noisy," he said. "Not exactly conducive to the element of surprise."

"Right. Well... new costume, too," I pointed out.

He nodded again, unimpressed. "Very... bright. Not good for night work."

"Well... yeah. But I don't do much night work."

"No, but I do. I'm doing it now, in case you hadn't noticed."

"I just... wanted to say hi," I said. Falcon again gave a cursory nod. "And to thank you again for getting me an interview with Scoutmaster." Another nod, this time with a grunt that could have meant anything.

"I understand your year with them hasn't been exactly... newsworthy."

I opened my mouth to justify myself, but the sinking feeling in my stomach reminded me he was right. I spent the first several months learning the ropes, a couple months sidelined from illness... I was a long way from being a household name.

Before I could make my excuses, he continued. "Sorry to hear about Ping Song."

I nodded, grateful to switch topics. "Hope she turns up, soon."

"Mm. Wouldn't hold my breath on that one."

I frowned, turned off by his attitude all around. "Right. Well, I'll leave you to your work," I said.

"One of us needs to do it," he said.

I flew off without replying.

In early December, I received a couple unexpected phone calls. The first was from Dr. Gray. He told me he was coming to town the following week for the Golden Gate Cells conference and was hoping I'd have time to get together for coffee or dinner. I agreed to coffee and we made arrangements to meet at a café near his hotel on the fourteenth, after the conference ended.

The second call was from the manager of the Red Devil Lounge asking if I'd be available to do a week-long stint at the bar to cover for someone out on vacation. They'd lost one bartender to medical leave and another to a "better offer." I'd been doing less and less bartending, but agreed, anyway. Extra money was never unwelcome, and since it was an evening shift, tips could be good.

The Red Devil is a small place on the corner of Clay and Post. The interior is very dark, lots of black paint and red trim. Strands of red lights adorn the walls and balcony and throughout the wrought ironwork around and above the mirror behind the bar. A devil gargoyle looks down from the top of the mirror. A tiny stage sits in the corner, waiting to host bands and standup comedians.

My first night, I met another bartender. I took one look at her and almost laughed. She was several inches shorter than I, with deep red skin, jet black hair, a stereotypical barbed tail, and a pair of cute little horns protruding from her forehead.

"Rachel," she said simply, thrusting out her hand. "And yes, it's all real. Including the tail and horns and no, you can't touch them." There was a hint of bitterness in her voice, despite the half-smile.

I shook her hand. "And those?" I nodded to her chest.

She blinked, then laughed. "They're real, too. And no, you can't touch them, either."

"Wait a minute," I said. And the look on her face told me she knew exactly what I was about to say, and was tired of hearing it. I said it, anyway. "You were that kid on TV."

She nodded wearily. "Yeah. That's me."

Li'l Devilgirl was a minor hit show when I was a teen. It was about the misadventures of a little girl who looked... well... like Rachel. She was an adorable, slightly precocious, but sweet child who simultaneously fascinated and freaked out the populace of her small Midwestern town. The "bad guy" of the show was a fairly clueless minister, who also happened to be her uncle. It ran for about five years.

"Why did the show end?" I asked.

Rachel grabbed her boobs. "Puberty." She chuckled. "We taped them down as much as possible, but there wasn't much to be done about the growth spurt. I was like Shirley Temple, a has-been at thirteen." She spread her hands. "Whaddayagonnado?"

"So now you're a bartender."

"Well, sort of," she said. "I'm mainly here for show, y'know? They pay me pretty well to work here and not elsewhere. I'm their token Red Devil, after all."

"But you do tend bar, right?" I was hoping I wouldn't have to carry the bulk of the burden for the week as a sub.

"Oh, sure. Memorizing drink recipes is easy compared to memorizing lines. And I went to flair school, too." She grabbed three bottles and began juggling them without a drop escaping the speed pourers. "I'm fun until someone asks me to 'make them something original.' I don't actually drink, and have no clue about mixology, so I have a list of really obscure recipes in my head to make for those people."

Over the course of the busy week, Rachel and I got to know one another. And the more we did, the more I liked her. Eventually, I asked the question that had been on my mind since meeting her. And the answer was yes, she did have some meta-abilities. She was pyrogenetic. "Starting fires, though," she said, "is of limited usefulness when you can't actually control the fire once you start it. Too much collateral damage. The meta-insurance companies won't even cover me."

It was a great week. Lots of fun, nice customers, a couple kickin' bands. And I have to admit, I really enjoyed watching Rachel's flair displays. Okay... I really enjoyed looking at Rachel.

On the fourteenth, I went to meet Dr. Gray for coffee, before going to my shift at the bar. I was early, as I usually am, so I got my drink, grabbed a table on the sidewalk, and waited.

At a table near me, a man was talking on his cell phone rather loudly. Big guy. Blond hair. He looked familiar, but I couldn't quite place him. I knew he was a meta, though, even before overhearing snippets of his conversation.

"No," he was saying. "The one with the 'a.' A-N-T." I looked around for Dr. Gray, but didn't see him anywhere. "Yeah, it's about the cereal and that 'special ingredient' you had them add." I sipped my coffee, not caring if he saw me eavesdropping. "No, Saul," he said, "it doesn't *give me* my powers, it *takes away* my powers."

Now I saw Dr. Gray and waved to him. "I don't care if it's harmless to non-metas, we're not selling breakfast cereal laced with the stuff, especially with my name on the box!" He looked over at me and gave a surprisingly shy smile before turning back to his call. "Well, of course they're going to use it to try and kill me, Saul!"

Dr. Gray arrived at my table, so I had to pull my attention from the increasingly amusing conversation. Making a mental note never to make any merchandising deals, I greeted my friend as he sat. After pleasantries, I said, "So, why were you in town, again?"

He frowned at me. "Golden Gate Cells Conference... American Society for Cell Biology? Wow, you really don't keep up, do you?"

I shook my head, feeling embarrassed that I didn't even know such a conference was happening in my own back yard. "So how was it?"

"It was good. Interesting. Might have gotten some ideas for possible drugs for PKD."

We chit-chatted for a while with general questions about each other's welfare. Finally, he said, "So where are you working, these days?"

I don't know why, but I'd never come up with a cover story for what I did. "Well, still a bartender," I said.

"You make enough as a bartender to live in the city?"

"Well... no." I knew that wasn't quite believable. "I also work as a receptionist. For the Coast Guard," I said, before I realized it.

"A receptionist," he said. "Dinah... you have a PhD! Why haven't you looked into doing lab work? I mean even a low-level position in science is better than being a receptionist!"

I nodded awkwardly, but was saved from responding by my phone buzzing for my attention. "Excuse me," I said. "This might be work." I pulled out my ultra-slim, government-issue, touch-screen smartphone. Yes, we had them a couple years before the public. The military always gets the good toys first. Ours were still in the early stages, but they were very handy. I swiped the screen, expecting to see a message from Scoutmaster. Instead, it was a text from Rachel telling me she was going to be slightly late for work. I shot off a quick acknowledgement, then tucked the phone away.

Dr. Gray was frowning, staring at my purse. "They give that kind of hardware to receptionists in the Coast Guard, huh?"

"It's... a rollout test," I lied. "They need a lot of users to give feedback to see if it's worth the investment."

I watched Dr. Gray's expression. I didn't think he believed me. And then I began to question why I needed to lie to him. He'd been as good a friend to me as anyone over the years. Why didn't I just tell him the truth? It's not as though I hadn't told others of my abilities. But, I reminded myself, the others I'd told had been metas. Dr. Gray wasn't one.

I'd already developed the "us vs. them" mindset.

After coffee, we parted ways. "Good seeing you," I said.

"You, too. Now, go make some killer drinks with your doctorate."

My job at the Red Devil ended the following evening, when their now-recuperated full-time bartender returned. After our shift, Rachel and I walked to Lori's Diner, a couple blocks from her apartment at Powell and Pine. There, we had greasy but yummy diner food and coffee and were able to talk without the distractions of customers and blaring music. I ended up telling her about my own abilities and my affiliation with the Bay Scouts.

And that's when I asked the question that had been on my mind almost as long as the meta question. It had been more than four years since Lee's death, after all. "I'm not seeing anyone right now, no," she said. Then she actually blushed, her cheeks becoming a darker red. "I've never been asked out by a woman, before. Which is pretty weird, living in San Francisco." Before my stomach could sink very far, she smiled. "I'm off tomorrow night. How about a movie? I've been wanting to see *Memoirs of a Geisha*."

"Perfect," I said. "Dinner after? Jardinière?"

"Pricey," she said.

I grinned. "I made good tips this week."

She smiled, then laughed softly. "Wow. My first lesbian date, and it's with a superhero."

I beamed, feeling a bit giddy. At the back of my head were the Maltese Falcon's parting words to me a couple weeks before.

I ignored them.

The following evening, over dinner, I told Rachel about my coffee meeting with Dr. Gray, which of course involved the entire tale of how I gained my abilities, the fire, and whatnot, eliciting the typical reactions of astonishment, sympathy, and so on.

Honestly, I was tired of telling the story, I told her. It was an embarrassment, destroying your place of employment while doing something you allegedly knew how to do.

"No more embarrassing than being put out to pasture as a teenager," she said. And I supposed I saw her point. But it didn't really help.

Embarrassing pasts weren't the only thing we had in common. There was also the fact that neither of us got along with our parents. "They pretty much disowned me as soon as I stopped making money for them. They don't like metas, and viewed me as an abomination from the first. If I'd been born at home, instead of a hospital, I'm sure I'd have ended up in a dumpster. Hospitals, of course, made a big deal over meta births. And back then, someone who put a meta child up for adoption was looked down upon."

"So different from today," I noted.

"Yeah. Anyway, they eventually started getting requests from photographers to shoot me and quickly figured out that I might be a spawn of Satan, but I was a moneymaker."

"That's terrible."

"I wouldn't mind so much if I'd gotten to keep any of that money. But I didn't."

"You're kidding."

She shook her head and poked her fork around her salad. "I wish. I was a minor, with no say over my own finances. And they never intended to share it with me."

"Well, couldn't you have sued them? I've read of some child stars doing that."

"Maybe. Except that, one, they spent it all on a big house, a big car, a big boat, lots of trips to Europe, and so on, and two, they died in a plane crash on one of those trips."

"Oh." I sipped my coffee. "Um... I'm sorry."

Rachel sighed. "Yeah. Me, too, for some stupid reason."

"Well," I offered, "they may have treated you like crap, but they were still your parents." I nearly choked on my own words. A little voice at the back of my head called me a hypocrite.

"Well, regarding your friend... Do you trust him?"

"That's the thing," I said, adding sugar to my third cup of coffee. "I do. I just don't know why I can't tell him."

"So how do you feel about him?" she asked, shifting slightly in her seat.

"What do you mean?"

"I mean, when you think of him, what's the first emotion that comes to you?"

My stomach sank. I stared into my cup. "Guilt." Rachel raised an inquisitive eyebrow. "I feel guilty because I was deceitful, working on my own project, using resources that didn't belong to me, and destroying the lab. He was my supervisor, so I know he caught some hell from the owners."

"And you don't think that admitting the truth would lessen the guilt?"

"No, because it would just make me feel even more guilty for not telling him before."

"Well, if you're screwed either way," she said, "just pick the path that hurts less."

The next day, I bought a Christmas card for Dr. Gray. In it, I enclosed a letter, pouring out my apology for not telling him the truth before. I included a promotional photo of the Bay Scouts taken after I joined and nervously mailed it off. I exhaled heavily as the mailbox door swung shut, immediately feeling a slight relief, but still not knowing whether I'd done the right thing.

As much as we metas try to "expect the unexpected," there are some scenarios too far-fetched to even think about, let alone prepare for. That winter, just such a scenario presented itself. Esteban and I were chatting in the kitchen of our base. We were talking about Rachel, and how well things were going. "We're spending Christmas together," I said with a smile.

"Ah," he said. "Romance is blooming?"

I blushed and smiled. "I think so."

Esteban grinned. "*Fabuloso*, Dyna! I'm happy for..." Suddenly, he stopped speaking, looked at me in alarm... and vanished with a quiet pop.

Mouth agape, I stared at the spot in which he'd stood. But before I could even utter a cry of astonishment, I felt the strangest sensation of my life. It was like I was falling. And rising. And being pulled back, pushed forward, and shoved to each side. All at once. I thought I was going to vomit.

Then everything went all swirly black, and when the nausea passed and I opened my eyes again, I was looking, surprisingly, into Valora's face.

Valora stared oddly at me, then grimaced. "*Damn* it, Dyna!" she spat, before planting a rock-hard fist in my face.

FIFTEEN

"Actioni contrariam semper et æqualem esse reactionem: sive corporum duorum actiones in se mutuo semper esse æquales et in partes contrarias dirigi."
~Newton's Third Law of Motion

It's been said that we only understand things in the context of their opposites. We wouldn't understand the concept of "light" if we didn't know darkness. We wouldn't comprehend "peace" if we didn't know war. Pick your pair. Wealth and poverty. Pain and pleasure. Wellness and sickness. Freedom and slavery. Sleeping and waking.

But this has always seemed to me to be too simplistic. Wellness, for example, is more than the absence of disease. Peace is more than the state of not being at war. There's more to things than such simple comparisons.

Opposites serve us well, allowing us to see the extremes. But we don't spend much of our times at the extremes in anything. We spend it in the gray areas or, if you prefer, the rainbow between black and white.

Dusk, for example, is not dark, but not really light, either. The ever-shrinking middle class is neither rich nor poor. And there is that hazy zone between sleeping and waking, a state of mind where we never quite know what is real and what is dream, which is conscious and which is subconscious.

I awoke with the all-too familiar feeling of a throbbing head. To my surprise, it was Valora jostling me awake, a frown on her face. Naturally, I immediately punched that face. It wasn't enhanced with energy, just a reflexive punch. I nearly broke my hand.

"I'll forgive that," she said.

I looked around me, now, and saw Esteban and the twins sitting on the ground, bruised and confused. I looked back at Valora, suspiciously.

Her eyes held a hint of panic and disorientation. She wasn't used to being in situations in which she wasn't in control, or at least had a hope of gaining it. At this moment, Valora seemed like a frightened girl hiding in an Amazon's body.

Val helped me to my feet and I looked around further. We appeared to be stranded in the middle of the desert. Not a building in sight. Mountains in the distance on nearly all sides.

I glanced at the others. Billy and Bobby each sported massive bruises on their cheeks and under their eyes. They didn't have a protective energy field, as I did. Then again, for all I knew, my face was as bruised as theirs. Valora hits hard. Which brought me back to the question of why she'd decked me – us – in the first place.

Except... the guys didn't seem troubled by it. I turned to her again, but before I could speak, I noticed something odd: Val was wearing different clothing now than when she'd smacked me. Seeing my confusion, she said, "Evidently, I have a doppelganger."

I glanced between her and the guys. "What, like an evil twin?"

"I got one'a those," Bobby joked. Billy backhanded him.

"If what the others reported is true," she said. "And judging from your reaction, you thought I'd struck you, as well." She frowned, clearly – and understandably – disturbed.

I was skeptical, but said nothing. I looked around again. "So where are we? And how'd we get here?"

"No ideas," said Esteban.

I pulled out my phone and hit the navigation button.

"Tried that," Billy said. "No signal."

He was right. I had nothing. "Well, let's try some aerial reconnaissance," I said. I kicked off my shoes and rolled up my pant legs. These were my favorite jeans, and I didn't need to shred them when I took off into the sky. From the air, I saw nothing resembling civilization, save for what appeared to be a road in the distance, in the low hills. I flew there, determining that it was, in fact, a road. But I still couldn't see any towns. Just lots and lots of scrub brush, hilly terrain, and desert.

Billy was shooting bursts of flame into the sky at regular intervals for me. Navigating back was no problem. I flew back low over the ground, blasting potholes into the dirt at regular intervals... my "bread crumb trail" back to the road.

We set off immediately and made it to the road by nightfall. I flew skyward again, this time looking for any city lights. Billy again shot flares for me. After a few minutes of flight, I saw what appeared to be dim lights quite a ways off. I returned to my team and they agreed that I should investigate. But I'd wait until morning. After all the flying, blasting, walking, and not eating for several hours, I needed rest.

We sat in a relatively level patch of scrub grass off the roadside, Billy keeping us warm by being a living campfire. We tossed around dozens of thoughts on what had happened, comparing notes on what we'd experienced. Everyone had felt the same weird sensations I had before suddenly being clobbered by Valora's twin. Beyond that, we were utterly clueless.

Whatever forces brought us here, we were grateful that Billy was with us. The desert gets awfully cold at night. I'm mostly immune to low temperatures, as my body generates a good bit of heat, but even I felt a chill that night. The problem with open flames in the dark, though, is that they draw attention.

I woke to the sound of Valora's yell. Instantly awake, I took stock of the situation. Valora was struggling with a group of men dressed in dark colored jumpsuits and helmets that covered their faces. They were attacking her with hi-tech looking weapons that shot out thick beams of reddish energy. Before we could rush to her aid, a second group opened fire on us.

To my astonishment, the beam felt very much like when Jack touched me during my Bay Scouts try-out. It was almost as cold and nearly as enervating.

Bobby was the first to fall. Then Billy. Esteban next. Valora continued to put up a great struggle, even managing to knock out one of the men before she fell. But I don't think they counted on someone who produced as much energy as I did. I'd taken three hits and was very weak, but was able to knock my assailants back with a sweeping, concussive wave. Then I took to the sky, hoping their weapons were short range. I only had enough left in me for a short flight, so I landed in the hills and hid in the brush, hoping they didn't have some way to track me.

I wasn't optimistic, though. Their helmets had goggles built in. Almost certainly with night vision capability, and possibly more. Heat sensing, perhaps. Naturally, my fears were correct. Within half an hour, I heard them approaching, and this time, one zap from their rifles took all the fight out of me. One more, and I was unconscious.

When I woke, I was alone in a cell. Instead of bars, the walls were made of energy fields, except for one, which was stone, roughhewn and cold to the touch. The entire cell was about eight feet wide and maybe twelve feet long, with a bunk, a toilet, and a small table bolted to the stone floor next to the bunk.

I examined the force fields. They appeared to be generated by metal pillars at the corners of the cell, the fields overlapping so that the pillars couldn't be reached from the inside. The reddish fields were translucent, to a degree. I could see somewhat clearly through the front panel, less so the side walls. One chilly touch told me the fields were the same energy used in the guns that defeated me. I felt weak when I came in contact with it. And it was firm, with no give whatsoever. An energy punch merely bounced me backward. And a blast dissipated harmlessly, like shooting at a glacier with a fire hose.

I turned my attention to the back wall. An energy blast chipped at it, slightly, but I soon determined I might have better luck using a good, sharp spoon. I was too weak to maintain any sort of prolonged effort into drilling through.

There wasn't a soul in sight within whatever sort of facility it was. The only sounds were the hum of the force field generators and my own movement. I wasn't sure whether the field was soundproof or the building was just that empty.

My head throbbed, and when I put a hand to it, I felt a crust of dried blood in my hair. Hours passed. My thoughts were scattered. I was concerned for my teammates. I was weak with hunger and thirst. And yes, I was scared. Helpless. And that was a feeling I was decidedly unused to.

I slept, but poorly, and when I woke, I forgot where I was for a moment, until I looked around. A tray of food and cup of water sat on the table, and I quickly devoured the meal.

Days passed, each the same. Hours of solitude, disturbing sleep, waking to find food, which was always delivered while I slept, no matter how hard I tried to stay awake for the delivery, like a child waiting for Santa on Christmas Eve. Lather, rinse, repeat. It was mind-numbing. No, that's actually not true at all. My mind was, if anything, hyperactive.

Where was I? Where were the others? Were they somewhere here, in other cells? Were they even alive? Who was posing as Valora and why? Were Scoutmaster and the others looking for us? Did they even know we were missing, or would it take a while, like it did for Ping Song?

For that matter, was Song here, too? Is that why she'd disappeared? And how in the world were we captured? Esteban had... popped... he'd just popped right out of existence, in front of my eyes. How was that even possible?

These were my thoughts for the first few days of my imprisonment. Then, still without having seen another person, my thoughts turned darker. I began to wonder if I'd die in this place. The silence was too much to bear, so I began talking to myself. The less said about that, the better.

When I tired of hearing my own voice, I calmed down and took stock of the situation, examining what I knew, little though it was.

Somehow, we had been plucked from our routine existence into an unfamiliar desert location. We were attacked and subdued by a team of men with weapons none of us had ever seen or heard of before. We were imprisoned – or at least I was – in advanced energy cages.

What else? Oh, yes. Someone was impersonating Valora, quite convincingly.

Five of us were taken. Six, if Ping Song's disappearance were related. All from the same team. This couldn't have been a random act. We were being targeted.

Or at least, some of us were. Daniel, Jack, and Sinta weren't here. Was there some unknown vendetta against the five or six of us? Or were the other three taken, too, but we just didn't know it?

And Song. She vanished a month or more before us. There had to be a reason for that. If, again, that's why she'd disappeared. I had to assume it was, mainly because I didn't like thinking about the alternative.

And back to the initial question: How did we get here? The only word I could think of for near-instantaneous relocation was "teleportation." But the very idea of teleportation defied even more scientific principles than my blasting did.

Or did it?

My understanding of physics is fuzzy at best, but on an atomic level, I knew a sort of teleportation exists, where changing the charge of one atom simultaneously changes the charge of its twin, in another location. And if it's possible on that level, it could theoretically be possible on a much greater, more complex level. Somehow. I can't imagine how, nor the energy required to teleport a living, organic being.

Twin atoms. Valora's twin. Doppelganger, she said. What if she were right? What if it hadn't been, as I'd been assuming, someone impersonating her? What if it really were some sort of evil twin? What implications could that have?

My head hurt, just thinking about it.

I'd mentally ticked off eight days before I saw a sign of life in my prison. I was awake, this time, when my food was brought. My jailers – three of them – approached my cell. One held my tray of food, while the other two held those damnable weapons.

They weren't wearing the helmets, but it didn't help me to identify them. All were clean-shaven with short hair, wearing dark glasses and black jumpsuits. They looked like a cross between soldiers and government agents.

I stood as they neared my cell. Only three? I could take three.

The food-bearer stepped to one of the pillars and appeared to punch some buttons on the far side. The front field began to fade, at which point the guns were trained on me.

My hands were pulsing, ready to let loose as soon as the field was gone completely. But the gunmen had the same idea. The moment the wall dissipated, they fired on me. I fell to my knees, glaring up at them.

After putting the food on the table, the man who seemed to be the senior officer of the party stood staring at me. He frowned. "Why did you attack us?"

I sat on the cold floor, willing my energy to return so I could blast the sunglasses off their faces. "Got that a little backward, ya think?"

The man sighed and his associates exchanged looks. Despite myself, I wondered whether I had things straight in my own head. Valora had already been fighting them when I woke. Had she been the instigator? A cool temperament wasn't her most shining attribute.

"What is it with you meta freaks?" he sneered. "Acting like you can do whatever you want... Is it any wonder normal people have to..." He cut off his words and clenched his jaw. "Again... why did you attack our base?"

I blinked. "What?"

"Weapons? Or something else?" he said, suggestively. "Who are you working for?"

I remained silent, wondering what he might have meant.

Finally, he gave up. "Fine. Maybe your memory will come back to you in another week."

With that, he turned and walked out, the gunmen backing out after him, weapons never wavering. Once they were out, he slapped the pillar and the energy field burst into existence again. The gunmen muttered to each other as they lagged behind their superior. In moments, they were gone, leaving me with a very sick feeling in my stomach.

I was beginning to panic, seeing no happy ending to this situation. I wracked my brain trying to figure out an escape, and tried the same things I'd done before, with identical results. The floor and ceiling were also solid rock. It was as though the structure had been built into the side of a mountain.

But I determined I'd get through, one way or another. In desperation, I gathered as much energy in my fists as I could, and began beating on one of the walls. But every strike drained me. I could see the bright blue glow around my fists dim, punch after punch.

I stopped, obviously needing a different approach. Maybe, I thought, I could overload the thing. Fully amped, maybe I had more energy than the machine could accommodate. It was worth a shot, anyway.

So I waited for another meal and some sleep. Fully charged, I approached one of the corners, intent to channel as much energy as I could toward one of the generators. I thrust my fists against the field and let loose with the largest sustained blast I could manage. Unfortunately, it wasn't much. I was being fed enough food to keep a normal human alive, but nowhere near enough to fuel me. When I'm not fueled, straining to blast trips my body into ketosis. Trouble is, I had hardly any fat content to convert to fuel. And converting protein to fuel was a bit counter-productive. Still, I kept at it, and was rewarded with a brightening of the energy field and a blinking red light on one of the pillars. But within seconds, I was spent. The blinking light ceased and the wall was as strong as ever.

I slumped against the wall, feeling it continue to suck my strength. I almost didn't care, at this point. Idly, I wondered if it would suck enough energy that it would actually kill me. Didn't seem likely. I expected to pass out again, as I'd done when they captured me.

And I did. I remember feeling woozy and tipping over. When I came to, though, I felt surprisingly energized. But it didn't last. Immediately, the energy drained from me. Then I noticed my bare foot was fetched up against the field. And it was sore. I pulled it back, frowning.

I examined my foot in the dim light. It was very tender where it had been touching the wall. It felt like a sunburn. But why had I felt so amped when I woke?

To test an idea, I stretched out on the floor and deliberately pushed my foot against the wall. Within a minute, I was unconscious. And then I woke again, feeling similarly energized. I pulled my aching foot away and sat there, pondering what it meant.

Sleeping... Awake.

Conscious... Unconscious.

Subconscious.

Instinct.

I stared at my hands, then at the wall. Then I stood. I took several calming breaths, eyes closed. Even though I'd never attempted, or thought to attempt, anything like this, my body evidently knew what to do, I told myself. I couldn't let my brain, or my emotions, get in the way.

When I was sufficiently Zen, I braced myself and pushed gently into the wall, fingers spread wide. But instead of trying to overload the mechanism, I opened myself to the energy. I let it suffuse me, and I drank it in.

The initial wave of lethargy passed, replaced quickly with a feeling of being supercharged. It was working. I was absorbing the energy from the machine. But it hurt. It was cold, but it burned. I didn't know whether it was just too much energy or that it wasn't "natural" biological energy like what I produced.

I cried out, every nerve in my hands on fire. I panicked and lost my concentration, and the force field now sucked my energy away. Weakening rapidly, I withdrew, silently cursing myself. I stared at my hands, watching the reddened flesh begin to blister. Fighting back tears of pain, I collapsed on my bunk, my mind racing.

It was just too much. I couldn't handle that much energy, or that kind of energy. Or, more likely, it was just a very dangerous thing for me to do. I stared at my hands again.

In a rare burst of inspiration, I thought of when I figured out how to fly. Wide dispersal, not concentrated blasts. Maybe it wasn't that it was too much energy. Maybe it was just too much to absorb through such a small area.

I got to my feet again, pushed the pain from my mind, and stepped to the wall. Calming breaths. And this time, I planted as much of my body against the field as I could, willing the absorption to come from everywhere, picturing myself in a bathtub of energy, drinking in the warmth from all sides.

I'm not exaggerating when I say it was the worst pain I'd ever experienced. It made being shot in the chest feel like a slap. It burned, both from touching the field, and inside, as I absorbed the energy. But thinking about the pain was only making the process last longer. I had to ignore it. No, I had to give in to it. Accept that it wasn't going to stop. As the energy soaked into me, I thought instead about the fact that, if I failed, I might never leave this place. And I felt everything fade, my nerves overwhelmed.

A century or two later, I pitched forward onto the floor outside the cell. I don't know how long I lay there, my numbness fading, the pain surging back into me. Eventually, I opened my eyes, seeing the energy wall solid again behind me.

Every bit of my body that had been in contact with the wall, whether or not covered by clothing, felt like a bad sunburn. My thighs, stomach, breasts, undersides of my arms, and the right side of my face screamed in pain. My palms and fingers were the worst, as this was their second exposure.

The energy I'd absorbed begged to be released. Every cell screamed at me, threatening to burst. I could literally feel it leaking out of me. Wisps of energy flickered from my fists. My whole body was glowing. My vision was hazy, and I saw similar flashes of energy in front of my eyes, as though leaking out of my eye sockets.

But I couldn't let it out, yet. Who knew how big this place was? Who knew how many adversaries I'd have to take on? And then there were those damn guns of theirs.

I got to my feet and looked at my week-long home. There were four identical cells next to it, two on each side, all empty. My teammates were here – the major had essentially said so – but imprisoned elsewhere.

I turned and took stock of my surroundings. Looking out away from the row of cells, I could barely see the far wall in the dim light, perhaps two hundred feet away. In between, there were what appeared to be racks of equipment, running the length of the building. I could, however, see people, moving among the racks. And it was only a matter of time before they'd see me.

Options. A set of double doors immediately to my left. To my right, a wide hallway with a single door at the far end. It wasn't a difficult choice. I was amped up, but every movement was excruciating. My thoughts were unfocused. I couldn't kid myself. I was in no shape to take on any of these guys, no matter how amped I was with energy. I needed to hide.

I crept toward the hallway, stepping lightly in my bare feet, and then saw that it branched off to the right. I peeked around the corner down the new hall. About ten yards down, there was a massive metal door, like the door to a vault, but one that raised up, rather than swung on a hinge. It was up high enough to walk under. And there was a sound coming from beyond it, a light thrumming noise, with the occasional crackling sound, as of electricity.

My curiosity won out and I headed to the door. It was solid steel, it seemed, and easily a foot thick. Peering past, I was relieved to see no people. I noticed, though, that the hallway narrowed quickly, and at the far end, I saw the source of the noise.

At the end of the hallway was a round, mechanical frame about six feet in diameter. But I took little notice of the frame itself, my attention fixed on what it was framing. Inside was pitch black, with lazy swirls of silver and occasional electric arcs of blue.

It was utterly mesmerizing, but I tore my gaze from it in order to examine the frame, which appeared to monitor whatever it was. A video screen embedded into one side showed a variety of readouts. I had no idea what it was measuring, but the green and red indicators were easy enough to understand. Green, good; red, bad. All readouts were in the green areas of the gauges. But what was it?

I carefully reached out a hand to touch it. There were no safeguards to prevent this, so I assumed it wasn't going to kill me. To my astonishment, my fingers met with some resistance, as though I'd stuck them into gelatin. I pulled my hand back slowly and examined it. Nothing seemed amiss.

I tested it again, this time watching the monitor as it scrolled through different unintelligible readings. But before I could examine it further, I heard voices and footfalls coming down the hallway. I turned to look and cursed myself for not being more careful. There were cameras mounted on the ceiling. A hundred thoughts raced through my head in a second. Then I turned and rushed toward the thick metal door.

I saw two men reach the entrance of the corridor, weapons ready. They fired, and the familiar bolts of red energy crackled past me. I slid to my knees and stretched my arms out in front of me, letting loose with a two-handed blast that filled the hallway, sending the men to the ground. Then I slapped the control panel to close the door.

Now I was committed. I returned to the strange construct and fiddled with it again. As I pushed my arm deep inside the thing, the gauges moved, but just barely. As I was up to my shoulder, I realized my fingers moved freely, with no gelatin feeling. But weirder, it seemed to be pulling me inside. With a glance back at the door, I sighed. Then I leaned my body into the blackness, allowing it to pull me in.

Immediately, the sensation hit me again. Falling, rising, pushing and pulling, all at the same time. I clamped my mouth and eyes shut against the nausea and disorientation. I tripped over my own feet and pitched forward, falling for what seemed more than the few feet to the ground. Naturally, I reflexively put my hands out to catch myself. I landed on my blistered stomach, gasping in pain. I quickly rolled over onto my back and opened my eyes, staring at the sky.

I was in the desert again. I immediately looked around to see if anyone had followed me through, and felt my stomach drop. I'd assumed I would just come out on the other side of wherever the portal was, seeing the entrance to my prison behind me. But there was nothing but a steep, scrub-strewn slope up into foothills indistinguishable from those in which we'd been captured, more than a week ago.

What had I been thinking? My teammates were still inside. I should have stayed. I should have hidden in one of the empty cells until my head was clearer. I should have tried to find and rescue them instead of running away.

I clenched my fists (painfully) and screamed at the sky, at myself. As I did so, all the stored energy demanded to be set free. So I let it go. Instead of forcing it through one part of my body, as I was used to doing, I simply stopped trying to contain it. The result was an explosion with my body at ground zero.

As the blast echoed to silence, I fell to my knees in a small crater now beneath my feet. I was utterly drained and knelt there looking around me. Ejecta from the blast splayed out in all directions from the crater. But it wasn't the only material thrown out. "Super," I muttered, seeing the almost unrecognizable shreds of most of my clothing. Judging by the scraps still left on me, the blast must have erupted from around my center of gravity, just above my waist. I panted in pain as my strength slowly returned, saved from embarrassment by the fact that I was alone with no one to see my bare flesh.

What had that been? It wasn't deliberate. Was it something I could reproduce, or was it unique to being "overloaded" with energy? I shook the questions from my mind as I cast off the remaining traces of what used to be clothing, focusing on my predicament. Several minutes passed as I sat there in my panicked desolation before I staggered to my feet. I needed to stay focused on the emergency at hand. I began pacing, my thoughts focused, now, trying to figure out a plan. Then I heard the noise of a vehicle.

I crouched low and looked toward the noise. It was a motorcycle, I saw, kicking up dust and heading straight toward me. Immediately, I was on guard and debated taking to the sky. But it was one lone figure, not an entire crew. I was weak, but I could handle one guy, no problem.

The bike slowed to a stop about ten yards from me. The small figure had black hair, shoulder length, and wore goggles with no helmet. The sun blazed behind the figure and I shaded my eyes from the glare, wary but curious. The stranger slowly dismounted, pulling what looked like one of the energy weapons from a holster on the bike. We looked at each other for several seconds, then the weapon lowered. "Dyna?"

My jaw dropped. "Song!" I ran toward her, not caring about my unclothed state. But as I approached, she raised the weapon again. I slowed to a stop. "Song, it's me!"

"Is it?" she said.

I nodded, but stared at her. She looked terrible, her face mottled with semi-healed cuts and bruises, her clothing torn. "Yes," I said, and a wave of relief spread over me, knowing she was safe.

She stepped over, looking me up and down, shock in her eyes. "What happened to you?"

I looked at my body, seeing for the first time the blisters covering my chest, breasts, and belly. Even my upper thighs. Many of them had burst and were oozing. And with the sight, my brain was reminded of the throbbing pain. I shrugged. "Something I ate," I said with a forced smirk. "How did you find me?"

"I wasn't trying to. I was investigating the explosion." She nodded to the crater several yards behind me. "Did you see what caused it?"

"Um... That would've been me."

She seemed to ponder that for a moment before offering me some of her clothing. I declined, since I didn't want anything rubbing against my wounds.

We spent several minutes explaining everything to each other. I told her about our abductions, our capture, imprisonment, and my escape.

In return she told me that she'd been abducted in much the same way, being pulled right from her apartment. She, too, had been pummeled by "Valora" upon arrival. "I came to inside some sort of facility," she said, and I nodded. "And that's when I saw the others. Esteban, Billy and Bobby..."

"And me," I said flatly, coming to the only logical conclusion.

Song frowned. "Seems likely. I didn't see her, though."

I kept thinking of what Valora's twin said before decking me. *Damn it, Dyna,* she'd said. As though I – or my twin – had done something to piss her off.

Song told me how they'd questioned her for hours before knocking her out. Like the rest of us, she regained consciousness in the desert. She indicated some of her injuries. "They were fairly persuasive." She frowned.

"What's really odd," she said, "is that they didn't ask anything you or I would consider to be private information. Just general questions about our world."

Our world. She said it so casually, as though everyone just *knew* there were other worlds than ours. But the words hit me like a kick to the gut.

She told me how she'd wandered for a couple days, eventually encountering a lone patroller on a motorcycle. She'd overpowered him, taken the bike and his uniform, and had been scouting around for the facility ever since.

"There's a tiny town about twenty miles north of here," she said. "I mean *tiny*. Not even a gas station."

"Yeah," I said. "Go back to the 'other world' bit."

"Well," Song said carefully, "that's the conclusion I came to with the information at hand. I'm not going to pretend I understand it, though."

"And right now, we're not in our world," I said.

"Correct."

"And... we're here because of some weird cosmic law that says we can't both be in the same world simultaneously."

"So it appears."

"Which means right now, our doubles are in our world, wreaking whatever havoc they have in mind."

I pondered this for a while, then we agreed that standing in the desert was accomplishing nothing. Any answers we might find, not to mention our teammates, were back inside that facility. We needed to find the entrance. "Where did you arrive?" Song asked. I jerked my thumb back in the direction of my crater. She nodded and walked over to the spot. I followed, wondering why that mattered. She paid little attention to the small crater and instead looked at the sloping landscape up into the small hills. And suddenly I understood. The entrance was camouflaged somehow. Given how complete it seemed to be, I assumed there was some holography at work.

I suggested this to Song and asked if she could detect the portal, or perhaps the holographic devices. She nodded. "If I'm close enough, I should..."

And then she fell silent and looked at me, a look of surprise on her face, and vanished with a quiet inrush of air.

SIXTEEN

"What lies behind us and what lies before us are tiny matters compared to what lies within us."
~*Ralph Waldo Emerson*

About ten miles from my hometown is a mall. When I was young, it had two anchor stores, a Montgomery Ward at one end and a Murphy's Mart at the other. The former no longer has brick and mortar stores and is now exclusively an online retailer. The latter chain is long gone. But both were alive and well in the late seventies.

Connecting the two, in the "mall" itself, were perhaps a dozen or so stores. I certainly can't remember them all, but there was a record store, a bookstore, a piano store that also sold other instruments (Dana would buy his guitar strings there), a jeweler, a few women's clothing stores, one men's store, a shoe store, the restaurant where I'd get ice cream, and a few others. But when we went shopping, we spent most of our time in the two anchor stores.

Mother would take us shopping. Dana was old enough to go off alone, but at five or six, I had to stick with our mother. At least for a while, until I became such a nuisance that she'd let me go find Dana, or she'd give me enough money for an ice cream cone and I'd go there.

Keep in mind that in those days, there was no rampant paranoia about your children being abducted the moment your back was turned. I'm sure it happened back then, but without instantaneous news relays via the internet or 24-hour news on TV, we just didn't hear about it. Either way, that sort of thing wasn't a concern.

It should be said that I'm an easily distracted person, and this was just as true when I was little as it is today. Mother would be strolling from one rack of clothing to another, and my attention would be drawn by a display of shiny bracelets or scarves or something. I'd examine the colorful items and, next thing I knew, Mother was no longer in view. And I'd panic.

My heart would begin pounding and I'd rush around the store, looking for her familiar dress. Invariably, I wouldn't need to search long. Certainly no more than a couple minutes. But it didn't feel that way.

Even then, I was sensing that Mother's affections for me were not like they once were. Sometimes I felt as though she didn't want me around. And the paranoia I had at that age was that she was hoping I'd get lost. Then she could collect Dana and skip out on me, leaving me behind.

Being lost like that, even for a couple minutes, wasn't the same as being allowed to go find my brother or get ice cream alone. In those cases, I had a purpose. I knew where I was going. Dana would be in one of the stores, looking at books, records, or guitars. And those were all small stores, not gargantuan, labyrinthine department stores.

Mother was never far away – sometimes just one aisle over – but to an insecure child, anything nearby but unseen might as well be a hundred miles away.

I'm not sure how long I stood there, staring at the emptiness in front of me. I don't know what I was expecting. Would I vanish soon, too, as I had after Esteban disappeared? Where was Ping Song's double? If I understood right, Song had vanished because her double had returned. But she wasn't standing in front of me. She wasn't in the scrub brush of the sloping hills. But she *had* to be there. So why *wasn't* she? It made no sense.

Who was I kidding? *None* of this made any sense.

I stood completely still, focusing my attention on the area around me, watching for any movement, listening for any sound. If she were here, I'd find her. And she wouldn't be at all happy about that.

But there was nothing. No movement more than the swish of dirt when a lizard scurried past. No sound but the low whistle of wind through the brush. Minute upon minute passed as I stood there, until the beating sun began to burn my blistered flesh.

Finally, I sighed and accepted that I wasn't going to find Song's double by standing around waiting for her to reveal herself. I'd have to find her by actually looking. And that meant looking for the hidden entrance to the facility.

It shouldn't be too difficult to find, I reasoned. It was a big place. I'd just have to walk up the slope and I'd eventually collide with one of its walls. But no sooner had I taken two steps before I realized the flaw in my reasoning. There were no walls to collide with. They didn't exist in this dimension. The only bit that existed here was the thinnest of windows, a hole between dimensions.

I looked back at my crater and cursed. That was my key. That was where I'd landed when I'd arrived. But what direction had I been facing when I hit the ground? I couldn't remember. In my pain of falling on my injuries, had I thrashed around? And how far from the portal had I fallen? A couple feet? Five? Ten?

With a sinking feeling, I realized I'd been assuming that travel through the interface was like going through a door, that you'd naturally just come out directly on the other side. But what if inter-dimensional physics was more complicated than that? What if I'd come out somewhere else? What if I'd come out as far from the portal as I'd been from the other portal when I was in the Bay Scouts base?

I couldn't think like that, I told myself. If that happened to be true, there was nothing I could do about it. But I had to act as though it were a simple thing, that it was nearby, and that I could find it.

So, feeling a bit ridiculous, I started at my little crater and walked in ever-widening circles, arms outstretched. Halfway through my fourth circle, I stopped. What if connecting with the portal edge-on wouldn't work? What if I had to connect face-on to even detect it? Almost as soon as this occurred to me, I berated myself for my own stupidity. There was an easier way to do this.

I returned to stand in my crater. Sweeping my arm in an arc, I let loose with a gentle ribbon of energy... if "gentle" is even a word that can apply to a blast of energy. I watched it extend outward until it dissipated. Then I turned forty-five degrees and repeated the process. And I saw what I'd hoped to. In the middle of the energy wave, the visible blast disappeared, while the waves on either side continued on.

Its bottom edge seemed to be about five feet from the ground. Not a problem for someone who could fly, though. But as I neared, the portal glowed and a body came through. It was the "other" Esteban. Unlike me, he landed on his feet when he hit the ground. He stood no more than a yard from me. He stared at me, breathing heavily, his bruised and bloodied face betraying confusion as to who I was, surprise at my nudity, and revulsion at my seeping blisters. Then astonishment as I planted a punch in his cheekbone.

I regretted it almost instantly. I was still weak from my mysterious full-body blast. He merely recoiled, then glared at me. "Unwise, *señorita*," he said, and lashed out in return.

The blow knocked me back several feet, but luckily for me, he never had the chance for a follow-up. "Bobby" fell through the portal and landed on him, allowing me to push aside the excruciating pain and let loose with as big a blast as I could manage. It wasn't much, but my aim was true. He buckled over as the blast hit his groin, taking all the remaining fight out of him. "Bobby" was already unconscious when he came through, it seemed.

I walked back to stand over his body, looking upward to where I knew the portal to be. I rested until "Esteban" began regaining consciousness, then power-jumped up from the ground into the portal, feeling the gelatinous resistance. Then I maneuvered my way through, collapsing inside, spent.

The heavy door was open now. In the corridor lay four of the paramilitary types, unconscious or dead, I couldn't tell. I crept down the corridor and poked my head around the corner. I couldn't see anything, but heard some commotion from further in.

I stepped out into the room and glanced to the right. What I saw made my heart drop. There, on the side of the corridor opposite where I'd been imprisoned, were five more holding cells. I'd not seen them before, since I'd taken to the hallway immediately upon seeing it. They were empty, but it didn't take a genius to know they had previously held my teammates, and that I could have freed them if I'd taken just another moment to explore my surroundings.

Before I had time to fully berate myself, something slammed into my left side. I pitched up against the wall, gasping in pain. I was certain I'd felt a rib break. I hadn't had much of a protective field around me, since I was so weak. But now I put all my remaining energy into it, to ward off another blow. But what had hit me? There was no one around, no wrecking ball hanging from a chain.

For some reason, my mind flashed to the portal I'd just come through, completely hidden from sight. Obviously, this world had some technological way of cloaking things from view. And if it could be done to an object, I reasoned, it could be done to a person.

I was up against an invisible enemy. And I'd have bet a month's rent that it was this world's Ping Song, the tech-head. And martial artist, as the blow to my ribs reminded me. It would explain why I never saw her when she was returned here.

I waited for her follow-up attack. I braced myself against the wall, panting from the exertion of keeping the energy field up. Every breath was painful, and I felt the field flickering from my lack of concentration. When the blow came, my field collapsed. And when the kick came to my stomach, it knocked the wind out of me. I didn't even feel myself collapse to the floor.

I woke to the sound of fighting, with no idea how long I'd been out. I struggled to my feet, hoping that my attacker was no longer around. I certainly couldn't engage in a battle. I didn't want to return through the portal. Glancing to my right, I saw the two doors I remembered from before.

I struggled painfully to my feet and hurried to the first door. I ducked inside to find a tiny conference room with a round table in the center and four chairs around it. A door in the left wall obviously connected with the other room, which I guessed to be an office. I went inside and found a large desk with a computer, file cabinets, and other standard office fixtures. I collapsed into the executive chair. I needed food. I rifled through the desk drawers, hoping to find a granola bar, an apple... anything.

I found something better. A bottle of whiskey, about a quarter full.

I chugged it, and soon felt the energy return.

I had to see what was going on, so I stepped out of the office and made my way to the fighting, hugging the walls as I did so. Finally, I peeked around a corner. In addition to at least half a dozen of the resident storm troopers, I saw fire. Lots of fire. It was Billy and his doppelganger in, if you'll pardon the expression, heated battle.

Figuring I could do some good, here, I rounded the corner and hid within the stacks of weaponry. I pulled one of the guns from the rack and examined it. On the bottom was the reservoir where a normal gun would have an ammunition cartridge. For these guns, it would be for some sort of battery pack, but those must have been stored elsewhere. I put the useless weapon back, trying my best to fight down the almost overwhelming fear that I was going to die here.

I turned my attention to the paramilitary guys I could see and began picking them off with focused blasts. After the third one fell, however, a bolt of familiar red energy flashed past my eyes.

I whirled, crouching behind a crate just as a second blast erupted. This time, I saw where it came from. But I saw no shooter. Because the shooter was the invisible Song.

I was too exposed, so I ducked low and worked my way back between the racks, barricading myself in. Song would have to be right in my face to shoot me. I was able to see, though, through small cracks between crates.

Even though I'd gotten some good energy from the whiskey, I was still starving. I was in horrible pain, and desperate to get out of there. And an invisible enemy was my main obstacle.

I couldn't see her, but maybe I could hear her, I thought. It was doubtful, over all the noise the others were making, but I tried. I did my best to ignore background noise and focus on what was nearby.

My heart pounded in my chest and I held my breath. Where was she? Had she decided I wasn't worth the effort? Or was she mere steps away? I turned my head to look through another gap and was shocked to see... something.

It was vaguely human-shaped, but without feature. A miasma of colors and patterns. I smiled to myself. Whatever technology Song was using to hide herself, it was evidently malfunctioning. I could see her, making her way around the corner to come down the aisle where I was hiding.

I carefully extended my arm along the side of a crate, taking careful aim. I built it up, aiming at the slow-moving pattern. But then two figures rounded the corner behind her and, in my surprise, I let the blast dissipate before firing.

The figures were two of the storm troopers, of course. I saw them clearly. What shocked me, though, was that I also saw similar glowy patterns in and around them. I blinked and shook my head, and when I looked again, I saw only their bodies. But now I couldn't detect Song. Her invisibility generator evidently wasn't completely broken, just working intermittently.

No question about it, now. I was screwed.

In desperation, I stepped out into the open, sending a sweeping wave of energy down the aisle. It wasn't strong enough to do much harm, but it knocked them off their feet. I sprinted out of the aisle behind the wave... and tripped over Song.

I landed on my probably broken ribs and cried out from the pain. But I fought it down and turned in alarm, knowing Song was probably on her feet by now. And she was. I again saw the strange aura type thing. She was approaching slowly, obviously believing I was easy prey. And she wasn't wrong.

To my surprise, though, she simply walked over to me. She apparently didn't realize her gizmo was malfunctioning and that I could see her. So I pretended I couldn't. And when she was near enough, I swept out my leg and brought her crashing to the floor next to me. One punch stopped her from getting up again.

I was still a target, though. The two goons were getting to their feet. Without thinking, I jumped up and agonizingly threw Song over my shoulder, then ran to the only safety I could think of. Back toward the portal.

My plan, such as it was, was to take Song's invisibility device for my own, then come back in through the portal with that as my protection. And it was a good plan, I thought. I could feel my rib grinding with every stride. I was in no shape to fight anyone, now.

In seconds, we were before the portal. And then oozing through it and tumbling out the other side. Where, of course, I fell again.

This time, the pain was so intense that I passed out.

I woke on the ground of the desert, each ragged breath sending a stabbing pain through my chest, much worse than before. There were voices. I saw feet in front of my face and another figure lying not far from me. Then I saw Valora lifting that body from a stretcher and placing it into a Trauma Pod.

A moment later, I was lifted and placed inside a second Pod. As I was lowered onto the stabilizing table inside, I looked up at the face of my rescuer. It was Jack. His face was bloody and one eye was swollen shut. His expression was of profound worry. He hesitated, seeing my eyes were open. Then he leaned in and kissed me on my unblistered cheek before closing the Pod door.

The autodoc kicked into action as the Pod's rotors lifted us off the ground. A screen in front of my face lit up and I looked blearily into the face of a trauma surgeon.

"Good morning, Dynamistress. Can you hear me?"

I nodded in reply as the autodoc lowered an oxygen mask over my mouth and nose. The surgeon glanced down and did something off-screen, then the autodoc swabbed my strapped-down arm and inserted an I.V.

"Good," the surgeon said. "You're in a Trauma Pod, in case you hadn't guessed. I'm about to perform a scan." The autodoc lowered a large arm, which traveled slowly over my torso. "Mm. Yes... broken rib," he said, confirming what I already knew. "Your rib has punctured your lung," he said in a serious tone. "I can begin treatment while you're in the Pod. You've got a long flight ahead of you." He glanced down again. "About three hundred and twenty miles, it looks like. So I don't want to wait."

Three hundred and twenty miles? How was that possible? Trauma Pods were for short flights, only. The doc evidently saw my confusion. "Mobile refueling," he said. "Even with the newer Pods that have much longer flight ranges than the older ones, refueling is still necessary." He smiled softly. "I'm going to sedate you now and will be using video cameras to perform thorascopic surgery on you during the flight. I'll see you when you get here."

I nodded as the sedative began to cloud my mind. But only one thought was going through it. What the hell was I doing in Nevada?

I woke in a hospital bed and looked around. Private room. I.V. in my arm. Pain. I was covered almost completely with a heavy layer of cream with gauze laid lightly over top. A thick pad of a bandage was loosely secured on my right side.

The door to my room opened and a nurse entered to check on me. I looked at her name tag. It said University Medical Center of Southern Nevada. I was in Las Vegas. A minute later, a doctor came in and, after a quick look-over, determined that I was able to receive a visitor.

The pair left the room and in walked an unfamiliar man of about fifty, in full Coast Guard dress blues. The gray at his temples stood out starkly against his dark brown skin. His name badge read, "T. Shepherd." The name, I knew. He was our liaison to the Coast Guard proper.

"Hello, Dyna," he said in a warm voice.

"Commander Shepherd," I said. "Nice to finally meet you in person."

"I was just about to say that," he said with a small smile. "I wish it was under better circumstances."

"I didn't think it was a social call."

He sighed softly. "Not entirely, though I'm pleased to see you're awake and on your way to a full recovery." He pulled a chair over to my bedside and sat on the backrest, his feet on the seat, and leaned forward. "My main reason for coming here, as you might expect, is to debrief you."

I barked a laugh, then winced in pain. "Wow. Impatient much?"

He smiled at my joke, and for the next several minutes, I told him in as much detail as possible what I'd been through from the moment I was plucked from the Scouts base until I woke in the Nevada desert. He nodded throughout the story. Clearly, he'd heard much of it from the others.

When I finished, he thanked me, and said, "I'm afraid this must all remain something you can never discuss outside of your team, Dyna."

I'm sure my mouth fell open. "You've got to be kidding," I said, before I could help it.

He shook his head. "I'm afraid not."

"You're seriously saying that the existence of another dimension is being kept a military secret? That citizens of our world are being replaced by those of the other and we're not allowed to tell anyone?"

He sighed heavily. "Unfortunately, that's exactly what I'm saying."

"Good god, why?"

"Mainly to prevent a panic," he said. "Seriously, think about it. Most people freak out over the least things, let alone something big."

I sighed, knowing he was right. People would absolutely freak. Hell, I was freaked. "So... what's being done?"

"I honestly don't know," he said with a hint of bitterness. "That decision was made well above my security level. It's a Homeland Security issue." I nodded. Of course it would be. "The Coast Guard is part of DHS, of course, but we're bottom level. The installation at Groom Lake is staffed by DHS personnel, not Air Force, in fact."

"Groom Lake," I said. "That's Area 51." Shepherd nodded in confirmation. "Guess there really are aliens there." I smiled softly at Shepherd's chuckle. "So this whole thing is a government project? How long have they known about it?"

"Project Echo, it's been named, and I don't know. Again... beyond my security level." He paused, looking at me seriously. "I need you to understand that this is no joke." He pulled out a piece of paper and opened it for me to see. The letterhead was from the FBI.

"What's that?"

"It's a national security letter. Essentially, it's a gag order. It states that members of the Bay Scouts are prohibited from speaking about Project Echo to anyone outside of the group. It carries forward, also, so you're bound by it whether you remain in the Scouts or not. The penalty for violation would be federal prosecution."

I lay there for several seconds, absorbing it all before I nodded. Shepherd thanked me, wished me well, and left.

Jack and Song visited me later. After confirming that they'd had the same debriefing and gag order from Shepherd, we talked about what all had gone on. As Song had determined, our doubles had come to Earth (even though they called their world that, too), which caused us to vanish, as we couldn't occupy the same dimension or world or whatever simultaneously.

"My double," Song said, "spent a couple months scouting, which included learning about our team. Our doubles planned to impersonate us."

"Why?" I asked.

Jack shrugged. "To make it easier to be accepted here? Not really sure. To be honest, we really were fooled for a while. We didn't see your double, at first, so we didn't have a clue that something like this could even have happened. We had no reason to try to detect what was different." I nodded, remembering well just how alike Valora and her twin looked. "In fact," Jack continued, "we weren't tipped off until their behavior became so obviously different."

And then the obvious hit me. "The others," I said. "The metas who turned criminal."

"Yeah," Jack said. "We're thinking they're quite likely doubles, also."

My mind was whirling, and I remembered what Commander Shepherd had said. "The facility in Nevada... Shepherd said it was staffed with DHS people. I imagine they're constantly monitoring the portal itself. So how did the others get through?"

"The monitoring is done remotely," Song said. "My double, as you know, has an invisibility device. She was able to enter unseen and use her abilities to disrupt the monitors, causing them to fail to detect the others coming through. How they then got out, I'm not entirely certain, but I figure they're pretty resourceful folks."

"So how did you guys get there? How'd you get through the military defenses?"

"That was Shepherd's doing," Jack said. "He got us through."

Everything about this sat wrong with me. It was big. No, it was gargantuan. It was the biggest story ever. And we had to keep mum about it.

Another thing struck me. "So, wait... what you said before... I take it there was something different about my double that would have revealed their imposter status."

Jack nodded faintly and reached inside his pocket. He held out for me a still photo from our security cameras. "Holy crap," was the only appropriate response I could think of. The figure in the photo looked very little like me. Oh, the facial structure was the same, and the hair was white.

But it was cut in a spiky mess. Energy leaked in tendrils from her eye sockets, which creeped me right the hell out, remembering what seemed like that same thing after I'd siphoned the energy from my prison cell. And her face had what appeared to be scars all over it. Thin, and in very straight-lined patterns, and it looked like there was something embedded, almost like...

"Is that... *circuitry*?" I looked up at my friends, the revulsion on my face almost certainly visible.

"Seems to be," Song said.

"Good lord... Why?"

"Her abilities, from what I've seen, are similar to yours, but not identical," Jack said. "Hers have a more electrical component to them."

"Imagine your bio-plasma with a lightning bolt inside," Song said.

I returned the photo to Jack. "Wow," I said. "I can see why she might stay hidden."

"Oh, she didn't stay hidden," Jack said. "She just didn't show up at our base until fairly recently." He frowned. "And... Dyna... she's also..." He hesitated before saying, "She's not quite right in the head."

I took that in, soberly. I didn't know why this bothered me, but it did. "My double is crazy?"

"To be non-PC about it, yeah," he said. Jack must have seen the effect this had on me, so he changed the subject. "How did you get all blistered?"

So I told them everything that had happened to me while I was in the other world. Song, especially, listened attentively. She'd been there, after all. In return, they told me how they'd finally ended things, with them making a concerted effort to capture the doppelgangers, mainly by deception and traps, then bringing them to the portal in our world.

"In Nevada," I said. "How did you know it was here?"

"Your double," Song said.

"Really," I said flatly. "How'd you get her to tell you?"

Jack smiled slightly. "Sinta asked her."

I nodded. "Sinta's claws can be very persuasive," I said.

"No," Jack said. "I mean she just asked her. The two... sort of became friends."

I blinked in surprise. "No shit."

"No shit," Jack said.

My mind snapped back to the Trauma Pod. "Who was the other one brought in?"

The two looked uncomfortable. "Daniel," Song finally said.

"What? How? And how is he?"

"He's... in a coma," Jack said quietly. "Valora's double," he said. "During our trip to the portal, she evidently broke free of her bonds, freed the others... so when we went to take them through..." He shrugged. "Song saved the day, really," he said, embarrassing her. "She went right into the portal to free you all. The rest of the doubles chased her. We tried to prevent them from getting through. Daniel tackled Valora's double, but she hit him really hard in the head. I mean, *really* hard. I thought he was dead, the way he fell."

As I absorbed this, my nurse entered and my friends were asked to leave. Jack smiled affectionately as they left.

The following day, Daniel and I were transferred to San Francisco General. I was in the hospital there for a week as I recovered from my surgery and allowed my blisters to heal.

Dana came down from Sacramento. He brought me a bag of things from my apartment and stayed with me at the hospital during the day, crashing at my apartment every night. I wanted him to know everything that had happened to me, but a paranoid part of me feared that my room might be bugged. So I had him read my thoughts.

He was suitably shocked.

My teammates and Rachel visited often while I was there. But by the time I was discharged, Daniel still hadn't come out of his coma, which had all of us worried.

It seemed like forever since I'd seen my apartment. I took my overnight bag to my room while Dana ordered pizza. Moving was still a bit painful. In my room, I dropped my bag on the chair in the corner. Then I saw the papers on my pillow, a black gel pen lying on top. I picked them up. Three sheets, front and back, of neat handwriting.

My handwriting.

A chill washed over me as I sat and read.

Dear "Me..."

My apologies for the uninvited visit. And for whatever discomfort comes from knowing I've been in your home, looking through your personal things. I let myself in using the spare key. You hid it in exactly the spot I would have chosen, if I lived here.

I came here because I felt a need to see how you live... what kind of life you have. To see what kind of life I might have had, if things had gone somewhat differently. That's really why I'm here in your world, despite what you might hear from others.

Oh, yes... I know you'll see this letter. I know they'll fail. Of course, I suppose it's possible that you may find this letter before you're fully brought up to speed by your friends. So I'll fill you in... or fill in the gaps, if most of this is known to you, already.

My world... Well, it's not a nice place. Once upon a time, it was. Very much like here. But things didn't stay all nice and pleasant. Over a couple/few decades, society pretty much went to hell.

There were many factors... perpetual wars in other countries, the public violently divided in ideologies, rampant corruption in many industries, and so on. Eventually, we had a massive economic collapse, class warfare, and all the fun things that go with it: businesses closing left and right, riots in the streets, a surge in homelessness, and so on. And then the diseases hit. Tuberculosis and pneumonia were a couple of the big killers, but there were others. Diseases tend to make nasty comebacks when people can't afford medicine.

With society crashing, those with power took over. Typically, that means politicians, but in this case, it was organized crime. Especially the metas. Opportunists like Valora, for example.

You're almost certainly wondering what my role was in all of that. Was I a villain in this drama? The answer is not "yes," but it's not much of a "no." I suppose, once, I was heroic. Some called me that, because of my accomplishments. But as I'm sure you understand, not all who call themselves heroes truly are. Some are sunshine heroes. Only when it suits them. Other times... Other times, we do whatever we please... or what we have to... or what just seems like a good idea at the time.

I think I fall into that last category. But to be fair, my ability to judge what is or is not a good idea is sometimes a bit impaired.

Our histories are not terribly dissimilar. Some minor differences, such as the fact that you're a few years younger than I am. But also a couple major differences, such as the immediate repercussions of our self-experimentation. From your scrapbook, I see you were fired and sued because you burned down your laboratory. I, on the other hand, was lauded as a genius in the scientific community. I was even nominated for a LeBon Prize. And so, I stayed active in research. I continued the self-experimentation, tweaking my genetic abilities about once a year. I even went so far as to implant a network of bio-circuitry into my flesh, which I determined would assist in bringing the flow of energy within my body to the surface, for better manipulation. I was right, but it was still not one of my better ideas. I became addicted to painkillers. The heavy duty kind. My thinking became a bit... confused.

Then there was Lee's suicide. A bit later in my life than in yours, it seems, but just as painful. And it was during that period immediately following, when I was psychologically vulnerable, that I met Valora. She befriended me, welcomed me into her circle, and helped me heal, for which I was deeply grateful.

Had I not been so emotionally ragged, and had my thinking been clearer, I might have realized sooner that these weren't the sort of people I needed as friends. I might have figured out earlier that Valora only wanted me as a tool.

Sometimes, you see, fame isn't all it's cracked up to be. Like many others, she knew my history. Her goal was for me to genetically alter others - ones who were already metahuman - to make them even more powerful. I didn't know if this was possible, and certainly didn't know what the results would be. But I didn't care. I began working on it.

Eventually, though, I learned the truth about her, how she planned to use these created pawns. But what could I do? For better or worse, I was part of Valora's crowd, and even though I was more powerful than some of them, Valora herself could defeat me easily. So I stayed out of fear. And... more. Valora is very charismatic. Truth is, I wanted her to like me. Silly, I guess, but I suspect you'll understand.

Val had a purpose for me and I did my best. I tried it out on one of her many admirers. I'd never met him before. I didn't need to know him, didn't want to know him. I suspect Val really wanted her boy toy, Jack, to be enhanced by my manipulations. But when I warned her of the danger, she gave me the other guy as a trial run.

And I failed. Spectacularly, in fact.

It wasn't pretty.

I apparently had one of my "episodes" during the process.

Yes, like you, I developed a fungal infection in my cerebrospinal fluid, which compounded my already shaky mental stability. My episodes take the form of... well... madness. I hallucinate, for example. I hear voices. I see things that aren't there. And my memory plays tricks on me, too.

At least, I attribute it to the meningitis. It's possible, I suppose, that my issues are due to nothing more than the repeated traumas I'd been through, from losing my parents, losing Lee, losing Rachel... losing Dana.

I can't tell you the feelings I have, seeing the photograph on your desk of the two of you standing, smiling, with Big Ben in the background. It warms me. It pains me. It makes me feel guilty.

Dana was one of the first to be put up against the wall when the revolution came. Because he fought. I'm surprised... no... I'm <u>stunned</u> to read in your diary that your brother, unlike mine, followed an academic path after his powers revealed themselves. Mine did not. He embraced his metahuman abilities. He, really, was my inspiration to give myself my powers.

Like you, I was bitter that Nature had not gifted me as she had Dana. I think, though, I was worse than you. You didn't learn of his abilities until you were sixteen. I learned of them a good decade earlier. And I had years to anticipate receiving my genetic gift, once puberty had its way with me. It was a crushing blow to learn that it wasn't to be.

And, as much as I respected and loved Dana, I resented him, just as you did. But worse. After I turned sixteen, I never spoke to him again. I followed his career in the news. And I cried when he was killed.

I'm grateful that, although my periods of madness are increasing and lasting longer, they are still the exception and not the rule. My periods of lucidity are still my "main" life. (I do admit, though, it has taken me three days to write this letter, so far. I want you to see the rational me.)

Yes, it was stupid of me to stay among Valora's group of killers. But it kept me alive. Even without my genetic skills at her disposal, I was nothing to sneeze at. Val knew this. So she kept me around.. And yes, to answer your other question, I did assist her. But I took no pleasure in it.

I don't know who it was who first learned of the portal's existence, though it was our tech-head who eventually figured out how to operate it. The girl's a genius, frankly. And when Valora saw this world, a warped mirror of our own, she hatched her plan.

I have no idea whether you saw it or not, since I don't know the method of your return, but there is a facility there... or not there. It lies in the overlap of the Venn bubbles of dimensions. We entered that place through the portal in the desert. Another on the opposite end of the in-between is the doorway to your world.

The facility was occupied by one of the many paramilitary groups in our world. Pains in the ass, they are. Fortunately, they were no match for us and we quickly routed them. You might have reason to be concerned, though. It seems unlikely that they would not have made use of the portal into your world. If so, and you encounter them, beware of their weapons. Val's puppet, Jack, invented them. They'll suck your energy right out of you.

As we understand it (and we may well not, really), there seems to be an active connection between the dimensions, between our worlds. They are not as distinct as we might believe. We learned this when we sent our tech-head through to your world. To our astonishment, her double ~ your friend, Ping Song ~ appeared in our world (bypassing the interdimensional space completely). As it happened, some of Valora's group were outside where she materialized and captured her.

Your friend is clever. She convinced Valora that killing her would strand her double in your world. I strongly doubt she's right, but it was a great ploy. It's why all of you are alive. Or were, when I left.

At any rate, our Ping Song returned, having done a good bit of reconnaissance. She told us about your team, the Bay Scouts, which had among its members several of our "twins." And that's when Valora decided we would impersonate you, gain the confidence of your friends, and... well... who knows what her plans really are? She keeps so much to herself.

Though, one part that wasn't in her plans was me. Our Ping Song told us of the vast differences in appearance between you and I. But I went through, anyway, without Valora's knowledge.

And so began my adventure in your world.

It's been interesting, though not without some embarrassment. Earlier this week, I apparently became good friends with a fire hydrant. Your Jack was "lucky" enough to witness that bit of entertainment. I applaud him (and thank him) for retaining some decorum during that. Valora's horde would simply laugh and make fun of me. At least, no one tried to abuse me physically, after the first time. An insane dynamo is nothing to poke a stick at.

So... Your friends...

For your own sake, I hope you count yourself among the truly blessed in the world.

I did not associate with many. I briefly met your friend Daniel. He distrusted me from the start, and therefore I liked him immediately.

Jack was the epitome of grace and understanding during my fire hydrant episode. He even bought me a pastrami burger. I will miss him when I'm gone. He is so unlike his counterpart, Valora's plaything.

Rachel... I did not want to see her. But I knew I had to. Just to see her face once more, alive. To erase the vision that has haunted me for years... that twisted death mask she wore as she lay there, a gaping hole in her chest, blood pooling in her eye sockets...

From your diary, I see you're just getting to know her. But she and I were together for nine months. We may as well have been together for nine years, the way her death hurt.

And seeing her alive did wonders for me. I don't know if I can explain it. I know it's a different world, but knowing that she lives, here, and has you, here... it makes my heart feel less burdened.

I completely avoided seeing Dana. I could not have handled that guilt, thank you very much.

I did, however, spend quite a lot of time with someone you don't seem to know well at all. You've not mentioned her in any detail in your journal. The only photo of her you seem to have is your team photo. I'm referring to someone who has a wisdom beyond her young years, but who needs, I think, someone older to help her break free of the walls she's erected around herself. When this girl blooms, she'll be nothing short of amazing. Dinah... do yourself a huge favor. Get to know Sinta. You won't regret it.

At any rate, I think that's all I really want to say.

I know that, on my world, you are probably suffering. Ten days ago, I'd have cared little. Today, I feel remorse. But if it's any consolation (and I feel it may be), please know that, by exchanging places with me for this short time, you have saved me. You and your friends.

Because I've seen, now, what I came here to see. In you, I've seen the heroic force I could have been.

Thank you.

And be well.

SEVENTEEN

"There's a period of life when we swallow a knowledge of ourselves and it becomes either good or sour inside."
~Pearl Bailey

When I was seven years old, I received my first (and so far, only) marriage proposal. His name was Chris. He was eight. Chris was the son of a couple who were friends with our next-door neighbors. He and I would play together when they visited, since we were about the same age.

His proposal took the form of a letter that arrived in our mailbox one Saturday. It was written in crayon, each word a different color. It was quite succinct: "Dear Dinah, Will You Marry Me? Thanks. Love, Christopher."

My memory tells me I replied with an affirmative answer, but I honestly don't remember if that's true or not. Not long after, our neighbors moved away and Chris and I wouldn't see each other again for almost a decade, when we happened to bump into each other at the mall.

I wouldn't have recognized him, except that he was with his parents, and they still looked very much like I remembered them. Chris, obviously, looked considerably different. The cute little boy was now absurdly good looking. I, on the other hand, was decidedly dumpy.

I stood next to him in line for ice cream and said hi to him. He said hello back. "Do you remember me?" I asked. He smiled and said he did. And then it was his turn to order. Aside from our farewells, that was the sum of our entire conversation. And I've never seen him since.

I often think about Chris. More accurately, I think about his crayon-scripted proposal. That he cared enough about me to do such a thing made me feel wonderful. I certainly didn't receive that sort of loved feeling from my parents. Dana was about fourteen at the time, and was still the person I was closest to. But having someone else express feelings for me was incredible.

I wish I still had that letter.

About a week after my discharge, Daniel came out of his coma. Unfortunately, there was brain damage. The doctors weren't sure if it had been caused by the blow itself or happened during the coma, and were still evaluating the extent of it.

Meanwhile, my blistering had healed up nicely and the silver sulfadiazine paste they'd applied prevented any but the most mild scarring. I was nowhere near ready for a return to action, however. My rib and lung both still had a good while left to fully heal. But I felt well enough for a date.

Rachel and I sat over coffee at the Red Devil before her shift. Gag order notwithstanding, I'd already told her all about the experience my teammates and I had shared. I wasn't worried that she'd go blabbing about it. What I hadn't mentioned to her was the note from the woman I referred to as my "other-self." After we sat down, I handed it to her and watched her while she read.

I watched as the confusion changed to astonishment. I saw all my own emotions on her face as she read of my other-self's history. And her eyes widened as she read of "her" own death. When she finished, she lowered the pages to the table and stared at them.

"Wow." She shook her head and then looked up at me. "Ever since you told me about it, I've been trying to wrap my head around the idea of alternate universes, wondering if I had a double there, too." She frowned a little. "It's... very strange... to know she was murdered." She folded up the letter and looked into my eyes. "I remember yours, now that I think about it. She was here one night. Came up and ordered a drink, then sat at a corner table and stared at me for about an hour." She shook her head. "Creepy, but I'm used to the stares." She handed back the letter and I tucked it away.

Rachel reached over and squeezed my hand. I squeezed back and forced a smile. "Dinah, I know how traumatized you must be over all this. But I'm sensing there's more than that. What else is going on?"

I nodded, surprised by her perceptiveness. "The letter's disturbing on a lot of levels, but the thing that's bothering me most is that she was wrong."

"About what?"

I hesitated and looked into her eyes, so dark and inviting. I didn't want to say what I'd been feeling, because voicing the words aloud would be to admit the truth of them, to give them a verity I could deny if they existed only in my head. I looked down and gently removed my hand from hers, cradling my coffee instead. "About me," I said quietly. "About why I do what I do. Why I did what I did." I stopped, not wanting to say more.

"Go on," she prompted.

It was time, I told myself. So I took a deep breath. "When I was a kid, dreaming of becoming a meta, it wasn't so that I could be a hero. It was so I could show off. So I could be famous."

"Well, that's what most kids want. Attention. And that would be especially true for you, given the relationship between you and your parents."

"Yeah, I get that," I said. "Abandonment issues. Attachment disorders. I understand the underlying reasons, but it doesn't help. I've never gotten past it. Once my abilities manifested, I just looked forward to the fame I thought was inevitable." I felt a heaviness in my chest.

"I'm no shrink, but it seems to me that you *are* getting past it. Otherwise, we wouldn't be having this conversation." She took my hand again.

I lowered my eyes, quietly voicing the bottom line. "I'm a fraud, Rach, not a hero."

I looked up at her, guilty tears stinging, to see her almost scowling. "Bullshit," she said. "Dinah, I get that you wanted the fame. As someone who had it for a while, I know how great being famous can be. But what I don't get is why you say you aren't a hero." I stared at her, not knowing what to say, and wondering why she'd think otherwise. "When you were stuck in that other world or dimension or whatever it is... you said your constant concern was about your teammates, that you needed to find and rescue them. That's not what a fraud would have been thinking about."

"They're my friends. That's different."

"And if you'd been with complete strangers when you were abducted, you wouldn't have been worried about them, wouldn't have tried to rescue them?"

I paused. Truth was, I would have. "Just because I'm not heartless doesn't mean I'm a hero."

"Come on. You knew the dangers. You knew of their weapons and you were already injured. Despite this, you still did your best. That sounds like a hero to me."

"Well, it's nice that you think so," I said, "but real heroes don't seem to agree. Last time I saw the Maltese Falcon, all I wanted to do was show off my new costume and ability to fly." I shook my head. "He was right to be dismissive of me."

"So what you're saying is that you don't think you fit the definition of hero as he would define it." As I shrugged, she said, "What about the people you've saved? Think they'd call you a hero?"

"They might," I said, "unless they knew that I wasn't really doing it for them. I was doing it for me." I paused. "There are heroic actions and heroic intent. I might have one, but clearly, I lack the other."

We sat in silence as Rachel absorbed this. Then she glanced at the clock. "I need to get to work, hon." I stood as she came around to my side of the table. She gave me a quick kiss and attempted in vain to tickle me. "Dammit," she said. "One of these days, I'm gonna find your ticklish spot."

"Unlikely," I said as she headed to the bar. Then I stepped out into the cold January air and walked home, wondering what my own definition of hero really was and, as I'd been doing practically non-stop, dwelling on the experience I'd had.

There were so many questions swirling through my head. One of the most irritating was the question of the portals themselves. Our "side" of the portal was under government's watchful eye. Why, then, was the portal on the other side so lightly protected? Jack said there were only about fifteen of those paramilitary guys in the facility. Song learned it had been more heavily guarded before the attack by the other Valora and her group. They'd killed many, she said. And her double had disabled the communications equipment, making it impossible for them to call for reinforcements.

When I got home, I went online to research as much as I could about Groom Lake, DHS, and anything I could think of that would be remotely connected to it. I also checked my email for the first time in more than a month. Sitting in my inbox was a message from Dr. Gray. In all honesty, I'd completely forgotten about sending him the card and letter before the holidays. I opened his reply with a bit of trepidation. It was short:

"Thank you for the lovely card and holiday wishes. Happy New Year to you. And thank you for your trust in me. I completely understand why you didn't tell me sooner and certainly don't feel slighted. It must be terribly satisfying to have proven your ideas correct. I've been fascinated with your work ever since reading it, so many years ago. Someday, I hope we can discuss your work in detail. And while I know your activity as a costumed hero is important, I have to say the Bay Scouts' gain is science's loss."

And that was it. I can't say exactly how I was expecting him to react, but I know that wasn't it.

Dana spent his birthday in San Francisco with me. I was feeling pretty good, so we went out to dinner and a movie. I bought him a book on home brewing, as he'd begun making beer at a brew-on-premises place in Sacramento. He promised I'd get samples of every beer he made. That's my favorite kind of "re-gifting."

By the end of January, Daniel was in an outpatient rehabilitation program. He had a CNA who assisted him at home and took him around, including to the Bay Scouts base.

Even though I wasn't on active duty, I went to our headquarters often, and was there during Daniel's first visit. He and I sat in the kitchen drinking hot tea. His motor skills were compromised and he had to drink his tea through a straw, since his hands shook so much. He could get around with the aid of a walker, though he was in a wheelchair on this day. He could speak, but his lips sometimes didn't cooperate fully. Fortunately, his mental cognition seemed good. His mood, on the other hand, was poor.

We spoke of the FBI gag order. He wasn't happy about it, either, but understood the wisdom of it. Better than I did, apparently. Finally, we spoke about his recovery.

"I'm done," he said in a voice I almost didn't recognize. His vocal cords were weakened and his face quivered as he spoke. "Never fight again." I began to protest, but he shook his head. "Truth."

It was, and I knew it. No wonder he seemed depressed. The Bay Scouts was his team, his baby. He had been the undisputed leader of the group since its inception. And now he couldn't even be an active part of it. We had great health insurance through the Coast Guard, so he'd never have to worry about getting the care he needed. But that wasn't as important to him as being able to be Scoutmaster. He was passionate about his work. And to reinforce my conviction that I wasn't a hero, not only did I not share his passion, I didn't really understand it.

"What 'bout you?" he said. "Troubled."

I nodded and, at his urging, explained to him everything I'd said to Rachel. "I'm not a hero," I said quietly, wrapping it up.

When I was done, he looked at me with a hint of a smile. "No," he said simply.

My first reaction was shock, with a little indignation. But then I just nodded. "I didn't realize I was that transparent," I said.

"Falcon," Daniel said.

I grimaced. "Yeah, he's never thought much of me."

He barked a laugh. "Sent you to me."

"I figured he did that to get me out of his neighborhood," I half-joked.

Daniel smiled, then sobered quickly. He sipped his tea. "You'll find it," he said. "Someday."

"Find... what?"

He looked me in the eye and smiled lopsidedly. "You'll know."

I frowned at him. I hate cryptic crap like that.

Four weeks after my surgery, I had a follow-up appointment with my doctor. He examined my X-ray with surprise. "And you say you have no pain?"

"I feel great," I said again. "Not even a twinge."

"Broken ribs," he said, "especially full breaks like yours, normally take much longer to fully heal. Not to mention punctured lungs." He turned away from the image of my ribcage and placed a stethoscope against my back, instructing me to breathe deeply. After a few such breaths, he stood. "Breathing sounds good," he said, tucking the business end of the stethoscope into his jacket pocket. "This is pretty remarkable, Dinah. You've healed in approximately half the time it would normally take." He shrugged as he said, "But one thing I've learned over the years is that, when it comes to treating metas, the expectations we learned in med school often go right out the window." He picked up a clipboard and scribbled his signature on the release form that would allow me to return to active duty without voiding my insurance coverage.

Not that I really had much in the way of active duty to return to. Because of recent events, including Daniel's physical state, we weren't being given any assignments. This didn't bother some members. Sinta was quite content to operate solo. Jack spent his time doing research. Song was wrapped up in a personal project that she wasn't talking about. Esteban and the twins had become withdrawn, still quite shaken by our experience. And Valora made no secret that she wanted command of the team, now that Daniel was effectively out of the picture.

I had no valid reason for not thinking Valora wouldn't be a decent leader for the team, if she could keep her ego in check. Even so, I didn't want to see her in charge. She seemed to have a sense of entitlement, as though she deserved the unswerving respect of others, and maybe the right to boss them around. And I didn't like being bossed around.

One piece of The Letter that kept nagging at me was the urge to get to know Sinta. The truth is, I knew virtually nothing about her. For that matter, I knew little about any of my teammates, and that was mostly intentional.

I knew Sinta had been born with her physical appearance. I knew she hated being referred to as a catgirl. I knew she had no living relatives. I knew she and I shared the same birthday and that she would be turning fifteen this year. I knew she had Type A-positive blood and that she was allergic to shellfish. But I knew these things because I'd read her personnel file, not because I'd asked her. I'd never asked anything personal of any of my teammates. And it wasn't because I respected their privacy. It was because I never cared to know more than the basics.

It was like my father and his baseball fixation. He could tell you the batting averages of just about anyone on the Pittsburgh Pirates, but had no interest in knowing what the pitcher's favorite beer was. It wasn't relevant to his enjoyment of the game. Knowing Sinta's favorite pizza toppings wouldn't help me appreciate her any more as a teammate, I reasoned.

Dana disagreed. "Look," he said. "Dad may not need to know what the pitcher's favorite beer is, but I'll bet you his coach knows. Dinah, your teammates aren't just pictures and statistics in magazines, now. They're flesh and blood. They're your partners... the people you're entrusting to protect your life, just as they do with you. I'd think you'd want to know as much about them as possible."

We were strolling through the shops on Fisherman's Wharf, weaving through the weekend tourist crowd. Dana had come down early in the day and taken me to brunch for my thirty-fifth birthday. He frowned, then muttered, "I hate what they did to you."

"Who?" I asked.

"Mom and Dad," he said bitterly. "You were such a caring kid before they hurt you." I frowned. I didn't recall being particularly caring, but who really does remember their personality at six years old? "I guess part of that is my fault, though," he said.

"How do you figure?"

"I should have been more careful in keeping my abilities secret. If they hadn't found out, maybe you and Mom could have had a good relationship."

"Only until she found out about my sexual preferences," I pointed out.

"Well... yeah," he conceded. "But that was later. Those formative years wouldn't have been so fucked up. You wouldn't have become so alienated."

I blinked in surprise. "Why do you think I'm alienated?"

"Seriously?" he said. "You don't see it?"

"I don't."

"Well, you distance yourself from people, for one thing."

"Only those who deserve it," I said, then amended, "or that I mistakenly think deserve it." I smiled apologetically at him.

"Really? How many close friends do you have?"

"Plenty," I said, growing more defensive by the moment.

"How many?"

"Well, how many do *you* have?"

"This is about you, not me. But I have about twenty close friends, six of whom I consider extremely close." He looked at me almost accusingly. "Do you even have one?"

I wanted to yell at him, to say that I most certainly did have close friends. But I couldn't, since it wasn't true. Dana was my closest friend...

really, my only friend... and he knew it. So I dropped it and steered us into the Ghirardelli store.

Chocolate wasn't enough to take the conversation from my head, though. So that night, after Dana left for Sacramento, I packed up the rest of the birthday cupcakes he'd brought, hopped on the Muni, and went to Sinta's apartment. Or, I should say, Daniel's apartment. He owned the place. Being a minor, Sinta couldn't sign a lease. Daniel let her stay there for free.

She answered the door wearing a baggy Star Wars T-shirt with the text written in Japanese, a pair of red running shorts, and SpongeBob slippers. As expected, she was surprised to see me. "Hi," I said, holding out the tray of cupcakes. "Happy Birthday!"

Sinta beamed after an initial look of disbelief. "Happy Birthday to you, too," she said, inviting me inside. I looked around her living room as she took the cupcakes and placed them on a small coffee table, then went to the kitchen to make tea.

It was a small place, but perfectly suited for one. Especially for a person who led as simple a life as Sinta. There was a bookcase, but no more than a couple dozen books on its shelves. A laptop computer sat open on her dining room table. A modest television faced a worn loveseat with a patchwork quilt thrown over the back.

I sat down on the loveseat as she returned. She set the tea on the coffee table, then hopped up to sit sideways, facing me. "I really shouldn't," she said, as she bit happily into the cupcake.

I snorted. "Like you're in any danger of getting fat," I said, taking one for myself.

She swallowed, shaking her head. "Not that. Sugar amps me up like crack for other people. I get all bouncy and jittery." She smiled, and I couldn't help but smile back, her grin being that infectious. "You want to ask me about your double," she said suddenly. Surprised at her directness, I hesitated, then nodded. "I thought she was nice. I mean, I guess she was strange, but..." She wiped frosting from the fur around her mouth. "She was nice to me."

"She liked you very much," I said.

Sinta cocked her head like an inquisitive kitten. "How do you know?"

"She left me a note." I smiled softly. "She said I should get to know you... and I realized she was right. I figured our birthday was a good time to start."

And in the hours that followed, I did get to know her. I learned that Sinta had grown up being shuffled from foster home to foster home, being met with ridicule and torment wherever she went, both from members of the foster families as well as children in the various schools she attended. Some was just verbal bullying, but occasionally it became physical. Kids throwing rocks at her, foster parents "disciplining" her.

She pulled down the neck of her shirt, revealing a thin line that ran over her left collarbone, extending down between her breasts. No fur grew there. "Is that a scar?"

"Mm hm," she said. "From a chainsaw blade. He used it as a whip. I left him much deeper scars, though." She said this with a shrug, nonchalantly licking frosting from another cupcake. "Wish I hadn't, though," she said.

"What? Why?" I said, astonished. "After he did that to you?"

"Well... mean people are usually ones who had others be mean to them," she explained. "I didn't need to add to that." I knew enough about psychology and sociology to know she was correct. But looking at that long line of scar tissue and imagining a child being whipped... I just didn't care. "Anyway, that's the night I left," she concluded.

At the age of eleven, she ran away, living on the streets for the next year, mainly in the Financial District, where she scored handouts of leftovers from the many different restaurants, and stopped the occasional purse snatcher or other petty criminal. One such action caught the notice of another meta, a friend of Scoutmaster's. In short order, she was on the Bay Scouts roster and living in this apartment.

I felt more humbled with each passing minute. This girl had more than enough reason to distrust anyone and everyone, but was instead filled with kindness and compassion, with a level of maturity I didn't possess, in some ways.

Riding home on the train, I stared out the windows at the city's populace and mentally compared myself to Sinta, feeling inferior in almost every conceivable way. Her childhood was worse than mine, by far. How did she not turn out bitter? Why did she choose to help strangers when no one had helped her? Was she that special, or was I the oddity? Were the majority of those people on the streets as understanding as Sinta? Did I have more in common with the ones I fought against than those I fought beside?

I walked home from my stop, feeling more of a fraud than ever. I felt empty inside and displaced. I didn't belong here in the city. I suddenly hated the noise, the smells, the closeness. In my apartment, I sat in the darkness, staring at the walls until I fell asleep in my chair, my brain torturing me with shameful memories.

Backstage, again, still flying from my performance covering Rose Royce's awesome disco/funk tune. Mrs. Martin hustles us all away from the back curtain and I smile up at her expectantly, waiting for her praise.

She smiles faintly at me and says, "Very good, Dinah."

She turns to the other girls, the backup singers and dancers. "You all were wonderful!" she says, and my spirit is crushed. They were "wonderful" and I was only "very good"?

I look at the others, their faces beaming from our teacher's words. I resent them for the rest of the school year.

I had taken to visiting Daniel at his home whenever I had time. His speech was improving, but his mobility was not. He still had the CNA helping him, though he did have a spiffier motorized wheelchair, now.

On one of my visits, we sat in his modest living room over tea. I was bemoaning my financial problems. While on our unofficial suspension, the Bay Scouts kept drawing a basic stipend, but it was nowhere near our active duty pay. I'd scrambled to add as many bartending shifts as I could, but was still struggling to make ends meet.

"Bounty... hunter," was Daniel's unexpected suggestion.

"I thought you didn't approve of such activities."

Daniel managed a shrug. "Not for... me." He smiled lopsidedly. "Falcon can give... contacts."

I nodded, considering this. It was, after all, how many metas unaffiliated with teams managed to make a living.

"Spoke with... Shepherd," Daniel said, changing the subject. "President... considering deploying metas... to Iraq."

I sighed. It was a subject that had been raised in political circles for years. Ever since Saddam Hussein's capture, the public had been calling for a withdrawal of forces from the Middle East. But, if anything, the war was escalating. "Think it'll happen?" I asked.

"Shepherd... is concerned. So... maybe."

I'd never paid a lot of attention to the war. Hell, I'd never paid attention to much that didn't directly affect or interest me. Current events were just trivia I could ignore. I smirked at Daniel. "I think you're safe from the draft."

He chuckled hoarsely. "You, too. Old woman."

I snorted, but was glad he had his sense of humor back.

We chatted for a while longer before I headed home.

Money wasn't the only concern I had. Another was the fact that gene therapy often needed additional treatments... sort of like "booster shots." It had been six and a half years since my first treatment and three years since its effects came to fruition. I was overdue for the second stage.

But I needed a lab. I knew Jack would happily offer me space and time in his labs, but he was a physicist. He wouldn't have sequencers, polymerase chain reaction equipment, and so on. Normally, my attachment to a government organization would have gotten me at least a foot in the door to a research facility, but my requests were all met with dead silence. So I turned to the one source that might be able to help me: Dr. Gray. I still couldn't bring myself to call him, so I sent an email to explain my needs.

"Let me see what I can do," was his simple reply.

I emailed my thanks and spent a while surfing the web for the latest in biotechnology news. I usually ignore the ads that clutter the news pages, but this day, one caught my eye. It was for a company that sold metabolic enhancers and a variety of supplements for bodybuilders, athletes, and people ashamed of their bodies. The picture accompanying the ad was of an emaciated kid looking in a mirror at an imagined muscular version of himself. The reflection was, inexplicably, a few inches taller, too. I wondered how a supplement was supposed to accomplish that. But as I stared at the bony kid in the picture, an idea struck me. I clicked through and was taken to the company's site, where I found the contact information I needed.

A week later, I sat in a meeting with that company's Vice President of Development and a couple of his senior staff. I pitched Dynapaste to them as a potential product. The science boys looked over the paperwork I'd provided and examined the sample I'd brought.

It was another week before they decided to license it. After negotiations were finalized, they had non-exclusive rights to the formula for the next five years. Our contract stipulated that my use of the formula would not be used in any way that would compete with their product line.

I walked away with a check for half a million dollars, one free case of the product per month, and the guarantee of five percent of net sales of the product. Not bad for negotiating without an attorney.

Once I received that check, though, I did call an attorney... the one who'd defended me in the GACTech case. I asked her to contact them to renegotiate my payments. A large lump sum, I figured, should reduce the amount I was paying monthly, or at least the amount of time I'd be repaying.

A week later, to my amazement, she called me back and said GACTech was willing to accept the half-million (which she was careful to say I may or may not have... this was all hypothetical) as payment in full. At the rate I'd been paying them back, it would have been another twenty years for them be paid off. Apparently, their immediate gratification was worth reducing the debt by a ridiculous amount.

To add frosting to that particular cake, she refused to charge me for the negotiation. "It was no big deal," she said. "I'm just happy to see this finally end for you."

I thanked her again and said goodbye.

The next day, I mailed off a certified check to settle my account with GACTech. Easy come, easy go. The sense of relief as the clerk took the registered letter from my hands was almost overwhelming.

After leaving the post office, I returned to the nutrition company to renegotiate the contract we'd so recently signed. They were, understandably, prepared to tell me to go climb my thumb. But when I told them I wanted to relinquish my claim to some residual profits, they gave me an audience.

In the meeting, I exchanged half of my royalties for the guarantee that Dynapaste would be sold at no more than five percent above production cost to any hospital in the country for their use in helping patients suffering from anorexia, other eating disorders, or any form of malnutrition. The company's marketing director loved the idea.

I slept very well that night.

EIGHTEEN

"Painful as it may be, a significant emotional event can be the catalyst for choosing a direction that serves us – and those around us – more effectively."
~ Louisa May Alcott

In May of 2006, *Nature* magazine published the final sequence of human DNA, the chromosome we call "number one." It's a treasure trove of genetic information, comprising eight percent of all genes in our DNA (out of 22 chromosomes, not counting the X and Y sex chromosomes). It contains two hundred forty-six million base pairs of genes, compared to only forty-nine million in chromosome twenty-two. Chromosome one's genes hold secrets to probably three or four hundred human diseases, from cataracts to prostate cancer.

This was, of course, fascinating to me. But the bulk of my focus had always been on the first significant part of the genome to be sequenced: mitochondrial DNA, the home of energy production. That and the elusive "meta gene."

The truth is, there isn't a "meta gene." Rather, what we call the "meta gene" is the combination of different genetic mutations that give rise to meta abilities. Which genes are included in this combination? Well, that depends on which abilities have been produced. The mutated genes of someone who has super-dense flesh and increased muscular strength will be a different combination from that of someone who has the ability to move objects telekinetically. If nothing else, the advent of metahumans and their abilities showed us in no uncertain terms that we didn't understand even remotely what amazing things we were capable of, if our genes were changed in certain ways.

Thinking about this, about the process I went through, brought to mind the letter my double had left me, of how that world's Valora forced her to use her process on others, and the horrendous results that came of it. I'd been puzzling over that, ever since, wondering why she couldn't make it work, wondering if I'd have the same bad results. I'd mulled this over frequently, and I wasn't liking the conclusion to which those thoughts were leading.

Not that I would ever get the chance to test my hypothesis. Our country had become so frightened of metas that, two years earlier, it slammed through a piece of legislation forcing hospitals to test newborns for the "meta gene." It hadn't mattered that scientists told them there wasn't a specific meta gene. Lawmakers (and the public) don't care about facts when fear is in the air. So the legislation passed and, in short order, a huge number of babies were identified as having "meta potential."

This meant little, though. Even if an infant had all the component mutations, it didn't mean they'd necessarily develop any abilities. It takes something more, something to light the figurative fuse to set off the explosion of meta abilities. It's like any other genetic trait. A person could inherit all the faulty genes that make him or her prone to a particular cancer, for example, yet live a long life free from it completely. Or an obese person who inherits a predisposition to high blood pressure and cholesterol can die at ninety years of age without ever having a heart attack. It takes something else, a catalyst, to set in motion major change.

"I'm leaving Penn State," Dr. Gray told me on the phone one day.

"Wow. Why?" I asked.

"QB3 is starting up a new program this year," he said. QB3 is the California Institute for Quantitative Biosciences, which is part of the University of California. It's devoted mainly to biomedical research. Exciting stuff, really. "The Synthetic Biology Engineering Research Center. SynBERC, for short. I'm going to be part of it."

"No kidding? That's fantastic!" Technically, the work I'd done on myself could be considered synthetic biology, since it was a tweaking of an existing system to obtain a specific result. "When do you start?"

"August first," he said. "I'll be living over in Berkeley. I'll be moving in mid-July."

"I'm not helping you unpack."

"Fine. I'll fly you out so you can do the packing."

"Not a chance," I laughed. "Well, congratulations, and I guess I'll see you in a month!"

"Dinah," he said, "once I get established there, it's likely that I'll be needing an assistant."

That caught me off-guard. "Wow. Um... I really appreciate the thought, but... you know... with the Scouts and all..."

"Right," he said. "It was just a thought."

I thanked him again and we hung up. And I immediately questioned why I'd dismissed the idea so quickly. Hadn't I been bemoaning the lack of facilities and equipment needed to check my DNA and tweak again, if needed? Talk about an opportunity falling into my lap.

After berating myself for turning down his offer so quickly, I shot off an email to him:

"I'll think about it. Thanks."

My life has been filled more than most, I think, with anticipation. As a little girl, I eagerly awaited the onset of puberty, so that my meta abilities would reveal themselves. At sixteen, I looked forward to the day when my brother would become famous with his own abilities. After becoming a registered meta, I looked forward to being "discovered" and enjoying overnight fame. And pretty much my entire life, I've been hoping for a mother who would love me.

My father, however, had a number of favorite expressions, one of which was, "Don't get your hopes up too high." I know he never meant it in a pessimistic way. He just didn't want me to be devastated when my dreams didn't come true.

And dreams seldom do come true. Nature didn't make me a meta. Dana chose a different path and wouldn't be famous. I was still mostly unknown. And mother was probably still a bitch.

Eventually, I learned that dreams have a better chance of coming true if you actually do something to help them. I gave myself meta abilities. Dana could have been famous if that was the path he'd wanted to take. My own fame would come only when I deserved it. And my relationship with my mother? Like the reconnection with Dana, maybe all I needed to do was make an effort.

So I was going home. And by that, I mean the town I grew up in... the house I grew up in.

"Fifteen and a half years," Dana had said during his last visit.

The number couldn't be right, I thought. I'd poured coffee for us and walked into the living room from my kitchen. Fine, so it *had* been that long. I conceded the accuracy of his memory. "So?" I said.

"So I think it's high time you go," he said, accepting the coffee. "The Scouts are still on hiatus; you're not really doing much. And you know how much you love the Fourth of July, there."

Dana was going home for his twenty-fifth year high school reunion, which I found weird, since he hated high school. But he hadn't missed a reunion, yet. "I don't know…"

He reached into his shirt pocket and pulled out a round-trip ticket, dropping it on the coffee table. "I'm going to be out there for a conference in Pittsburgh a couple weeks before, so I'm just going to stick around. But you should come."

I picked up the ticket envelope and looked inside. July first to eighth. Dana was right about the holiday. Our home town does a big celebration on the Fourth. Art shows, barbecues, classic car shows, and of course, a great fireworks display.

He also gave me a check to pay for a rental car and whatever else I needed. "Thanks," I told him. "I'll think about it."

And I did.

I don't like long flights, so I changed the ticket Dana had bought me. I took a red-eye out of the city and slept on the plane. I landed in Pittsburgh sometime after ten the next morning and rented a car. Home is still about a hundred miles or so up Route 28, which is actually Main Street there. The drive is through the rolling hills of western Pennsylvania and it gave me a solid two hours in which to think. Mostly what I did was remember… key events of the past… major emotional periods. It had been so long.

I often try to remember good times about my life at home… and I can. But they're fairly shallow. I remember festive times. Birthday parties. Easter egg hunts. Picnics on Memorial Day, the Fourth of July, and Labor Day. Thanksgiving dinners and football on TV. Carols and presents at Christmas.

The same things every other person remembers, typically.

But I always think of stories. Other peoples' stories. Stories Lee told me. Stories my teammates told me. Stories of real family closeness, of sharing in each other's joys and successes, fears and failures.

I have none of those. Not past a certain age, anyway. Eight or nine, maybe. After that, Mom and Dad stopped heaping praise for my report cards. Now, of course, I realize this was around the time my folks would have learned of Dana's telepathic abilities and Mom got deeply into religion. She'd always been active in church, but then she discovered television evangelists. Billy Graham, Jimmy Swaggart, Jim Bakker, Jerry Falwell, Pat Robertson, Benny Hinn… She never cares when one of them is caught with his pants down, or his hands in the cookie jars… these are holy men, righteous men, and God would forgive them, so everyone else should, too, gosh darn it.

There were, to be fair, bits of sanity that would creep in. Usually when she'd transition from one huckster to the next, there would be a period of a few weeks in between… a period when I'd get a phone call that wasn't laced with condemnations about my lifestyle choices and pleas to allow God into my life again. A phone call where she actually sounded like I always figured a mother should sound. Concerned. Caring. But they weren't enough. A year of abuse can't be erased by a week of kindness. Not for me, anyway.

Dwelling on the past made the drive go quickly, but it put me in a pretty foul mood. The closer I got to town, the more I was inclined to just turn around and go somewhere else. Anywhere else.

It was around one in the afternoon when I arrived. It was a beautiful day, in the mid-'70s. I was glad it wasn't oppressively hot and humid, as it so often was in the summer. Even so, it was warmer than I was used to in San Francisco.

I was a bit surprised to receive hugs from both parents when I walked in. Then I felt guilty for feeling surprised. Did I really think they cared so little for me? Then another surprise hit me. They looked so much older. Of course, they *were* so much older. Fifteen years, I reminded myself. That's a big chunk of life. To be fair, they stared at me with equal astonishment. I guess they'd never seen a picture of me with white hair.

I took my luggage upstairs, where I found surprise number three. My old bedroom waited for me, looking much the same as it had when I was a teenager. It seemed so ridiculously small, now. I couldn't believe I'd spent so much time there, curled up on the bed, reading magazines, listening to the stereo, wishing to be allowed to have a phone in my room.

I unpacked, then joined the folks downstairs. Dana was out with one of his high school buddies, they told me. We talked for a bit. The conversation was subdued, superficial. They asked no questions about my life. No surprise, there. They'll never ask how my love life is, since it's "that kind" of love. They'll never ask about my "job," since it would only remind them that their daughter is an "abomination."

So I answered questions about San Francisco and the weather there. We talked about politics, which bored me to tears, but it beat the weather.

Dana got home around four and immediately headed up to take a shower. We had dinner around five, which was only two in the afternoon to my California-tuned stomach, but was still fine with me. I'm always hungry. Mother took note of how much I ate, making a subtly snide comment about my weight. It's as though she still saw my heavy teenage body instead of the athletic adult one.

After dinner, Dad collapsed into his recliner and opened the newspaper to the crossword puzzle. As always. Mom did the dishes, then settled in to watch *Wheel of Fortune* and *Jeopardy*. Again, as always.

I went for a walk.

My home town is small... about 2000 people, give or take. Seven churches and as many bars. Not sure if there's a correlation there or not.

The street where I grew up is a cul-de-sac, nestled between railroad tracks on the west and a diked creek on the east. A great analogy for how I felt there… hemmed in on all sides with no way out but the way you came in.

I walked past the houses of childhood friends, none of whom lived there, anymore. I idly wondered where they ended up. We all drifted apart after high school. No… it wasn't that we drifted; it was that I ran away, turning my back on this little borough, my eyes set on larger, less rural, settings.

On Main Street, I turned west, crossing the railroad tracks before the road's gentle rise to "uptown." Many of the businesses I remembered had closed, some due to the economy, some due to the retirement or deaths of the owners of these little mom and pop operations.

On the opposite side of the road, just past the tracks, was a credit union. But when I was a kid, the building was a diner. I remember Dana taking me there for hot chocolate on cold winter days, and another time losing a loose tooth on some breaded "cutlet" thing.

Those were the days, I realized, that I treasured. Early childhood. Before mother's xenophobic prejudices alienated us. Before Dana had gone off to college. Back when we still felt like a family.

But it wasn't just that. In those days, in this bucolic little borough, people didn't lock their doors. Parents never worried about bad things happening to their children. If they were gone for three hours on a bike ride around town, it wasn't a big deal. I don't know if it truly was, but it always felt safe, there.

I continued walking through the business district. The stores, though, were almost all different from those in my memory. When I was little, there was a tiny shop where we could buy hot peanuts in the shell and fresh popcorn. I have no recollection of whatever else they might have sold. The variety store was closed, where my teenaged self would purchase my magazines and 45-rpm records. The five and ten was gone, too, as was the Rexall where I'd worked. This surprised me, as it had always been such a fixture. So many new businesses. An Asian restaurant. A thrift store. Gone were the men's clothing store, the butcher, and the furniture store. My dentist's office was still there, but his son's name was on the window, now. Across the street had been the barber shop where I'd watched Dana get haircuts. Now it was a gift shop. Everything else there seemed new, too. I found myself oddly depressed.

Memories came and went during my walk, but it wasn't until I crossed back over to the east side of the tracks that nostalgia hit me really hard. And it was a smell that did it. That mix of fresh, unpolluted air graced with the aroma of baking pizza… I can't believe how much it affects me, even today. It was at this moment that I knew just how firmly I was tied to this town, despite all the changes. Even if I never live there again, even if I never feel comfortable in my parents' house, I know it will always be "home."

I stepped inside Josephine's, my old pizza haunt, where we'd gather to play pinball and video games. It was larger, now, having expanded into the building that used to be the dry cleaner. And it was a bar now, too. I don't know how old the place was. It had been around long before Dana was born. Josephine herself had passed before I ever met her. The place was now run by her grandson, I soon learned. That explained why it now had a liquor license, I thought cynically. Of course a *guy* would take it in that direction.

I grabbed a stool and ordered a slice and a Dr Pepper. I ate the pizza at heat lamp temperature, as I often did when I was a teen. For some reason, I liked it better that way.

Boys barely old enough to purchase the drinks in their hands checked me out. I watched them from behind my mirrored sunglasses, unsure what to make of this unfamiliar woman with the shocking white hair and toned bod. I smiled to myself, imagining how they'd react if they knew what tortures kept me in this shape. And then I questioned it, myself, thinking of all the bruises, the concussion, the blisters, the broken rib and punctured lung...

I glanced at the boys again and repositioned myself on the stool, my leather duster falling open, giving them a good look. It wasn't teasing, exactly. Or maybe it was.

It was hot inside, with the pizza oven going. It reminded me of the muggy summers spent wishing in vain that we'd finally get air conditioning in our house. At least in the biting cold winters, I could always put on more clothes. There are only so many layers you can remove to beat the heat.

I glanced out the door, which hung open for ventilation. It was getting dark, so I dropped a tip and headed out, ignoring the eyes that followed me. As soon as I was free of inquisitive stares, I took to the sky, to fly my concerns away.

I'd never before seen my town from the air. It was slightly disconcerting. Everything I remembered, all the landmarks, took on a completely different sense. It was darkening and I couldn't see much, but I flew over the small playground, the swimming pool, the Little League field. I watched cars cruising up and down Main Street and took in the view of roads illuminated by street lamps and porch lights. I flew higher and soon could hear nothing beyond the susurration of energy dispersing from my body to keep me aloft.

I'd missed the quiet of this town. Since leaving, I'd lived in much more populated areas, from a large university town to the city on the bay. The noise of human activity was pervasive there, but here, a person could have the peace to think. In my case, my thinking had been about how to get away from this town, away from my family, away from who I was, in the hopes of becoming someone new.

I looked at my hands, fingers spread, pulsing wide sprays of energy.

Mission accomplished.

The following days were much like the first. Mom and Dad treated me not as a guest, but as though I'd been there all along. In other words, they didn't pay much attention to me at all. Dana spent most of his time away from the house. I knew he was hanging out with lots of friends who were similarly only home for the reunion or the holiday, but I know he was also wanting to give me a chance to connect with our folks. I just didn't know where to begin with them. I was hoping things would heal all by themselves.

They didn't seem to want to make an effort more than I did. They kept to their routine of the same conversations, and every night, the same game shows, followed by either "reality TV" or whatever variant of *CSI* happened to be on.

On the morning of the fourth, I sat in the living room, looking over the brochure of Independence Day events. "So what all are you going to, today?" I asked my parents.

"Oh, nothing," Mother said. "Just the fireworks."

"Really? What about the parade?"

She shook her head. "It's gonna rain."

"Old-Timer's Baseball Game, Dad?"

"Maybe... if it don't rain," he said from his recliner.

I frowned. He never missed the game. Sometimes, he was an umpire. And Mother loved the parade.

I didn't try to figure out what was behind their unexpected replies, deciding I'd made enough of an effort at connecting with them for one day, and headed out into the activities.

Stepping outside, I was immediately struck by the smell of chicken cooking on the barbecue. Wisps of white smoke rose from the other side of the creek, the huge cookout courtesy of the Kaimann Club. This and the other concessions were gathered in the parking lot of the football field.

As I strolled through the concession area, munching on soft pretzel nuggets and other goodies, I watched people. I had my hair pulled back in a ponytail and wore my sunglasses to make the observation less apparent. I wandered from the food area to the tiny craft show, to the car show, watching people all the while. And there were a lot of them. The festivities drew people from all around, adding about fifteen thousand people to the two thousand who lived there.

In the huge crowd, I didn't draw a lot of attention. I didn't recognize anyone. This surprised me a little. I blamed it on the fact that most of the people I encountered were from other towns, rather than the fact that I was eighteen years out of high school.

As it turns out, it didn't rain on the parade. I stood in my traditional spot, where our street intersects with Main Street, just near the tracks. And I watched the marching bands, the gymnasts, cheerleaders, and color guard;

the displays of police cars, fire/rescue vehicles, and farm machinery; the stream of elected officials in their cars, the troops of Girl and Boy Scouts, and of course, the clowns and animals.

I didn't spend much time looking at the people, but plenty of them stared at me, especially the adults. The kids were too intent on candy being tossed from the fire trucks and floats. No one asked for an autograph, though.

The fireworks were just as great as I remembered. Dana and I sat on the dike across the road from our house and watched them explode overhead. It was like we were kids again, smiling and laughing as the rockets burst and we felt the concussions. Our folks watched from chairs on our lawn, almost as though they didn't want to be with us.

The next day, I drove into the neighboring "city," ten miles away. It's a city only by virtue of having ten thousand people, barely making city status when the census is done. But it has a mall, anyway, and even though the selections are slim and the prices are higher than they should be, it was still a break from the monotony.

It was 2006, but you wouldn't know it by walking through the mall. It was as though the entire place got stuck twenty years in the past. Men sported mullets and 80s hair band shirts. Probably originals, rather than retro reproductions. Women had "mall hair" and wore legwarmers. I found it mildly disturbing.

I bought a couple new outfits, a pair of slingbacks, and some CDs, then decided to get an ice cream cone. The ice cream counter faces the main mall area. It was crowded, with nearly a dozen people waiting in nothing resembling a line. One woman waiting stared at me the whole time my cone was being put together, her face pointed toward a magazine in her hands, but her eyes betraying her voyeurism. Finally, I got my cone and was putting my change in my purse when the woman stepped over to me. Her voice was soft, tentative. "Dinah?"

I was shocked. I didn't expect to be recognized. I hadn't been home in a long time, and I sure didn't look like I did when I lived there. I was wearing the shades, too, which, though obviously not enough to hide my identity, should have been enough to hide my surprise as I looked at her. I was hoping they hid my confusion, too, because I had no idea who this lady was. She was probably about forty or so. Some friend of Dana's, I assumed.

"It *is* you," she said, and I couldn't tell whether she was happy to see me or not. Her voice had a strange tone to it. "A scoop of Pistachio and a scoop of Black Cherry... you always got that."

Now that weirded me out. No friend of Dana's would know my ice cream habits. I fought down the discomfort, smiled faintly, and nodded, reaching up to remove my sunglasses. "It's me," I confirmed, and paused, hoping she'd take the hint.

Mercifully, she told me her name, and I was even more astounded. It was Rhonda, my childhood friend. I voiced my surprise, asked her how she'd been and all that, as we stepped away from the crowd and into the wide hallway. As she spoke, I wondered to myself how she became so old. I did the quick assessment and surmised nearly everything she said, before she said it. Ring on her finger. Kids, too, because... well... that's just what you do when you live there. And of course, she gave it all to me in recitation. Married. Three kids. Divorced. Remarried. Two step-kids. Oldest was...

"What?" I blurted, hoping I misheard her.

She smiled. Her oldest was starting college in the fall. She may have *looked* old, but now she was making me *feel* it. I wanted to beg her to tell me she was just kidding, that her oldest child was maybe ten, at most... that she didn't really get knocked up at seventeen, like those trampy girls we used to talk shit about. But instead, she turned the conversation around to me. Her hand was to her mouth, and her eyes were, to my amazement, welling with tears. "Dinah... I thought you were dead."

"What?" I repeated. "Why?"

There was an explosion, her mom had told her, years ago... and I was caught in it. It was bad. A laboratory or something. I nodded, but corrected the story. No explosion... at least, I don't think so. But I asked her why she thought I was dead.

She blinked, shaking her head in puzzlement. "Because that's what your mother told mine."

The shocks kept getting bigger and bigger. I was beyond stunned by this bit of information. She had to be mistaken. Mother and I might not be close... she might disapprove of my "orientation" and my "profession," but she wouldn't... she couldn't...

There was a long silence, while I took this in, and Rhonda stared at me apologetically while ice cream dripped all over my hand. Suddenly sick to my stomach, I pitched the cone into the trash. I felt like I was either going to cry or throw up. Maybe both.

My hand was sticky, and without another word, I walked down the hall to the rest rooms. Inside, I rinsed my shaky hands in the sink and suddenly my legs wouldn't support me, anymore. I crumpled to the floor, pitching up against the wall. Sobs heaved from me as I finally realized just how deeply my mother was embarrassed of me. She'd tell her neighbors and acquaintances that I was dead rather than run the risk of them learning that I'm either gay or a metahuman or both.

How sick and twisted was that? How could she even look me in the eye? How could my father put up with it? Did he feel the same way? Did all his old cronies feel sorry for poor Richard, who lost his daughter in a lab explosion over in Bellefonte?

I wiped tears away, the sobs abating, and saw Rhonda standing there. She looked probably as bad as I felt. I climbed to my feet and she wrapped her arms around me. I returned the embrace, thrusting this new revelation out of my head, remembering instead my days as a pre-teen, playing with the child version of this woman... Barbies and Parcheesi and Chinese Checkers and Old Maid. She was my best friend for about five years, up until we were fourteen. Why did that end, again?

And then I remembered, and my heart skipped a beat. I broke from the comforting hug and held her at arm's length. I looked at her face, the memory surfacing. I removed my hands from her shoulders and folded my arms across my chest. And her sympathetic look faded, to be replaced with one of self-conscious guilt.

"Sometimes," she said softly, "kids can be heartless and mean. Even to their friends."

I took a deep breath, accepting the truth of these simple words. She was right, of course. I had only to look at my behavior toward my own brother. Compared to that, her betrayal of my trust, by telling others at school that I thought I might like girls, was nothing. Not to mention compared to spreading false rumors of a daughter's death.

So I nodded, with a sigh. She apologized, and of course, I accepted. We hugged again, and though it was a bit strained this time, it was all good.

"How long are you in town for?" she asked as we walked together back out into the mall.

"Just a few more days," I said. "I need to get back to San Francisco."

"Wow. You must have a good job to afford that!" Then Rhonda reached out and tousled my ponytail. "How do you get it so white? It looks so natural."

"Oh, well..." And then I noticed her eyes growing a little bigger.

I really wasn't ready to take another shock.

"San Francisco!" she blurted, practically beside herself. She pulled out and opened the magazine she'd been reading before and thrust it toward me, her finger pointing to a photo.

It was *Supers* magazine. The photo was a paparazzi pic of a memorial service in Golden Gate Park for a fallen hero. Rhonda looked at me, pointing to a white-haired woman in the crowd. "You're a meta!" she said, the caption of the photo naming the woman in the picture.

It wasn't me, I told her. And it wasn't. It was another San Francisco meta who just happens to look a fair bit like me, white hair and all. Others have remarked on it. But Rhonda looked at me skeptically as she flicked her gaze between me and the picture.

I hesitated a moment, then opened my purse. "However," I said, and handed her my meta registration card. She looked it over. As her eyes widened again, I allowed myself to smile a little.

She began with the deluge of questions, acting like a star-struck schoolgirl. I saw in this a hint of the friend I remembered. But I begged off. I wasn't in the mood. We exchanged phone numbers. I promised to call her before I left town. We hugged again, and I headed "home."

There are no words, really, to sum up the explosion that occurred when I confronted my mother. I just lit into her, calling her every name in the book. I verbally eviscerated this woman, who sat there and said virtually nothing the entire time. And it wasn't only the "my daughter's dead" thing. It was a venting of a quarter century of hurt and resentment.

I flashed back to the last time I exploded on this woman, on the day I smugly told her I was a godless, lesbian, wannabe meta. And I expected her to argue back. I expected hellfire and damnation. I expected righteous indignation. Or even another slap across the face.

But I got none of that. Instead, I got a woman so wracked with guilt that she was incapable of opening her mouth to defend herself. And I took full advantage. By the time I finished, she was a quivering mess.

And then I learned a few things. Between occasional sobs, she vomited out a string of apology and explanation. She didn't mean to say I was dead. But she couldn't bring herself to explain the truth. Inexplicably, she never expected Rhonda's mother to do anything beyond express sympathy. It was as though she forgot what small towns are like. Not to mention human nature. Naturally, Rhonda's mother told others, who told others, who told others... Soon, the whole town knew and she was having to explain to everyone that, yes, her dear daughter had perished in a terrible accident, but please, she was trying to just get through her grief and would appreciate it not being brought up, thanks for understanding.

My father was present for this scene. I wasn't happy with him for putting up with her betrayal of me, but was grateful that he didn't try to stop me from erupting on her. He knew she deserved it. Dana walked into the house at the end of it. He stepped into the living room, saw our blubbering mother, and turned to me.

I narrowed my eyes and growled at him. "Did you *know*?"

"No," our mother said, before he could even ask what it was he might or might not know. "He never knew." This only added to Dana's confusion, but was a great relief to me. I could never forgive him for keeping my "death" a secret.

I packed my things and left, checking into the town's motel for the last days of my visit. I spent those days mostly at Rhonda's, getting to know her and her whole brood... husband and all five of their collective kids. Rhonda had, of course, told them I was Dynamistress. Naturally, none of them had ever heard of me.

I felt obliged to show off. No, I didn't go blasting the landscape, but I did little tricks for them, like gently pushing them away with a force bubble, or power punching through cinder blocks. After dark, I carried them, one by one, a hundred feet into the sky.

I thought about the very near future, of how my mother was going to have a lot to answer for. But I gave Rhonda a cover story. My mother had been under instructions to tell everyone I was dead. Top secret stuff. Couldn't trust anyone. Rhonda's kids ate this up. Even the 17-year old. They're good kids. She's a good mom.

My own mother's contrition didn't last, which was, I told her when I stopped by to say goodbye to my father, something she must have learned from all her idolized evangelists. She chided me for my attitude, and said she didn't understand my continued resentment of her. God will forgive her, she said, so why can't I?

I told her it's because I'm not some fictitious, perfect being who will do whatever someone wants, if only they beg just right, and who'll have unconditional love for all, no matter what insensitive fucking things they do to others. I told her that, contrary to popular myth, *real* love *is* conditional, as is trust, as is respect. Love is an overused word, and any love that lacks trust, that lacks respect, is hollow. It's clear that she doesn't respect me, so any claims of loving me are fairly empty. And it's also clear that I neither respect nor trust her. The difference between us is that I don't claim to love her. Not in any significant way.

So maybe one day, if she's truly ready to make a sincere apology, I told her, I might be able to forgive her. But I'm not holding my breath on her ability to do so.

And that was the last speech I made before I climbed in the car and headed home. And by that, I mean San Francisco.

It was another long drive to the airport.

I called Rhonda from my cell and we talked and laughed the whole way to Pittsburgh.

NINETEEN

*"Nobody can go back and start a new beginning, but anyone can start to-
day and make a new ending."*
~Maria Robinson

The dynamics of family life have always been beyond my ability to
comprehend. Dana tells me this isn't unusual. Families are complex. The
larger the family, the more complex it becomes. Each member has emotional
ties to every other member, and emotions are themselves barely
comprehensible.

In my own family, with a mere four members, there are eleven
distinct relationships. Six two-person relationships, four three-person
relationships, and the quad in sum. Of those, the only one I actually enjoyed
was my relationship with Dana. Nevertheless, I couldn't deny how all the
other relationships affected me.

The Bay Scouts had nine members. That's a total of 502
relationships. As with my genetic family, I felt closer with some of the Scouts
than others. Sinta and Jack had become very important to me. I respected
Daniel. The others... well... we had a professional relationship. And even
though we weren't best friends, I knew they'd all have my back. Unlike, say,
my mother. And I couldn't imagine the Scouts being as dysfunctional as my
birth family. Not by a long shot.

If I'd learned anything about families on my recent trip home, it was
that no matter how horrible the relationship might be, it's impossible to
completely sever the connection. Not without a lobotomy or fortuitous
amnesia, anyway.

On the last day of July, Commander Shepherd called a special meeting of the Bay Scouts. As we gathered in our base, I realized this was the first time our entire crew had been together since "the exchange." It felt good to be with all of them again.

Daniel sat in his wheelchair, but not at his customary place at our conference table. That head spot was reserved for Shepherd. I studied the rest of my team. Billy and Bobby were uncharacteristically quiet; it seemed odd not to have them bantering with everyone before the meeting. Esteban was similarly quiet, but this was normal for him. Jack and Song were deep into a discussion about something beyond my tech expertise. Valora clearly did not want to be present. She practically glared at Shepherd when he entered the room. Sinta sat next to me, eager to hear what our Coast Guard liaison had to say.

Shepherd greeted us cordially, but casually. "It's good to see you," he said. "I know the past months have been very difficult for the Scouts, and I appreciate your patience as we've dealt with the fallout of everything that's happened. That brings me to the first item on the agenda, which is to tell you that Project Echo has officially ended." This got our attention. Several of us exchanged glances. "Not because DHS wanted to end it, but because the gateway has closed. Apparently, there was a failure in the apparatus that was keeping the aperture open, and... well... now it isn't." He was quick to remind us, though, that this didn't lift the gag order. "Until DHS or the FBI says otherwise, this is still Top Secret."

"What about those who've infiltrated our society?" Jack asked.

"DHS is handling that. And no, I don't know how," Shepherd admitted. He paused for several seconds, staring at his hands. I looked across the table at Daniel, who wore an expression of profound sadness. And I suddenly knew what was coming next. "I wish there was some sort of painless way to say this next part," he finally said, looking up to meet our expectant gazes. "DHS has decided to disband the Bay Scouts."

The Commander went silent, allowing all of us to absorb this. We looked around the table at each other, too stunned to speak. All of us but Valora, that is. She pushed herself back from the table and stood. "You and your government agencies," she spat. "Politics and posturing! You disgust me." And with that, she stormed out of the room.

Shepherd went on to advise us all that we'd receive severance packages of one month's active duty pay per year of service. For me, that meant only two months. We'd also receive 180 days of our benefits through the Transitional Assistance Management Program, after which we could purchase a package through the Continued Health Care Benefit Program as a further transition to a non-military health plan. But there was no way I'd be able to afford a thousand dollars a month. We metas pay roughly triple what non-metas pay. That would be fine if we made three times as much money, over all, but few of us do.

After Shepherd departed, we sat around in silence for a while before hitting Daniel with our inevitable question. He told us that, yes, the Scouts could continue, in a manner of speaking. But DHS was our source of funding. The base belonged to them. So we'd have to find a new headquarters and revenue stream. "Frankly," he said, "that's... not likely." He shook his head. "And I don't have... energy to pursue it."

The rest of us exchanged defeated glances, knowing this was the last time many of us would see each other. Eventually, we got out of our seats and exchanged hugs and farewells, then went to empty our lockers before leaving the Bay Scouts base for the final time.

I was the last member to join the Bay Scouts, so my bond to the group wasn't as strong as that of others. Even so, I felt adrift. I had just begun to feel like I belonged, to feel as though I'd found a sort of "family" that my life had been missing. And now it was gone, dissolved the way a family is with a divorce. The whole thing just served to inflame my attachment issues and plunge me into a depression.

And like after a divorce, one of my main issues to address was money. Dynapaste, or whatever the company was going to call it, hadn't yet gone into production for sale, so I was seeing nothing from that. Rachel was able to exercise her clout at the Red Devil to get me some regular shifts and I immediately set out to secure as many floater shifts at other bars as I could get.

My mind flashed back to Dr. Gray's offer the previous month. But he hadn't even started at his job, yet. And likely as not, it would be at least two months before he could take on an assistant. I couldn't wait that long for a steady paycheck. So I took Daniel's advice and spoke with Falcon about some freelance work.

Falcon explained that one needed a license to be recovery agent, but that my meta license allowed me to bypass getting a separate one. I decided that "recovery agent" sounded better than "bounty hunter."

"So how do I get jobs?" I asked. "You have a contact you can share?"

Falcon paused before answering. "I'll introduce you to one or two. Just don't expect much."

"What do you mean?"

"Dyna, look... You're a meta. You're used to dealing with high-powered baddies. And while there are certainly meta-worthy fugitives, competition for those jobs is fierce. And since you don't have an established track record as a recovery agent, you're not likely to get those jobs."

"So... I'll be getting what?"

"Small fries. And your competition for those will be every bail bondsman in the city."

"How many is that?"

Falcon chuckled at my naïveté. "I know of at least thirty agencies within an easy walk of where we're standing. Most of them down on Bryant Street."

And Falcon was right. Competition was fierce and the jobs I got, at first, were nothing to get excited about. I started with non-violent cases... check bouncers, shoplifters, and DUIs. My bank account barely registered the income from these bail jumpers and I regretted not having kept some of the funds I'd gotten from the sale of Dynapaste. I resigned myself, for the near future, at least, to living as frugally as I had been while still making payments on the debt.

Dana offered to help out, and I thanked him, but wanted to do this on my own. "Well," he said, "can I at least treat you to something special?" And so it was that on August 11, Dana and I drove to Reno for my very first Alice Cooper concert. It was a high-energy show, despite Alice no longer being exactly a young man. Dana bought me a tour t-shirt and a little white teddy bear adorned with black, Cooper-style eye makeup. It was a great night, and just what I needed to boost my spirits.

Despite my financial situation, life was surprisingly good. Rachel and I shared many shifts at the club and would hang out at my apartment afterward. I'd make breakfast in the morning before she had to leave. I wasn't entirely clear on where our relationship was going, but that was okay. We were having a good time. I loved her. Not in a burning, passionate way, but certainly enough to continue seeing her and maintaining whatever it was. Friends with benefits, I suppose, though the emphasis was decidedly on the friends part.

Sinta was becoming like a little sister to me. She knew the city much better than I did and I learned a lot from her. In return, I helped her with some tutoring. She was working on her GED and needed some help with math. We talked about college for her, but she didn't seem interested.

Jack busied himself with lab work, mostly. Sometimes I'd visit him and discuss sciencey stuff. Other times, we'd discuss the Scouts. No one had heard from Valora. The twins had moved back to Texas, finding a home with the Lone Star Rangers in Dallas. Esteban had joined the small but respected Los Campeónes down in San Diego. Ping Song had just accepted a job with the computer science division at the University of California in Berkeley. And Daniel was as retired as his team.

Dr. Gray and I got together for coffee or dinner every weekend. He filled me in on SynBERC and his job there and said he would be able to hire an assistant to start in January, when the new budgets went into effect.

"But," he said, "I could bring you in as an unpaid assistant until that time, for whatever hours you can manage."

I jumped at the chance. First, I had to go through a mandatory safety training and pass a certification test. But once that was out of the way, I had access to the lab, under Dr. Gray's supervision.

This was the first opportunity I'd had to see how my genes had been altered by my first stage of the process, eight years earlier. And I was pleased with what I saw. Examination of the DNA showed it to be healthy, with no obvious problems. I expected this, of course, since I hadn't yet come down with a nasty disease or died. Still, it was nice to see this reaffirmed by solid evidence.

Over the next month, I carefully mapped every change in my DNA, comparing the current version to samples I'd kept from before the procedure. The resulting map was interesting, but only gave me vague ideas on how to continue the process. It would be easy enough to simply do a "booster," using the same formula as before. I could recreate it. But I wanted improvements. I wanted to tweak my code to boost my powers, increasing stamina and efficiency.

As I mentioned, though, there is no specific "meta gene." My experiment, from day one, had been educated guesswork, doing what I thought might enhance specific genes that controlled – or at least influenced – specific bodily functions. Further tweaks would be more of the same.

"What vector will you be using?" Dr. Gray asked.

It was a question I'd been struggling with for years. When I'd done my first run, I needed to absolutely minimize any potential for error. I needed the least amount of degradation of the altered DNA and the highest amount of gene expression. So I used the laborious process of microinjection. Meaning I delivered the altered genetic material directly into cells using a glass pipette under a microscope, one at a time. Took forever.

But now, the sensible approach would be to use one of the many viral vectors at my disposal. Using a virus as the delivery method is quite efficient. A virus's sole purpose in life is to attack its host and shove its nastiness into the host's cells. That's how they replicate, and they're good at it. So if you want to deliver something into a cell, you could certainly use a much slower way to do it.

Different viruses have their own advantages and disadvantages, and sometimes outright dangers. For example, to use a virus as a vector, first you've got to remove from it the genes that cause disease, replacing it with whatever you're wanting to deliver. There's always the possibility that the removal process is not perfect and a little of the disease-inducing material gets left behind. Since we're typically talking about nasty viruses, this isn't a good thing.

The long and the short of it is that I wanted a virus that would integrate with my cells (meaning it would carry over when my own cells divided), be long-lasting, and have a low chance of giving me cancer, since, well, that would suck. Though, all things considered, cancer was certainly not the biggest danger in what I was doing.

At any rate, all this pointed to an obvious delivery vector: a lentivirus. There were two drawbacks that bothered me, however. One is that, while most viruses had incubation periods measured in days, this particular virus had an incubation period measured in weeks or months. Sometimes longer. The other drawback was the particular lentivirus to be used.

"HIV," I said to Dr. Gray. And despite knowing the risk of actually contracting HIV from this was slim-to-none, those three little letters felt huge coming out of my mouth.

As October arrived, though, my positive mood darkened, as it did every year. The eleventh would be the fifth anniversary of Lee's death. I always thought of her at this time of year, but this year was worse than others, probably because of the loss of the Scouts. As irrational as it seems, I carried with me a certain amount of guilt over her suicide. It didn't matter that it wasn't my direct fault. I told myself I still should have been more concerned over her behavior, should have urged her to seek help, rather than just avoid her. Out of sight, out of mind. That's how I treated her. But her issues, whatever their origin, were only out of my mind, not hers. I should have been able to see it, should have talked things through with her.

"You can't change the past," Dana would say to me when we spoke of it. "You can only make peace with it."

"I don't think I'll ever be able to do that," I told him. But maybe, I thought, I could lessen its chokehold on me. On the anniversary of Lee's death, I called San Francisco Suicide Prevention and inquired about volunteering as a crisis counselor.

That same month, the U.S. population passed 300 million. The Bay Area was nearing seven million. This meant the estimated number of metas in the country numbered about three thousand, a hundred or more of which were in San Francisco.

I did some checking and learned that in 2006 there were 92 registered metas in the Bay Area. There were also a dozen or so suspected metas who were wanted by the authorities for one crime or another. And probably a similar number of unregistered metas.

It's common knowledge that negative sentiments in the country have made it so that metas increasingly keep their self-discoveries secret. Unfortunately, this also prevents any accurate studies on whether the rate of meta births has changed over the past decades. So the best we can do is guesstimate.

Truthfully, whether or not the rate had increased was of little interest to me. But Dr. Gray thought it was important to know. "Imagine, Dinah," he said as we sat over coffee in my apartment, "if we learned that the rate was increasing at a measurable rate, it could indicate that humans are going through a sort of accelerated evolutionary spurt."

I was skeptical. "I'm no expert in evolution theory," I told him, "but that sort of thing requires some type of environmental stressors to bring about the change." I poured myself another cup. "And I sure don't see what stressors we have that could possibly be doing it."

Instead of arguing the point, Dr. Gray leaned back in the chair and looked at me thoughtfully. "You don't really want the lab assistant job, do you?" When I gave a confused look in response, he continued. "I mean, even disregarding lab work, you're a clever theoretician. Your research was terrifically insightful, as far as it went, long before you had any actual experimental evidence to support it. But you never went any further with that. And in the lab, now, you've not shown any actual interest in my work or much else that SynBERC is working on."

Because I'm selfish, I thought, but said, "I didn't really have a reason to continue. I'd succeeded in my goal, which was to make myself into a meta. That was always my entire reason for pursuing my degree. I never intended to make this process available to anyone else."

Dr. Gray shook his head. "But think of all the good it could do! I mean, leave aside the whole meta-ability thing. Just the benefits you could introduce in terms of longevity alone – such as your use of sirtuins – would be immense!" He frowned and shook his head again. "I just think it's a travesty that your work is essentially lost to science."

"First of all," I said, "it's not lost at all. You know a good bit about it, after all. You read my dissertation, which is, I assume, still sitting on a shelf back at Pattee Library, available for anyone to study and follow in my footsteps." I frowned. "However, I hope they don't," I said. "Invariably, it would fall into the wrong hands. Imagine opposing armies creating metahumans to fight others, each side tweaking the process to get the desired outcomes, then tweaking further to maximize those traits in their creations, as though human beings were crops to crossbreed. Eventually, you'd have armies of monsters."

"Oh, come on," Dr. Gray said. "That's an unlikely scenario, don't you think?"

"No, in fact I think it would be inevitable. The more radical a change you make to the DNA, the higher the likelihood that you'll get undesired changes. My white hair is a particularly innocuous example of it." I shook my head as I poured the last of the coffee into Dr. Gray's cup. "But a radical group wouldn't care about those things. They'd manipulate the DNA to reap the greatest weapons. So long as the walking tank could rip through their enemies, they wouldn't care if it had two heads with tongues two feet long and a life span measured in months."

Dr. Gray shook his head and sipped from his cup. "Subjects with such exaggerated mutations wouldn't survive to maturity."

I looked at him for several long seconds. "These aren't 'subjects.' They're people."

He waved off my words. "You know what I mean."

"Yeah, I do," I said. "But the point is that the ones who'd pursue such ends wouldn't care that their subjects are people." I sighed. "I dunno... maybe we disagree because you spend your life dealing with scientists and students and I spend mine dealing with somewhat less pleasant people."

"You're saying I'm naïve." He nodded. "And you may be right. I concede your point, even though I still can't accept it as an inevitability." He said it casually enough, but his face betrayed an unspoken concern.

Thanksgiving Day, November 23, 2006. I'd begun the day with an early shift on the suicide hotline dealing with people who couldn't find much to give thanks for. Not that they were suicidal; most callers to the hotline aren't. Rather, they're individuals in crisis of some sort, feeling lost or lonely, and mainly wanting someone to listen to them, to really hear them. In the short time I'd been taking calls, still under supervision with another counselor listening in on a separate headset, I'd dealt with people of all ages, from thirteen to seventy. Some were disheartened, some were drunk, and some were mentally ill "frequent flyers." By that, I mean people – usually with diagnoses and on meds – who called the line often. We had a file full of information on them all. There was also the occasional pervert, but the less said about those calls, the better.

After my shift, which had consisted of more calls than usual, likely due to the holiday and the family-related stresses that came with it, I returned home and began my computer routine. This consisted first of checking the news, then browsing the many recovery agent internet boards, and finally using social media to track down my latest jobs. It's shocking to me how stupid some people are about announcing their whereabouts online. I spent a lot of time on MySpace, which at that time was still the primary outlet, Facebook having not yet surpassed it.

At the time, I was trying to track down a meta by the name of Oscar Helman, a small-time thug, built like a truck, who could throw balls of flaming plasma and went by the oh-so-original name of Hellion. He was wanted for failure to report to his parole officer. There was a good price for him, since he was a violent offender, and I really wanted to be the one to find him.

As I was in the middle of my research, Rachel showed up. We'd planned to spend the day together, Dana having gone home to Pennsylvania to spend the holiday with our parents. She came in and sat with me on the sofa and we began chatting about our plans, which included a picnic in the park. As we discussed details, she glanced at my laptop, sitting open on the coffee table. Her eyes widened as she looked at the screen.

She lifted the computer onto her lap. "Dinah, what's this?"

"My latest mark. Got out on parole and never once checked in, so he's wanted."

"Fuck," Rachel breathed. I looked at her, seeing the look on her face, and realized she knew the guy. She nodded when I said as much. "He's my ex." As I swallowed that surprising fact, she lifted her eyes from the screen. "He's dangerous, Dinah. You have to find him." There was more than a hint of panic in her voice and in her eyes.

Immediately, I remembered the words my other-dimensional self had left me in her note. The Rachel of her world was dead, murdered in horrid fashion. And of course, Rachel had read that note, too. "You're afraid of him."

Rachel averted her eyes. "Well... I was the one who turned him in."

"Right. Okay, so you're going to stay with me until he's behind bars, again." To my surprise, she didn't hesitate to agree.

I sent her back to her place to pack for a long stay, while I made space in my closet and drawers for her clothes and cleared some room in the bathroom for her other things. Then I sat down at the computer again and learned everything I could about Mr. Oscar Helman.

Eventually, I tore my gaze from the screen and realized it had been nearly an hour since Rachel had left. I pulled out my cell phone, lamenting not for the first time the loss of the spiffy smartphone I'd had with the Scouts. I called Rachel, but it went straight to voicemail. And my stomach went straight to my feet.

I didn't wait for a taxi. I blasted straight into the sky to fly the dozen blocks to Rachel's apartment. As soon as I was above rooftop level, I saw the smoke. I rocketed to her building to see flames licking at the windows from inside a third floor unit. Rachel's, of course.

Fire trucks were on the scene, dousing the flames. A ladder truck was slowly maneuvering a firefighter toward Rachel's window. But I couldn't wait. I dove straight toward the building and shot through the broken glass and into her bedroom. On the bed was a suitcase, open and in flames. I screamed her name over the roar of the fire.

The heat was almost unbearable, and would have been overwhelming if I hadn't been constantly pulsing energy from my body, which kept some of the heat and smoke from me. I dashed from room to room, finding all of them empty. Now panicked, I blasted out the living room window and flew home, heart pounding.

I stood in my living room, reeking of smoke, paralyzed with dread. I stared at my laptop, still sitting on the coffee table. Then I pulled out my phone and stared at it before calling the police. I told them what I knew, explaining that I was a recovery agent working on the Helman case. I told them about Rachel and her past involvement with him. I gave them everything I had, withholding only the fact that I'd been in the burning apartment.

Then I called my friends for help. Sinta and Jack, of course. I also told Daniel, who promised to get word to the Maltese Falcon.

I went to the Red Devil and spoke with those who knew Rachel best. Two of them remembered Oscar and promised to keep an eye out for him or any of his friends. I knew it was a long shot, but I had to cover all the bases.

My phone rang and I answered without even looking at the Caller ID, hoping against hope that it was Rachel. But it was Dana, calling to wish me a Happy Thanksgiving from the other side of the country. I told him everything, of course, and he offered to fly home the next day. I told him not to bother, since I had no idea how he could help.

When I'd contacted everyone I thought could possibly help, I collapsed onto the sofa and resumed my online hunt for Hellion.

It never crossed my mind that he might also be hunting me.

TWENTY

"It is easier to forgive an enemy than to forgive a friend."
~William Blake

Bullying.

Today, the very word carries a weight of indignation. Adults are shocked and appalled at the cruelty one child can inflict upon another. It's as though they've completely forgotten what it's like to be a kid. There are probably those who never experienced bullying and never witnessed or heard of others being bullied. But I've never met such a person.

I don't think bullying is more rampant now than during my childhood or earlier, but it's different, today. Social media makes it easy to bully someone 24/7, rather than just at school. Fewer kids in the closet makes anti-gay bullying more prevalent. As a child, I never heard of any suicides attributed to bullying. But again, we lacked the instantaneous news reports we have today.

Back then, bullying was viewed as just a part of childhood. Kids were told to suck it up, to stand up to the bullies, or to bide their time until it passed. Today, we treat bullying as the big deal it always has been, and that's gratifying. But to my mind, there's not enough focus put on the causes of bullying.

Lest anyone think I'm some sort of profound thinker on human nature, let me be clear that my brother is the expert on that (as much as anyone can be). From our talks, I've learned that there are several reasons why kids become bullies.

One reason is because the kid is reacting to something frustrating. Frustration, as most of us know, can lead to aggressive behavior. Take me and computers, for example. I love computers and enjoy using them. And I'm fairly savvy, I think. But I do expect them to work as advertised. When they don't, I get frustrated. This is fine, and expected. What wouldn't be fine is if I vented my frustration by hitting my laptop with a hammer. Some bullying is the result of not being able to handle frustrations properly. And these frustrations can come from any source, be it something as simple as a car that won't start or something as complex as a poor home environment. Many bullies, it turns out, are themselves the victim of aggressive behavior in another aspect of their lives.

Another primary reason kids bully is, to me, more disturbing. Essentially, it's done in order to get something, typically a level of status in the eyes of one's peers. It's a very calculated behavior, a display of dominance. A child who successfully teases or humiliates another is viewed as more powerful or, sadly, "cooler" than the victim.

I should point out that bullying is certainly not limited to the young. It exists in the adult world, too. In academia, in the workplace... any place where people haven't outgrown the need to make themselves look better by tearing down someone else, i.e., everywhere.

Including among metas.

The only real lead we had was that Helman was from Sunnydale, a neighborhood I'd never been to. "Be thankful," Daniel told me. "Improving, but still... not a nice place." I'd gotten into the habit of calling him regularly regarding my work. Not only because he was a valuable source of information, but because I knew it would make him feel useful. "You think the Tenderloin is bad..."

Daniel described for me vast housing projects with irregular trash pickup, scant public transportation, high crime, and extreme poverty. It was a neighborhood for those who can't afford to live anywhere else in the city. That's the environment that produced Hellion.

Sinta joined me in exploring the neighborhood and I soon understood why it was sometimes called "The Swamp." The place was a mess. Trash was everywhere, it seemed. Grass competed with weeds... and was losing. Daniel had urged us to go during the day, and I was glad I'd listened to him. I couldn't imagine the place at night.

I wore my old leathers, wanting to give the impression that I was tough enough to handle The Swamp. I didn't think my blue and white unitard would pull that off. Of course, people paid more attention to Sinta's furry face than my clothing. She made sure to show a lot of fang.

We spent hours there, hitting up every bar and liquor store, every convenience store and barber shop, every pawn shop and quick loan facility, flashing photos of Oscar Helman and demanding any information. Despite Sinta's growls and my own power-enhanced posturing, we got the distinct impression that people were more afraid of Hellion than of us.

When we'd finally accepted as many "No ideas" and "Get losts" as we could take, we left, dejectedly making the trek back to the city. We took the bus to the Market Street stop nearest my place, then walked to a little Asian fast food joint for a cheap dinner. Sinta did her best to convince me that we'd soon find Rachel. "What bothers me most," I told her, "is that we haven't heard a word. It's been a week, with no ransom demands or anything." I didn't say it, but I feared she was already dead.

After eating, I walked the short distance to my apartment, while Sinta headed for the Muni. I entered the lobby, checked my mailbox, and walked up to the third floor. I put the key in the lock and turned it.

The blast was strong enough to literally embed me into the wall behind me. Flames and smoke poured out my doorway. My vision swum as I gasped for breath, but I saw what I hoped were other residents running for the stairs at either end of the hall. I heard laughter as a figure walked out of my burning apartment. Hellion.

He continued chuckling as he stood in front of me and took stock of my situation, looking at my body stuck halfway through the flimsy wall of the hallway. I could barely think straight, too stunned from the shock to do anything to free myself.

"Nice," he said with a smile. "Good blowback on that one." Then his voice hardened. "So you're the dyke my ex has been screwing. And you're a do-gooder hero, she says." He lowered his face to mine. "Always looking to raise my street cred, y'know. Even a nobody hero helps."

"Where... is she?" I managed to croak. "If you've... hurt her."

He gave a guttural bark of a laugh. "Like I'm gonna talk to you while you get some strength back. Stupid bitch." With that, he extended a hand toward me and let loose a searing bolt of flame.

Instinctively, I put as much energy as I could into my protective shield, knowing it wouldn't help much. Holding back solid things? Fine. Holding back heat? Not so much. Anger flared inside me and my head began to clear. But my efforts weren't enough. The walls and ceiling were already burning around me, and I could feel my skin beginning to blister.

Suddenly, the barrage stopped and I heard thumping noises through the dense smoke and crackling fire. I wrenched myself free of the wall. Then I heard a cry of pain that quickly turned to a scream. It was Sinta, who knelt on top of Hellion, engulfed in flame. He shoved the burning girl from his chest and got to his feet.

I braced my feet and let loose with a diffused blast, which whisked the flames from Sinta's body. As she rolled to the side, I sent a focused shot at Hellion, blowing him back onto the floor.

He fired off another geyser of flame as he rose, but I was able to avoid it as I rushed him. "Your turn," I said, and hit him with a double blast that crunched him into the wall at the end of the hallway. I followed up with an energy punch that knocked the wind out of him. He crumpled to the floor.

The fire was spreading and I had to get us out of there. Sinta was able to hobble out on her own, but not Hellion. I blasted through the wall behind him and, figuring he could survive the drop, shoved his heavy body through the hole. Then Sinta and I headed down the stairs at the end of the hall.

In the hospital, I was relieved to find that Sinta was not badly burned. Her fur was virtually gone from her torso, but her skin was only mildly scorched. The doctors said she'd be fine and the fur would regrow.

Hellion was under armed police guard in his room, handcuffed to his bed, when I was brought in to identify him. Then I spent an hour with a cop out in the hallway, giving my statements. And I implicated Hellion in the firebombing of Rachel's apartment and her disappearance, explaining the connection between them.

"Was this information reported at the time of her disappearance?" asked the lieutenant.

"It was," I said. "But I'm not sure how seriously they took it." In response to his puzzled expression, I explained. "Let's just say that the officer I spoke to didn't strike me as being sympathetic to metas."

To my surprise, the cop frowned and apologized. "There's no excuse for that," he said. "You have my word that I'll make this case a priority." He paused, then said, "You know... not everyone has an irrational fear of you guys. To me, you're people, no different than anyone else in any way that matters."

I smiled and thanked him, feeling my eyes sting with tears of gratitude. Or from smoke residue. One of the two.

The next day, I watched Hellion through the thick glass of the jail's visitor station as he took a seat. "This should be entertaining," he said. "What do you want, dyke?" He frowned when he saw I wasn't alone. "Who's this asshole?"

"Where's Rachel?" I asked.

"You know," he chuckled, "I'm not done with you. When I get out, I'll finish what I started."

"Think you can do it without incendiary explosives?"

"Sure. That was just for show."

"Where is she, Oscar?"

He smiled. "Fuck you."

"Unlikely."

He smirked. "Your loss. Be the best you ever had." Then he frowned and rubbed his temple, as though in pain. He stood up. "We're done here."

I looked at Dana, who nodded. "Guess we are," I said.

For the second time, I traveled to Sunnydale. This time, I knew where I was going. Ironically, it was one of the convenience stores Sinta and I had visited. I waited until there were no customers, then went inside. The guy behind the counter was one of the accomplices. He recognized me and reached under the counter, pulling out a gun. "Go ahead," I said. "Give me an excuse to punch you through a wall."

It disappointed me that he thought better of it and put the gun down. I really felt like punching someone through a wall. He said, "She's in the back."

"Good boy." He looked up as two police cruisers came to a stop in front of the store. I'd tipped my meta-friendly lieutenant, who called it in to the Ingleside station. He looked at his gun again. "Don't," I said.

With a sigh, he put his hands atop his head as the officers came in. I headed for the back room, where I found Rachel lying on a futon, mostly naked. She was bound, gagged, and semi-conscious. Her face was deep red where it was bruised. On the floor next to the futon was a bottle tank with a gas mask attached. Nitrous oxide.

Rachel managed a bleary-eyed smile as I removed the gag and cut through her bonds with the pocket knife I carried. As I rubbed her wrists to restore circulation, I relaxed for the first time since Thanksgiving.

"Police!" came a voice from the doorway. "Drop the weapon!"

I spun around to see the cop pointing his firearm at another of Hellion's goons, who put down his weapon and slowly raised his hands. My stomach sank as I saw the all-too-familiar energy-sucking weapon of my double's world.

There's no question it was the same weapon. The officer at the scene let me examine it before it was taken as evidence. I asked Hellion's goon where he got it, but he said Hellion gave it to him. Helman had posted bail, so I couldn't drag Dana back for another visit. But that was okay. I knew I'd be seeing him again.

Once again, I was indebted to my brother for footing the bill for new clothes, food, and a new laptop, since mine had been in the apartment and was now so much slag, along with virtually everything else I owned. All the truly important stuff, i.e., my research, was safe on USB drives and CDs in a fireproof box, which was now with me at Sinta's apartment.

She'd saved my life, without a doubt. Such dumb luck that we'd chosen to have dinner not far from my apartment, and that her sensitive ears heard the sound of the blast from half a dozen blocks away. I was deeply grateful that her injuries were minor.

Rachel was being kept overnight in the hospital. She was dehydrated and malnourished, but otherwise fine. Unfortunately, she'd been kept barely conscious the whole time she'd been there, so she knew nothing about the weapon. She didn't even remember seeing it.

Daniel wasn't happy with the news, when I told him. "Afraid of this," he told me.

I paced Sinta's living room as we talked on the phone. "My double warned that some of those weapons could have made their way into our world. I wonder how many are out there." Then, after an awkward silence, I said, "Did you believe Shepherd when he told us that Project Echo had been terminated?"

Daniel was quiet for a moment before answering. "Honestly... I don't know what to believe, anymore."

I wasn't afraid of Hellion, but had to accept that he was a danger to me, since he knew my identity. Rachel told me that he hadn't known anything about me other than the fact that she and I were involved. But Hellion had one of his guys lingering near Rachel's apartment after the abduction. He'd seen me fly in and out of the burning building and was bright enough to make the connection, since they had my name and description from someone at the Red Devil.

But I clearly needed to do everything I could to keep a low profile. Hellion's actions made plain the danger of having my identity known. Every two-bit idiot trying to make a name for himself would be coming after me. And let's face it, I have a standout surname, thanks to my paternal grandparents, who chose to do a weird, name-blending, hyphenated thing. They died before I was born, so I never got to ask what possessed them to create such a peculiar appellation. "It is what it is," was all my father had to say about it.

The likelihood of attacks also meant a lot of potential property damage and bystander casualties. Luckily, no one else had been badly hurt during Hellion's two firebombings. I needed somewhere private, somewhere safe. And there was only one location I could think of that would qualify.

It took a lot of phone calls, a lot of pleading, and a lot of promises, but I was able to secure access to the Bay Scouts' old base. It wasn't exactly homey. There was no natural light, since it was underground. The original heating units were long dead and space heaters were the norm. But there was electricity and running water, and plenty of space to convert into living quarters. By Christmas, Rachel and I were moved in.

I'd asked Daniel and Falcon to put some feelers out to see if there were any other reports of these energy weapons showing up anywhere. I checked with Marcus in Sacramento, too. All their searches came up negative. So it was vital to find out where this specific one came from.

My plan for finding this out, however, hit a major snag when Dana refused to help. "I told you before, Dinah," he said. "I won't read someone's thoughts without their permission. Doing it to find Rachel was one thing, as it was likely a life or death situation. But this doesn't even compare."

I wanted to argue, but couldn't. Despite how much easier my job would be if he'd do so, it really was ethically questionable. "If every telepath, even with the best intentions, invaded other minds for just any reason, we would become the very threat the public already feels we are," Dana had said. And he was right. So I had to come up with another way to get the information out of him. And since a deceptive approach wasn't an option, I thought I'd try a direct one. I spoke with my new police friend and explained in vague terms what I needed. In turn, he spoke to the prosecuting attorney and said that the weapon confiscated at the scene was used in another crime and we needed to learn where they'd gotten it. The prosecutor spoke to the defense attorney who suggested that cooperation might reduce any sentencing and within days, I had an answer. I didn't know if it was the truth, but it was all I had: the name of a gun shop in Oakland.

In retrospect, I think my reasoning was a bit on the paranoid side. But at the time, it seemed logical enough. This was the only weapon of this type I'd heard of in the city. The point of entry was in the middle of the Nevada desert five hundred miles away. That what seemed to be the one and only weapon from the other world had made its way to San Francisco was too coincidental. My Bay Scouts friends and I were among the very few who knew the truth about that other world. The weapon was given to Hellion, my girlfriend's ex. Again, maybe paranoid, but I believed it was intended from the start to be used against me, for some reason.

The weapon itself should, if things were happening properly, find its way into the government's hands after the trial. But knowing the speed at which government operates, I wasn't about to wait. I wanted to find out how this particular gun shop had acquired such a weapon in the first place.

It was a small shop in a rundown neighborhood, in a brick building with bars over the windows. The other establishments on the street were mostly out of business. I stepped inside, pulling the heavy door closed behind me, and taking stock of the store's layout.

I was the only customer. Behind the counter was a heavily muscled, short-haired man of about forty with a tattoo of Animal from The Muppet Show on his forearm. In the ceiling corner behind him was a security camera.

I idly looked over the wares on display, wearing my clueless female face. After a minute, "Animal" came over to me. "Help you find something?" he asked, his eyes definitely not on my face.

I was wearing my leathers, exposing a good bit of skin. I smiled vapidly. "Yes, please! A friend of mine got a gun here," I said. "I want one just like it, but I don't see any."

The man shrugged. "So what was it?"

"It was... um... an energy gun," I said, feigning embarrassment.

At this, the man frowned. "Who's the friend?"

"Oscar," I said with a smile. "Oscar Helman."

Another frown. "You're a friend of Hellion's?" he asked, clearly not believing it. I just smiled again. The man stared at me for another second, then said, "Only had the one."

"Oh," I pouted. "Well, where did you get it?"

"Can't remember," he said.

"Really?" I said. "Anything I can do, maybe, to jog your memory?"

The man hesitated at that, his eyes wandering over my leather-clad body. "Maybe," he said, and after another long look-over, walked to the front door and threw the deadbolt, flipped the sign to "closed," and pulled the shades. Then he walked back to me, practically leering. "What did you have in mind, sweetheart?"

I smiled coyly. "I don't know," I said.

"I have a few things in mind," he said, reaching to touch my bare midriff.

"Was this one of them?" I asked, grabbing his hand and violently twisting his wrist.

He grimaced and yanked his hand back. "What the hell?" he said and shoved me back into the counter, as I'd hoped he would. I didn't know if the security camera was real or fake, but in case it was live, the recording would show that he was the instigator in what was to follow. He moved in again, this time not so slowly, and with anger on his face. I slapped that face, using enough energy so that it probably felt like a full-fledged punch. He recoiled, shocked, and looked at me warily.

"Was that enough of a jog?" I asked, dropping my ditzy blonde voice. In response, he took a full swing at me. I easily avoided it and planted a punch of my own to his side, just below the ribs. Then I kicked his legs out from under him and slammed him to the floor, dropping to land one knee on his chest. "How 'bout now?"

He glared at me, but the fight was out of him. "Fuck," he said, catching his breath. "Fine. Just lemme up." I got off him. I even helped him up. "I'll get it for you," he said, moving behind the counter again. He reached under and, perhaps predictably, pulled out a gun. Without hesitation, he shot me in the chest.

I had a tight, dense, energy field around me. But being shot still hurts like hell and leaves deep, ugly bruises. And pain tends to inflame my anger. I reached over and grabbed the guy's gun and the hand holding it and slammed it down, smashing his already hurt wrist into the hard countertop. He yelped in pain.

"Quit fucking around," I said, pulling the gun from his limp hand and tossing it across the room behind me. "Give me a name."

"Don't... have one," he said around the pain.

"So you're a liar." I ground his wrist into the countertop. "Were you lying about not having any more of those weapons, too?"

He shook his head, grimacing. "It was the only one." He struggled vainly to pull his hand free.

"Why so protective of your source? And why the hell did you shoot me?" At this, I allowed him to have his hand back. He rubbed his wrist gingerly. He'd figured out that fighting me or trying to escape wasn't going to work and didn't try anything else. But he stayed silent. I frowned. "Your source. Who is he?"

He hesitated again, this time a bit nervously. His eyes flickered to the clock on the wall. And then it hit me. He wasn't nervous. He was impatient. He'd triggered an alarm when he went down for his gun.

"You think the police are going to stop me from getting the information from you?" I said.

To my surprise, he actually chuckled. "I didn't call the cops," he said.

At that moment, there was the scream of tearing metal as the store's front door was ripped from its frame. I whirled in time to see it crash across the floor. Two figures stood in the doorway. The one in the front, a man dressed in familiar paramilitary garb, held an energy weapon pointed at me.

The beam struck me fully in the chest, immediately draining a large chunk of my energy reserves. I summoned enough for a blast and aimed it directly at the weapon, which sparked and began smoking. It was out of commission, but it didn't matter. Because the other figure was Valora. And I knew it wasn't the one who was my former teammate.

I also knew I stood no chance against her. My only hope was to hit her with as many blasts as I could before she could get to me. Even my shields wouldn't stand up for long against her incredible strength.

But I could escape, I thought. I summoned a dense energy field around my fists and launched myself full-blast toward the barred window. The iron and glass gave way upon impact and I flew through the shards.

Only to be tackled ten feet from the ground. Valora couldn't fly, but she could sure jump. We fell to the pavement and began pummeling each other. It was a hopeless battle for me, but I did my best. And that wasn't nearly good enough.

Valora rained blow upon blow. "Don't hurt her!" I heard her accomplice yell, just as my shields finally gave out. It was a familiar voice.

I came to with my head throbbing from the pounding Valora had given it. My breastbone ached with the bruise from the bullet. My mouth tasted of blood. One eye was swollen half shut. I was weak and hungry and had no idea where I was.

I half expected to wake in an energy prison, as in the other world. But in fact, I was in what appeared to be someone's living room, save for the fact that it didn't appear "lived in." I was in a comfortable armchair at one end of the room. At the other end, the front door stood on the right and an entrance to a hallway on the left. Along the left wall was a sofa, and seated in it was who I assumed to be the same ally of Valora's from the store, holding another one of those damned guns. He never took his goggled eyes from me.

I was, however, unbound. But as I sat up, I realized I was, indeed, restrained. I felt something around my neck. My fingers told me it was a metal band, more than an inch thick.

"It's a bomb," Valora said as she strolled in from the kitchen, at my left. She was wearing casual clothes and carried a plate of cold fried chicken. After taking a breast, she handed the rest to me. "It's pretty fancy, really," she said as I accepted the plate. "An acquaintance of mine made it. There are sensors built in to monitor your energy levels. Any unusual build up, such as for your impressive blasts, will trip the explosive. So... I recommend staying calm and not..." she smiled "...losing your head." She smirked again and said, "I found it very helpful in keeping 'you' under control in my world." She sat on the arm of the sofa, facing me, picking at her chicken. "Go ahead and eat," she said. "You might as well."

She was right. I was starving and there was no sense in staying that way. I truly hated this woman, I thought as I devoured the chicken. She had crippled Daniel, taking from my friend the thing most important to him. And then there was the question of my world's Valora. I swallowed a mouthful of meat. "Is she alive?" I asked flatly.

The woman looked at me in confusion. "Who?"

"Valora, of course!"

"Oh," she said as she tore another strip from the chicken breast. "Not likely." So casually, she said it. As though it didn't matter. So little did she care that verifying her double's fate wasn't worth her time. She nibbled the strip of meat and spoke without looking at me. "Speaking of alive, I imagine you're wondering why you still are."

I put the plate aside. "No," I said simply. And it was true. I remembered well my double's story, her tale of why this Valora kept her around. The irony would have made me laugh, in other circumstances.

"It's because I have need of your talents," she said.

"I'm not going to help you create an army of enhanced metas."

Now she looked at me, surprised. After a moment's silence, she sighed. "Then just tell me where your research is. I don't need *you*, after all. I have my own scientist." She smiled, then looked at her accomplice. "Don't I, Professor?"

A chill washed over me and I shook my head in denial as the man hesitated, then put down his weapon, removed his goggles and stood. Now I knew why the last voice I'd heard before losing consciousness had sounded familiar. Dr. Gray removed his mask and looked at me, not quite concealing the shame on his face.

I just stared at him, not wanting to believe this was possible. Finally, he averted his eyes, causing Valora to chuckle. "I'll leave you two to catch up," she said. "Oh, Dinah, darling... I should mention there are three other triggers for your new necklace. One, obviously, is a remote that is always in my possession. Another is if you try to tamper with it. And the last is if you pass a certain radius of this house. And trust me, it's not a great distance." She smiled smugly and walked out the front door into the night.

I stared at "Dr. Gray" and felt a pang at the loss of my friend. "How long ago?" I demanded. "And is he alive?" The man just looked at me blankly. I pushed myself out of the chair and got up into his face. "When did you switch with the real Dr. Gray, dammit? What have you done with him?"

To my surprise, the shame returned to his face. "I'm... Dinah, I'm me. I'm him." He looked at me with puppy dog eyes. "No switching."

My stomach dropped. "Liar!" But even as I spat the word, I knew he'd told the truth.

"Valora contacted me. She'd worked with my twin. She knew about what you could do, and that I was familiar with your work."

"You realize your twin is dead, right? Otherwise, he'd be here and you wouldn't be." He hesitated, evidently not having thought of that, before. "In fact, she's probably the one who killed him," I said. "And she'll do the same to you, when she has no more use for you."

"You have to believe me... it was never supposed to come to this!"

I narrowed my eyes. "*What*, exactly, was never supposed to come to this?" My exasperation was too great to contain. "I mean... what the *fuck*? Can't you see how evil she is?"

At this, he glowered at me. "*Evil?* You must have a perverse sense of the word." He clenched his jaw before launching into his rant. "When I was ten years old, my twin brother was diagnosed with cancer. It was aggressive. Standard treatments did little more than make his hair fall out and feel even worse. Eventually, the doctors said there was nothing to be done. Our parents didn't want to believe that, so they did as much research as they could. And they learned of an experimental drug that had the potential to help. They brought this information to the doctors. But some bureaucratic

FDA bullshit red tape prevented us from getting that treatment. And he died, Dinah! He *died!*" He stared back into my eyes. "*That* is evil."

I really couldn't argue that one. "I'm sorry," I said, and meant it.

"Withholding lifesaving treatments is just wrong," he said, turning his back to me and pacing the room. "People should have access to what exists, whether or not some government agency decides someone is a good candidate for it or whether the treatment is safe." He spun and screamed at me, "So that drug wasn't proven safe? Cancer wasn't safe, either!"

I let him rage, not really seeing another option. This history was new to me, as was his passion. I just nodded in agreement.

"And your work," he said, moving closer to me, "is no different." He shook his head and chuckled ironically. "You know, there are at least twenty top geneticists in the world working on the exact same thing, all of them failing where you somehow succeeded." He glared at me, sneering. "And let's be honest. You're no genius. You're competent, no question. But there is no reason why your experiment should have worked – and worked so well – when no one else has been able to find success." Despite the fact that I have never thought of myself as a genius, his words still stung. I started to offer some sort of placating words, but he cut me off. "And that's why I've been trying to get you to tell me your secrets for so many years. But you've always kept it from me." He shrugged. "So here we are."

I frowned. "I don't see how you can equate my work to cancer treatment."

"Anything that can prolong or better our lives falls in the same category," he said. "You have become so much more than human. I know enough about your work to know that you've got more going on than your energy abilities. Like I said before, your sirtuin enhancement alone will probably extend your life expectancy by a decade or two. Unless, of course, you get yourself killed with your idiotic superheroics."

A sick feeling began to fill me, remembering the last time he'd mentioned the sirtuin process. I hadn't placed it at the time, but now I realized why I felt odd when he mentioned it.

"How did you know about the sirtuins?" I asked, even though the answer was forming in my head.

His indignation disappeared. "What? I..." He sighed in exasperation. "You mentioned it over coffee or something."

"I didn't," I said. The sirtuin enhancement hadn't been included in my dissertation. That idea didn't fully gel until after I'd been working at GACTech... a job I now knew he'd gotten me in order to monitor my work. The sense of betrayal grew and I stared at him. It all made sense, now. Every twisted bit of it. "So the fire at GACTech really *wasn't* my fault."

Dr. Gray stood stiffly, seemingly offended at my implication. Then he softened and looked away. "I told you before, I had no idea the company would hold you responsible. But," he said, "you *were* drunk, after all."

I nodded slowly. "Yes. They tested my breath for alcohol. But they never tested my blood or urine for drugs." I glared at him. "What would they have found? GHB? Rohypnol? And when did you spike my drink?"

"When you used the rest room, of course," he said casually. "And once you passed out, I got what I wanted... the remainder of your altered DNA. There was enough left in the bag and tube for me to examine."

I felt the tell-tale tingle in my fists of energy accumulation. I took a calming breath, staring at my hands, not knowing what to say or feel. "God damn you," I growled. "Because of you, I've lived with uncertainty and guilt for almost a decade. Because of you, I went through years of garnisheed wages and living hand-to-mouth. The stress of the lawsuit led to me having an affair, and to Lee's eventual suicide..."

"You can't blame me for your infidelity," he said.

"I'll blame you for whatever the hell I want," I said, advancing on him, fists clenched.

He stared at my fists and pointed nervously at them. "You better be careful. You can't use your powers." He glanced at his weapon, just out of reach on the sofa.

"I don't need my fucking powers to deal with you." I punched him in the face. He stumbled backward, tripping over a coffee table, sprawling on the floor. He looked up at me in shock and fear as I leaned down, grabbed his shirt, and hoisted him off his feet. I certainly don't have Valora's strength, but years of working out and training made me pretty buff. "Now you listen to me, you son of a bitch," I said directly into his face. "You're going to tell me where I am, what Valora has planned, and you're going to get this fucking thing off my neck."

He said nothing, but fumbled in his pocket while staring at my "necklace." Perhaps I shouldn't have been surprised, but he pulled out a pistol instead of a key. I was pretty sick of guns by this point. So I let go of his shirt. As he fell, I grabbed the hand holding the pistol. Then I wrenched it from his grasp and aimed it down at him.

"You really want to play this game?" He stared at the weapon for a moment, but only glared back at me. "The key. Now."

The door opened, sending a gust of winter air into the room.

"I don't have it," Dr. Gray said.

"That's true," Valora said, closing the door behind her, a steaming Starbucks cup in hand. "Put down the gun, Dyna."

"Mmm, no," I said. "I think I'll just kill him."

"We all know you won't," she said, "so stop posturing." But she didn't move toward me.

"Really?" I said, looking at her. "He knows the hell he's put me through because of his actions." I moved the gun to point at his head. "Ask him if he thinks I'll do it or not." Valora frowned and cast a look at Dr. Gray, who was clearly not so sure. "You think you know me? I can assure you, you don't."

She was quiet for a long minute. "Val," Dr. Gray whispered. "Please."

I needed to do something to break this stalemate. It was time for the big reveal. "You want to know why I won't help you?" I said. "Because it's impossible." This caused Valora to look at me with a frown. "Ask him," I said. "He knows. He's just not admitting it." I glanced back at the man, who now blinked curiously at me. "He said it himself. There's no reason my experiment should have succeeded when better minds have failed repeatedly. And it's why my double's experiment in your world failed so badly." I paused, looking at Valora. "You had his twin try it, too, didn't you? And when he also failed, you killed him." Valora's eyes narrowed, but she merely looked toward Dr. Gray, waiting for him to say something. When he remained silent, I said, "Are you both so stupid that you haven't figured it out?"

This wasn't false bravado. Dr. Gray's words had simply caused me to accept a truth I'd long suspected. It's not that I wasn't aware of the work others had been doing. I just figured I'd gotten lucky, but in the back of my head, I think I always knew the truth.

"Figured out what?" Valora asked flatly.

The signs had all been there throughout my research. I just didn't recognize them for what they were. And even before... going back to my very first hospital stay. I'd come to understand what that was. Or rather, what it was trying to be.

I looked her in the eye. "The process can only work on someone who already has the mutations." I glanced at Dr. Gray, whose eyes held a flicker of comprehension. "Tell her what I mean."

He blinked at me, then glanced at Valora. After a moment, he licked his lips and spoke quietly. "She means... that she was born with the meta mutation. But for whatever reason, it didn't activate at puberty... like it did for her brother."

I nodded. "All my work only served to enhance what my body was already set up to do. That, and to jump start the process."

Dr. Gray slumped, his dreams evidently destroyed. Valora, however, only shrugged. "So you can't create metas from non-metas. But you should still be able to enhance an existing meta."

"Not exactly," I said. "Tell her why, doc."

With a sigh, he mumbled the explanation. "She would need to have a thorough understanding of the individual, of the scope and type of mutations they have. Any enhancement would need to be custom to that person. Far too time-intensive to be what you want, Val."

Now she frowned. "I don't believe you."

I'm glad she didn't, because I knew the minute she accepted the truth, I would be a dead woman. "Your choice," I said with forced nonchalance as I prepared myself. "Either way, we're done, here."

I took a deep yoga breath and lowered the gun. "No!" Dr. Gray yelled as I closed my eyes and slammed every erg of energy into my tight body shield.

The bomb's explosion knocked Valora off her feet, giving me the opportunity to blast through the door and into the sky. I was deafened and felt as though I'd broken my neck. But I was alive.

TWENTY-ONE

"As long as the world shall last there will be wrongs, and if no man objected and no man rebelled, those wrongs would last forever."
~Clarence Darrow

When I was a little girl, Dana and I played together a lot. My earliest memories of our games involved that childhood standard, Hide and Seek. I loved the game, especially when it was my turn to find Dana. I always got more satisfaction out of discovery than deception.

And in truth, I wasn't very good at hiding. Or maybe Dana was just good at finding me. It never took him long. But I didn't care. Being found quickly just meant I didn't have as long to wait before I got to find him again.

A few short years later, my mother's changing attitude toward me would lay the groundwork for the many issues that would taint so many of my future relationships. So the idea of enjoying a game wherein someone was deliberately avoiding me strikes me as more than a little ironic.

Or perhaps my desperate need for affection and attention is why I'm good at finding things. Those picture puzzles where objects are camouflaged? I love them. Word jumbles, too. And maybe that's why I was good as a recovery agent. It was a lot like playing Hide and Seek, only I got to be the Seeker all the time. True, it wasn't as fun. There was no thrill involved in finding my target, other than knowing I'd be able to make rent that month.

Of course, even the best detective sometimes can't see the forest for the trees.

The month following my escape from Valora was frustrating, and I don't mean just because I visited a chiropractor every morning for two weeks and spent a week in a neck brace. For one thing, I had no idea where to look for her or Dr. Gray. They were, of course, long gone from their temporary home by the time I managed to locate the house in which I'd been held, with Jack and Sinta as backup. I spent much of my spare time trying vainly to predict their next moves, and wondering if they'd believed my explanation of why their intentions were doomed to spectacular failure.

Obviously, there was the unspoken but overriding concern: if Valora had been replaced, all of us were at risk. Then there was Captain Shepherd's reaction to my news. (He'd received a promotion since our last contact.) Daniel agreed that a call to him might be a good idea. Even though he was no longer attached to us in an official capacity, we all respected him and he seemed willing to help us in any way he could. We joined him on a video conference line and I brought him up to speed, from tracking the energy weapon to my escape from faux Valora. "Project Echo might be closed," I said, "but the portal obviously isn't." He pondered this for a moment, then said he would look into it. Perhaps it was my imagination, or paranoia, but he seemed to say it in a conciliatory fashion.

And finally, there was the fact that my relationship with Rachel had become strained. She had been staying mostly underground. She wasn't working at the bar. We didn't pay rent, so her biggest expense was gone, and she was able to pay her other bills out of the settlement from her insurance claim. I ran errands for her, including picking up her mail from the post office and buying all the groceries. She only really went outside to get fresh air, and mostly at night. And she never strayed far from the hidden entrance to our haven. I knew it was beginning to wear on her. But more than that, she was still recovering from the trauma of being abducted. I empathized, remembering the hell I went through imprisoned in an alien world, but she didn't seem inclined to use me as any sort of support in her recovery. She had begun to pull away, and I didn't know how to stop her.

About a week after our call to Shepherd, I woke to my phone ringing. After fumbling in the dark for it, I answered. It was Daniel. "Shepherd swears it's dead," he said in a quiet voice. "Went to Nevada himself. Inspected the site. Place being packed up. Minimal staff. No portal."

I hung up, my heart heavy. Our Valora was lost to us. She and I weren't close. Heck, we didn't even like each other very much. But I wanted her here, in our world.

I looked at the time. It was after nine, but you'd never know, living underground as we were. Rachel must already be up, I realized. And just as I thought this, I also knew she was in the kitchen. I got out of bed and pulled on a pair of jeans, then frowned.

How would I know she was in the kitchen? It was three rooms away. I looked in the direction of the kitchen and, of course, saw the bedroom wall. But I saw more. I saw Rachel.

Or rather, I saw *something*.

My mind flashed back to when I could "see" the other Ping Song because her invisibility mechanism was faulty. What I was now looking at was the same sort of image. I sat down on the bed again, staring in shock. It was similar to looking at a weird sort of thermal imaging. I could see her plainly, though I could see no identifying features. I closed my eyes and could still "see" it just as plainly. And it was as though I could feel it... almost as a tangible presence.

This, of course, freaked me the hell out.

I shook my head to clear it, but when I opened my eyes, I could still see the image. And it was moving. Rachel was approaching from the kitchen. My heart was pounding and I stared, wide-eyed, as she entered the doorway, cradling a cup of coffee.

"Morning," she said, flicking on the light, which snapped me out of whatever this was. Now she looked normal. "You okay?"

I nodded. "Yeah," I said, my voice shaky.

"Who called?"

"Daniel," I said, and told her the news. She absorbed it with a sympathetic look, but said nothing. I stood and pulled on a t-shirt. Rachel was staring vacantly into her coffee. I stepped over and put a hand on her arm, asking what was wrong.

When she looked up at me, I was surprised to see her eyes were damp. "I... don't know if I can keep doing this."

"Doing what?"

"Everything," she said, turning her eyes away from mine. "Being with you. Being in the city. Always hiding from my past."

I frowned. "I don't understand. What about your past?"

"Oscar," she said.

I reminded her that Helman had multiple felony charges against him. "He's going to prison. Probably for the rest of his life." He would certainly appeal, but I didn't think it would get him anywhere.

She shook her head. "He could escape."

"Well, even if he does," I said, "so what? He's a punk!"

She cast an accusing glance at me. "A punk who nearly killed you. And yeah, I know he caught you off guard with his bomb, but if he did it once, he can do it again. You don't know him, Dinah. He holds a grudge, and he always gets even with those who cross him."

"I'm not afraid of him, Rach."

"Well *I* am! And it's not just him! His gang is probably out there looking for us, now. Only the fact that we've been living in a goddamn bunker for two months is saving us. And I'm tired of it!"

She turned abruptly and walked to the base's living room area, plopping onto the sofa and setting her coffee heavily on the end table. I followed and joined her.

"I'm just tired."

I nodded. "I know you are. But I think you're just a bit paranoid," I said, without a hint of irony. "I don't think anyone's looking for you."

"I'm not eager to test that theory," she said.

"Rach, why have you never tried to gain more control over your abilities? You could learn to use them effectively and offensively. So you could stop being so afraid."

Rachel shrugged. "Never had that kind of dedication," she said. "Never had anyone to help me."

"I'll help you," I said.

"You have any clue how to do that?" When I hesitated, she said, "I didn't think so. But thanks for offering." She let out a long breath. "I need to move, Dinah. Get away from the city. Maybe leave California altogether."

My stomach sank. "No!"

"It's something I'm considering."

I reached over and ran my fingers through her hair and just stared at her, my devilgirl. While it's true that we didn't have what anyone would consider a passionate romance, the thought of losing her brought back all the pain of losing Sharon and Jackie, forced all my abandonment fears to the front of my mind. Rachel smiled softly at me, reaching up to squeeze my hand. And that only made the pain worse.

In the ensuing days, I focused on easing Rachel's fears. I convinced her to go out in public. We went out to dinners, for walks in the park, and after a lot of persuasion, I even convinced her to resume her job at the Red Devil. Her condition for doing that, though, was that I always be there, whether tending bar or just hanging out. And I was okay with that.

During this time, I also practiced detecting the strange patterns in others as I'd done with Rachel. I found that, with effort, I could shift into whatever state of perception allowed such sensitivity. As near as I've been able to figure it, I'm able to sense bio-organic energy. I hesitate to use the term "aura," because it isn't something that is outside a person's body. Rather, it seems to be contained within it.

This sense is limited only to energy generated by living things. I can detect it in a human being, but I could look right at a nuclear power plant and sense nothing. Obviously, the larger and more energetic the source, the easier it is to sense. A horse registers more strongly than a rabbit. The rabbit, in turn, registers more than a tree. Humans, for some reason, are easier to "read" than other creatures.

I discovered that no two patterns and color combinations are identical. And the more often I observe the pattern, the more easily I can recognize it later. The patterns aren't static. They have a movement to them, but there is so little variation in the way they move from day to day that they may as well be fixed. Memorizing them is no different than memorizing someone's face. As with faces, there are certain similarities between these patterns, certain constants. And yes, the energy patterns of metas can look different from those of non-metas, but not often. The more "normal" a meta looks, physically, the more likely his or her energy pattern will look "normal" to me.

The other thing occupying my mind was a growing conviction that Shepherd was lying. Or was being lied to. I just couldn't accept that the portal was gone. The idea of a government cover-up seemed perfectly plausible. Or perhaps it was less a cover-up than a takeover. Who knew how many had come through? Maybe Shepherd himself had been replaced.

I needed verification from someone I could trust completely. And the truth is, there were precious few people who fell into that category. In fact, they numbered exactly six: Dana, Rachel, Daniel, Sinta, Song, and Jack.

The problem, of course, was how to get this verification. The facility housing the portal was at the northern end of Groom Lake. Shepherd had told me that Project Echo was staffed by DHS personnel, not Air Force. If the project really was shut down, there's a chance it might have been vacated. But I certainly didn't want to count on that.

Then again, just getting to the site undetected would take a lot of effort. Area 51 is heavily monitored around the entire perimeter. Motion sensitive cameras, radar, civilian and military patrols... the works. Which, now that I stopped to think about it, raised a very interesting question. With all that surveillance, how did anyone coming through the portal manage to get outside of Area 51?

The answer, of course, was that they couldn't. Not without a hell of a fight, collusion with someone on our side, or some method to prevent detection, such as the invisibility mechanism the other Ping Song used. I had to admit the latter was not only the most likely, but pretty much a given.

Whatever the situation, I knew I couldn't let it go. I had to see for myself that the portal was truly gone. But I'd only ever seen the portal into the other world, not the one into ours. I needed someone who'd been part of the original mission to return the imposters to their world.

I looked around Jack's home, a small house in a quiet Alameda neighborhood. It was my first time there and I was impressed by how tidy it was. But not surprised. Jack wasn't the stereotypical single guy, living on beer and pizza with ESPN always on the TV. He wasn't a stereotypical guy in any sense, really.

"Yes, I think I can give you a pretty accurate diagram of the layout of the place," he said. "But Dyna... what you're talking about borders on criminal."

"I know," I said, toying with my now empty coffee cup and shifting in my seat to face him. "But can you blame me for not trusting Shepherd? Or, really, anyone?"

Jack was silent a moment, then shook his head. "No. No, I suppose not," he said as he sank back into his overstuffed chair. "What does Daniel think about this?"

"I haven't told him, yet. You know him. He doesn't question authority. He'll believe anything Shepherd tells him."

"Yeah. But still..."

"What if I'm right?" I said. "What if Val wasn't the only one replaced? What if Shepherd was? What if half of DHS has been? What if Song has been, or someone else from the team? Can we afford *not* to do this?"

"And what if the portal really is closed?" he said. "What if Shepherd is telling the truth?" I frowned, not willing to accept that possibility. Finally, he sighed and said, "We need to tell Daniel. And we'll need backup."

Jack went with me to Daniel's home. As expected, our former boss wasn't at all happy about it. "We're not asking you to be an active part of this," I said. "We just wanted you to know what was going on, just in case things go badly."

Daniel fidgeted in his wheelchair. "Making me... accessory, Dyna," he grumbled.

"I know. And I'm sorry for that. But you told me before that you weren't sure what to believe, anymore. And neither are the rest of us. And I guess... I guess what I'm asking is for you to believe in us. To believe in me."

He looked at me for a while, then said, "What if portal... really is closed?"

I glanced at Jack before answering. "Well... then we're screwed. But I just don't believe it."

"Enough to risk prison?" Daniel asked.

Jack saved me the trouble of answering. "The implications are huge, Daniel. What if others really have been replaced? People in key positions, such as Shepherd..."

"I know!" Daniel snapped. Then he sighed. "I know."

"We already suspect certain metas of having been replaced," I said, remembering the ones we believed had simply turned to the criminal side of life, before we knew about the other world.

Daniel nodded slowly. "You'll need more than just... two of you."

"We're going to try to get Ping Song," I said.

"More than three... too," Daniel said. When I didn't agree with him, he said, "Serious."

"I dunno. If things go well, it'll be fine."

"Big if."

"Speaking of Song," I said, "have either of you heard from her, lately?" Neither of them had. I'd left two phone messages for her, but hadn't heard back. I feared the worst. "I was thinking of paying her a visit on campus tomorrow. Want to go with me, Jack?"

"Just in case?"

I nodded. "Just in case." I didn't like thinking that she'd been replaced again, but obviously had to consider it a possibility.

I turned back to Daniel. "There's something else," I said. And this was something I hadn't told Jack, yet. I took a breath. "I think this needs to be made public at some point." My friends stared at me in surprise.

"Dyna," Jack said slowly, "we're sworn to secrecy." Daniel nodded in agreement, staring at me.

"I know! But I don't care about the gag order," I said. I looked at them and could see they were far more concerned about it than I was. Violating the order could result in imprisonment, we all knew. "Look," I said, "it may not be necessary. We could find everything is on the level, that the portal is gone, that Shepherd is right. If that's the case, then fine. Jack and I – and Song, if she's part of it – will face the consequences." I smiled at Jack, acknowledging the risk he was taking. "But if it's not," I continued, "and the portal is still there... if it's clear that this is as huge as we fear... we have to bring it to light. It's just the right thing to do. The public deserves to know." I paused, surprised at the thought I was about to voice. "And if we don't tell them," I said, my pulse pounding, "then... we're just hypocrites."

Jack stared at the floor, but his eyes told me I'd hit a nerve. As for Daniel, I looked to find him staring at me with an odd expression on his face. Bemused, almost.

"Besides," I said, "once the public knows how big it is, the FBI wouldn't dare prosecute us."

"So you think," Jack said.

I sighed. "Right. It's just my opinion. But can we agree to have that fallback? Just in case?"

Both men nodded. I looked at Daniel. "You'd naturally be the one to talk to the media."

But he shook his head. "Bay Scouts never... esteemed... like Gatekeepers."

"No," I agreed, "but..."

"And," he continued, "I'm... crippled. Brain injury. Not what you'd call... reliable." He sighed. "Besides... metas not exactly... in high regard."

I had to admit he was right. But, not completely. Certain metas were still regarded as heroes, despite public distrust and fear. And I happened to know one of them. I pulled a phone number from my cell and texted it to

Daniel. "If things go badly, one of us will text you. Then you can explain everything to Marcus. I assume The Golden Bear is respected enough."

Neither opposed, though I didn't think they believed Marcus would go for it. And as it was getting late, we said our goodbyes. Daniel shook my hand at the door. He wore a sort of half-smile and nodded faintly as he looked into my eyes. I began to ask why, but he yawned. "Good night, Dyna." I shrugged it off. I had too many other things on my mind to try to figure out what was going on in his head.

Two days later, Jack and I called Shepherd from the base's videophone. His face came into focus and he nodded a greeting. "Hello, Dinah. Jack," he said with a hint of impatience. "What can I do for you?"

I cast a glance at Jack before replying. "I'm afraid we have disturbing news," I said. "Valora isn't the only former Bay Scout who's been replaced."

That got his full attention. "What? Who?"

I moved aside, so Shepherd could see behind me, where Ping Song slumped motionless in a chair, gagged, her hands behind her.

"We feared that Ping Song had been replaced," Jack said.

I moved back into the frame. "Obviously, we're curious what to do with her. She doesn't belong here. She needs to be returned to her world so we can get our Ping Song back."

Shepherd frowned. "Yes, but as I've told you... the portal has closed."

"Captain?" Jack interrupted.

"Yes?"

"I may have a solution to that."

Shepherd blinked. "Go on."

"You know my background and my area of expertise. I have reason to believe my abilities may make it possible to re-open the portal."

Another frown. "How certain are you?"

"Not certain at all. But I think it's worth a shot."

Shepherd was quiet for a moment, then put us on hold. He was away for ten very long minutes. When he finally returned to the line, he said, "All right. Tomorrow at 0900, have her ready for transport." He sighed. "Still no luck finding the other Valora?"

"No, sir," I said. "We're hoping you'll be able to learn something from this one."

He nodded. "Let's hope. See you in the morning at the base."

I disconnected the call. "So much for the easy part," I said.

Jack nodded. "Now for the illegal part."

Song lifted her head and removed her gag. "Who else feels like tea?"

✧   ✧   ✧

I called Dana that night. He asked a lot of questions; I gave a lot of vague answers. It was a draining conversation, and I regretted ever having brought it up. I couldn't imagine how he could possibly have been more worried than he was.

In bed, I curled up with Rachel, but sleep wasn't easy in coming. I was virtually certain that at least one person we'd encounter the next day would be working with Valora. And the implications of that scared the crap out of me.

TWENTY-TWO

"No yesterdays are ever wasted for those who give themselves to today."
~Brendan Francis

The first time I ever lost a loved one was when I was thirteen. It was our dog, Scooter. I realize there are some out there who can never equate the loss of an animal to the loss of a human, but I'll never understand those people. I grew up with that dog. We got him when I was two, so I have no memory of him not being around. He was a presence every single day of my life until he died. Dana was off at college. I called him, bawling my eyes out, the day it happened. Dana cried, too.

It wasn't old age that took Scooter. Nor was it death by vehicle. It was cancer, of a particularly aggressive nature. One day he was acting oddly, and when it continued for two more days, Dad took him to the vet. They ran tests. The diagnosis came two days later. And two days after that, Scooter went outside, plopped down in the grass beside the front steps, and took his last nap.

My whole world was different, overnight. After Dana left for college, Scooter had been my main companion. Whenever Mother and I would fight, he'd be there to comfort me... whether he knew or not why I was upset. When I'd have one of my many nightmares, I'd wake to find him lying in bed at my side, nuzzling my hand, as though he knew to wake me.

For years after, I would wake in the night, certain that I'd heard his quiet snoring beside me. I'd come home from school and my heart would ache when a ball of curly fur didn't come bounding across the room to jump on me as I came through the door. Decades later, I can mentally go back to the moment Dad told me he'd died, and the memory immediately plunges me into deep sorrow.

Time heals, of course. But for me, the wounds from having those I care about leave my life only seem to heal superficially. On the outside, I look fine, but inside I'm still bleeding from Lee, Sharon, Jackie, Dana, Rhonda, Scooter, and, of course, my mother. Even when some of those – such as Dana and Rhonda – came back into my life, it only lessened the pain. It didn't erase it.

I often wonder how many more departures I can handle before the accumulated grief renders me numb to the world.

At nine sharp, Shepherd arrived with a DHS escort at our former base, now my temporary home. Jack and I ushered our prisoner outside toward the waiting car. We were dressed in our "official" Bay Scouts uniforms, he in his black jumpsuit thing and me in my blue and whites. Song was gagged again, and her hands truly bound, this time. Jack and I flanked her in the back seat, while the escort drove and Shepherd rode shotgun.

We rode mostly in silence to the air station, where a medium-range helicopter waited for us. It was black with gold accents and adorned with Homeland Security insignia. Two pilots were already aboard. The five of us took seats in the back. Song sat between Jack and me, with Shepherd and the escort sitting across from and facing us.

The flight lasted about ninety minutes, during which Shepherd grilled us on how we'd determined Song had been replaced and how we'd captured her. I recited the story I'd made up, Jack nodding at appropriate spots.

Shepherd frowned a lot during my tale. But was he frowning because he was concerned over widespread world-swapping? Was it because he knew I was lying and he didn't know what to do about it? Or did he just not have his coffee, yet? I wished, for the millionth time, that I had Dana's abilities.

"So how do you think you can re-open the portal?" he said to Jack.

"How much do you know about particle physics?"

"About as much as I know about how to win the lottery."

Jack laughed. "Well, then."

But Shepherd wasn't my main concern during the flight. It was the escort. He spent the flight staring at Ping Song. We'd discussed the possibility that someone we encountered might be familiar with the other Ping Song, so she sat with her head lowered, to prevent him from studying her face in great detail. This didn't deter him, though. He barely looked at anyone but her.

The closer to Area 51 we flew, the more nervous I became. I was convinced we were going to screw up. Why had I been so sure this would work? There were too many things that could go wrong. I'd been arrogant in my thinking.

Eventually, we landed at the north end of Groom Lake. The five of us left our ride, the pilots then took to the air again, headed to the south end of the lake for refueling. There was only one building at this end. A single Jeep sat out front.

We entered the building and followed Shepherd to the check-in. Here, we were required to surrender any weapons (of which we had none) and communication devices. Our phones were plucked from our hands and placed in safekeeping until our departure.

I tried not to panic over the loss of the phone. True, we had communication equipment built into our suits, but when the Scouts were disbanded, they ceased to serve any useful purpose, since they were all routed through the central computers at our base.

We were led down another hallway. The building itself was a modular, temporary building. Shepherd had explained that this installation had only been set up for the purpose of containing and monitoring the portal. It was scheduled to be dismantled soon. I cynically disbelieved him. The building was still here because the portal was still here.

The layout matched the rough sketches made from Jack's recollection of the place. But there were few people in evidence. We passed by empty workstations and areas in disarray. For the first time, my conviction wavered. I might, I thought, end up needing a good attorney for the second time in a decade.

Finally, we reached an office. An armed guard opened the door for us, saluting Shepherd. We filed inside the small room. Seated behind a desk was a man whose face I instantly recognized. Dane Weatherford, Director of the Office of Metahuman Affairs, the division of DHS devoted to all things meta, including enforcement of the Meta Registration Act. Maybe I shouldn't have been surprised to see him, but I was.

We filed in, the DHS agent herding Jack and me in to the left, while he stayed near Song. Weatherford and Shepherd exchanged greetings, then Shepherd began to introduce us. Weatherford cut him short as he stood and stepped out from behind the desk. He was a big man, and none of it flab. "Dinah Geof-Craigs and Jack Fullerton. Dynamistress and Zero-Point, formerly of the Bay Scouts. Yes." He didn't greet us so much as acknowledge our presence. Then he frowned and spoke to Shepherd. "And why are they here, Captain?"

To his credit, Shepherd spoke with a confidence I suspected he didn't feel. "Zero-Point has expertise that might allow the portal to be re-opened, so we may send back those who've infiltrated our world and retrieve our own citizens."

"Interesting," Weatherford said.

"And Dynamistress is here because she has direct experience with the other world and those who have come here, including the other Valora."

"That would be helpful if the other Valora were here," said Weatherford. Then he turned to me. "I've read the report," he said. "It stated you also had fought against this one." He jerked his head toward Ping Song.

I nodded. "That's correct."

He frowned and cast his gaze to the floor. "Now, according to the report, you stated that she possessed some sort of apparatus that rendered her invisible."

My stomach began to knot. "That... was what I believed to be the case, yes."

He looked back up and glanced at Song. "She seems quite visible to me," he said. "Oh, but I forgot. You also said the device was malfunctioning." He raised his eyebrows mockingly. "A technological wizard... with a malfunctioning device?"

I frowned. "Why not? Nobody's perfect."

Weatherford conceded the point. "Even so... I would think she'd have been able to repair it since then. Wouldn't you?"

"I suppose," I mumbled, beginning to hate this man. "Assuming available resources were at hand."

He turned and reached up, removing Song's gag. "Or you could just admit that this isn't her."

My stomach sank. I cast quick glances at the others. Jack looked worried; Shepherd, confused. "What are you talking about?" I asked, hoping my voice didn't betray my concern.

Before he could reply, the DHS agent yelled, "Enough!" I looked up to see him holding a handgun version of those damned energy weapons. He held it against Song's ribcage.

I stared at him. He was on the far side of the room from me. I had no clear shot without hitting someone else.

"What are you doing, son?" Shepherd said, holding up a placating hand toward him. For his effort, he took a shot from the weapon and fell to the floor.

Ping Song took advantage of this to hammer her head into the DHS agent's face. He cursed, blood shooting from his nose, and shot her, then Jack, who was in the process of diving toward him.

He began to raise the gun toward me, but I blasted him into the wall before he could get the shot off. He crumpled to the floor, the gun skidding to Weatherford's feet. The big man stooped to pick it up.

"I'll take that," I said.

"I'm afraid not. DHS property," he said, turning to face me. "I do apologize. This agent is clearly a bit jumpy."

I stepped toward him, frowning. "Right."

"Ms. Geof-Craigs," he said. "Please don't entertain the idea of trying to take this weapon from me."

"Why not?"

"Because I will have you arrested."

I shrugged. "You were going to do that, anyway, though. Right?"

Weatherford frowned at me, then apparently realized I was within striking distance. He raised the gun. "Stop."

Instead, I gave him a gentle energy shove, which for most people of his size, would have been enough to topple him backward. But Weatherford didn't even teeter. And then he shot me.

I staggered, cursing myself, realizing now that Weatherford was a meta. I surged forward to give him a solid punch, but he backhanded me easily. I fell to one knee, thinking I might have made a big mistake.

I looked up, expecting another blow, but Weatherford was staggering. Jack was barely conscious, but had reached out to grip the man's ankle.

Before Weatherford could shoot Jack, I jumped up and laid into him. Between the two of us, he was unconscious in seconds. As he fell, I took the weapon.

Jack sat up, his back against the wall, recovering his strength. "Wow," he said. "So that's what it feels like."

"Yeah," I said, pulling out a tube of Dynapaste from a cape pocket. I squeezed some of it out for Jack. "Your double invented it."

Then I turned and checked on Song and Shepherd, rousing them and giving them some Dynapaste, too.

Shepherd looked around the room. "...the hell?"

I handed the gun to him. "Captain Shepherd," I said seriously, "you're an intelligent man and I hope you know that I... all of us... respect you and appreciate everything you've done for us. I'm sorry for the deception, but..."

He looked down at Weatherford as he stood. "You think he's one of them."

"I don't know," I said. Jack and Song looked at me expectantly. "But I do know I don't trust him."

Shepherd looked at me with a mix of emotions, clearly unsure. "Jesus, Dyna. This," he said, "this is why the government doesn't like working with meta groups, anymore. You don't deal well with rules."

"True enough," I said. When Jack and Song were sufficiently recovered, I said, "Which way to the portal?"

Shepherd gave us directions, but added, "Be careful. By now, the alert has gone out." He nodded toward the door. "The guard should have come in when things started up."

"Crap," I said. "Come on." We dashed to the portal room, expecting at any moment to be attacked. But we saw no one at all. Puzzling, but I didn't waste time thinking about it. Gift horses and all that.

The room itself was unguarded and unstaffed. Inside, we found a computer station, active, with cables extending to the center of the room, where the portal mechanism stood, thrumming with power.

Jack nodded. "Just as I remember."

The structure was quite similar to the portal into the other world from within the "in-between" zone. A huge mechanical circle, embedded with sensors feeding data to the computer. But there was one critical difference. The area in the center of the circle was nothing but empty space.

I reached my hand inside. There was nothing. No weird, gelatin-like resistance. No swirl of colors. Just air. I turned and looked at Song, who was studying the computer readouts.

"History shows energy levels suddenly dropped to effectively zero... let's see... ten days ago. Almost as though..." Song studied the data more closely. "Yes. There's a small gap in the data where nothing was recorded. It could have been due to power being lost, then restored."

"Valora," I said.

"Probably, yes." Song plugged a USB drive into the computer and began downloading data.

Jack looked over her shoulder at the screen. "They've got a lot of sensors in that thing," he said, obviously impressed. "Measuring everything you could think of."

It didn't matter to me what they were measuring if the portal itself was gone. I turned to look back at the structure, wishing we really did have a way to open it again.

"What's that?" Song asked. I looked back to see her pointing at the screen. "That reading is unchanged."

"P· a," Jack said. "Pascal. It's measuring pressure."

I frowned and stepped over to the computer. "Pressure of what?"

Jack shrugged. "No idea. But it's a ridiculously small amount. You wouldn't even feel it." He looked at the numbers again. "Weird thing is that it's only the sensors on one side of the frame that are registering it, as if..."

"What?" I said.

"Well, it's almost as if something in there were trying to move in one direction, bumping against one side of the frame." He looked up from the monitor. "Dyna... I think it's still there, in some respect."

"But... movement? What?"

"Okay, look... I don't even play a cosmologist on TV, but we figure what we've got here is two... dimensions... universes... whatever you want to call them... that have rubbed up against each other. Now, we know everything in our universe is moving. Planets, solar systems, galaxies... spinning and moving through the universe, which itself is expanding. There's no reason to assume these dimensions or whatever are stationary. They could be sort of sliding against each other."

I blinked. "That means the portals move?"

"Apparently so, unless anchored somehow, such as by these mechanisms. Don't even ask me how that all works. But it seems that when the power was cut, it evidently wasn't off long enough for it to completely close and move outside the frame's influence, but long enough for it to shrink beyond its ability to hold it open."

"Well, that's fascinating. But we need it open. Is there anything in all that data that might give us a hint how to do that?"

"A big bang," Song said. "That's how it started."

"Sorry," I said. "I don't know how to recreate the universe."

"No," Song said. "I mean an explosion. That's what brought people to this spot in the first place. A tremendous blast was detected and, upon investigation, they discovered the portal." She nodded toward the screen. "Pretty extensive notes in here," she said. "But... it was estimated at several megatons," she said. "And when they found the rift, it was pretty big. Twenty feet, this says."

I pondered this for a moment, then pulled a tube of Dynapaste from my cape pocket and started sucking it down. I certainly couldn't come close to a blast of that size, but neither did I need to create a rift twenty feet wide.

"Right," Song nodded, picking up on my intentions. "Jack? We need to move the frame. And the computer." She stopped her download and yanked out the USB drive.

I removed my belt, head band, and my electronics and tossed them to Song, who carried them out of the room. When she returned, I pointed to a tiny seam at the top and bottom of the portal. "It looks like it breaks down into two halves."

Jack looked confused as he unplugged the cables from the computer and moved it and the monitor out of the room, but said nothing. Song came over to the machine. I hovered in the exact center of the frame as she laid a hand gently on one side of it and closed her eyes. Then she began "singing" to the machine in her click-and-hum fashion. A moment later, the halves separated. She opened her eyes. "Quickly," she said to Jack as he returned. Together, they pushed the mechanism into the hallway. When they were safely out of the room, I let loose with as big a blast as I could.

The sound of rending metal filled my ears as I fell to the floor, spent. When I opened my eyes, I saw half the room was gone. Walls were flattened and the ceiling was in shreds littering the ground. And at "ground zero" of my blast was a small, shining rift, shrinking rapidly. Without thinking, I thrust my hand into it, then watched as it settled in snugly around my wrist. My arm prevented it from closing completely. It looked like my hand had been amputated. I pulled another tube of Dynapaste from my pocket and ripped it open with my teeth.

"Whoa," Jack said from the doorway. "If that doesn't bring someone running, I don't know what will." Then he ducked away, and he and Song brought the equipment back in. But again, no one else arrived. This worried me.

Once the portal frame was reconnected, Song booted up the computer. A seeming eternity later, she said, "I'm not getting any readings."

Jack said, "The portal isn't making contact with the sensors. It isn't filling the framework."

"Great," I muttered. "Well, let's see..." I tried sticking my other hand inside, but my finger couldn't penetrate into the rift, slipping instead through empty space. Then I tried dragging my arm toward the portal frame. But I may as well have been trying to move it through solid rock. I stood there, stumped. The others had no ideas, either.

Then a thought struck me. "If Muhammad can't come to the mountain..."

"Good thinking," Jack said as he came over to me. He pushed the framework assembly until one edge of the frame came in contact with my wrist.

I felt the frame "grab" the rift. "Okay," I said. "Let's see if this works, now." With great effort, I attempted to drag my arm downward, gratified that it budged, however slightly. But after an inch or two, it grew easier to move. After a foot, even easier. I was careful to keep my wrist in contact with the frame as I worked it around the circumference. The rift stretched and crackled as I did so. When I finally returned to the origin point, the familiar swirling pattern erupted as the rift filled the entire opening.

"We have data," Song said from her position near the computer.

"Awesome." I said. "I don't want to waste any time. I'm going in, hopefully to return with Val." I quickly replaced my belt and whatnot, then said, "See if you can figure out why no one responded to all this." The others nodded, and I stepped/oozed through the portal.

I emerged on the other side, ready to blast whoever happened to be waiting for me. But I was in what appeared to be an empty office. To my right was a computer on a desk. There were file cabinets and bookcases. I looked back at the portal. It was framed with a similar mechanism, but it was silent, not operating.

I stepped to the other end of the room and out into a hallway. Two more doors to my left. A quick peek revealed these rooms to be vacant, as well. I turned down the hallway in the other direction. At the end was another familiar thing: a thick set of doors like I'd encountered at the other portal in this area. Thankfully, these were open.

On the other side of the doors, I walked into the huge open area filled with weapon racks. There were no overhead lights on but there was a dim ambient glow. I had no idea what the source was, but I had no time to solve that mystery. I tapped the jewel in my head band, bringing forth its pale bluish white rays.

The place seemed devoid of people, which I found hard to believe. I concentrated and shifted into my weird, energy perception state. I wasn't sure what kind of range I had, or what could impede it, but I sensed nothing. I headed toward the holding cells at the other end of the complex, keeping alert for anyone who might be there.

Two of the cells were in use, and I assumed Valora would be in one of them. However, I was surprised to find that one contained the otherworld Ping Song. She had a gag in her mouth and gave me a hateful look when I peeked in on her. The other one held the otherworld version of Jack. The look he gave me was more of a leer.

I wondered why they were in there, but I didn't waste time asking them, or inquiring about Val's location. I still needed to find her and I had a very bad sense that I wasn't going to like what I found. That sense being smell.

In the farthest cell, I found a body. My heart sank as I saw it was Valora. She was dressed only in her underwear. A metal spear was stuck through her, the sharp, bloody tip of it protruding just under her breastbone, sticking out more than a foot. I recognized the spear as Valora's own... or one that looked just like hers, anyway.

Blood pooled around her, mixing with a puddle of urine. I knelt next to my former teammate, overcome with emotion. This isn't how we're supposed to go out, I thought. Stabbed in the back. What a cowardly attack. It bothered me to think of how it must have been done. Because of the nature of Valora's flesh, this couldn't have been a quick impalement, but slow and deliberate. And agonizing.

Though it turned my stomach to do so, I rolled her sideways and pulled the spear out, tossing it aside. I looked at her carefully. Her skin was mottled and veins were visible. Her abdomen was swollen, but not bloated. If Valora had been a normal human, I would have said she'd died maybe four days previously. But I had no idea of the rate of putrefaction for someone like her. She could have been dead a month, for all I knew.

I brushed the tousled hair away from her face and tried to wipe away the line of blood from her mouth, but it was dried. Her eyes were closed. I assumed, therefore, that she'd lingered a while before death.

After another minute or so, once I'd collected myself, I took a deep breath and shoved my arms underneath her body. I stood, hoisting her dead weight. I looked down at her pale face and spoke softly. "Time to go home, Val."

I emerged into Area 51 prepared for chaos. Instead, the room housing the portal – or what was left of the room – was empty. Jack and Song were gone. Over the oscillating drone of the portal construct, I heard the chop of a helicopter outside. I didn't like what that might imply.

Lowering Val's body to the floor near the computer station, I stepped out into the hallway and back to the room where we'd met Weatherford. As I feared, Shepherd, Weatherford, and the DHS escort were also gone.

I dashed back to the portal room, since it was the quickest way outside, but skidded to a stop as I got there. Standing over Valora's body was, impossibly, the other Valora.

And now I understood why my teammate was clad only in underwear. Her doppelganger had taken her clothing. Insultingly, she was dressed in my Val's full combat regalia, including her golden chainmail tunic, studded leather armor skirt, and thick golden helmet with sleek wings.

She looked up, her face reflecting the surprise on my own. "It seems death defies displacement." She smirked. "How fortunate for me."

"Maybe not so much," I said, and let loose with a blast that blew her across the floor. Then I attacked her, my disbelief replaced by rage. This woman killed my teammate, and frankly, I wanted to beat the shit out of her.

My energy-enhanced punches are pretty powerful. If I can punch through a brick wall, it's not hard to imagine what I can do to skin and bone. Unless, of course, you have flesh like Valora's. As much as I pummeled her, it was as though I was just slapping her. The best I could do was knock or blast her away from me. And I did need to keep her away. My protective energy shield prevented her from killing me, but her blows still hurt like hell.

There was no question that I'd run out of energy before she tired. So, with a last blast that sent her skidding across the floor, I took to the air, out into the open desert.

I scanned the sky and saw a black combat helicopter heading east, toward Freedom Ridge, if my memory served correctly. Most likely, this was an Air Force 'copter, not a DHS aircraft. As I watched it receding, I noticed a plume of dust rising from the ground on the far side of the lake, as though a vehicle were approaching. The 'copter was obviously on an intercept course. There were also flashes of flame coming from the ground.

But before I could speculate on the situation, a searing pain raked across the back of my neck. I spun in the air to see my attacker. Wheeling around for another swipe was a woman with dark skin and deep brown hair. And wings. Big, feathery wings, mostly brown with bits of white, but the primaries showed the white more than the brown. Another talon ripped at my throat, but my shield now repelled it. I hit her with a close-up blast that propelled her backward, but didn't seem to do much damage. She rolled... or flew... with the blow. But it seemed to give her pause, as she flew off instead of attacking me again. I watched as she met up with Valora, who was getting a bit too close for my liking. I took off toward Freedom Ridge.

It took me about a minute at full thrust to reach the commotion. The helicopter was just hovering, the pilots observing the action. Two vehicles sat nearby. One was a small Jeep that appeared to have come down from the ridge. The other was a larger personnel carrier that had evidently come from the base. About a dozen DHS agents, each with a zero-point weapon, were in the process of having their asses kicked by a small bundle of fur. I grinned as I saw Sinta bouncing from one agent to another, clawing and kicking.

There were two strangers, one of whom I recognized, the other being a blond guy built like a tank. The bursts of flame I'd seen had come from one of the Texas twins. His brother dampened the area with sprays of water splashing off his targets. And the big tank guy had his hands full with a certain Mexican hammer.

It took me only a moment to realize how my friends must have come to be here. I reached up and switched my radio to our team channel. I nearly laughed aloud as I heard the chatter.

"Wow, they'll let anyone in here," I said.

"About time you... joined the party," came Daniel's voice.

I took careful aim at the massive guy beating on Esteban and built up a powerful shot. "That's me," I said, firing off the blast. "Always a day late and a dollar short." I smiled in satisfaction as he spun to look up, allowing Esteban to land a couple great hits. "Thanks for inviting some friends. You're at the base?"

"Yes."

"Sorry I didn't vacuum."

I dove in and continued blasting the big guy. I recognized him, now. Powerhaus. A solo meta out of San Jose who'd been one to "turn bad." Which we now knew to have been one of the replaced.

"Don't mind that," Daniel drawled, "but... you're out of coffee." I grinned despite myself. Gallows humor, I suppose. It helped to ease the tension of being in such dangerous spots.

"Have Rachel go get some," I suggested.

"Not here," he replied.

That surprised me. I'd been joking about sending her for coffee, knowing she wouldn't go, anyway. But I had no time to waste thinking about it. "Bring me up to speed."

Daniel did so, explaining that he'd called our former teammates and arranged for them to meet up with Sinta in Las Vegas. From there, they rented the Jeep and drove up to Freedom Ridge, awaiting a signal from Daniel. If things had gone south, I was supposed to contact him. But my explosion served as a better signal than any other would have.

I wondered how they'd gotten past the security, both civilian and military. Then I realized that's probably why the helicopter was there, having been dispatched to see who'd gotten past the guard shack and how.

"What's with the 'copter?" I said, just to be sure.

"Probably trying to... figure who to shoot."

I laughed, even though I knew he was serious. "And the flying chickie?" I asked, blasting Powerhaus again.

"Caracara," Daniel said. "Records say she's from... French Guiana."

"Replacement?"

"Seems so."

I wasn't surprised that the otherworlders were here. Powerhaus. This Caracara person. And, over fighting the twins, Kimera. I'd suspected there must be some sort of connection between them and the otherworld Valora. I just didn't know what it was.

Daniel spoke up again, saying simply, "Valora?"

Now wasn't the time to break that news. "Daniel, where are Jack and Song?"

"I... don't know," he said. "Never made... radio contact."

A zero-point beam struck me and I staggered to the ground. I waited for a follow-up, but there wasn't one. "Sorry about that," Sinta said, behind me. I turned to see that she'd disarmed the last DHS agent and knocked him out. At least, I thought that was all she'd done.

Esteban had Powerhaus on the ropes, now, so I looked to see how Billy and Bobby were faring against Kimera, a creature you have to see to believe. A female body covered with tan fur, sharp feline claws, the tail of a lion, a face with somewhat reptilian features and three-inch fangs, and ram horns coming out of her forehead.

Despite the twins' abilities, they were having a difficult time with her. Kimera is fast. Really fast. Also very strong, very nimble, and very smart. She seemed able to predict the attacks aimed at her, and could evade almost all of them. Even against two foes. Three, I decided, would probably do the trick.

I swooped in and aimed a blast. Just as I let loose, though, something heavy hit me from above. Or someone, I should say. It was Valora. The flying woman had carried her over and dropped her on me. Valora clung to me, wrapping her hands around my throat.

Despite my shield, she was hurting me. Breaking her grip wasn't likely, as she was far stronger than I. So I pivoted in the air and blasted us straight toward the ground.

As we hit, Valora tumbled off of me, landing in front of Sinta, who held one of the zero-point weapons. She immediately fired it at Valora.

My satisfaction evaporated, though, when Caracara swooped in and plucked Sinta from the ground, knocking the weapon from her hands and carrying her into the sky. Valora was quicker than I in recovering. Just as I got to my feet, she tackled me.

Sinta's nervous voice came over my headset. "Dyna?"

"Coming," I said, though I was not at all sure I was. Valora was pummeling me. I was completely on the defensive, unable to get a blast in to knock her away.

A deep voice came from behind Valora. "*Perdóname, señorita.*" And then Esteban pulled Valora from me and commenced hammering. I blasted into the sky after Sinta.

"*Dyna!*" The panic in Sinta's voice sent a chill through me. And what I saw about tore my heart from my chest. Caracara had carried Sinta up above the vortex of the helicopter blades... and dropped her.

Time stood still.

I was blasting as fast as I could to reach her, but knew I couldn't catch her before she hit the blades. I might be able to destroy the blades, though not without causing considerable harm to the personnel on board. The crash from this height might even kill them.

I made my decision in a split second and fired off a massive blast. My aim was true, and I altered my trajectory to catch Sinta. The blast had knocked her far enough away from the 'copter to miss the blades. She was out cold when I caught her, limp and bleeding. I'd hit her hard. I hoped there wasn't serious internal damage, but couldn't assume there wasn't.

I maneuvered back up to the helicopter and hovered near the open cabin doorway. The gunner swung his mounted weapon at me, but paused, seeing that I was holding an unconscious Sinta. I placed her gently on the floor of the cabin and spoke to the gunner. "She needs medical care. Now." He looked at Sinta, then at his comrades. After a moment's hesitation, he let go of his gun and pulled Sinta further into the cabin. I breathed a sigh of relief as the 'copter wheeled and headed south to the base.

I relayed this information to the team, then turned my attention back to Caracara. And that's when everything went to shit.

"*No!*"

It was Billy's voice that split our eardrums over the comm. I turned to look in the twins' direction, in time to see Kimera dropping Bobby to the ground. Even from my distance, I could see the fang punctures in his shoulder. Kimera's venom – or at least, "our" Kimera's – was extremely potent, which was why she didn't use it much. She had no desire to kill her opponents. And while it's true that she could meter the dosage at will, I doubted her doppelganger had done so in this case.

Ignoring Caracara, I dove down toward the twins. I landed next to Bobby, sending a wide blast at Kimera as I hit the ground. It wasn't enough to hurt, but it sent her flying backward several yards. I hoped it would buy me enough time.

I reached into my cape, opening the Velcro-sealed pocket that held my emergency kit. One of the items in the kit was polyvalent snake antivenin. I had no idea if it would be effective against Kimera's venom, though. I began injecting Bobby, whose face was contorted in agony and fear. He looked at me in gratitude.

To his credit, Billy stayed out of my way and kept Kimera at bay with huge swaths of flame. "Watch out for Caracara," I said as I pulled out

Bobby's own med-kit and used his antivenin. And just at that moment, she came swooping in. Billy whirled and angrily shot a bolt that hit the woman dead on. Her wings erupted in flames and she came crashing to the ground in a cloud of feathers and smoke, screaming in pain.

Lifting his glazed eyes from my injections, Bobby turned his head toward Caracara, who clearly was unable to extinguish her burning wings. And, despite his pain, despite the fact that she was fighting against us, he extended a hand and sent a geyser of water shooting over the woman, dousing the flames. Then his arm dropped to the ground and he lost consciousness.

Caracara was curled into a ball on the ground, coughing from the water. Huge patches of feathers were gone, the rest blackened. She made squeaky pain noises. She was out of the fight, I decided.

Billy was furiously attacking Kimera, who evaded his flames, but wasn't able to close the gap between them. It was just a question of which of them would tire first. My money was on Billy to drop, as soon as his adrenaline surge wore off.

I joined in, and between the two of us, we soon had her on the ropes. But Billy's flames were growing weaker by the second.

Despite the huge horns on her head and the claws, tail, and fur of a lion, when I looked at Kimera, all I saw was snake. And it wasn't just the fangs. There was no fur on her face. It tapered off around her shoulders, transitioning to fine, golden scales up her neck and face. Her green eyes were much larger than a human's and serpentine in appearance. I dug into my memory of animal biology classes. And then I wondered just how much Kimera was like a snake.

The vast majority of snakes have monocular vision, but Kimera's eyes were closer together than most snakes, more like a human's. So her depth perception was probably fairly accurate. Snake vision ranges from crappy to excellent. I was going to have to assume the latter for Kimera.

Snakes smell by using their forked tongues, which pull in the particles that a human would inhale through the nose. But I knew Kimera didn't have a forked tongue, and she did have a human-looking nose, so I tossed this out as irrelevant.

But her nose also had deep grooves flanking it, like those of pit vipers and some other snakes. If the similarity held true, these would be receptors that detected infrared. Heat signatures, in other words.

That was it.

I battered her with a series of sweeping energy bursts. The wider they are, the less damage they do, but she couldn't avoid them as she could my focused blasts. I knocked her back a bit with each one, until soon we were in the scrub brush of the foothills to the ridge.

On my command, Billy set the brush all around her in flames, stoking them continually so they were quite high. Thick smoke filled the air around her and the heat obscured her infrared. But my ability to sense her energy pattern was unhindered.

One high-energy, focused shot, and Kimera went down. Billy turned and ran back to his brother as I bound her hands and feet. I left her lying there and headed back to the others.

Valora was nowhere to be seen. Esteban was on the ground. Powerhaus was gone, as was the Jeep my friends had arrived in. I scanned the area and saw the tell-tale cloud of dust of a vehicle, moving in the direction of the portal building. I let them go. I had more immediate concerns and held no illusion that I could hope to beat the two of them even if I should catch them.

Caracara was sitting up, but was clearly no threat. The dozen DHS goons were still unconscious. Or perhaps dead. I didn't check. I flew over to check on Esteban. He was unconscious and blood trickled from his ear.

"Daniel?" I said into my mic. "We're in a bad way. I need immediate medical attention for Esteban and Bobby. Any way you could make that happen?"

"Will try," he said.

From my med-kit, I pulled a chemical ice pack. I ruptured the liquid core, shook it up, and put it on Esteban's head to help minimize any brain swelling.

I looked over at the twins. Billy sat in the dirt, cradling his brother's head. "Is he conscious?" I asked over the team comm.

"No," Billy said. "But he's breathin'."

"Good," I said. "I need your ice packs." Billy brought over the ones he and his brother carried, and I activated them, placing them around Esteban's head.

Billy returned to Bobby, and I sat there, holding the ice packs in place, waiting to hear from Daniel, and wondering what the hell we were to do now.

TWENTY-THREE

"A child begins to reach maturity when he realizes that other people are equally worthy of the spotlight."
~ Jonathan Heid

Anger is a funny thing.

I once asked Dana about it, because the more thought I gave to my own unresolved anger, the less I understood it. In fact, it took years for me to accept that I even had unresolved anger issues. I believed that anger was an end unto itself.

But anger, he said, was the emotional response to an event that we consider unjust or threatening. It's often a protective sort of thing. Anger "gets our blood boiling," so the expression goes. That means it gets our adrenaline pumping, so it's helpful in situations that truly are threatening.

But obviously, not all anger-inducing events require that sort of physical protection. And sometimes, our anger is displaced. In many people, chronic anger reveals itself as depression, cynicism, fatigue, or other conditions.

I've become better at understanding my anger and letting go of some of it. I came to understand that my anger at Dana wasn't really anger at him. Unlike anger at my mother, which most certainly is exactly that.

And in some cases, I can't deny the usefulness of a good, old-fashioned rage.

The atmosphere in the Air Force infirmary was tense, to say the least. Bobby and Caracara occupied beds on opposite ends of the room. Kimera was in custody elsewhere in the base.

Sinta's and Esteban's injuries were severe enough for them to be flown to a hospital in Las Vegas. I'm not sure where the DHS agents were taken.

Billy had been treated for dehydration. He sat next to his brother, who had been given additional antivenin. I had the back of my neck tended to. Shepherd was there, as well. He said the DHS escort had gotten the drop on him and clocked him in the head. Weatherford brought him to the infirmary.

All of us were under the watchful eye of armed airmen. We weren't prisoners, exactly. Or maybe we were, as far as they were concerned. And honestly, I didn't blame the Air Force for being pissed about all of this. They'd been ordered by DHS to refrain from interfering with their operation. I was just grateful that they didn't feel observation was "interference." And that they were willing to help out at Daniel's request, though I had no idea how he'd accomplished that.

I stood next to Caracara. Part of me wanted to beat her senseless for what she tried to do to Sinta. Had she succeeded, I probably... well, honestly, I don't know what I would have done. As it was, I looked at the blistered flesh of her torso and wings and the huge expanses of missing feathers, and I actually felt for her. She sat upright in a bed, her injuries slathered in silver sulfadiazine.

She ignored me when I first stepped to her bedside. But when I'd remained for a minute, she finally acknowledged me. "*Quoi?*" she said, without looking at me.

"*Anglais?*"

She nodded. "Some."

"Good. I don't remember enough French to trust it." I took a breath, trying to control my emotions. The last thing I needed to be right now was confrontational. I nodded toward her wings. "Will they grow back?" I asked.

"*Oui.* If the roots are not too badly hurt."

"That salve will help," I said. "Will you answer some questions?"

"*Peut-être,*" she said.

I decided to start easy. "How long have you been in this world?"

She glanced up at me for the first time. "Four days."

"And what is your relationship to Valora?"

"*Rien.* She controlled the way."

"Then why were you helping her?"

"*C'est notre accord.* She gave me... transport? Passage. I agreed to assist when she asked."

I frowned. "So... this was just payment for that?"

She nodded. "*Oui.*"

I looked again at her injuries. "I think you overpaid."

She looked up at me. "*Vraiment.*"

"Same deal for Kimera?"

Caracara's eyes flashed. "*Démon!*"

"Yeah... I'm not a fan, either." I sighed. "I imagine it would be pointless to ask you what Valora's plans are."

"I know nothing."

"You realize we're sending you back, right?"

The woman looked up at me, surprised. "Not prison?"

I shook my head, initially baffled that she'd even suggest that. Then a strange thought struck me. "How did you learn of this world?"

Caracara chose her words carefully. "On the computer. Valora had posted messages. A fresh start for any who wanted."

"And what did she tell you about this world, exactly?"

The woman shook her head. "Little."

"So you don't understand what's going on..." I let out a heavy breath and gave her the nutshell version of how she came to be here and what that meant for our world. Her eyes grew with each passing moment.

"*Merde,*" was her verbal reaction. "You are saying that when I came here, someone just like me went to my world?"

"Yes," I nodded. "And we'd like her back." I cleared my throat. "One last question," I said. "What did Valora tell you about those of us you were fighting?"

She looked up at me. "That you were here to kill us." She lowered her eyes. "*Putain!*" She clenched her talons, ripping great tears in the mattress of her bed. "The liar!" Then she stiffened. "*Mon dieu.* Your little friend..." She looked up at me in horror at what she'd nearly done.

"It's okay," I said. And I meant it. My anger at her was now just more for Valora, something I hadn't thought possible. "Anyway... Thanks for talking with me."

Caracara nodded, then I went to check on the twins before heading into the hallway, where I spoke to Daniel again on a private channel. I brought him up to speed on the others. I asked him to call Rachel's cell phone, mine being still back in the building at the north end of the lake. But she didn't answer when he called. He left a voicemail for her to call him. "Can you let my brother know I'm okay?"

"Of course."

I sat in a folding chair against the wall, out of earshot, but not sight, of an armed airman. "You were right. This was a bad idea. I can't imagine how badly it would have gone if you hadn't arranged for the others to join us." I waited for him to offer words of comfort, to tell me it wasn't a bad plan. But he didn't.

"What now?" he asked.

"Maybe you should tell me," I said. "I'm clearly not a tactician."

"Find Valora. Find Jack and Song."

I hesitated. "Yeah, well... Finding Valora isn't as high a priority as it was before."

Daniel was quiet for a moment, then said, "You didn't answer... before. About Val." He lowered his voice. "Dead, isn't she?" I let out a heavy breath, then told him how I'd found her. How I'd brought her back. How this hadn't sent the otherworld Valora back. "Good of you," he said, "to not let others know, yet."

"Yeah, well... if they wander into the portal room, they'll know."

"So. Jack and Song."

I hung my head and slumped back against the wall. "I've been trying to consider all the possibilities, there," I told him. "One is that they're dead. But I'm not going to think about that one."

He grunted an acceptance of that. Then he said, "Why are you... still at infirmary?"

"Because I don't know where to look!"

"Options... limited."

I frowned. He was right, as usual. I was wasting precious time. I thanked him again and clicked off. I stood and headed for the nearest exit. Time to find out if we were prisoners or not.

Turned out we weren't.

I saw the abandoned Jeep outside as I landed in the portal room. The portal was still active, the interface swirling, the mechanism humming. I was nearly certain my foes had gone to the in-between, or even into their world, either of which would be safer than here.

I walked past Valora's body, out of the room into the hallway. And for the next half hour or more, I roamed down every hall, checking every room, only to find everything empty. No DHS agents anywhere.

Could they have gone with Valora and Powerhaus? It didn't seem as though there was another possibility. I stopped and closed my eyes, relaxing and switching to my energy-perception state. Though I didn't need to, I turned in a circle, "looking" in every direction. And there was something.

It was very faint. But it was there.

And it was coming from beneath my feet.

It took me nearly an hour to find the hidden stairs. The entrance was in Weatherford's office, hidden behind a bookcase like a bad cliché.

It was dark, the only light in the stairwell coming from plastic light strips on each step. I listened carefully before descending slowly and as quietly as I could. I heard muffled voices.

At the bottom, I listened to the voices, but was unable to make out anything being said. I inched my forehead along the wall, just enough to get an eyeball in the open.

The stairs opened into a single, large room. An impressive amount of machinery and scientific equipment sat around the perimeter, but my full attention was on the very center of the room. There stood, floor to ceiling, an energy cell, virtually identical to the ones in the in-between.

Standing next to it, looking into the cell, was a familiar figure: the DHS escort. He held a zero-point rifle, slung over his back and was observing the figures in the cell: Jack and Song. Both were seated in folding camp chairs. I could see Jack's profile as he looked out at the escort.

Scanning the rest of the room and seeing no one, I took careful aim at the escort's weapon and hit it with as narrow a blast as I could conjure. The weapon took the brunt of the impact and began sparking. The escort himself was knocked back a foot or so and froze when he saw me dashing toward him.

He swung the rifle around, but by the time he realized it was damaged, I'd reached him. I took him down with a punch. Jack jumped up from his chair when he saw me. I stepped over to the cell. Song, however, remained slumped, her head lolled to the side.

I examined the pillars of the cell. Like the one in which I'd been imprisoned, this one had its controls on one of the corner pillars. I frowned when I saw the numerical keypad. Deactivating the energy walls wouldn't be as simple as slapping a single button. Then again, I thought, I wasn't interested in reusing it.

Jack stood back as I hammered the pillar with an energized fist. Sparks crackled and flew; the energy walls flickered and died. I rushed to Song's side and examined her.

"Drugged, it seems," Jack said. "She's been like that since I woke up."

I nodded. That made sense. An energy cell wouldn't hold someone who could "speak" to the machinery.

Jack told me that, moments after I'd stepped through the portal, half a dozen black-suited men came in with the zero-point rifles and took them down. He had regained consciousness there in the cell. "No idea where anyone else is. I've only been conscious maybe an hour or so." He looked me over. "You look a little the worse for wear. What's going on?"

Now it was my turn to fill him in on everything, including Valora's death, the arrival of the other Valora and her allies, as well as our teammates, who were now mostly out of commission.

"Any idea where Valora and Powerhaus might have gone?"

"No." I looked down at the escort. "But I suspect this guy might have the answer."

"Yeah, maybe you shouldn't have hit him so hard."

I appreciated Jack's attempt at levity, but I just couldn't smile. Too much had gone wrong. Too many people were hurt. And there were too many implications I didn't like.

I turned and nodded at the energy cell. "This bothers me," I said. "This technology, of the weapons and the walls of this cell, are almost certainly the work of your counterpart."

"Clever guy."

"This being here tells me that infiltration from their world is more profound than we expected. Who knows how many otherworlders have replaced members of Homeland Security? And why have they done so? How does that fit into Valora's intentions?"

Jack shrugged. "Who says it has to?"

I hadn't actually considered that. But Jack had a good point. Just because Valora seemed to be the one in charge didn't mean that others couldn't have agendas of their own. Caracara's words seemed to support that idea.

I nodded toward Song. "Anything you can do for her?"

"I'll see," he said, and went over to the girl.

Since I wasn't going to get anything out of the escort, I pulled out a pair of nylon cuffs and bound his hands behind him. Then I turned my thoughts to the other problem.

"What do you think she wants, Jack? Aside from living in a world that's not such a shithole, what is Valora after? I mean, she knows now that I can't create metas, or make existing metas into... super-metas or whatever."

"Maybe she doesn't believe you."

That was what she'd claimed, anyway. Maybe she thought Gray could do it, as she'd implied. I turned to see what progress Jack was making with Song, to find him looking back at me. "What?" I said.

"Hm?"

"Why are you looking at me like that?"

He smiled faintly. "When's the last time I told you how beautiful you are?"

I frowned. "Seriously? That's where your head is?"

He chuckled. "Just an observation." Then he looked down at Song, who was stirring. "Ah. Here we go."

Song opened her eyes and looked around. She nodded at me and thanked Jack.

After filling Song in on recent events, I said, "I hate to say it, but I think we need to go in. Valora is either back in her world or in the in-between zone. Let's take the fight to her."

The others agreed. I tapped my radio to the team channel. "Daniel, I've got Jack and Song."

"Good!"

"Have you heard anything about our injured friends?"

"Spoke with the hospital," he said. "Sinta is conscious. Internal damage minimal. Will be fine." He paused a moment. "Esteban still out. Brain swelling is going down, though. Expect full recovery, in time."

"Great to hear. Billy, how's your brother?"

"Stable, Dyna. Thank God."

"We're going in," I said. "Could use your help, if you're up for it."

"Be there pronto."

Once through the portal, I led the way, stepping through the office-type room into the hallway, then down through the open blast doors and into the room filled with weapon racks. I led the others through the room, extending my senses to detect anyone else nearby. I still wasn't sure what kind of range I had with it, so I didn't rely on it to do much more than keep me out of immediate danger.

"What if Valora's gone through?" Billy asked. "How you expect to find her?"

"Let's first see if she's done so."

"How will you know?" Jack asked.

I nodded toward the cells ahead of us. "The otherworld Jack and Song were imprisoned here," I told them. "If they still are, then it stands to reason Valora hasn't come here at all, let alone gone through."

Song grabbed a pair of zero-point rifles from a rack and tossed one to Jack. To my curious look, she said, "We don't all have the luxury of offensive abilities we can use from a distance."

"Right," I said, annoyed that I hadn't thought of that, first.

Moments later, we stood before the cells. And there they were, still captive, and both evidently asleep. So much for my theory.

"Now what?" Song asked.

I heaved a sigh and stared vacantly into Jack's cell. "I don't know," I muttered. I'd been so certain that Valora had come here. The Jeep had been parked outside, after all. I should have watched the surveillance videos, just to be sure, but simply hadn't thought of it.

As my teammates shifted uneasily, I stared at the sleeping other-Jack. Would it be worth it to wake and question him? Could we intimidate him enough to spill anything worthwhile? Unlikely. Valora undoubtedly inspired more fear than I could impart.

"Dyna?" Billy said. "What's the plan?"

I wished I had an answer to that question. I stared at the other-Jack's sleeping face, noting the thin trail of drool at the corner of his gagged mouth. I remembered the smirk on that mouth the other time I'd seen him, and the leering look he'd given me. A chill swept through me, then. His mouth hadn't been gagged when I saw him before.

I cursed myself for not realizing I'd been set up. I slammed energy into my shield and spun around in time to see Song smack the butt of her weapon into Billy's head, sending him sprawling to the floor. Then the energy bolt from Jack's gun hit me.

To my astonishment, I felt my shield collapse as I fell to one knee. This weapon was different. My energy was draining much more rapidly than from the other weapons.

Jack laughed as he fired again, and I suddenly understood. He was somehow able to use his own abilities to boost the gun's power, making it into a super-weapon in his hands.

Song shoved Billy into a vacant cell and activated the walls. And then I collapsed fully to the floor in a heap, arms sprawling in front of me, eyes closed. As I'd hoped, Jack stopped shooting me. I lay still, becoming as passive as I could, feeling my left toes touching the front wall of Jack's cell. I allowed the energy to invade me.

"Give me a hand," I heard Jack say to Song.

"Wimp," she said.

My foot blazed with pain, but I focused only on sensing the location of my adversaries. They stood in front of me, stooping to each grab an arm.

I reached out and grabbed each of them by an ankle and blasted myself from the floor to the high ceiling in the middle of the cavern-like room and hovered there. Blasting through my left foot made it feel as though it was in a meat grinder, so I was using only my right to keep us aloft.

"Here's how this works, now," I said, as they dangled upside-down more than twenty feet above the floor. "You're going to answer my questions. Any struggling and I drop you. And since I'm not the strongest woman around, I'm not sure how long I can hold you. Which means you might want to answer before my grip gives out. So... Where's Valora?"

Hovering with only one source of propulsion is tricky, at best. Add the weight of a couple slightly squirmy bad guys and it was a recipe for disaster. Or comedy, depending on your perspective. I couldn't maintain a steady position and kept jerking left and right, dropping a few feet, then going back up. They might have been too frightened to speak, but I never got the chance to find out.

I remember feeling an impact, as though something bumped me in the back, causing me to drop my passengers. I looked down and, to my surprise, saw Powerhaus standing below me, waiting to catch them.

Even more surprising, though, was something partially obstructing my view of him. It was a piece of metal, long and blood-stained. Peculiarly, it was protruding from my torso, below my ribs on my right side.

And then I was falling toward Powerhaus. Thinking he was more likely waiting to break my face than my fall, I blasted, propelling myself back toward the cells. I landed hard and skidded to a stop.

I didn't understand what was happening. Had I been impaled? No. Valora had been impaled, not me. Why was I on the ground? Looking toward the cells, I saw Billy standing close to the front of his prison, staring in horror at me. Without really knowing why I was doing so, I extended an arm in his direction and blasted.

The energy pulse struck the corner pillar directly, sending sparks flying. The walls disappeared. And out charged a very angry ball of Texan fire.

I dragged myself into a sitting position and tried to clear my head. I examined myself and admitted that, yes, I had a spear sticking through me. Oddly, it didn't hurt badly. I didn't seem to be bleeding much, at least externally. But my breathing was rapid and shallow. I felt cold and slightly nauseated.

Wrapping my cape around myself, I closed my eyes and cleared my thoughts. I was going into shock. I was probably bleeding badly, internally. Despite my confusion, I knew I had to do something. Medical treatment wasn't going to be coming anytime soon. In all likelihood, I was going to die, here.

I should be lying down, I knew. But that was hard to do with a rod of metal sticking through me. Where had that come from, anyway? Powerhaus? No. That's not something he'd do. Valora, of course. I could sense her, now.

My head was clearing, and I took stock of my situation. I had a spear sticking through me. If I pulled it out, I'd probably bleed all over the place. But if I kept it in place, I couldn't maneuver at all. Not that I had the energy to do much maneuvering.

I berated myself for this. I'd had little energy into my shield when I flew Jack and Song up to the ceiling, thinking no one else was around. And with the pain in my foot, I'd barely been able to stay aloft, let alone concentrate on defense.

I was no longer cold, I realized. The MPET lining in my cape really worked, I remember thinking. But then I opened my eyes and saw the inferno Billy had started.

Flames rose in a ring so thick I couldn't see through them. Our enemies were contained for the moment, but maintaining such high-intensity fire took a lot of energy. Billy would tire before the flames used up enough oxygen for them to pass out, or for them to collapse from the heat.

Perhaps it was this knowledge and desperation that caused him to do what he did. Or maybe it was just anger. But he collapsed the flames onto them.

He meant to kill them.

I can tell you now that I fully wished him to succeed, at least where Valora was concerned. But the others didn't necessarily deserve that. Not that I could prevent it. I tried to yell, but he couldn't hear my weak voice over the roar of the blaze.

Just then, Valora burst out from the pyre and lunged toward Billy. This was a woman who had crippled Daniel, who could go one-on-one with

The Hammer. Compared to them, Billy was about as tough as a pane of glass. He'd be dead before he hit the floor.

Fortunately, Billy had presence of mind enough to shoot a jet of flame directly into Valora's onrushing face. It scorched her, but she quickly ducked under the blast and rolled, leaping up to swing at Billy. But he'd sidestepped just enough that her punch only glanced his head. It still sent him pitching up against a burning rack of weapons.

The others were getting to their feet, now. Billy looked over at me. I wasn't sure why. To ask for guidance? To see if I was alive? To say goodbye?

I wasn't ready for that, yet. I stared back at Billy and, taking a deep breath, began yanking the spear out of my body. I let out a scream as I did so, which drew attention away from Billy for the moment, giving him the chance to set up a wall of fire between him and Valora.

The spear actually came out easier than I'd expected. After the initial agony, the pain faded. Once I caught my breath, I used the weapon as a crutch to get to my feet. Valora turned her back to Billy and crossed the floor to me. Her face was burnt red. She stopped a few paces from me and sized me up.

"Not looking too good, Dinah."

I was in no mood to exchange quips. "Why are you still here?" To my surprise, her face relaxed, showing weariness and pain. "I told you," I continued, "I can't do what you want. And neither can Dr. Gray."

"Oh, certainly not," she said. "He's dead." Seeing the shock on my face, she smirked. "No, I didn't kill him," she said. "You did." I shook my head in denial, but she nodded. "Surprised you didn't see it on the news. Mysterious explosion in a house in the suburbs, one man dead…"

I felt sick to my stomach, but had no time to dwell on this. "What do you want, then?"

"You're going to make me the most powerful meta on the planet."

"I told you. I can't do that. But even if I could, why would you trust me?"

"Oh, I don't. Not for a second. I just need all your notes. Others can take those and proceed."

"Trying to kill me is a funny way of getting my notes."

"Give me some credit, Dinah. That injury isn't going to kill you." She gave me a funny look. "Don't tell me I know more about your abilities than you do."

As curious as I was about that statement, I had to get out of there. Powerhaus was waiting for Billy's flames to weaken. And even though I felt my own strength returning, I was in no shape to fight off anyone. "Let him go," I said, nodding over at Billy.

Valora glanced over her shoulder, then back at me. "No."

"I'm fine with giving you my notes, because I know you'll never be able to do anything with them. But you've got to let him go."

She shook her head. "Again, no. I don't need your agreement. I just need you alive. Plenty of telepaths out there who'll extract every bit of information I need from your pretty little head." Valora reached up and removed her winged helmet. Then she spun and hurled it with incredible force across the room. I watched as it disappeared into Billy's wall of fire. A moment later, the flames vanished. Billy was slumped on the ground, the helmet stuck into his shoulder by one of its golden wings. Laughing, Powerhaus moved in for the kill.

Adrenaline surged in me and I felt my energy increasing. I probably bellowed something stupid, like, "Get away from him." I'm not sure. But before I could even rationalize what I was doing, I was blasting across the room, holding the spear in both hands like an axle. Powerhaus turned in time to see me, but not in time to duck. I caught him in the forehead. He went down, stunned. I landed next to him, trying to ignore the spatter of my blood as I did so. One energy punch to the head and he was out.

A wide blast sent Jack and Song flying. Neither showed much inclination to fight, anyway, having taken the most damage from Billy's attack.

Valora clapped condescendingly as she strode casually toward me. I clasped the spear as a bar again and blasted toward her. She braced herself, preparing to knock it out of my hands. At the last moment, I flipped the weapon point first. It struck Valora squarely between her breasts, catching her by surprise.

Naturally, it didn't pierce her bizarre flesh. She tried to swat the weapon away, only to find that it had, in fact, become lodged in the chain mail. It wouldn't budge.

I levered the spear to scoop her up like a lacrosse ball and blasted straight up to the cavern's ceiling. I slammed her into it and kept her pinned in place, and would do so until I passed out. Which probably wasn't going to be long.

Valora growled in anger at me and in frustration at the situation. She held the spear and tried twisting it away, but I was able to compensate for her actions by shifting my thrust. I wondered if she appreciated the irony of the situation on any level.

I was weakening. I could feel my energy levels dwindling rapidly. I couldn't maintain enough thrust to keep her pinned to the ceiling. We began to drop.

Valora smiled, realizing I was nearly spent. Then suddenly she stopped, her face showing confusion as she stared at the spear in her breast. Then she gasped in pain.

The spear, slick with my blood, had worked its way through the chain mail and now only gravity kept her atop it. And this force was slight enough to allow the point to penetrate her skin.

She redoubled her efforts, trying to push the weapon away from her. But my resistance was enough to prevent that, despite the fact that we were slowly falling.

Her cries of pain turned to curses and finally to anguished silence. Her blood flowed freely down the shaft of the spear, coating my hands and arms. We hit the ground and I dropped Valora to the floor. She stared up at me with a look of pure hatred for a long minute... until the light left her eyes.

I stared at the blood on my arms. And then I saw it on my legs. Except that blood was mine, flowing again from my wound. I looked up to see the others staring in shock at the scene, including Billy, who held a hand to his injured shoulder. Then my adrenaline wore off and I fell unconscious to the floor.

I'm in the audience, sitting with my family, watching my six-year old self singing and shaking my little booty to "Car Wash." I feel strangely detached from the performance and am a bit too critical, perhaps, in my analysis. Hit an off-note, there. Timing was off by a tad on that dance move. But I'm only six, I remind myself, and try to just enjoy the show.

I pay attention to the others on stage with me, the girls with the buckets and rags, twirling around in unison. I smile at how much their performance adds to mine. They really make me look good.

It strikes me, as I look more closely at them, that I'm not the prettiest girl on stage, despite my adorable dimples and shining, golden tresses. And I note that at least two of the girls are much better dancers than I am.

To my surprise, this pleases me.

Then I am above the audience, looking down on it. I see myself sitting beside my brother and parents. Except I'm my current age, while they are all decades younger. On the other side of me sit Sharon and Jackie. Lee is there, too. She holds Scooter in her lap.

And suddenly, I'm lying on the stage, staring straight up into a blinding spotlight. I can't turn my head away. It hurts my eyes. I want to fly up and turn it off.

I hear people talking urgently, then yelling, but I can't see who it is. The other dancers gather around, staring down at me. They take their white rags and put them on me. When they lift them again, they're red. They put them in their buckets, look at me sadly, and wave goodbye.

The song is over. And I don't know what I'm supposed to do, now.

TWENTY-FOUR

"People often say that this or that person has not yet found himself. But the self is not something one finds, it is something one creates."
~Thomas Szasz

My father was never much of a disciplinarian. Even before our parents discovered Dana's abilities, I don't remember either of us ever receiving a spanking. A verbal admonishment now and then, but nothing major. Not that either of us ever did much to deserve more than a minor dressing-down.

Some would claim that we were well-behaved because we were afraid of what would happen if we ever did something bad. And that's true, but it wasn't a fear of any punishment he might inflict. It was a fear of disappointing him.

I was a daddy's girl, no question, up until things started to go south. And as an adult, I lost respect for him for allowing my mother to get away with all her crap. But as a child, I looked up quite a bit to my dad. And even though his doting on me started to fade around the same time Mother began to detach from me, it didn't lessen my feelings for him. I always wanted him to be proud of me.

I suspect Dana felt the same. And that's why we were good kids. We never wanted to see an expression of disapproval on Dad's face. To us, that would hurt more than any spanking.

Dad taught us at an early age that there are always repercussions to our actions. He taught us about accountability, about responsibility. And he taught us the concept of "paying forward" rather than "paying back."

Somewhere along the way, these lessons faded in my mind, and I began living in my own warped reality, where being famous was the ultimate, where being loved by a multitude of strangers would make up for the lack of mother love.

But when it came right down to it, I didn't see anything wrong with my attitude. What did it matter if I wanted to be famous? What difference did it make that I intended to use my scientific knowledge for entirely selfish reasons? It didn't make me a bad person. I paid for the education. I didn't owe it to anyone to use that knowledge for anyone but me.

I can see the disappointment on my father's face, even as I write those words. And even after all these years, that look still forms a pit in my stomach.

Another lesson he laid down for us was that of having to deal with the consequences of our mistakes. When Dana accidentally broke a neighbor's window while playing baseball in the yard, he had to pay for the new window out of his allowance. But sometimes the price we paid wasn't financial or in punishment, but in the form of our own guilt, such as when I said something mean to a classmate during a bratty phase. I apologized, but felt bad for weeks from seeing how much I'd hurt her feelings.

One thing Dad's lessons never prepared me for, though, was a situation in which there would be intense guilt in addition to severe material consequences. But then, I'm sure it never entered my father's head that I'd someday kill a person.

Let alone two.

I woke in the now too-familiar hospital in Las Vegas. I glanced idly at the tubes running into my arms, felt the bandages over my midsection, and shifted uneasily from the pain of my injuries. But that was the lesser pain.

Better them than me, right?

I'd flippantly said those words to Dana when he'd warned me about my abilities potentially being deadly. It seemed so long ago. In fact, it seemed as though someone else said it, not me.

I wasn't likely to shed a tear for the death of the otherworld Valora. It truly had been a "better her than me" situation. I had no doubt that she would have killed me without a second thought. Even so, I wished it hadn't been me who'd brought about her demise.

I kept remembering the slickness of her blood on my gloves as it slid down the shaft of the spear. I saw, over and over and over again, her eyes as they went from glaring at me to focusing on nothing.

Her death troubled me not at all compared to the gnawing guilt of Dr. Gray's death. I was still hoping Valora had lied about that, as a tactic to unnerve me. But I couldn't imagine such deceptions being her style. She had no need to psych me out. And when I replayed it in my mind, I couldn't help but see that the explosion easily could have killed him. A piece of shrapnel from the bomb could have done him in. But even without that, he could have died from the concussive blast alone.

Hollywood does many disservices to the general public, largely by making them think certain things are possible. In a movie, a person will be shot by a handgun and die instantly. A vehicle will go over a small cliff and erupt into a fireball. An action hero will be lifted and thrown fifty feet by the shockwave from an explosion, then get up, brush off the dust, and continue with his heroics.

In reality, unless it's to the head, death by gunshot is rarely quick. Unless that vehicle is hauling explosives, it's just going to burn, not blow up. And any blast strong enough to do much more than knock a person down will very likely cause massive damage to internal organs.

Many metas have bodies that can survive such things, such as Valora with her non-Newtonian flesh or me with my energy shield. The force of my blast had blown Valora into the wall, and she was immeasurably tougher than Dr. Gray.

And despite the fact that he'd been working with her... despite his betrayals of me, going back to that night so long ago at GACTech... he didn't deserve to die.

Dana was right. Even though it wasn't my abilities that directly killed him, I should have foreseen the possibility. I should have, and easily could have, avoided injury to him. I could have run past Valora before detonating the bomb. I could have used her as a shield between us. I could have done many things. I *should* have done any one of them.

But I didn't.

I had a few visitors while in the hospital. Jack and Song brought me up to speed on our former teammates, who were all recovering nicely and sent their well wishes. I asked them to tell Sinta that I'd come visit on our birthday, which was rapidly approaching. Jack joked that the hospital was giving me a frequent visitor card. After ten stays, I'd get one free. I was just happy that the extension on our health care coverage wouldn't expire for a few more weeks.

When Shepherd visited, he told me that the otherworlders were all being held in custody back at Groom Lake while DHS decided what to do with them. I shared some suggestions with him, and he promised to pass them along. Further, he assured me that I'd face no charges for Valora's death. It was clearly self-defense. Besides, it took place somewhere not even in our world. No court had jurisdiction over that. He confirmed Dr. Gray's death and, hearing my account of the situation, said he'd see what help he could offer.

Dana flew in from Sacramento and we had a long talk. It wasn't very pleasant. He was clearly upset at seeing me in the hospital again and feared that I'd end up as dead as Valora. I filled him in on everything that had happened, finishing with the confirmation of the death of Dr. Gray. Dana suggested counseling, naturally. Finally, I told him about my suggestions to Shepherd regarding the otherworlders, and how there was a role for him in them, should DHS agree. Needless to say, he wasn't happy about it.

I had too many things on my mind to get any actual rest during my recovery. I slept in short bouts, until my dreams would wake me and I'd lie there most of the night, trying to make sense of things.

I kept thinking of Valora's words after she'd impaled me. *Don't tell me I know more about your abilities than you do.* What had she meant by that? So I asked my doctor if there had been anything unusual about my injury. Turns out there was significantly less bleeding and internal damage than he would have expected, he said, after scolding me for removing the spear.

After pondering this for hours, rolling Valora's words over and over in my head, I concluded that my energy shield may somehow function internally. My primary hypothesis is that a weak, internal force formed a sort of cannula around the impalement, preventing much blood from escaping. Only when I was at my weakest did the field fail.

My secondary hypothesis is that it was just dumb luck.

I'm in the hospital. My mother sits in a chair near the door, opposite the foot of my bed. I look at her from my inclined position. She scowls at me, and I remember when I was eleven, and she believed I was faking a prolonged pain. She looks as she did, then. I want to yell at her for not taking me seriously, not just about my pain, but ever in my life. But I don't.

"She wasn't always like this," says my father, who stands next to my bed, holding my hand. My fingers are so tiny, child-like, in his grip. I look up at him, knowing he's speaking about his wife, but not understanding what he means. He smiles sadly. "She used to be... well... like you remember her being when you were very little. Kind and considerate."

"She's isn't always like this," says Dana, and I turn to see him standing at the other side of my bed, holding my other hand. My fingers are mature, like his, in his grip. I know he's speaking about me, but talking to our parents. "She can be really... well... like you remember her being when she was very little. Kind and considerate."

"But after learning of your brother's abilities," Dad says, "she changed." He shrugs. "Maybe I should have been more assertive, forced her to deal with it... or maybe seek help. But I didn't."

"But after learning of my abilities," Dana says, "she changed." He sighs. "Maybe I should have done something, forced you to stop being so small-minded... and become what you always feared I was. But I couldn't."

"It's probably too late," Dad says, *"for her to change again. And I'm sorry, sweetheart."* He squeezes my hand before fading away.

I look up at Dana, waiting for his words to echo Dad's. I wait for him to say it's not too late for me. But he just squeezes my hand as he looks at me. Then he, too, fades away.

Days after my discharge, I stood in front of Director Weatherford in an *ad hoc* DHS hearing. Shepherd was there, as were a few other DHS officers I didn't recognize.

Weatherford spoke as the others did little more than stare at me. "After considerable discussion, the Department has agreed with your suggestions on how to deal with the otherworlders. We will begin carrying them out immediately."

I nodded. "If I can be of any help, please let me know."

"Oh, we will. Have no doubt."

I shuffled uncomfortably, casting a glance at Shepherd. He noted this and leaned over to whisper something to Weatherford. The Director nodded, then said, "Anything at all involving the otherworlders is considered to be a DHS matter." I nodded, not sure what relevance that had to me. "Including the unfortunate death of Dr. Philip Gray." Seeing the blank look on my face, he said, "That means there will be no charges against you."

"I see," I said after a second. I questioned the ethicality – and legality – of this, but only in my head. I kept my mouth shut and grudgingly thanked Weatherford for that intervention. I still didn't trust him, but I wasn't going to turn down his assistance.

I've been through one trial in my life. I certainly didn't want another. Especially not one for murder or manslaughter or whatever charge it would have been. But honestly, a conviction couldn't have made me feel worse than I already did.

Under Weatherford's watchful eye, we carried out the exchanges. To his credit, Dana did exactly as I asked, without complaint.

Since his "other-self" was dead, there was no risk for him entering the other world. First, he telepathically rendered the otherworlders unconscious. Then he blocked from their memories any details of the location of the portal. Finally, he took them through to the other world, where he telekinetically "flew" them to the tiny town miles from the portal. By the time they regained consciousness, he was on his way back to the portal, the location of which he'd marked in some fashion.

I knew the psychic surgery was distasteful to him, but he still did it. I felt guilty for asking him to do it, but could think of no other way to guarantee (inasmuch as we could) that they wouldn't find their way back.

And watching him work, I couldn't help but understand the fear of telepaths that many people had.

As they were carried through, their counterparts from our world materialized on our side of the portal. I spoke with Kimera and Caracara, explaining some things they hadn't already figured out, and gave them each my phone number before Weatherford took them aside for debriefing.

Powerhaus never materialized. We searched the in-between zone for him, to no avail, so assumed this meant he died on the other side. DHS would notify his next of kin, I was told.

This left one outstanding issue: the problem of otherworlders who'd exchanged places with those from our world that had not yet been identified. I had a possible solution to that, too. And it again involved Dana, after a fashion.

Telepaths, I explained to Weatherford and Shepherd, could easily determine if a suspected individual was, in fact, from our world or not. The public had a distrust of metas, of course, and it was especially bad for telepaths. If DHS let the world know of the replacements, rather than keeping it a secret, as it was inclined to do, it could serve to improve the meta image. Those who'd "gone bad" would be revealed as imposters. Telepaths would be the ones rooting them out, thus protecting the public. Win-win, as far as I could see.

It took some arguing of my case, but DHS finally agreed. And for this reason, the portal at Groom Lake was kept active. Those of us with direct knowledge of it were given approved access passes from DHS. For this, we were expected to be called upon to assist in "relocating" the replacements, if needed.

As expected, my temporary home – the Bay Scouts' old base – was half empty when I returned. Rachel's things were gone. On our bed... on *my* bed... was a note. It said what I'd been fearing ever since Daniel said she wasn't here. She was gone from San Francisco, off to build another life for herself, to get away from Hellion and his gang.

And to get away from me, too. She thought she was putting me in danger from Hellion, for one thing. But for another, she knew she was going to hurt me and chose to do it sooner than later.

She never had known what to make of our relationship, I knew. She didn't think of herself as a lesbian, or even bi. She was with me because it was comfortable. Because she'd been lonely. Because I'd been the first person in a long time who looked at her without seeing a sideshow attraction.

Her message said, of course, that I would always be incredibly special to her, and so on and so forth. I filed the note away with the rest of my romantic memorabilia.

I filed the pain away with the rest of my heartaches.

Daniel and I accompanied Valerie Andersen's body to the grieving bosom of her family in St. Paul, Minnesota, where she was buried in a quiet service attended by her parents, four siblings, and a dozen other relatives. Many of them spoke with us afterward, thanking us for bringing her home. I felt awkward, having known nothing about Valora's family, but honored to have known her at all. And I told them so.

I knew nothing about Dr. Gray's family, but wouldn't have known what to say to them, anyway.

DHS carried out "their" plans to the letter. Rumors of the existence of the portal had been around since its discovery. But the existence of the portal, and the other world, were confirmed in a White House press conference. Homeland Security Secretary Chertoff spoke at length about the presumed origin of the portals in an attempt to quell rumors that the things had been deliberately created by American scientists working for the government.

Those metas who were known to have been replaced were named. In addition to Kim, Cara, Powerhaus, and my former teammates, there were six others suspected. These six were confirmed by a special contingent of telepaths working for DHS. They were returned to their world in similar fashion as the others had been.

The portals would remain "open" for at least another year, the Secretary said, in order to deal with any other "replacements" they might discover. He finished by thanking the meta population for their cooperation, and for their service to the country.

"PowerPaste" had gone on sale to the public several months earlier, marketed in little packets a bit larger than fast food ketchup, each holding about 500 calories of the nutrient-dense goop. It sold for about five bucks a pop. PowerPaste differed from DynaPaste mainly in the addition of vitamins and minerals. My goal in making it was purely for calories, for energy. To market it as a supplement, though, it needed to have more nutritional value.

The company added other flavors, too, beyond my initial few. My favorite is the Cookies & Cream.

My first residual check arrived in June. It was for more than I'd expected. Not a fortune, but it was in the low five figures. So after getting current on my bills, I did something I decided I desperately needed. I went on vacation.

I rented a convertible and drove north, up the incredibly gorgeous California Route 1. It's a breathtaking drive, with ocean views nearly the entire way. I stopped often to walk on beaches and enjoy the sea wind on my face. I stayed in cabins rather than hotels.

My cell phone was off during this journey. I didn't check my email. I needed to be alone with my thoughts, to figure out who I was and what I wanted. My youthful expectations had been turned upside-down and sideways. My ambitions, I came to realize, were petty, and I was embarrassed by them.

Route 1 moves inland in Mendocino County, ending as it hits U.S. Route 101. There, I continued north, stopping for walks in the redwoods along the Avenue of the Giants. The majority of these trees have been here since before our country was founded and will still be around for hundreds of additional years. The length of a human lifespan is paltry compared to that of these giants. Standing among them, I felt small, insignificant, and stupid.

It's as though I never really grasped what I was reading when I went through the pages of those magazines when I was a teen. I never really understood why some metas were famous. I equated them with movie or TV stars, many of whom were popular only because they were sexy, not because they were particularly accomplished. I saw only the glamour of being in the spotlight, not caring whether the spotlight was deserved. I viewed super teams as I would pop bands, rather than police or fire departments. Had I never actually read the articles? Had I only looked at the pictures and read the captions? Had I really been that shallow?

Route 101 took me out of California and into Oregon. More ocean-front driving and beaches, great seafood, and introspection.

The word "hero" kept sticking in my head. It was a word that didn't hold a lot of meaning to me, maybe because it was so overused. Some people seemed to think a person became a hero without having to do much. Enlisting in the military, for example. It seemed the default view was that all soldiers were heroes unless they did something particularly bad. But if I knew anything at all about heroism, it was that it was not something so casually attained. Most soldiers – or police officers or firefighters – were not heroes. Even within those ranks, it took exceptional actions to be considered a hero. The same is true for super-powered metas. Putting on a costume doesn't make you a hero any more than does putting on fatigues, a badge, or a funky red helmet.

Astoria, Oregon, sits at the mouth of the Columbia River, just south of Washington, and here my journey ended. Over the next few days, I discovered that the town has a lot of similarities to San Francisco, with one obvious exception being the size. San Francisco has about eighty times as many people. I learned that Astoria is even sometimes referred to as "Little San Francisco." Both are peninsulas with multiple bridges. Both have lots of hills. San Francisco has Coit Tower; Astoria has the Astoria Column. One thing Astoria seems to lack, though, is a meta presence. I wondered if it needed one. I liked Astoria. I could see myself living there. And I'd definitely be a big fish in the little pond. It could be an easy life.

On a lazy Saturday, I sat sipping a cappuccino at Coffee Girl, enjoying the view of the bay from Pier 39, and thinking about this little trip I was on and what I was really doing. And it occurred to me that I wasn't on some search to find myself.

I was running away.

I'd chosen my path, after all. Maybe the reasons hadn't been the best ones, but that didn't seem important, anymore. Things hadn't really gone how I'd planned, but that was hardly uncommon for anyone. And here I was, hundreds of miles away, expecting to find answers.

But the answers I sought weren't in Astoria. They weren't on a beach or in the woods. And maybe there weren't really any true answers. Maybe there were just ideas and inclinations.

Did I still want to be a big fish? Perhaps a part of me did. But if that was in my future, I knew I wanted it to be because I deserved it, not because I was the only game in town, because I looked great on a magazine cover, or because I had a good P.R. firm.

I packed up and departed that afternoon, my thoughts now on the future, not the past. I'd figured out who I was: no one of consequence. Now I had to figure out who I wanted to be. And how to become her.

A few days after my return, I rented a two-bedroom apartment on Page Street. Dana helped me move, of course. It always helps to have a telekinetic for the heavy lifting. I wasn't worried much about the cost. I'd manage, somehow, even if my quarterly profits from "PowerPaste" weren't always good.

But given the ending of the Bay Scouts and his ongoing health issues, I suspected Daniel was going to need some income if he didn't want to drain his savings. I suggested that, if Sinta lived with me, he could get some income by renting out or selling the apartment in which she'd been living. Daniel initially declined, not wanting to displace Sinta. But then he saw how excited Sinta was about the idea. She couldn't wait to move in with me.

I finally took Dana's advice and found myself a good counselor. I had a lot of emotional healing to do, and talking helps. We talked mostly about my guilt over Dr. Gray's death. I knew it would take a long time before I could forgive myself, if I ever could.

I spent time talking with others, too, but for them, not me. I took on more hours on the suicide hotline. Turns out I'm pretty good at helping people in crisis find the bright spots in their lives, even though I'm not the best at finding my own.

One day, I received in the mail an envelope with no return address, but a Los Angeles postmark. It contained only a clipping from one of the movie industry rags. It was a short missive, only a paragraph, and referred to the trend of resurrecting old television classics as movies. The latest show to be part of this was rumored to be *Devilgirl*. The buzz was that it would feature the same actress, reinventing her character as an adult, dealing with the problems of being a housewife and mother in suburbia.

Drawn in red felt-tip at the bottom of the clipping was a little heart with horns. I stuck it on my fridge next to a picture of Rachel and me behind the bar at the Red Devil.

Caracara and Kimera eventually contacted me, wanting more information about their other-selves than DHS had given them. I told them the whole story as I knew it. Caracara seemed pleased to know her other-self wasn't a heartless bitch. But I felt badly for Kimera, as her double had been particularly vicious, and now Kim was dealing with a tarnished image, despite DHS publicly clearing her of any criminal activity. Of course, being a member of the Gatekeepers, I figured that image would shine again before too long.

Speaking of the Gatekeepers... a month later, Kimera invited me to visit their headquarters. It's an impressive building. Yeah, they have an actual building, not a bunker. But then, they also have dozens of members and much more government funding.

To my surprise, there was an ulterior motive for the invitation. On the good words of Kimera, Daniel, and Shepherd, I was invited to join the most prestigious team on the west coast. This was quickly – and unrelatedly – followed by an interview request from *Supers* magazine.

I was terribly flattered, I told both of them.

But I'd have to think about it.

AFTERWORD

When I was asked to take part in capturing Dinah's life in book form, I actually laughed. I write fiction, I said. What do I know about memoirs and biographies? Almost nothing, that's what.

I suppose the rationale was that, when dealing with a larger-than-life person, hiring someone with a penchant for the grandiose and fantastical isn't too terribly strange. But what I found in reading Dinah's journals, and in interviewing her teammates and friends, is that neither "grandiose" nor "fantastical" truly describes Dinah's life, each being both an exaggeration and inadequate. And that just made this project all the more fascinating.

My role in this first book was primarily organizational. Her words are her own, with very little of my influence. In the two volumes to follow, you will continue to see her words, as there are plenty of her journals remaining. But given the events that took place from 2008 through 2010, it's impossible to tell the remainder of her story without the input of others.

I'm honored to be part of this project, and I hope you all find her story as inspirational as I do.

Vincent M. Wales
January, 2013

About the Author

Vincent M. Wales was raised in the small town of Brockway, Pennsylvania, where he frequently complained about the weather. Since then, he has worn many hats, including writing instructor, suicide prevention crisis counselor, essayist, Big Brother, freethought activist, wannabe rock star, and award-winning novelist.

He spends most of his writing time in coffee shops, since his cats fail to grasp the entire concept of "writing time."

He currently lives in Sacramento, California, where he frequently complains about the weather.

www.vincentmwales.com